TRANSITIONS

Transitions

Twenty-Four Bilingual Short Stories
by
JOSÉ L RECIO

BOOKS

Adelaide Books
New York / Lisbon
2021

TRANSITIONS
Twenty-Four Bilingual Short Stories
By José L Recio

Copyright © by José L Recio
Cover design © 2021 Adelaide Books

Published by Adelaide Books, New York / Lisbon
adelaidebooks.org

Editor-in-Chief
Stevan V. Nikolic

For any information, please address Adelaide Books
at info@adelaidebooks.org

or write to:

Adelaide Books
244 Fifth Ave. Suite D27
New York, NY, 10001

ISBN: 978-1-954351-46-2

Printed in the United States of America

Contents

TRANSITIONS

Preface **9**

An Old Cemetery **11**

Ernestine's Struggle **24**

Lucas Parra **36**

Never Too Late **53**

Palmiro **55**

Three Black Birds **60**

El Teso Village **65**

The Ambler **88**

A Beautiful Afternoon in April **103**

Pietro's Dilemma **112**

At the Gate **123**

Marie **126**

The Easel on the Beach   *130*

The Bridge   *135*

The Deer   *139*

The Hiker and the Hawk   *143*

Feeding the Family   *145*

The Pot-Bellied Man   *147*

A Gift of Love   *148*

The Solitary Tree   *149*

The Mongrel Dog   *151*

Winding Roads   *166*

Grandpa's Old Neighborhood   *179*

Bertha's House   *185*

TRANSICIONES

Prefacio   *209*

Un antiguo cementerio   *213*

El conflicto de Ernestina   *228*

Lucas Parra   *243*

Nunca es demasiado tarde   *264*

Palmiro   *267*

Tres pájaros negros   *272*

El Teso Pueblo   *277*

El Paseante   *303*

Una hermosa tarde en abril   *320*

El dilema de Pietro   *330*

La verja del jardín   *342*

Marie   *346*

El caballete en la playa   *350*

El puente   *355*

El ciervo   *360*

El caminante y el halcón   *364*

Alimentando a la familia   *366*

El hombre barrigudo   *368*

Un regalo de amor   *369*

El árbol solitario   *370*

El Perro de raza mixta   *372*

Caminos tortuosos   *389*

El viejo barrio del abuelo   *403*

La casa de Berta   *410*

List of First and only Publications   *431*

About the Author   *433*

Preface

Over the last five years, I have written the stories in this collection in English and published them in different American and European literary magazines; once published, I translated them into Spanish (my native language). Why did I not proceed in reverse? To explain it, I must take a brief biographical detour.

Regardless of the chronological age, as we grow older, we become aware of periodically entering new phases in life that require adjustments. The degree of personal satisfaction, as we move on, depends in part on achieving a successful adaptation throughout these periods of transition.

When health problems forced me to retire from a long career as a physician, in addition to recovering my health, I knew I had to figure out what to do post-retirement. The answer didn't come seamlessly. At first, I was only thinking about getting my health back and working in the medical field again, the only alternative that seemed logical, despite the contrary advice, based on my still fragile health, from friends and family. It took about two years and quite a bit of exploration and experimentation before giving up the idea of continuing to do something in the medical field. By then, I had, in a significant part, recovered my health.

The thought of becoming a medical translator came to supplant prior plans. After entering and graduating from a one-year Master's in translation in preparation for the task, I gave it up. It was at that point when it dawned on me that what I wanted to do was to write. Why write? I believe there is an inborn tendency in every individual to be creative, and being creative is an essential part of my life; it has always been. I write because I want to express myself artistically, writing is the only tool I have to use for a creative purpose.

After I retired (December 2008) in California, my wife and I moved to Spain, and it was there that I started writing in Spanish. A new set of circumstances, however, brought us back to California in the summer of 2012.

I came to America from Spain when I was in my mid-thirties and can testify that the process of absorption of the language and culture—that is, adaptation—is gradual and prolonged. If one is born and raised in a country and then moves to another, an appropriate adaptation requires not only that one acquires the new language but also integrates the two cultures. From a pragmatic point of view, however, popular culture, including language, dominates the daily social activity of a country. The acknowledgment of this reality, along with encouragement from my American wife, determined that I switch languages and write in English.

The majority of the stories in this collection are mainstream fiction, and the characters reflect some autobiographical, albeit fictionalized, and transitional phases in life. As a character in one of the stories ("Never Too Late") says, 'Nobody's completely alone in life,' and writing a book, any book, cannot be entirely done in solitude; the writer needs feedback from editors, critics, and readers. I much appreciate the help I have received from my family, writing professionals, friends and fellow writers; too many to list here.

José L Recio
Pasadena, California, 2020

An Old Cemetery

They were in Angelica's bedroom, her lying on the bed and her mother standing by the door.

"You must do something to get out of the black hole in which you are," her mother had said.

Over the last few years, Angelica had gone through an ordeal—her father died, and she married her good-for-nothing high school sweetheart, who proved incapable of dealing with a miscarriage she'd had a few months after they were married and divorced her.

"Like what?" She wished she were dead—no more trying and failing.

"Like... taking a vacation?"

Angelica lifted her head a little. "I've no place to go, Mom."

She had returned to live with her mother because, at twenty-three, she had no other place where to go.

"You could go to Guadalajara. I'll cover your expenses."

What was there for her? Angelica's breathing slowed down. "You mean the city where you and dad met?"

"I was on vacation and met your father there. What's wrong with that? At first, we were happy," her mother said and gazed at her daughter as if expecting her approval.

Angelica pulled herself up and sat on the bed. "You have often blamed yourself for bringing Dad to Los Angeles and marrying him."

"And I still do. But I didn't know then that alcohol addiction is a disease."

Angelica turned pensive. Her dad was a drunkard. He used to come home loaded from work and demand to be served: dinner at 8:00 pm a bottle of wine on the table, the paper by his side, and bring me this, and take this plate away. She had missed having fun with her friends because of his exigencies.

"Mom, I don't see why you try to justify dad's behaviors."

Mom seemed to reflect. "We all make mistakes, Angelica," she said. "Often, I wonder how would life be for you now if you had married a more mature man." She walked to the edge of the bed, leaned forward, and kissed her daughter on the forehead. "I only want the best for you, dear." She left the room.

Over the course of the next month, Angelica spent long hours in her room, lying on her bed or sitting on a chair by the window, ruminating and crying. Who was she to reproach her mother for marrying the man of her choice? What about her own decisions?

"Mom, I've been thinking about your suggestion," she told her mother a day they had sat down for dinner. "I mean, about taking a vacation."

"I'll help you with the expenses for two weeks," said her mother, and her eyes brightened. She seemed happy that her daughter was eating the soup with a healthy appetite.

"I appreciate your generosity, Mom, but I'll accept your help for a week's time, in Guadalajara."

"But I thought—"

"Now, I see things differently," she cut her mother short. "It isn't your or my fault that we married the wrong men," she

said. "I'm glad to have this opportunity to visit my father's town."
She paused. "The only trouble though," she added, "I dread to
come across dad's relatives there."

"Your dad had only two living sisters left, and I don't know
where they live now."

Hearing these words, Angelica produced a sigh of relief.

"Thank you, Mom, for such a delicious dinner!"

"You're welcome."

They finished eating.

A week later, Angelica flew to Guadalajara. She had re-
served a room at a hotel downtown. She checked in at mid-
morning, unpacked, took a shower, changed into comfortable
clothes –linen pants, cotton blouse, and tennis shoes—and
walked out, ready to explore the Historic Area.

When she hit the streets, she felt an upwelling of contentment rising inside her. She strolled down the street, mingling
with the crowds and looking around: the historic buildings,
the shops loaded with merchandise, the Cathedral. She went
inside the temple. A few tourists meandered through the aisles,
and some locals knelt on the benches. Angelica admired the
art in the religious figures, the ornamented pulpit, and the
stained glass windows. She also liked the arrangement of several bouquets of flowers someone had distributed around the
main altar. She too knelt on a single prie-dieu to say a prayer,
but intrusive thoughts invaded her mind. Did she forget about
the loss of her unborn baby, the divorce, and her father's de-
manding behavior?

During the rest of the day, she tried to maintain an open
mind and absorb the newness around her, but in the evening,
after she returned to her hotel, feelings of happiness intermin-
gled with those of sadness, and the excitement of coming back

to life with grief from her past losses. Nevertheless, she forced herself to get up early the next morning to visit an old cemetery.

When she arrived, all she found was a long stone wall, built along the sidewalk of a narrow street, and an iron gate, which gave way to the graveyard. A man in a blue shirt and khaki pants stood near the gate.

"The next tour starts at 11:30, this morning," he said. He held a gray fabric satchel that he was distractedly swinging back and forth.

Is he a beggar? "Next tour did you say?"

"Yes." He lifted and thrust his chin forward to indicate a piece of paper stuck on the gate.

"Oh! I see. Thank you."

She didn't quite 'see' it, though; her thoughts were still on the man. Something in him attracted her. She read the note—a handwritten time table of the tours for visiting the cemetery.

"You're right. Twenty minutes left before the next visit," Angelica said.

He took a few steps away from her and sat down on one of two big, ornamental boulders that lay one beside the other in front of the gate. She decided to wait for the next tour and sat down on the other rock.

"Are you interested in the legends about this cemetery?" He touched the satchel with the tip of his index finger.

"What legends do you mean?"

He opened the satchel and took a pamphlet out of it. Angelica watched his moves, his brownish face, his curly hair— But was he missing an eye?

"You can read all about it here." He waggled the booklet.

She didn't pay attention to his motion. She wanted to know what was wrong with his left eye.

"No, thank you," she said.

14

The man, who seemed to be in his mid-thirties, returned the pamphlet into the satchel. She glanced at him.

"This," he said, "happened to me in a fight." He opened the eyelid of the sick eye with his thumb and index fingers to show it to her. She leaned forward and looked into a hollow eye socket with a whitish membrane at its bottom.

"How awful!" she said and covered her face. "Can you see well with your other eye?"

"I see, but I get bad headaches if I force myself to read. I'm like a living dead!"

"I'm sorry." She turned her head away from him.

"Please, forgive me if I have hurt your sensibility," the man stated in a polite tone.

A touch of distinction was apparent, and she struggled to identify its origin.

"Please, excuse my sensitivity." She turned back to him. "Angelica, my name. I live in Los Angeles."

"I'm pleased to meet you. Rodolfo."

She liked the way he shook hands: a light pressure and a slight bowing.

"You speak Spanish very well," he said.

"My dad was from this city. He spoke to me in Spanish." She tried to focus on his only eye.

"Did you say *he was?*"

"My father died a few years ago. I'm an only child."

"I'm sorry." He made the sign of the cross.

Angelica interpreted that Rodolfo had shown respect for the deceased. Had she ever shown respect for her father? She withdrew into herself. Meanwhile, Rodolfo gazed at her long, curly black hair, and the blueness of her eyes.

"Is your mother an American?" he broke the silence.

"Yes," she muttered.

Two young women arrived at the gate, and Angelica heard them speaking in English. She checked her phone. "It's time to join the tour," she said.

"I feel sorry about your father," Rodolfo said. She had joined the two women on their way in.

The cemetery was a small place. The young Mexican tour guide explained the ins and outs of the site in English, but his talk didn't trigger Angelica's interest. To her, it looked like a poorly maintained graveyard. The other two girls on tour asked nothing but silly questions. She was growing disappointed. The guide led the group to a corner where a thick oak tree sat, encircled by a two-foot-high brick fence.

"Underneath this tree, as the story goes," the guide said, "a vampire lives. Many people believe—"

"Excuse me," Angelica called fretfully, "I didn't know these tours were on a schedule. The time I spent waiting outside for this one to start has put me behind in my plans for the day, so I must leave now."

She handed a tip to the tour guide and walked down the mean path toward the gate. The three watched her leaving.

When she came to the gate, she saw Rodolfo still sitting on the same rock. This guy didn't seem to sell many pamphlets. She opened her purse and took a hundred pesos bill out of it.

"I don't care much about the legends in your pamphlets, but, please, accept my contribution to your cause," she said.

"Thank you. What cause do you mean?"

"I don't know. I feel upset about your eye."

He got up and started swinging his bag like a pendulum. Was he sad?

"I appreciate your feelings towards me," he said. "It would be a pleasure to get to know you better."

"I can't stay. I got a ticket for a show downtown."

"I'll be at the gazebo in front of the Cathedral at 6:00 pm, tomorrow," he said.

That night, Angelica could hardly fall asleep. She liked many things about Rodolfo, his mustache, his long sideburns, and his manners. But what did he want from her?

The next day, after she had taken a downtown walking tour, she returned to the hotel. Still thinking about Rodolfo, she showered, brushed her hair, changed into a white blouse, red skirt, and black shoes, and walked out to meet him.

In the vicinity of the gazebo, Rodolfo was pacing back and forth seemly anxious. He was wearing the same clothes from the prior day plus a black jacket. Something was missing, though. Oh, the satchel! He looked elegant without it. When he spotted her, he came to meet her, waving hello. Both remained quiet, walking down the avenue, behaving as if they were used to going out together. He suggested taking her to dinner, and she accepted the invitation. They went to a classy restaurant on Av. Chapultepec.

"A mariachi group performs in this restaurant," Rodolfo said after they had entered the place.

Angelica liked the looks of and the atmosphere in the restaurant.

"This may cost you a fortune," she said.

"Don't worry. I keep some savings from the time when I worked. The selling of the booklets is just to keep me busy."

The busboy was leading them to a table.

"What was your occupation?" she asked after they had sat at the table.

"Before the fight, I owned a small bookshop." He seemed to pride himself on it.

A waiter came to their table. "*Pierna de cordero con mole y ensalada mixta.*" They both ordered.

"I'll pay for the wine," Angelica said.

"We better drink lemonade."

She circled the rim of her plate with her finger and glanced at him wondering. "Fine with me," she agreed. "So, you were saying you had a business, but then you fought somebody and lost everything?"

"Yes."

"You'll excuse me, but isn't that unusual?"

Rodolfo's only eye started quivering.

"Tell me, Rodolfo," she went on, "what drew you to the fight?"

"I was drunk in a bar. Somehow I started a quarrel with a couple of thugs there, and they beat me up."

Angelica looked at him directly. "Are you an alcoholic?"

The bus boy brought a jar of lemonade to their table, and Rodolfo began pouring the refreshment into the glasses. His hand was shaky.

He raised his glass, nevertheless. "For us!"

Angelica clicked on his glass and smiled at him. The waiter returned with the dishes.

"I've been an alcoholic, but I am not one anymore," he said—a declaration Angelica had heard before from other alcoholics, and she knew it had proved to be false for the majority of them.

"I've learned at Al-Anon that—"

"Bullshit!"

She was startled. But his anger appeared to mix with an expression of firmness and determination that she liked.

"What then?" she asked.

"Alcoholics are not all made out of the same pattern. I know some who go to AA meetings but fall off the wagon quickly. I don't go to any meetings, and I've been sober for a year. I'm not an alcoholic anymore." He went back to chewing his *cordero con mole* and drinking his lemonade.

The waiter approached them again. "Dessert?" They both declined.

"Rodolfo, please, let's calm down. After all, we're getting to know each other," she said. They had finished eating. "Perhaps we should leave now and breathe the fresh air?" she suggested.

"I'll walk you to your hotel," he replied, visibly a bit upset.

Rodolfo paid the bill. On their way out, Angelica threw a last glance at the mariachi group: she loved their colorful suits and wide-wing hats. Outside, they walked slowly. They didn't talk much but often smiled at each other. Occasionally, their bodies were brought together, jostled by the waves of people walking in both directions, and then Rodolfo purposely encircled her waist with his arm. She enjoyed his contact, which brought memories of the beginning of her past marital life.

"Can I see you tomorrow?" Rodolfo asked when they arrived at her hotel.

Angelica had hoped he would ask her to go out again.

"You can leave me a message, room thirteen." She walked into the hall.

The next day, they met again at the gazebo. He took her to the neighborhood where he was born and raised. They walked around, and he pointed out the building of the high school he had attended and the grounds where he used to play soccer. In his company, she experienced a child's joy, something she had only rarely felt with her ex-husband.

"Where did you have the bookshop?" she asked.

"It was located near the restaurant where we dined yesterday. Let's take a bus there, and I'll show you."

When they got off the bus, he took her into an area of narrow streets with aligned small shops.

"This one was once 'Rodolfo's Bookshop.'" He had stopped in front of a shop filled with colorful *quinceañera* dresses. A cloud of sadness came in his only eye.

"I'll buy you a latte," she proposed.

They walked across the street and entered *Café Galeria*. Rodolfo talked nostalgically about his former bookshop and his passion for books and love for reading. "Do you like to read?" he asked.

Angelica had not read a novel for a long time, and knowing this, she took a long sip of coffee as she wanting to think about it. "I should read more," she then said. "After high school, I started my way to becoming a teacher, but I married, and I quit reading."

"You're married?" He looked shocked.

"No, I mean I was married. We were high school sweethearts. We're divorced now."

She was dying to find out about him, but didn't want to appear intrusive—should she ask questions.

"Another cup of coffee?" Rodolfo pointed to the empty cup.

"No, thank you. We better keep going."

They left the coffee shop and walked back to her hotel. Before she went in, Rodolfo kissed her. Her chest swelled with satisfaction.

That night, before falling sleep, Angelica thought they were getting to know each other. She had enjoyed his company.

The next day was Sunday, and Rodolfo called for her early. He wanted to take her to an Indian market, about an hour by bus. "In the morning, the market is at its best," he said.

The market, set along the main drag, consisted of stalls lined up to the right and left of the sidewalk. A mass of human bodies slowly moved between the booths. Immersed in a sea of bodies and things, when Rodolfo passed his arm around her shoulders, Angelica felt happy.

On their way back to town on the bus, it started pouring. Big drops slid down the window panels, blurring the outside view. Inside the bus, it felt cozy, beside Rodolfo. He took her hand—it felt warm—and pulled her a little bit closer to him.

"I can't see why any man would divorce you," he whispered.

"We were young, inexperienced. A few months into our marriage, I had a miscarriage. My ex-husband couldn't deal with it."

She was disclosing intimate details. She turned to look outside, but it all appeared opaque.

"What about you? Are you married?" She turned back to him.

"No. I lived with my girlfriend for years until she left me after I had the fight."

Why would a woman leave her boyfriend at a moment of crisis?

"I was drinking too much," he said, and she thought he had read her mind.

"Oh, that!"

The bus stopped a stone's throw from the hotel, and they stepped out. The rain had ceased. When they entered the hall, Angelica said she was tired, and Rodolfo kissed her goodbye and left.

The next evening, Angelica's last one in Guadalajara, she invited Rodolfo to a farewell dinner. "It will be my pleasure," she said. She had spotted a cute little restaurant a couple of days before during her touristic rounds. At dinner, the conversation focused, once again, on them.

"Do you live alone?" She reached over and lightly laid her hand on his arm.

"After my girlfriend and I split, I moved into my mother's. My father passed away five years ago. He was an alcoholic. I'm the only child, like you."

Angelica left her fork on the table and drank a sip of sparkling water. "A lot of coincidences in our lives!" she said.

They smiled at each other with complicity. What would her mother think if she told her that she had met an attractive Mexican man?

"I'm curious, Rodolfo, what are your plans for the future?"

He swallowed his last bite from his beefsteak and looked her directly.

"To be honest, now that I've met you and I've quit drinking, I feel like going back into business."

"But you said you get bad headaches—"

"True," he cut her off. "Look, Angelica, I like you a lot. I think we could do business together. I mean, you'd be the reader and I the business adviser," he added jubilantly.

"That's very kind and loving, Rodolfo. I've got good feelings about you, too. Unfortunately, I'm leaving tomorrow."

He seemed to be taken aback, and she realized she had not told him yet she was leaving the next day.

"Will you come back soon? I'll be waiting for you."

"I need time to heal, Rodolfo. Emotionally, this week has been a rolling coaster. I'll let you know about me. I promise."

When they came out of the restaurant, the breeze was cool; however, both preferred walking back to her hotel. He looked down, perhaps defeated? She had learned from Al-anon that alcoholics often expect somebody will rescue them from their falls. Rodolfo despised AA, why? After her father had attended his first and only meeting, he also disliked AA meetings, and he never achieved sobriety. Would Rodolfo be capable of staying sober?

"I think you should attend AA meetings," she said.

"We've talked about it. You know where I stand in that regard."

She didn't know what to think, what to believe, what to do. She needed time to reflect on it all. For now, she argued, they should leave the matter the way it was—they should remain friends.

Back in L.A., Angelica told her mother about Rodolfo while they were having tea in the kitchen. Her mother was surprised that her daughter had set eyes on a one-eyed man.

"He swears he will never drink again," Angelica said.

"Does he have a sponsor?"

"No. He feels capable of doing it on his own." Angelica's voice dropped. "He wants me back."

Her mother made a grimace, which Angelica read as an expression of skepticism.

"Do you think, Mom, he will be capable of staying sober?"

Her mother had a sip of tea before she answered.

"I can't say, but I'll tell you this," she said. "It's awfully difficult to love an active alcoholic."

Silence reigned for some time. Then, Angelica retired to her bedroom, that first night back home, and tried to relax and fall asleep, but images from the time spent with Rodolfo filled her consciousness until, drained out, she fell asleep. At day breaking, she awoke up startled, cupping an eye with her hand. 'I'm blind!' She jumped out of bed, and still patching her eye, she ran to the window. Trembling, she uncovered her eye: the clarity of the rising sun hit her face. "I've been blindfolded my entire life," she spoke to the morning breeze, "crippled by my father's tyranny, my ex-husband's obfuscation, and yes, impressed by Rodolfo's only eye and his false optimism and need to be rescued. My mother helped me to get out of the black hole, and I must stay out of it. Enough!"

Ernestine's Struggle

As a child, I spent a lot of time with Grandma (Ernestine for the family) while my parents were at work. After school, she would take me to the park, to Disney movies, sometimes to musicals, a lot of fun. I loved her.

The day I started the fifth grade, Ernestine walked me to school, near home, in San Francisco. On our way there, she asked whether I knew where Boston was.

"Yeees!" I said.

In the year 2001, however, I didn't know where exactly Boston was on the map but I had heard my father talking about it when referring to his parents.

"You really know where Boston is, Martina?"

"Dad says it's a far away but nice place."

"Yes. He's right."

Then she told me that she and Grandpa Arthur were the same age and that they grew up in Boston, but at twenty-eight, they came to San Francisco, where Dad was born. Of course, I don't remember the exact words she spoke to me at the time, but I knew this was what she meant. I did the numbers in my mind.

"Grandma, aren't you sixty years older than me?"

"Why—?" "Well, let me see, I was born in 1931, and you were—"

"So, yes, Grandma, you're sixty years older than me!"
I couldn't imagine myself growing up fast enough to fill up the gap. So I asked my father how old he was. He said thirty-eight. I looked at him and Mom, a year younger than he is, and I still couldn't fancy my catching up to their age. I suspected that I was missing something; there had to be other people in Grandma's family that were older than me but younger than Dad or something like that I thought. I was aware of belonging to a tiny family. I knew my mother's folks only in photos because they died before I was born.

Seeing Grandma after school was a happy time. She answered all my questions. My friends also felt at ease with Ernestine when they came along. Although not a funny lady, she always listened to us, and we appreciated how fair she was when judging everything. From her, I learned that she was the youngest of three sisters and a brother. Her parents and sisters died of alcohol complications, but Ernestine and her brother, Theodore, who was married and had two daughters, didn't drink. He was the only family member back East she kept in touch with. Grandma didn't like, she said, that her family used to drink a lot and she and Grandpa decided to come to California. In Boston, both had worked for different insurance companies, and in San Francisco, each found a similar job, but Ernestine retired soon after I was born.

In middle school, I began to hear with increasing frequency that Grandpa, who had just retired, was showing odd behaviors. Although I was not as close to him as I was with Ernestine—Grandpa was still at work when Grandma used to pick me up after school—once retired, I liked him better because he would sometimes take me for an ice-cream or come to my soccer games. Every time I heard somebody saying that he was acting bizarre, I wouldn't believe it because he looked fine to me. One day, though, I caught him peeing by the side of the house.

"What are you doing, Grandpa?"

He didn't flinch.

"I'm taking a leak," he said.

"Why don't you do it in your bathroom?"

"The rats pee there!"

Perplexed, yet I must admit also amused, I ran into the house. Grandma was wondering where he would be. I told her.

"Martina, dear," she said, "Grandpa is sick in his head. I think he's getting worse by the day."

That was the day I realized that Grandpa was not okay. His oddities evolved in crescendo, which made the family feel nervous. Even today (I am writing these notes in 2014), I'm amazed at the change in personality that Grandpa Arthur went through. He would voice insults against Grandma for no reason, and he often walked outside naked to everybody's embarrassment and made passes at any female who came across his reach. An ordeal, Ernestine used to say. The doctors diagnosed a brain tumor, a frontal lobe... something. I've never retained the exact medical word they used. They discouraged having surgery due to the location of the tumor and favored radiation. However, nobody noticed improvement, and he died a couple of years later.

After he passed away, I understood that his odd behavior had been due to the brain cancer, which made me feel sorry for him because for long, everybody had been critical. I missed Grandpa, in particular the time after he retired and used to take me places. Thinking of him made me feel sad. But many things were changing in my life. My middle school was not at a walking distance. Instead of Ernestine walking me there, now Dad, or sometimes Mom, would drive me to and from school, and the same happened when I had to attend other activities outside the home.

I missed the time spent with Ernestine. My mother visited her often, and sometimes she would take me along. One day, Dorothy, Ernestine's best friend of many years, was there too, consoling her. The two of them were seated at the kitchen table, drinking tea and talking in low voices. When Grandma saw me, she opened her arms. I ran toward her, and she hugged me and kissed. Then she said hello to Mom and went back to her quiet moments. No questions about how I was doing, or if I liked the school, or anything else. I moved away from them and pretended to be busy reading one of the books I kept at her house, but my ears were attentive to their talking. Dorothy said to Mom that Ernestine was hardly eating anything. I looked askance at Grandma and noticed her sunken cheekbones. It broke my heart how bad she looked. It occurred to me that it should be in reverse: Grandpa being gone, peace should return to the house. Of course, my mind omitted the fact that he was gone forever; an omission further reinforced by a comment Grandma made a minute later. She declared to be unable to sleep at night because "Arthur enters my bedroom, sits on the edge of my bed, and calls me a whore." She said *whore*. That night, after I went to bed, I cried. I wanted to understand why things had to go so badly for Ernestine, why everything had to be so confusing? I should know better.

As time went on, Ernestine remained reclusive. My eyes got used to seeing her in a blue mood, but my heart wept every time I saw her.

"What's wrong with Grandma?" I asked my mother.

"She is mourning. She misses your grandpa, but she is also mixed up about her feelings toward him because, as you know, he acted so strangely in his final years that she's confused."

"Is Dad mourning too?"

"We're all in grief, but each of us expresses it differently," Mom said.

I thought my sorrow had to do mainly with Ernestine's suffering. My parents believed she was in need of some extra help. We helped her with housework, but that wasn't enough to keep her safe and healthy. Mom hired Amelia through Social Services, a Guatemalan woman in her mid-twenties with a great sensibility for seniors. I immediately liked Amelia. Instead of my blond hair, blue eyes, and pale countenance, I wished I had Amelia's shiny, tanned skin, sparkling black eyes, and straight, coal-black hair. I delighted in the way she spoke English, with a subtle foreign accent I hadn't before heard from anybody else. Her parents had immigrated to this country and brought her with them when she was a child. She attended school and also helped with the family business, making and selling Guatemalan crafts in street markets.

The thought of my connection with Ernestine never going back to the way it had been before Grandpa died frightened me. Amelia behaved very friendly towards me, and I often asked her about how Grandma was doing. Nevertheless, I felt the need to track my grandmother's situation at a personal level and decided to start a diary when I was still in middle school.

Reviewing my journal, I felt the desire to write this current account. For a long time, my entries contain only a pessimistic view of Ernestine's condition: her not eating, not sleeping, not talking to people, withdrawing to her bedroom in the dark, and so on. A year after I had started the diary, the first optimistic note shows up: *Ernestine wants to come to my school and see me perform in our ballet play,* I wrote.

Ernestine came to see our show, and I felt happier than I remembered having been in a long time. Grandma's attitude had changed. I was unsure of when the change had started, but it didn't matter because from that day on, she returned to go places and be active again. It seemed like a miracle. But once she regained her self-confidence, she asked Amelia to stop coming, which I thought was a mistake.

Grandma went on living her life as a widow without significant problems until one day in September 2007 when she received news that Theodore died of a heart attack. One of his daughters called from Boston. He had divorced and lived alone. Ernestine managed to communicate the news to my parents, and they called me at school, so I phoned Grandma during the recess.

"I'm very sorry about your brother," I said.

"Thank you, dear. Theodore's passing—"

She went silent.

"Are you OK?" I asked.

I heard her weeping over the phone.

"I don't feel like living anymore," she said.

How could I console her? "We'll help you go through this loss," I said.

"Thanks, Martina, my child."

My parents accompanied Ernestine to Boston for Theodore's funeral. After their return, I noticed a change in Grandma's expression, but I couldn't figure out what it was. When she'd had a chance to rest a little, I took her out for dessert at a small café I knew she would like. Ernestine wore a black cotton dress—her dark-blue eyes and gray hair highlighting her features—and on the dress's neckline, a gold necklace stood out. She looked pale, and I remember my father had said that when younger, she was a slim lady, with long arms and legs, and freckled, pale skin, but on this occasion, she looked too pale.

"I'm sorry about your brother passing," I said again.

"Thank you. Theodore's passing—" She stopped.

She remained silent, staring at the cup of steaming tea in front of her. Her hands dropped to her lap, and all expression on her face vanished. I felt sad, and it dawned on me that the change I had observed in Grandma on her return from Boston was due to sadness.

"What's wrong?" I asked.

She was startled. Tears rolled down her cheeks. With difficulty, she got a handkerchief out of her purse and dabbed her eyes.

"Nothing makes me feel happy anymore," she said.

I got up from my chair, went around the table and hugged her. We wept together, and when we resumed talking, we addressed unrelated issues, such as my plans after finishing school, the beauty of her necklace, which had belonged to my great grandmother, she said, and little more. While we chatted, I realized Ernestine's sorrow seemed profound, and maybe she would never recover completely from her loss. After I had taken Grandma back home, I let myself cry.

Although bereaved, Grandma tried to make a comeback, but she often complained of back pain. Her doctor, Dr. Morgan, a tall, lean, mature, well-mannered man, whom I had met once at Grandma's place when she had a bout of diarrhea and he came to do a home visit, diagnosed osteoporosis of the vertebrae. He also said she was at risk of falling.

My parents were concerned about Ernestine living alone. When my grandparents had arrived in San Francisco, they leased an apartment until they purchased the house in which she lived. She argued that she was capable of taking care of herself. She also wanted to do some volunteer work at the local hospital. And it didn't take long for Ernestine to start working a few hours three days a week. Her duties consisted of delivering mail, magazines, and cheer to the patients. They called her the zucchini bread lady, she told us, because she often baked large loaves of zucchini bread, sliced them, and offered them to the staff. She kept herself busy, and I thought she had regained her vitality. I was far from anticipating that in that winter (2008), one evening, she felt chest pain and called for an ambulance. The doctors diagnosed a heart attack. They contacted my father before performing a bypass operation.

The surgeon recommended that she not live alone. I was present when the doctor made his recommendation because my parents had asked me to accompany them to pick up Ernestine upon her discharge. She looked weak. Amelia was called back to help her. But in spite of all the care, about a month later, she fell. At lunch time, Grandma said she needed to go to the bathroom before sitting at the table. A moment later, Amelia heard a loud thump. She rushed to seeing what happened and found Ernestine on the floor 'all confused.' She called an ambulance.

My parents and I went to the hospital where Ernestine was admitted. My mother talked to one of the doctors taking care of her. Mom worked in the front office of a medical group and knew a lot of medical terms. She shared with my father and me that, according to the doctor, Ernestine had two fractured vertebrae and was in pain. She needed an operation to take care of the problem.

After the operation, the doctors referred Ernestine to a rehabilitation center. I often accompanied Dorothy to visit when my parents were busy. Weeks of uncertainty went by before she returned home. When she did, she had to use a three-legged walking cane. She still complained of pain in her back and legs. She looked older and thinner to me, and her mood was dark. We tried to cheer her up, and I took her out to the park for short walks. Mom convinced Amelia to move in with Ernestine. Amelia is an angel.

In the spring of 2008, I was about to graduate from high school and I hoped Ernestine would be able to attend the ceremony. Shortly before the actual date, however, one evening, while sitting on the sofa, watching TV, she felt dizzy, and her body lurched to the left side, falling. Amelia phoned my father, who advised taking Ernestine to the ER. The doctors said she had just had a stroke, which weakened the left side of her body. She complained of burning pain in her left shoulder and arm.

Four days later, the doctors discharged her in a wheelchair, with more medications and prescribed physical therapy. Dr. Morgan came home to see her. He had been in touch with the hospital doctors who attended Grandma. Her further complaint of burning pain, he said, was due to the stroke. She's going to need a lot of rest and care, he warned.

"I don't want to live like this," Ernestine said after Dr. Morgan had left.

She was lying in bed in a light nightgown because she couldn't stand any heavy clothes without feeling more pain.

"We'll help you with everything, and you'll get better," I said.

"I don't think so, dear. I believe I'll become a burden to you all."

"Dad says he'll hire a nurse—"

"I can't take this pain. I would like you to take me to see Father Damian."

A seasoned Catholic priest, with a good reputation, Father Damian had met my grandparents through the parish church.

"OK," I said. "I'll drive you there."

Mom had bought a new car and passed her old Toyota Corolla on to me. So the following morning, Amelia helped me to put Ernestine's wheelchair and walking cane in the trunk, and I drove her to church. I wanted Amelia to come along, but Ernestine shook her head.

When we arrived at the church, the priest wheeled Ernestine through the vestry into a room to receive parishioners and we helped her onto a chair at a round table, near a window. Ernestine kept holding her cane. I got up to leave the room, but she stopped me. "You can stay," she said. I sat by her side, and Father Damian across the table, facing the window. A tray with a teapot, cookies, and a few books of devotion lay on the table.

"I do not wish to keep on living," she said.

Father Damian looked surprised.

"Do you feel depressed?" he said.

"I'm in pain, an invalid, and don't want to become a burden to anyone. I pray God takes me."

Father Damian served tea, and he and I grabbed a cookie.

"I'm afraid God won't listen to you," he said.

He dunked the cookie in his tea, and I did the same in my cup.

"Why do you say that, Father?" Ernestine asked.

The priest hesitated. "You're asking the Lord to change His plans for you."

She grew impatient, sighing in pain.

"I find your opinion hard to accept," she said in a sarcastic tone.

The priest looked annoyed.

"What do you expect from me?" he said.

"I want you to help me die."

"That would be euthanasia!"

Father Damian looked at me: Please help me with this! I read on his face. I reached for Grandma and held her left hand; it felt cold. Her face showed disapproval, and I remembered she could not stand anything touching the paralyzed side of her body. I withdrew my hand. She produced a sigh of relief.

"Let's calm down," Father Damian said. "Would you like a cookie?" He picked one up, but Grandma shook her head.

"Your issue is a matter of faith," he said.

Ernestine lifted her cane into the air. She looked fatigued. She glanced at me and made it clear she wanted to leave. I thought she had run out of an argument. Since the brain injury, she had a hard time staying focused and finding the right words to say, which further irritated her. Father Damian seemed to understand her situation and remained silent, gazing out the window as if looking for an answer. We made it back home safely.

My mother hired an LVN to help Amelia with the care of Ernestine. Dr. Morgan facilitated the installation of a hospital bed in her room. About a month after her visit to Father Damian, Ernestine had another stroke. I thought that the devil had something to do with it, for she now became nearly blind. I couldn't look at her without breaking into tears. She found a smidgen of energy to ask for her doctor. He came to see her, and they talked privately. My parents and I were there when Dr. Morgan arrived. When he came out of her room, he looked concerned.

"She wants to die," he said. "Even if I wanted to, I can't help her."

My mother offered him a cup of tea, and we all sat down in the living room.

"Ernestine has also asked me to help her die. I couldn't find words to respond to her request," my father said.

"Who's to say where the limit of human life ends?" Dr. Morgan said.

The issue raised by the doctor struck me as mysterious. What kind of help did Ernestine mean? I felt impelled to get up and go see Grandma. She was awake. She briefly explained to me what she was expecting somebody do to her. I listened in astonishment. Now I knew what exactly she wished from others. Why didn't any of them do it?

"I'm disappointed at Father Damian and Dr. Morgan," she said.

I started crying. I said nothing. I didn't find any words that could sound fair to her. I caressed her forehead. I kept touching her.

Ernestine got worse. She remained bedridden and in pain. We all helped to wash her body, dispose of her waste, keep her hydrated, and administer her meds until she entered a coma. Within two weeks, her fingertips and lips turned blue, she produced a final sigh, and she died.

After the funeral, vivid memories of the times Grandma and I had spent together piled up in my mind with disregard for chronology. Images of her grasping for the last breath in her deathbed scrambled with those in the park when she used to push me on the swing while I enjoyed my childhood fear-lessness. Now, in my junior year, during moments of solitude while writing these notes, I reflect on Ernestine's struggle. She had anticipated the end of her life. She wished to become nei-ther a burden nor commit suicide. She called upon the people she trusted, her family, her pastor, her doctor, to piously and peacefully help her die, but she received no convincing answer. What do other doctors, priests, and wise men in society think about the struggle between life and death that people faced in their late days? What did I do to help Ernestine? What would I tell her now if I saw her again? Please forgive me, Grandma. I love you. I'll miss you. I'm sorry I didn't know how to help. I won't forget. Goodbye.

Lucas Parra

It's the year 2010, and Lucas Parra can't wait to be there! He's returning to his old town in Spain, where he was born and raised. His parents immigrated to America when he was a teen and settled in California.

On the train, after landing in Madrid, Lucas occupies a window seat and takes in the early morning view. It's the end of summer, and the plains appear bereft of crops. Now and then, a flock of birds crosses the sky, and a lonely village shows in the distance. When the train enters the station of Lucas' destination, he gets off and takes a taxi to the hotel he has booked.

"Welcome, Mr. Parra," a young male receptionist greets him—his name carved on the tag pinned to his lapel: Armando. His stylish haircut, up-curved mustache, and gold buttons of his jacket match the hotel's atmosphere, a two-story building with a touch of Italian taste.

"Thank you."

A porter leads him to his room. He unpacks and hangs his clothes in the closet. A blue turtleneck sweater brings the memory of Patricia, his wife, also an immigrant from Spain. They had met in USA after they graduated from college. She died of cancer, six months ago, and he misses her terribly. Lucas gets the last pair of socks out of his suitcase and pushes the luggage rack into a corner. He takes a shower and changes into fresh clothes, and around noon, he steps out of the hotel.

He strolls along a broad avenue lined with office and apartment buildings and little gardens along the side. The sound of bells coming from an old church squeezed between two apartment buildings calls his attention. As he looks up to the turret, it begins to pour, and a raindrop splashes on his eye. Lucas wears a brown leather jacket and shoes but carries no umbrella; he hurries down the street. He wishes Patricia walked by his side, but she is gone forever, and he must carry on the plans they had made before she died. They had agreed to move to Spain. 'It'll be great,' she had said.

In his haste, his feet slide on the slippery pavement, and he's propelled forward until he crashes into a young man in a yellow poncho who sweeps pools of water with a wicker broom.

"Hey, Old Man, watch your step!" the sweeper voices. "At your age, a fall means a broken hip. I've seen it happen when it rains."

"Sorry!" Lucas slows down.

Old man. The phrase touches a sore point. When Lucas announced his decision to retire, the director of the corporation of nursing homes, where he had worked for decades, used the same phrase: 'You've contributed to the excellence of this institution, Lucas. Now that you're an *old man*, you might consider moving here,' he had said. 'Thank you,' Lucas replied. For the time being, though, I have other plans.'

Rushing in the rain, Lucas feels optimistic. He can't hide the crow's feet around his eyes and his gray hair, but he feels healthy, and his mind works fine. His vision is not great anymore, but the crashing into the sweeper was an accident. Why bring up this crap about his being an old man? As he walks down the street, he tilts his head down to avoid the raindrops that wet and fog his glasses. Soaked from head to toe, he reaches the Central Plaza when the clock from the City Hall strikes twelve. Coincidently, the rain stops, and sunlight break through the clouds. Lucas finds himself in an urban space, surrounded by offices, boutiques, and restaurants. He navigates his way to one of the terraces and occupies a table next to a young man—a plate with a sandwich and a cup of coffee lay on his table, and he reads a newspaper, which he moves aside to glance at the newly arrived.

"I did not expect rain," Lucas says. With his fingertips, he brushes his wet hair.

"It's been cloudy all morning," the man says.

Lucas shakes raindrops off the lapels of his jacket. "You are right."

"You aren't from here, are you?" The man folds his newspaper and leaves it on the table.

"Why do you—"

The waiter approaches Lucas. "What would you like to have?"

"A ham sandwich, espresso, and a glass of water, please," Lucas says.

He turns back to the conversation. "Why do you ask?"

"The way you talk."

"I have lived abroad for a long time."

"I guessed so," his neighbor says and takes a bite of his sandwich.

"What do you mean?"

"That you're a returnee."

Lucas remains silent.

"They all come back," the man says. "Some of them hope to do great things here. It's funny. I'm looking for work myself. That's why I got this paper. Not many jobs available around here."

The waiter brings the order, and Lucas waits until he's gone before he talks again.

"Tough!" he then says.

"Very! Let me introduced myself. I'm Marco, an unemployed business administrator."

"Lucas Parra, a retired accountant."

"Well, Old Man, welcome back." Marco picks up his paper.

"Thank you."

Lucas eats his sandwich, sips coffee, and watches the activity on the plaza. He imagines Patricia and him strolling around and getting acquainted with local people. After a while, he feels sleepy, and guesses it might be due to jet lag. He calls for the waiter, pays the bill, smiles to Marco, and leaves straight to his hotel to rest.

The next day, and for the next couple of weeks, Lucas journeys through town on foot. He goes from one office to another to formalize his status in Spain. At some point during his journey, he comes across a city park in which he used to play as a child. Sadly, it's missing the enchantment it once had, for he notices fewer birds in the trees and ducks on the pond, and more people around. From this park, he and his pals used to walk along the edges of farmland to the river. Lucas feels nostalgic and decides to stroll down there.

Three youngsters are fishing. Fish-catching nets, bamboo rods, and fishing kits lay on the ground. Lucas observes them. He wishes he were a grandfather, but his only son Oscar and his Chinese wife, Sue, are childless. They moved to Hong Kong soon after they married. Lucas saw them last at Patricia's funeral. Sue didn't look healthy. They struggle to make ends meet, but they have never accepted help. Lucas walks to the edge of the water.

"Hey! boys, any luck?"

"We just got here," says one of the boys.

"What do you use as bait?"

A second boy turns to him. "We use artificial lure-flies, of course."

"I see. When I was your age, my friends and I used to dig right at the riverbank to find the worms."

"We live in a different world now, Old Man," the third boy, taller and stronger than the other two, shouts.

Lucas stands still. Does this boy think I am less of a person because I am a senior? He moves away. A real estate agent expects him at his downtown office in an hour. Patricia had planned to lease a flat until they sold their house. A warm autumn sun spreads throughout the countryside, and he hates taking a bus or taxi; he walks.

The realtor, a tall man in his forties, wearing a gray jacket and blue tie and speaking with an Argentinean accent, suggests walking to see a flat he thinks will comply with Lucas requirements.

The flat forms part of a three-story building, located in a quiet area, and it has two bedrooms, two baths, and a dining and living area with French windows facing a park.

"In tip-top condition," the realtor emphasizes.

"Beautiful." Lucas stands in front of the French window and looks out. "What are the leasing terms?"

"Before signing the contract, the corporation that owns the building expects the future tenant to provide a deposit."

"A deposit?" Lucas scratches his head and turns to face his interlocutor.

"I beg your pardon, Mr. Parra, but that's the requirement, along with paying the realtor's fee, the community fees, a two months lease, and—"

"Really? I have never heard of such a string of obligations."

"The building is a historical landmark."

Lucas swallows and turns to look out the window again. He becomes more interested in a willow tree he sees in the park than he is in the flat. He looks for a pond nearby; willow trees love water.

"Something less pretentious," he says, still looking out.

"I should have advised you—"

"It is not your fault," Lucas interrupts, turning to face the realtor. "I am a widower. I am trying to follow my late wife's wishes. She never said we ought to live in a historic building," he adds with a smile.

"I certainly can show you other properties, Mr. Parra, but, may I say, you being a respectable old man, I would suggest—"

"A nursing home!" Lucas heads towards the door.

"A living community for seniors, Sir."

"I will think about it. Thanks for showing me this apartment anyway. Now I must go."

Outside, a late afternoon sun lends a purple hue to the streets. From afar, dense clouds approach the city. Lucas heads toward his hotel. He wishes he were settled in town. He has placed a call to a company that is looking for a part-time financial advisor. When he arrives at the hotel, Armando hands him a piece of paper with a message. Lucas reads, *Mr. Miranda would like to see you at 11:00*, and he guesses it's about the job. He eats dinner at the hotel restaurant and then goes up to his room.

The next morning Lucas goes to meet Mr. Miranda—his office is half a mile away from the hotel. It smells of rain. On this occasion, though, Lucas carries an umbrella. When he arrives, he sees a three-story historic building. Another landmark! He rings the bell. A female secretary in a dark blue skirt and jacket opens the door.

"Please, Mr. Parra, come on in. Mr. Miranda will receive you shortly."

"Thank you."

In the antechamber, Lucas deposits his umbrella in the stand by the door and takes a seat. He grabs an issue of *Forbes* magazine from a coffee-table and leafs through, but after a few pages, the secretary comes back. "Mr. Miranda will see you now," she says and escorts him to the office. Lucas had expected a luxurious setting, but the place, while spacious and well lit, looks humbly furnished. After shaking hands, Mr. Miranda sits at his desk and gestures Lucas to sit across from him. Fifteen minutes into the interview, Lucas has spelled out his credentials.

"Your background in accounting fits our expectations," Mr. Miranda says. "However, this position requires extensive traveling both national and international."

Lucas reacts like a puppy does to his master's command. "I have no problem with traveling."

"It's the level of resilience needed that worries me," Mr. Miranda says.

Lucas glances at the family pictures spread on the desk, shifting from one to another, trying to disguise his disappointment. "The level of resilience?"

"Please, don't get me wrong, Mr. Parra. Age in itself is not, of course, a factor—"

"What is it, then?" Lucas lifts his chin and stares at his interviewer quizzically.

"It's the reality that matters."

Dejected, Lucas leans back on his chair. Mr. Miranda has hurt his pride like his former employer, the street sweeper, Marco, the boys at the river, and the realtor did. He feels as if he is going to explode. Suddenly, he pounds on the desk, knocking over some of the framed pictures.

"I get it!" he says. I mean, *reality*."

Mr. Miranda raises his eyes. "Well," he says, "I'll let you know the outcome of this interview as soon as possible."

They shake hands again. Lucas feels strangely at ease. Mr. Miranda phones his secretary to let her know that Mr. Parra is leaving. Lucas walks out of the main office and goes to pick up his umbrella. He sees a young man sitting on the chair he had occupied before.

"Marco?" he calls.

"Yes, and you're—"

"Lucas Parra."

"Sure. How are you?"

"I feel strangely at ease! Listen, Marco, coincidently, we have applied for the same job. I don't think I'll get it, but if you do, please call me (Lucas tells him the name of his hotel), and we'll celebrate together."

"Will do."

Outside, it's raining. Lucas walks under his umbrella to the hotel. He reflects on the many changes he has witnessed in his life: the vinyl records replaced by the CDs, the typewriter by the PC. . . Seamlessly, we go from one to another reality. Distractedly, he comes across the street-sweeper he had encountered before, wearing a yellow poncho and sweeping the pools of water away from the sidewalk.

"Hey! Old Man," the sweeper shouts. "Good to see you again. I see you've learned how to protect yourself from the heavy rain."

"That is the reality, Young Man," Lucas replies and keeps on walking.

When he arrives at the hotel, Armando greets him.

"Hello, Mr. Parra, you've got another message." With a smile, he tears the top page from a hotel notebook and passes it to him.

Lucas grabs the piece of paper and holds it between two fingers. He takes a look at the young man with his curved mustache and his uniform with gold buttons like a character from past times.

"I wonder, Armando," he says, "after you get off work, do you find it hard to shift to your other daily realities?"

"It isn't. I switch really fast."

"You mean you get in and out your roles like some tourists hop on and off a bus?"

"Well, I never thought of it that way, but, yes, pretty much so."

Lucas smiles and walks away. When he gets to his room, he holds the paper with the message in between the lips while he fishes for the keycard in his pockets and then opens the door. Inside, he walks to the window, and looking out, he reflects on his experiences of the last few weeks. For Mr. Miranda, age dictates the level of endurance a person can display at work; for Marco, the chances of finding employment; for the realtor, the setting where one should live, for—a jet crossing the sky, leaving a trail of white smoke, cuts short his musings. He grabs the piece of paper held between his lips and reads the message: *I got the job. We'll be celebrating at the Grand Hotel lounge, downtown, this evening after six. Please join. Marco.*

At 6:15 pm Lucas steps into the Grand Hotel lounge and spots Marco in the bar, standing at the counter and surrounded by half-a-dozen friends—all men. He makes his way to Marco, past dark Italian-leather couches placed on a red carpet, and joins the group.

"This is my friend Lucas, the retired accountant," Marco says, introducing him to the others.

Lucas likes that Marco refers to him as *my friend*. He smiles widely. Someone hands him a glass of Bourbon-on-the-rocks, and he raises his glass towards Marco, gesturing a toast. "Ah!" he exclaims after taking a sip. Marco keeps ordering drinks and appetizers for all, and they chat about jobs and women—small talk. Lucas smiles and listens.

"I'm also an accountant," someone whispers in his ear. "Ruben's the name."

Lucas turns to make eye contact: a short, lean man in his mid-forties, with sallow skin. "You are the first colleague I have met in this country," he says. Ruben smiles, and Lucas opens up to befriend all of these men.

After the party, Lucas returns to his hotel, feeling a little tipsy and very elated. He enters his room and switches on all the lights. He paces the floor as if looking for something he is missing. It's ten o'clock. Should he go to sleep? Take a shower? Watch a movie? Have another drink? He throws a look at the mini-bar. No! He sits on the edge of the bed and gets a couple of business cards out of the breast pocket of his shirt, reaches for the phone and dials the number printed on one of them.

"Hello?"

The voice sounds strange, disengaged.

"Marco?"

"Yes."

"It's Lucas—"

"Sorry, I've got company."

"Oh! I just wanted to thank you again—"

"You're welcome."

The conversation ends. Oh, well! He wishes he could share the welcoming experience he has had at Marco's party with Patricia. He goes back to pacing the room until, fatigued, he begins to undress. In his pajamas, he sits up on the bed. Before going to sleep, he dials the number on the other card.

"Hello?"

Lucas recognizes this voice.

"Hello, Ruben, it's Lucas. Hope I'm not intruding. I know it's late and—"

"Don't worry, Lucas, my wife and I go to bed late. What's up?"

Lucas feels at ease. "I wanted to thank you—"

"Oh! No need. It's been a pleasure. If we can help in any way— After all, I know you've just landed in this country—"

"Yes, a little over a month ago." Lucas repositions the pillows behind his back and leans on them.

"Do you live alone?"

Lucas crosses his feet together. "My wife died six months ago." He senses how lonely he feels.

"If I may ask, why are you here?"

Lucas perceives no reproach, and he succinctly tells Ruben his story.

"That's amazing. What's your next step?"

"I don't know. I'm staying in a hotel. I would like—"

"I see. Well, I work for a private firm that owns a residential living complex for seniors. Perhaps you—"

"Interesting, a real estate agent advised that I should take a look at that type of dwellings."

"Listen, I'll talk to the administrator, a woman. Everybody knows her by her first name, Maria. She'll give you a call, and you can check it out. What do you say?"

"It would be great."

"We'll talk again. Good night."

"Good night, Ruben, and thank you."

Lucas receives Maria's call, and although a bit skeptical, he sets off to visit the senior living complex on an exceptionally bright autumn morning. When he arrives, he notices the wrought-iron gate that leads to the interior courtyard is ajar and decides to go in and take a peek. A circular water fountain in the center of the yard with a statue of The Fallen Angel in the middle and a choir of water-jets around it captivates him. Sparrows bathe in the fountain and then extend their wings in the sun. Landscaped plots of different sizes and shapes, carefully cared for, spread throughout the entire yard. He imagines roses, pansies, and camellias coloring the little gardens in the spring.

"Sir, can I help you?" a male voice asks.

Lucas turns to him. He is a gardener.

"I have an appointment with the administrator."

"It's this way, Sir." The gardener leads him.

At the administration office, Lucas meets Maria: short-cut, black-amber hair, black eyes, and shiny teeth matching her white dress. He hadn't anticipated her being a lady of color and such a pleasant appearance, a young-looking senior.

"Please sit down," she says and points to a pair of armchairs set around a coffee table in the middle of the room.

"A beautiful fountain," he says and points to the courtyard. "I can imagine how colorful the flowers might be in the spring."

"They have a lovely fragrance, too. But please, allow me to inform you briefly about our facility."

The property, rectangular in shape, covers one acre of real estate, with three blocks of buildings, each harboring ten living units, facing the central yard on one side and the street on the other, and a white, solid wall, with the wrought-iron gate, providing the forth side of the rectangle.

"Would you like to see the available units?" Maria asks.

"Yes, please.

"I suppose Ruben has mentioned to you that I am a widower—"

"He has. I'm sorry about your wife, Mr. Parra. Ruben also said you are a returnee?"

Lucas draws a brief smile. "Yes, I am an *old man* returning to my old country."

He feels relaxed. Maria is accommodating, and the office aesthetics pleasing. A vase with white lilies sits on her desk, a tea set on the coffee table, and landscape pictures hang on the walls.

"Someone from my office will give you a tour before our real estate agent shows you the available units. I hope you like our facility." She gets up, goes to her desk, and makes a phone call; then, she comes back to Lucas. "Arrangements made. Please, don't hesitate to ask any question, any time."

"Thank you."

A woman from PR guides Lucas through several activity areas of the building and gives him a brief explanation about their features and use until the loudspeaker calls his name. They return to the administration office where he meets the real estate agent, a young, red-haired man with freckles who introduces himself as Angel.

"*Angel* as in *The Fallen Angel?*" Lucas tries to be funny.

The real estate agent, a soft-spoken and friendly man, smiles. He shows three furnished apartments to Lucas, each one equipped for comfort. Lucas likes what he sees, and back in the administrator's office, he signs a one-year lease. When he leaves the complex in the afternoon, he strolls through the streets, enjoying the city's atmosphere, until he feels hungry. He stops for dinner at a restaurant serving local food, and later, he walks to his hotel.

Lying on his bed, Lucas wishes he could communicate with Patricia. In his imagination, he evokes her voice.

"It's so wonderful to hear your voice, Patricia," he speaks aloud. "I miss you so much."

I hope you're well.

"Yes, I am."

How is Oscar?

"He is well, too, but Sue continues having flare-ups of her illness."

They are going to need your help.

"I'll be ready. Listen, Patricia, I have lots of things to share with you—"

Lucas stops talking; he's weeping. He realizes the futility of his endeavor: Patricia is gone, and he is alone facing life. He takes his glasses off and goes to sleep. He wakes up in the morning feeling pressure as if he ought to dispatch some urgent matter. The move! That's what he tried to tell Patricia last night. He takes a shower, gets dressed, and goes to the senior living complex. When he arrives, he sees that the gate to the yard is again unlatched. He pushes it open and enters.

"Sir—?" somebody calls. The gardener stands a few yards away, watering the plants. "Do you need any help?"

"You showed me the way to the administration. Remember?"

"Yes, Sir, I do."

"Thank you, though."

Inside the building, Lucas stops at the reception office and asks to see Maria. The receptionist dials the extension number.

"She'll be available in ten minutes," she says.

"Thank you."

Lucas sits and waits. Once in the office, Maria invites him to take a seat. Lucas tries to describe his needs, but hesitates.

"Perhaps you should make a list?" she says and passes a pad of paper to him.

Lucas makes a list.

"I've got a suggestion," Maria says. "Some residents would be happy to help you."

A week later, he finds himself sitting on the couch in the living room of his new home, sipping coffee and looking out the glass door to the courtyard. In the fountain, the water jets shoot up and fall synchronously. He feels lucky.

Approaching winter, Lucas goes out to enjoy the scenes in town. He delights in hearing the crunch of fresh snow under the soles of his shoes and seeing the bell towers covered with a white cape. But in December, though, he feels lonely. He calls Maria.

"Hello?"

Lucas remains silent. "This is Lucas," he finally says.

"Is there a problem?"

"No. I don't know how to put it. I wish I knew more people around here?"

"Throw a party!"

"Excuse me?"

Maria explains that a team of volunteers from the complex love to organize welcome parties for new tenants. Lucas mood brightens.

A couple of days later, Maria guides Lucas around a room set up for the purpose, making their way around the tables and chairs, and introduces him to other residents in the complex. He worries he won't remember everybody's name and strives to retain some details from the new faces he encounters. After he has met a few people, he asks Maria whether she minds if they sit down for a while. They occupy a table on which there are appetizers and wine. They serve themselves some slices of cold meat and a glass of rosé, and they chat. Lucas learns that Maria divorced ten years ago and has no children. From Lucas, Maria hears about Patricia, and Oscar and Sue. He, Lucas, can't understand why they remain aloof. While they chat, they also glance around, and Lucas spots Ruben and his wife Iris, sitting at a table. Lucas excuses himself and goes to greet them. A minute later, he is back with his friends. They all engage in conversation. Iris tells him that she volunteers as an events coordinator at the complex. She needs someone to help with the accounting of fundraisers and expenses. Would Lucas be interested? Other people stop at their table and join the conversation. Lucas enjoys his time thoroughly.

When the party ends, Lucas feels gratified. Slowly, he walks to his apartment through the courtyard and briefly stops near the fountain to let the breeze refresh him. It's time to go home.

Following the open-house party, Lucas receives phone calls and thank you cards. Maria invites him to a Christmas Party at her home, and Iris encourages him to volunteer his expertise as an accountant to help with the setting of forthcoming events. These demonstrations of affection reassure him that he has chosen the right community. Today, though, in the mailbox there is only one letter. It's from Oscar. Lucas takes it, steps inside, and puts it on the kitchen table while he pours some coffee for himself. Then, he sits and stares at the envelope like a greyhound at a still rabbit. He takes a sip of coffee, then grabs the letter opener and tears the envelope open. After the second sentence, he stops reading. Sue has died. Suddenly, buzz upsets his ears. His hands are shaking, but he manages to keep on reading. Sue died in the hospital after she had a severe flare-up of the blood illness. Oscar writes of his profound sense of loss. He feels isolated in Hong-Kong (Sue's family lives in Beijing) and longs to return to California. He pleads with his father to also return home; he needs him. Lucas finishes reading the letter and tosses it onto the table like a heavy piece of lead. The buzzing in his ears gets louder, and he can't think straight. He gets up, grabs his coat from the closet, and goes out.

On the streets, he roams through the city park of his childhood, the river, and back to the Central Plaza. There, he enters the terrace of the restaurant where he had met Marco on his first day in town. But Marco has a job, so he walks away and returns home. He takes his coat and shoes off and lies on the bed looking at the ceiling, thinking of Patricia until he falls asleep.

In the morning, Lucas wakes up feeling at ease. He is convinced Patricia spoke to him during his sleep. He gets dressed and goes to the administration office.

"Maria, I must return to California."

Taken aback, the administrator stares at him.

"Is that so?" she asks.

They are standing in the middle of the office, facing each other. Maria invites Lucas to sit down. He declines.

"Sue, Oscar's wife, died," he says. My son is going back to California. He needs me. I promised Patricia I would be ready for him if he called for help."

"I'm sorry." A pause follows. "To break the lease contract is going to take some time, though," Maria adds.

"I know the process."

"Perhaps you ought to leave some money in the bank to pay the monthly fee in case the reality in your life pushes you to come back?"

Lucas reflects on Maria's advice. "I might," he says. "Circumstances mark an individual's destiny, like the wind guides the weather vane."

Maria nods. She moves closer to him, and they hug each other in an emotional goodbye.

Never Too Late

From her last alcohol binge, instinctively, she ended up at his door. They had been drinking buddies, and later, lovers—a long time ago.

With whatever remained of her, and her seventy years of age weighing on her shoulders, she sat down at his kitchen table across from him.

"What's left of you besides bones and a flicker of spirit in your eyes?" he asked, fearful of smothering her last breath of hope.

"Habits, we develop over the years. Some bring happiness and others tears," she said in a shaky voice.

"You're consumed by alcohol. But you won't admit it, will you?" His confrontational approach, though, softened as he viewed her pathetic appearance.

"Perhaps this is my last port. I drop anchor."

She had a coughing spell; then, she lit a cigarette.

"Sure," he said. "I guess next you're going to make smoke rings and tell me stories of years gone by."

"Why should I?" she said and exhaled halos of smoke through her protruded lips. "You know them all. Alcohol, nicotine, gambling—"

"Indeed, I know all your *habits*, your joys, and hurts."

Through ringlets of smoke, she threw him an avid look.

"Maybe we pray to break these bad habits," she said.

"I doubt praying alone will do it. I also struggle to stay sober."

She offered him a cigarette. He shook his head; then, he got up and brought two glasses and a bottle of water.

"Please," she said and pushed a glass toward him. So he poured a glass of water for her. "I guess you're happy," she added. "Spring is here. You made it through winter."

He poured water into the other glass for himself. "I'm listening," he said.

She drained her glass.

"I want to quit my drinking," she said. Now her voice didn't sound shaky.

He became aware of her return to life.

"You took off on your own," he said, trying to dissipate any tone of reproach in his voice, "and now you return to my door, wasted and in need of compassion."

She dropped the cigarette butt inside the empty water glass. "Without alcohol, I fear my life will turn dull," she said.

He rapped his fingers on the table. "I fear alcohol will soon kill you."

She raised her eyes toward him, and now her facial features softened, and tears ran down her cheeks. "I don't want to face life, stripped bare."

"Nobody's completely alone with life."

A silence followed. She tried to recompose herself. "I need help," she said, dabbing her tears. "I need your guidance."

"Not so," he said. "Alcoholic Anonymous ought to be your guide. I can only support your initiative."

"I'll start tomorrow," she said.

"Why not next month?" he replied ironically.

She hesitated. "Today," she said.

"Now."

She nodded. They got up and left together.

Palmiro

"I'm tired of your laziness!" Silvia leaves the apartment and slams the door behind her. Palmiro, feeling harassed, jumps out of bed and walks into the bathroom; he hates that she wakes him at dawn.

A few minutes later, he dresses in a sweatshirt, hangs a Marlboro from his lips, and storms out to the streets in downtown Madrid. "I'll light your cigarette—" He hears the song through his earbuds as he lights up.

Six-foot tall, lean, and pale, Palmiro strides aimlessly. When he feels hungry, he checks his pocket—some money left. He takes one last drag from his third Marlboro and walks into a little café, located at the corner of two narrow streets. A couple of customers sit at one of the available tables, but Palmiro chooses to stand at the counter.

"A cup of coffee, no cream, no sugar, and toast," he commands the angelic-looking waitress behind the counter. "Fuck the bitch!" he mutters under his breath.

"Excuse me, are you talking about me?" The waitress, who appears to be of his age, in the early twenties, looks perplexed.

"I'm saying that soon I'll compose a hit song, and she'll know who I am."

She relaxes her shoulders. With her fingertips, she styles her short, dark hair. "Are you a musician?" Her eyes shine with expectation.

"I'm a songwriter."

She smiles and moves away to make the toast and pour the coffee.

"And who is she?" she asks when she returns.

"She's my girlfriend. She looks like you, slim and graceful; only she is blond and blue eyes. For some reason, this morning she woke up feeling mad and left, slamming the door."

"She may have her reasons," says the waitress. She stands behind the counter, near him.

"She wants me to find a job and forget my dream." He shakes his head.

"What dream?"

I'm an artist, he thinks but doesn't say. Instead, he hurries to finish his breakfast and pays the bill.

"Soon, you'll find out who I am, sweetie," he yells to the waitress and walks out the door.

Outside, a bright spring sun blinds him; he has forgotten his sunglasses. He reaches for the shady side of the street and walks slowly, tightening the earbuds in his ears: "You don't bring me anything, but down—" the voice sings. He keeps on going towards Puerta del Sol. There, he enters the subway. In the Metro carriage, the air feels thick and hot. He sweats profusely and wipes his forehead with his sleeve. Man kills his girlfriend with an ax, Palmiro reads in the paper that another passenger holds unfolded in front of his eyes. He turns his head away to avoid throwing up. He gets out two stops later.

Palmiro emerges to the street surface at Calle Fuencarral. He takes a deep breath and walks down the street, looking for a particular three-story building. Once there, he enters, climbs the stairs to the second floor, and stops in front of one of the apartments, whose door is painted with a vivid red color. He turns his phone off and rings the bell. Silvia opens the door.

"How dare you come to my sister's place?"

"You can't leave me like that, Silvia."

"Who's to stop me?" She straightens her shoulders.

"I love you—"

"No, Palmiro. You love yourself. For two years, I've been going to work—"

"I can't hold a job, and you know it," he cuts her off.

"That's your problem! I'm fed up with listening to your excuses." she takes both her palms to her belly as if in pain.

"I'm an artist!" Palmiro says.

"And I am pregnant. You're going to be a father." She looks straight at him.

Thunderstruck, Palmiro pushes the door, but Silvia closes it shut. Damn it! She is pregnant. I'm going to be a father, she says. What does all this mean? He remains standing there, immobile, until the brightness of the red color blurs his sight. Then, he puts another cigarette in his mouth and turns around. Silvia's news that she is pregnant has shaken his insides. What is he supposed to do? "Soon, I'll compose a hit song," he babbles on his way out of the building.

He can't make up his mind toward where to head. The memory of the young waitress at the little cafe pops into his mind, and he goes back there. Now a crowded place, he walks to the counter and sits on a stool between other customers.

"Hey, sweetie," he calls to the same waitress, "I need a beer."

In spite of his bravado, his stomach shakes, and his heart weeps. The customer on his right, a senior man, glances at him with an expression of disapproval. The waitress approaches him.

"Has somebody beaten you up?" she murmurs.

"I'm not sure of where I belong," he says.

She throws him a look of compassion. "I'm Monica," she says and smiles.

"I'm Palmiro."

"What type of beer?" Monica asks.

"A draft of any beer."

The customer on his left, a middle-aged woman, a little bald, glances at him with a grimace of disdain.

"I'm an artist!" Palmiro yells.

Nobody makes any comments regarding his statement. Monica brings him the beer and calmly asks what his trouble is.

"I can't hold a job, damn it!" he yells and grips the glass of beer with such pressure that his arm trembles, and he gets glances of contempt from the people around him.

Tension arises. With an air of indifference, he puts his earbuds on, aware of being the focus of attention. Quietly, Monica leans forward and knocks on the wooden counter in front of him like she would have done on the door at his place. Palmiro pulls his left earphone out.

"We, artists," she whispers, "can also work." Palmiro, disconcerted, stares at her. His brain doesn't hear the music from his phone anymore. "I'm on my way to becoming a professional ballerina," she adds with a smile. "If I didn't work, I wouldn't be able to afford my training."

Monica's words bring calmness to the customers, but Palmiro feels uneasy.

"How much is it?" he asks.

"The beer is on me," Monica replies.

"Thanks," he says and, eyes cast down, leaves the place.

Absentmindedly, he goes back to stroll in the streets, no longer listening to the music. At the turn of a corner, his eyes come across a sign, set on the façade of a building. It's made of white tiles, with the name of the street —Calle Clavel—at the bottom and a large pink carnation painted in the middle, surrounded by several smaller ones. Something on it calls his attention. Suddenly, the carnations rearrange themselves in front of his eyes into words: Do something practical, he reads. Such a weird vision!

Palmiro, shaking his head, emerges from the spell feeling scared; he also feels compelled to take action. "I can do better," he utters to the clouds. He hesitates between going back to the little café and thank Monica for her wise words or back to Silvia's sister's apartment and share with her his determination to look for a job.

Three Black Birds

At dawn, Anna, Carolina, and I set to hike on steep trails from the foot of the Pico de las Espadas onward to the top of that Aragon Mountain.

Recently graduated from med school, I started to work in the emergency room of the county hospital. Ana worked there too, and the Department Director determined I should join her shift. Soon, I realized that Ana displayed much endurance at work, which I admired. When she shared with me her fondness for mountaineering, I thought that perhaps her physical strength came from her practicing that sport.

"Are you interested in mountaineering? she asked.

I had no experience with the sport. Anna passed me a small book about it she had published, which I found interesting.

"I'll give it a trial," I said.

That's how I met Carolina. When Anna introduced me to her, an Art student, I quickly sensed she had a sweet nature.

I started dating Carolina. She suggested that we join Anna in her Pyrenean excursions. I couldn't fancy Carolina—a small girl with a pale complexion— climbing on steep trails, but the idea of exercising outdoor appealed to me.

The three of us often ventured out together. Anna's ability to show how to battle weather and terrain adversities became apparent. I admired Anna and loved Carolina. Also, I became aware of a strong bond that existed between these two women.

So today, at dawn, the three of us set off to hike on up-hill trails, committed to reaching the summit—Anna leading, marking the pace, Carolina in the middle, and then me, not quite as tall as Anna was but physically in good shape. A little after two hours of marching, I began to feel my backpack heavier on my shoulders and wondered about Carolina's.

"Do you feel tired?" I asked.

She nodded but uttered no complaints. I realized Anna had taught her how to develop stamina. During the excursion, Anna was pending of our safety; she appeared self-confident and aware of her leadership role. Carolina, on the other hand, needed reassurance now and then.

Halfway up, we stopped to rest. We sat on a flat rock off the trail, ate a snack from our backpacks, and drank a sip of water from our canteens. Anna noticed the presence of clouds where before the sky had been clear.

"It smells like rain," she said. "We should hurry a little."

We resumed the walking. A cooler breeze had made its presence, and a smell of ozone floated in the air as if a thunderstorm was forthcoming. I trusted Ana's guidance. She pulled us faster over the last stretch until, at the edge of noon, perspiring but happy, we crown the apex. The sun appeared blurred out among thick clouds, and the atmosphere gray and oppressive. I felt difficulty in breathing, and Carolina claimed she felt dizzy.

"Listen to a rumbling noise in the distance. It's the wind," Anna warned. "We got to be strong!"

The howling wind seemed to gallop toward us, whirling among the rocks. Moments later, dense clouds broke, thunder resounded, and a long serpent of fire tore through space. Three big black birds in flight just above us were shaken violently. They lost their way, and before the lifeless remnants from one of them had fallen to our feet, another flash of fire intertwined with Anna's body, and she collapsed onto the rocky ground. Immediately, I walked to her side and checked her pulse.

"Very feeble," I murmured to Carolina.

She had crouched down five or six feet away. Trembling, she gazed at us as if contemplating an apparition, as if Anna and I were the inhabitants in a different world, a world unknown to her. I proceeded to do mouth-to-mouth resuscitation, checking and rechecking for Anna's heartbeat, until I realized that her heart had stopped functioning forever.

I moved away from Ana's dead body and went to Carolina. She looked as if she was in a trance: her teeth gnashed, her hands shook, and her eyes opened widely. The windstorm was whirling very strongly around us. Carefully, I pulled her toward me first, and then, down to the ground. She let herself do. We lay immobile, in shock, until a torrential rain woke us up from our lethargy. Darkness had taken over. The Pico de las Espadas had blackened; the sun had gone out of our lives.

"Anna is dead," I said. "We must notify the police." I could hardly stand. I grabbed my cellular to make the call, but it showed no sign of reception. I asked Carolina to let me use hers. With shaking hands, she passed it to me. No sign of reception either.

"Let's go back to the valley," I said. "We need help."

With a great effort, Carolina took a thin blanket out of her backpack, passed it to me, and then pointed toward Anna. I grabbed the blanket, walked back to Anna's dead body and covered it. I didn't touch anything else.

We tried to retrace the way we had climbed at dawn; now trackless trails, for the wind and the rain had erased all markings. With Carolina sobbing by my side, I being afraid of losing our route, and struggling to overcome obstacles, we walked down to the valley and back to the small house the three of us had rented the day before. Filled with apprehension, I stepped in, and Carolina followed me. At that moment, reality hit me hard: We had been three in the house; now, we were only two. I felt bewildered, uncertain of what to do, what to think, what to say to Carolina.

"I love you," I said, but my words sounded as if pronounced at the wrong time.

"Anna is not longer with us," she replied in a distant, ghostly voice, and her words sounded like the announcement of the end of a trip, a terminal station.

Drained out, I sat down on the couch in the living room. Carolina retired to rest in the bedroom. I called the police. As I tried to describe what had happened, I had a flashback about a county employee who was taken to the ER two nights before. He was almost dead due to an electric shock he had received while he was working on a public installation. Anna took charge of the case. She applied the defibrillator to the patient's chest and saved him.

"I couldn't save her," I automatically said to the officer on the phone. He assured me a rescue helicopter would be dispatched to the area right away. He also requested that Carolina and I remained where we were until they came to meet with us.

After the phone conversation, I lay down on the sofa and tried to relax, but images of the awful event crept into my mind. Would the two black birds that lost their friend while on flight survive? Had we lost Anna forever? I fell asleep.

I have woken up a short while ago—two o'clock in the morning. For a few moments, I was unsure of what had happened until I remembered Caroline was resting in the bedroom. We had not talked to each other since we came back to the house. I went to check on her. She was awake. "Yesterday, we lost Anna, our loved one," she said with a distant, ghostly voice.

I left her resting and returned to the living room, where I'm now sitting on the couch, waiting for the police to arrive and wondering whether Carolina and I will be capable of loving each other without Anna.

El Teso Village

Father Lionel Guzman had been the parish priest of Cruz-Santa Church for thirty-seven years and was feeling too old to keep pace with the demands of his ministry. His hair had turned gray and his muscles often ached, but his life as a rural priest helped him to stay slim. He was a Ladino, a descendant of the colonial Europeans, taller than the average man in town. Rarely did he wear a cassock outside of religious services, but he never failed to wear a large crucifix on a thin chain. In the past, it had not been unusual for him to walk several miles on dusty paths to visit a family in need, conduct a burial, a wedding, and so on.

A couple of years ago, on a night of thunder and rain, someone knocked violently on his door. It was after midnight.

"Father Guzman!" a female voice called.

He put his pants and shirt over his pajamas.

"Who's there?"

"It's Irma. My husband Ulil went to the woods at sundown to gather pine straws. He isn't back. I've a bad feeling. Please help me." Irma had married Ulil four months earlier, and they were expecting their first baby.

He opened the door. Irma, a young, handsome Mayan woman, was wearing a dark-reddish huipil and nagua, and had covered her shoulders with a small green blanket. She looked apprehensive and was soaked.

"Please help me."

He wasn't sure if this was a dream.

"Let me put my boots on and grab a couple of lanterns," he said.

They walked hastily, in silence, side by side, near the mountain slope, holding their breath and their lanterns. She knew the area well because she had accompanied her husband many times to collect pine straws. They were basket weavers. She called her husband's name. Father Guzman called it too. But they heard no response, only the sounds of the wind and rain beating against the leaves of the trees. Suddenly, the priest stumbled over a large, blackened lump surrounded by bundles of pine rods. Probably a charred trunk of a tree, he thought. But Irma had fainted beside him, and when he saw it was Ulil's dead body, he knew that lightning had struck him.

It took several weeks for Father Guzman to recover from that shock. Gradually, though, he went back to his mission of gaining terrain over the Protestants in favor of Catholicism. The Evangelists had already built a church, and this was killing him. Convinced that the Catholic iconography and rituals made a better match for the native people than the Protestant liturgy did, at the beginning of 1981, he maintained his enthusiasm for the mission. To complicate matters, an armed conflict between the military forces of the Guatemalan Government and civilian guerrilla groups was going on in different parts of the country, including the Highlands, cradle of the Maya Civilization. Although the actual fight had not reached El Teso Pueblo, an atmosphere of stress prevailed as news about the atrocities committed not far from there filtered in.

Father Guzman had written to the Bishop asking for another priest for Cruz-Santa Church, which would be a blessing. The Diocese replied at first that it was not possible to honor his petition *due to a shortage of priests and an extreme need for religious services, from those priests available, in the war zone.* A response to his third letter, though, arrived days prior to the celebration of the annual town festivities, in March. He adjusted his glasses to read it: "It will now be possible to provide your church with the assistance requested." He was reading to Ismael, the mestizo church administrator. "Father Francis Palenque, a young Jesuit with a clear vocation to help the humble with their spiritual needs, is expected to join the parish church of Cruz-Santa shortly." The letter was signed by the Bishop's personal secretary. While reading, Father Guzman's hands were shaking. Ismael made him aware of it. The old priest was taken aback by the clerk's remark. "Wouldn't your hands shake, Ismael if you were as happy as I feel now?" he said. They were in the vestry, also used as an office. The priest stood beside his desk and the clerk near the door to the main church, fixing a candlestick.

The priest released the letter onto his desk and silently sat in his chair. He looked weary. He remembered that Ismael had also noticed his hands shaking while lifting the Holy Host, during Consecration. Even Indalecia, the Mayan woman who was his housekeeper and cook for so many years, had seen his trembling. 'Your hand is shaking, Father,' she once said as he brought a spoonful of soup to his mouth. He wondered if other people had also witnessed this quivering. Maybe Irma, who was just about to give birth, had also noticed it. Would it become a problem? He needed his physical entirety to continue his ministry. Father Guzman stared out the window toward the big volcano. Then, he got up as if in a hurry. "We have work to do, Ismael," he said. "We better get going."

The townspeople busied themselves setting up the stands for the market and decorating the streets with colorful paper flags for the annual festival. It was the hot season. Some two thousand people lived in town, most of them of Mayan descent: farmers, weavers, and artisans. El Teso Pueblo had had a more relevant past when the capital of Guatemala was in the Panchoy Valley and magnificent buildings were raised in the city and the valley villages. It still counted with an ancient bridge and a few Spanish colonial buildings, one of which served as City Hall and another as Court of Law, both located in the Central Plaza. The narrow cobbled streets about the plaza were the ones being decorated.

During these days, Francis Palenque arrived in town. One morning, he knocked on the door of the vicarage, adjacent to the church. Indalecia opened it, and they silently glanced at each other.

"I'm Father Palenque," he said.

"Father—?" she inquired as if she hadn't heard him.

"Francis Palenque. I just came on the bus," he spoke in Kaqchiquel, the local indigenous language.

Indalecia was in the presence of a very young Mayan man.

"Welcome, Father Palenque. I'm Indalecia, Father Guzman's housekeeper," she said in Spanish.

"Sorry I didn't let you know the exact time of my arrival," he said, also in Spanish.

He was wearing a dark blue shirt with the sleeves rolled up; black, smooth corduroy pants; and dusty, military-type, black boots. For luggage, he had a crumpled leather bag slung over his right shoulder.

"Father Guzman was expecting you at any moment," Indalecia said.

Lionel Guzman was anxious to meet him. Standing in front of him—short, slim, with dark hair and black eyes—in the lounge hall, though, he felt very old. This was a child!

"You entered priesthood very young, I presume?" He said.

"I don't remember ever wishing to do anything else."

Father Guzman nodded. "I'm a Franciscan, a soldier of Christ," he said.

They looked at each other silently.

"Well, welcome to El Teso Pueblo," Guzman finally said. "Indalecia, my housekeeper will take you to your lodging. I'm sure you would like to rest for a while."

In addition to the vicarage, the church had a small dwelling annexed to the property, where Francis Palenque was going to lodge.

Francis liked the church—a sturdy, concrete-and-stone construction, showing no particular architectonic style. Located on First Street, about one hundred yards from the Central Plaza, it stood in the middle of a broad esplanade with magnificent views of the big volcano.

"Built before the independence of Guatemala," Father Guzman said as they walked inside.

"What was here before?" Palenque asked as he glanced at a large figure of Christ on the cross carved in wood and hanging behind the altar.

Father Guzman didn't know what had been standing on that ground before the church was built.

"Nice work isn't it?" he said instead, pointing to the statute of Christ.

"Yes, very nice."

Having walked around the entire church, Father Guzman led Francis Palenque to the vestry where they found the parish clerk at work.

"Ismael helps with everything from weddings to funerals, and he is also our administrator," he said as a way of introduction.

"Great," Francis said, "I'm pleased to meet you."

The two men shook hands. Ismael, a few years younger than the parish priest, was a stocky man, of healthy appearance, and well grounded. He lived with his wife, not far from the church; they had no children.

"Father Palenque was asking me what was here before this church was built," Father Guzman said.

"As far as I know," Ismael said, "nobody has ever heard of anything important being on these grounds before this church."

"It's a good question, though," Father Guzman said, turning to Ismael. "See what's happening now with the old bridge."

They each sat on wicker chairs around a coffee table placed in the middle of the vestry.

"Indalecia will bring us coffee and biscuits in a minute," Guzman said.

Francis stretched out his legs in front of him and crossed his hands on his lap.

"What's happening with the bridge?" he asked.

Father Guzman also stretched his legs and leaned back.

"Two archeologists came here a couple of months ago and declared the bridge is over a thousand years old," he said.

"Interesting," Francis remarked.

Lionel Guzman said nothing.

"The Government has money available, we guess from the Americans, to invest in this valley," Ismael said. "The plan is to re-channel the flow of water running under the bridge and build a road along its current course."

"They plan to get rid of the bridge altogether?" Palenque asked.

"Yes, but many oppose the idea of knocking down a historical bridge. Besides, most people believe a road would bring soldiers into town, and that scares them," Ismael said.

"I can see why," Francis said.

Indalecia arrived holding a tray with the coffee.

"It's their river, people say," Father Guzman spoke.

"Isn't that true?" Palenque remarked.

Father Guzman tried a piece of sweetened bread and helped himself with a cup of coffee.

"The issue has two sides," he said. On one hand, in people's eyes, the Government will deprive them of the water they need to grow their crops. On the other hand, a road might benefit the village at large."

"Where does the Church stand on this?" Palenque asked.

"It's their river, people say," Father Guzman repeated.

"Isn't that true?" Palenque asked.

Father Guzman dipped another biscuit in his coffee and took it to his mouth carefully to avoid shaking. Ismael took the thread again.

"Cruz-Santa is not alone in this dilemma. The parish of *Piedras Blancas* is also affected by this plan."

"I see," Palenque said.

All three continued chatting for a while longer while drinking their coffee.

The next morning, Francis Palenque went back to the church by himself. At that hour, it looked brighter. Indigenous women were washing the floor, setting bouquets and chandeliers around the altar and polishing the pews. They had turned on the lights. Palenque smiled at them.

"I'm Father Palenque, the new priest," he introduced himself. "Who uses these pews?" he asked smiling.

"These are for the important people," one woman answered.

"Where are the pews for the ordinary people?" he inquired still with a smile.

The woman looked surprised as if he should know better.

"They prefer the benches," she finally replied.

"I guess so," he said and waved them goodbye as he continued his route through the church.

Every year, Father Guzman said a solemn Mass at noon to honor the patron saint. Attired in a colorful chasuble, he headed a slow-paced procession from the back of the church toward the high altar along the central aisle. This year, Francis Palenque, wearing a black cassock and holding a tall, light-weight metal cross, walked behind him. Six children in white tunics followed them, swinging a censer and spreading incense throughout the space. Open mouthed, the peasants looked at Father Guzman as if he were a deity. He was happy to see his church full of people. He saw Irma, standing in the back—she would soon give birth to her baby. He glanced at Dr. Julian Bruno, the general practitioner, a man in his mid-fifties who lived in *Piedras Blancas*, six miles away, but never failed to attend the yearly solemn mass in El Teso Pueblo. He greeted the people in the pews. When he reached the altar, he made a genuflection and turned his attention to God's matters. At the end of the mass, he blessed his congregation. "The Lord opens the doors of our Faith to all," he said.

That day, the market was at its best: an amazing display of shapes and colors, and smells of chilies, tortillas, grappa, and coffee. Father Guzman swung by in the early afternoon. For him, moving around those crowded stalls every year was a reminder of the passing of time. The swineherd sold baby pigs as he had done from years back; only presently, his body stooped and new wrinkles appeared on his face. Father Guzman thought about himself getting old when he heard a voice calling him. It was Irma. She was standing a few yards away. Colorful baskets hung from her shoulders. She signaled him to move to First Street, and he went there, wondering what she would want him see.

A juggler, surrounded by a circle of admirers, performed. Lionel Guzman came across another circle of people standing around a man who talked to them. He got closer and recognized Francis Palenque. "I've been in the Highlands, and I realize there is no compassion for the humble and poor there," he was saying. Lionel Guzman guessed that was the reason Irma asked him to come to this street. Francis sounded credible. Sooner or later, the old priest reflected, all of us will have to face reality. One only had to listen to the clandestine radio broadcasting from Cuba to know that the fight was not between Christians and pagans but the powerful and the oppressed. Francis spared no effort to connect with the townspeople. Father Guzman decided the wise thing to do at that moment would be to leave him alone, and he moved away.

April marked the beginning of the rainy season. Along with the rain, a Government military commissioner, Lieutenant Atilano, a tall, blond Ladino man in his thirties, with a loud voice, arrived in El Teso Pueblo to supervise the obligatory military draft ordered by the President of the Republic. The rain kept falling relentlessly, and by the end of May, the streets were muddy and the milpa, the maize fields, flooded. The mayor, Ulmil Zunc, a Mayan man in his forties with the air and cunning of an ambition politician, issued a proclamation to notify the townspeople of the urgency to discuss a possible course of action to deal with the flood. He called for a meeting at the City Hall. The handcrafted ceiling of the room where they gathered attracted glances of admiration.

"First thing is to prevent a mudslide," Lieutenant Atilano told the audience.

He, the mayor, and the police chief occupied seats in a slightly raised platform at the front. Ulmil Zunc grabbed a pen and made an entry in a notebook.

"With my respects, officer, we need more resources," Zoylo, a small Mayan man, a representative of the farmers, said.

"What do you need?" The lieutenant asked.

Silence ensued, except for the raindrops knocking on the window panels.

"With the sewers clogged," the physician said, "we fear an outbreak of dysentery."

"If so, the Army will help to evacuate the sick," the military man said.

Ulmil wrote something else in his notebook.

"Sir," Zoylo called again, "the milpa is our wealth," he stated humbly.

"Don't panic," the officer Atilano said. "The new road will facilitate economic development."

He referred to the Government's intention to rechanneling the river and building a road where the ancient bridge stood, which would link with the Pan American Highway and bring wealth into town. Ulmil added a new entry in his notebook. Dr. Bruno seemed attentive to whatever could apply to his cause, and Father Guzman, his fingers intertwined to avoid quivering, envisioned his dream of filling the empty niches on the front facade of his church with new stone sculptures.

"If I may say," the physician raised his hand, "we need ambulances and another doctor."

His words triggered utterances of approval from the benches, including the natural herbs medicine-man and the midwife. Many people, when feeling sick, chose to look for the local medicine man first, but if they did not improve they recurred to Dr. Bruno.

"Our church—" Father Guzman started. "The niches on the front façade are empty. Before I came, stone-carved figures of saints filled them. But now, now," he repeated, "with Father Palenque aboard, now, it would be possible to fill them again."

His voice trailed off. Ismael, who sat by his side, kindly grabbed his hand to keep it from shaking, and Francis nodded. Lieutenant Atilano looked at the clock, which hung on a wall in the room—almost an hour had passed—and grinned at the mayor. The latter seemed to interpret the gesture as meaning it was the end of the discussion. "The meeting is adjourned," Ulmil said. "Thank you all for your attendance."

People picked up their ponchos from the racks by the sides of the Conference Room and exited the place. Outside, Ismael invited the old priest to come under his umbrella, and they walked home together. Father Guzman stooped and stepped on the pebbles awkwardly.

"I hope this lieutenant will bring us some good," he said.

"He's convinced the Government will," Ismael affirmed as he kicked a banana skin away.

"Thanks for the kick," Father Guzman said. "A lot of work remains to be done, tough."

When they arrived to his home, he opened the door, and after thanking Ismael for his company, he stepped inside.

On June, the independent farmers gathered in the milpa fields to perform their traditional ritual under the full-moon light in preparation for the harvest. The rain had ceased, but sadness prevailed because the damage caused by the flooding meant a reduction in the volume of crops. But there they were, men wearing allegoric masks and women ceremonial huipiles embroidered with patterns of animals and flowers. They were at the point of initiating the traditional dance to honor their deity, *Maximon,* and ask Mother Earth for fertility when they saw a helicopter landing not too far from where they were. They witnessed men in military uniform getting out from it and moving away across the field.

The next day, the story of the helicopter, along with Irma's just born baby boy, Ulil junior, became the talk of the town. The appearance of the helicopter brought forward different interpretations. Some people voiced the existence of communist pockets nested in the town, and the soldiers had come to remove them. For others, the soldiers arrived to help the local authorities with the forced draft, and the civilians were Government agents. And a few opined that El Teso Pueblo was in the crosshairs of the Government for an unknown reason. Perhaps the mayor knew what was going on.

Ulmil informed the townspeople that the civilians who descended from the helicopter were Canadian experts in matters of oil drilling. The Government had expanded the search for oil to include the Panchoy Valley, starting in El Teso Pueblo. As for the soldiers, they were in town only to help the lieutenant—as many had guessed—supervise the ongoing enlistment.

Father Guzman summoned Francis Palenque and Ismael to the sacristy to talk about the plans to expand their church.

It was one of those days of down-pouring rain, and they could hear the drops splashing on the roof. They had coffee and pastries served by Indalecia. Lionel Guzman took his cup to his mouth with great care, holding it with both hands to avoid spilling the coffee because of his shaking.

"There are many things we need to do," he said. "A new baptismal font, a granite altar table, statues to fill the niches on the front façade—"

"More schools, potable water, a lot of things we need," Father Palenque interjected. "A matter of priorities, I guess," he added.

"What would be your priority?" Ismael asked him.

"Unity, a single voice," Palenque said.

The pastor and the parish clerk looked at each other wondering.

"Speaking of unity," Father Guzman said after a few moments, "Julian and I plan to write to the Bishopric detailing what we need for our church and his patients."

"I suppose you should rather write to the Government," Ismael said.

Father Guzman made a gesture as if feeling uncomfortable. He tried to cross his legs, but immediately gave up because he felt awkward while attempting the movements. "The President of the Republic and the Bishop sometimes dine together," he said. "As for the unity you speak of, Francis," he added, "I find the concept difficult to explain in a letter."

Following those words, and lacking further matters to bring up for discussion, they ended their meeting.

Meanwhile, a group of dissident recruits escaped into the mountains after refusing to enlist in mandatory military service.

Nevertheless, some people in town saw an opportunity to prosper economically under the wings of the Government. Under an overall atmosphere of uncertainties, however, a public protest took place.

Zoylo managed to convene about fifty farmers at the old bridge on the morning scheduled for its demolition. Standing up and holding each other's arms, they surrounded the bridge to manifest their opposition to its destruction. The lieutenant, the mayor, the police chief, and a crowd of observers, including the two priests, arrived at the scene. The Lieutenant Atilano and Zoylo talked at a distance and tried to cut a deal. "The lieutenant acknowledges your interest in saving this bridge," Ulmil announced afterwards, speaking through a megaphone. Shortly after, people dispersed peacefully.

Coincidently, Ulmil's daughter was getting married to a diplomat, at noon, on that same day, in Cruz-Santa Church. Father Guzman performed the religious ceremony and then attended a reception set at the mayor's home. Tables and chairs were set in the yard, and people moved around chatting, laughing, eating, and drinking. Local musicians played Marimba music. When Father Guzman arrived, he spotted a table in the shade and was on his way toward it when Dr. Bruno met him midway.

"Hey, Lionel, listen, I've got news for you." Privately, the doctor and the priest addressed each other by their first names.

"Let's sit down first, Julian," Father Guzman said, pointing to the table in the shade.

"Shall I bring you a drink?" the physician asked.

"Punch with a splash of gin, please."

Father Guzman went to occupy the table while the doctor went to the corner of the garden where a provisional bar had been installed and procured the drink. Two people were already sitting at the table chosen by Father Guzman. They greeted the priest with a smile, but he did not engage them in conversation. When the doctor came to the table, Father Guzman asked what news he meant. The other people got up from their seats, respectfully bowed to them, and moved away.

"The Government has agreed to concede everything we asked for in our letter to the bishop."

"I can't believe—"

"Not only to that. They want you to grow a garden in the esplanade of your church," the physician added.

The priest stared at him. "But I haven't requested a garden."

"It's a gift from the Government."

Lionel Guzman meant to say something else when Irma unexpectedly showed up by their table.

"I didn't expect that man to be here, at this wedding," she said.

"What man?" Dr. Bruno asked.

"That Lieutenant Atilano."

"What's wrong with him?" Father Guzman wondered.

"Yesterday, I went to my stall in the market," Irma replied and glanced at Father Guzman as she talked. "The lieutenant looked at me with lust," Irma jerked her face to a side in disgust. "I'm a widow and the mother of this baby. I hate him." She started sobbing.

Irma's presence, her holding the baby over her hips, her breasts bouncing with her agitated breathing; everything about her triggered his sexual arousal. Silently, he prayed and held the hanging crucifix tightly in his hand.

"Zoylo and Father Palenque," Irma went on, "think the lieutenant and the other foreigners are here to oppress the poor and favor the rich." With a hand, she wiped her cheek.

Father Guzman, his mouth half open and his lower lip visibly trembling, cast his eyes on her—only his eyes expressed his amazement. Just then, the newlyweds along with some of their guests and the lieutenant approached them.

"For the bright future of El Teso Pueblo," Lieutenant Atilano shouted, raising his glass.

Irma barely got a hold of her temper. She adjusted her black hair, which was tied back in a thick braid, and holding her baby tightly against herself, moved away. The tension dissipated, and the party went on.

When ready to leave the party, though, Father Guzman was feeling sick. It had been a long and emotional day. First, the protest about the old bridge in the morning; then, the wedding in church at noon; and finally, the evening celebration, and Irma's scene. He tried to get up from his chair, but his muscles cramped, and his legs froze.

"I'll take you home. Get some rest, and you'll soon feel better," the doctor said.

Dr. Julian Bruno had arrived in Piedras Blancas some fifteen years after Father Lionel Guzman had started his parish mission in El Teso Pueblo, and the two men soon became friends. To care for his patients, the physician traveled from village to village by bicycle until he bought a Honda motorcycle, which he still had, and later, a black Volkswagen Beetle.

As the doctor had anticipated at Ulmil's daughter's wedding party, the old priest got better after a few days. He wondered what was wrong with him, but he didn't dare to ask the doctor. Not that he was afraid of dying, rather he was afraid of becoming crippled, and therefore, unable to complete his plans for the church. The temple, Cruz-Santa, or his vision of an improved inside and outside building, had become a symbol of his legacy as the village's priest.

"My hand trembles, Francis, but I don't feel like consulting with Julian Bruno," he confided to the young priest when he came to visit during those days of home rest.

They were in the vicarage, a rather unpretentious dwelling: one bedroom, dining and living area, kitchen, bathroom, and a little room used as an office. When Francis came to visit, they sat in the living room, near the window through which they could see the volcano across the splanade.

"A glass of brandy?" the old priest asked.

"No, thank you."

"I will," he said and rang a handbell to call his housekeeper to bring a bottle of brandy.

"Why don't you ask the local medicine man, then?" Francis wondered.

"Ask what?"

Francis Palenque stretched his legs in front of him. "Does he know of a healing brew for your shaking?"

"I'll ask Julian when I'm ready."

Indalecia came back with a bottle of brandy and two small glasses on a tray. Francis served Father Guzman the liquor.

"I need a steadier hand than mine to deal with these times," the old priest said.

"I'm here to help," Francis said.

"Things are more complicated than I had anticipated."

"Things never remain pure in times of war," Francis drew a benevolent smile.

"Sure, but I particularly worry about our community."

It was evening, and the room, facing north, stayed cold. Father Guzman rang the bell again to request a blanket from Indalecia.

"What's the trouble?" Francis asked.

"Irma speaks of a split in people's opinions about what's going on in town," he said.

"Differences in point of view are inevitable under these circumstances."

Indalecia returned with a small wool blanket.

"None of us should get political," said Father Guzman, comforted now by the blanket extended over his belly and the brandy in his system.

"But we must get involved somehow."

Father Guzman turned to him as if troubled.

"You aren't a communist, are you?" he asked point blank.

Francisco did not flinch. He leaned forward to get the bottle of brandy and poured another glass to his master.

"Irma speaks of the 'oppressed,'" Father Guzman insisted.

Francis set the bottle of brandy back on the table. Publicly, he had identified himself with the poor, born into a family of farmers from the Highlands.

"Let's be clear," he emphasized. "We Mayan people are chapines, of sharp instincts. The authorities of this country impede our progress because if we did progress, they wouldn't be able to manipulate us."

The old priest leaned back on his chair and crossed his arms over his chest. "I hope you don't turn political."

"I'm only a catechist."

Father Guzman smiled at him. "I just want our church to look nice, as the House of God should look," he concluded.

Francis Palenque gave himself up to his catechesis with enthusiasm. He convinced Dr. Bruno to sell him the Honda motorcycle since the physician hardly used it after he had bought his VW. Riding the motocicle, he ventured into the Highlands—Sololá, Cobán, Petén—where the armed conflict was rooted. As a consequence, Father Guzman noticed an increase in church attendants, which released him from the obligation of himself preaching to the unfaithful and gave him the opportunity to concentrate on improving the church's looks. The growing of a garden in the esplanade had started, but not so the other projects, for he heard from the Diocese the approval of these other projects would take longer. Francis Palenque realized the importance of spreading the right message among those receptive to hear it so he could promote unity. He understood the concept of economizing energy, and he was an advocate for the poor and oppressed.

"What we need is a place where we can teach people how to speak with a single voice," he said to Guzman.

The parish priest wrote to the Bishop, requesting authorization, and soon after, an abandoned building, located at the junction with the Pan-American Highway, served as a Catechist Training Center.

"What part of the Gospel will you preach, Francis?" Father Guzman wondered.

The two men strolled in the new and almost finished garden by the esplanade of the church one warm morning at the beginning of November. They were getting acquainted with the kinds of plants and trees already growing there.

"Respect for human rights."

"*Palo de jiote*"

"Excuse me?"

"I'm reading the label attached to this tree, here."

Francis looked at the young tree, crooked and leafless. "I see."

"It will grow into a tortuous tree," Guzman said.

Slowly, he moved on. Then he stopped again.

"Did you know that?" he asked.

"What?"

"That the branches of the Palo de jiote grow in a tangle."

"Yes."

They approached another young tree.

"This one is a cypress," Guzman said. "It will grow up straight."

Francis nodded.

"I heard you," the old priest said now.

"Excuse me?"

"'Respect for human rights,'" you said.

They stopped walking and glanced at each other.

"Fairness, unity—" Francis began saying.

"Those are difficult concepts to explain." Lionel Guzman cut him short.

They courteously smiled at each other and kept on walking.

"I guess you mean it sounds *political*?" Francis asked.

"Lieutenant Atilano may disagree with the way you impart catechism. It's—"

"Tortuous?"

"Yes, it isn't straight, like the cypress."

Francis broke away from his companion and, as he walked, began talking to the flowers as if they were an audience: "Love, as Christ taught us, consists in going the extra mile to do good without expecting any benefit for oneself," he said emphatically.

"That's straight Christian talk," Guzman approved.

"I know. I'm a Jesuit. But I'm not convinced that everything attributed to Christ's teaching is right."

At that moment, they heard Indalecia, standing by the vicarage door, calling Father Guzman.

"Telephone," she shouted.

"Sorry, Francis, I must go back. We'll continue our exploration of this garden at another time."

He turned around, and with shuffling steps, he went to answer the phone while Francis kept on strolling.

Not every change that went on in town happened seamlessly. Prosperity did not reach all corners, and change was not always advantageous for all farmers. Jealousy and revenge proliferated in the new El Teso Pueblo. Families whose sons were involved in the civilian patrols, away from the field, saw a decrease in the volume of production of crops. There were also unexpected outcomes. Irma, for example, went to live with Lieutenant Atilano. Under his wing, she led a group of women, embroidery and basket weavers she had organized into a cooperative, throughout the intricacies of exporting their articles. Father Guzman could hardly take the betrayal. He refused to keep her present in his prayers—he confidentially told Ismael.

In the midst of this landscape of changes, Father Guzman woke up on the night of December eleventh startled by people shouting and banging on his door. This sense of urgency triggered a flashback to the night in which Irma had lost her husband. He tried to jump out of bed to see what all the noise was about, but his body would not move. The people outside, though, did not wait for him to open the door; they knocked it down.

Julian Bruno, Ismael, Indalecia, and a few other neighbors bounced into his house and his room. They helped him to come to the window, and he saw, under a full moon, his church in flames. It was burning on all sides. He had never seen a more spectacular fire in his life. He was in a state of awe. Why had that happened?—he wondered—those massive flames, that inferno, why? He felt pressure in his chest as if a tourniquet gripped his heart, and his eyes suddenly went blind to everything around him. Instead, he saw with the mind's eye a parade of flashes from his life in front of him. Was God angry at him because of his sinful attitude toward Irma? Nevertheless, he was conscious of, despite his weaknesses, having never trespassed on her limits. Although during his life as a priest he had to fight moments of lust, he never failed to hold on the crucifix he carried, asking for forgiveness. Occasionally, he doubted his religious vocation, but he was fully committed to doing God's will. Why then this punishment of seeing his church in fire?

"Father Palenque's headquarters is also on fire," Julian Bruno said, and his words shook the priest out of his trance and back to see the real flames.

"Where is Francis?" he asked.

"He was taken away," Dr. Bruno responded.

The old priest felt betrayed. Francis had set the fires on purpose, he thought, an act of revenge because he—Father Guzman—was not providing him with enough support in his crusade against those who oppressed the humble and the poor. Suddenly, he punched the panel of the window with surprising force.

"Is he a communist?" he asked infuriated, keeping his eyes on the flames.

"Please, Lionel, calm down. He isn't," Ismael intervened.

Hearing these words, Father Guzman calmed down.

"Why then—?" He was unsure of what he tried to ask.

"He is an advocate of the New Christ," Ismael whispered.

The priest turned his head toward him for an instant—his face reddish from the reflection of the flames through the window. "What do you mean?" he asked, glancing back at his church.

The fire blazed out of control. This building was his dearest parish church, a symbol of his dedication to God's will, his only meaning in life, and his commitment to keeping El Teso Pueblo parish a Community of obedience to the Lord. This destruction came as an indescribable loss for him.

The specks of ash floated in the air and their silhouettes, illuminated by the moonlight, resembled flocks of ugly birds that the breeze pushed toward the new garden on the esplanade.

"Francis is accused of being part of the Guerrilla Army of the Poor," Dr. Bruno said.

"Is he a guerrilla?" the priest asked, his eyes fixed on the floating ash.

"No," the physician said. "He is a catechist."

Lionel Guzman, his hands trembling, moved his head away from the window and toward Julian Bruno.

"Will the military execute him?" he asked.

"His teaching implies the poor can and should have access to power," Julian Bruno said. "That's why nationalist soldiers are in a rampant revenge, burning churches and catechist centers, and arresting the priests who preach in them, from the Highlands down to El Teso Pueblo."

More people arrived at the vicarage. Lionel Guzman hoped to see Irma among them, and his heart pumped stronger for a minute, but she was not there. He wondered which side she would join. Then, he addressed the physician again, "Julian, what is wrong with me?"

"You've got Parkinson's," the physician said.

Father Guzman nodded as if he understood everything about it.

"Indalecia, would you please help me go back to bed?" he said.

She helped him to lie on his bed. With his crucifix quivering between his fingers, he let himself fall asleep.

The Ambler

Luis Vela had adopted the *Cadets Decalogue of the Army* of his country as his model for conduct and manners.

"One day, you'll outrank your father," his mother had proclaimed when he entered the military academy at eighteen. After he had graduated, however, he declined to volunteer to fight in Western Sahara to defend the Spanish colonies there against the Moroccan invasion. He realized, then, that he loved everything military except going to war. His father had reached the rank of Colonel before he died, but he, an only child, at fifty-eight, wore on the shoulder pads of his uniform the emblem of captain. Now, it was too late. All he could do was to conceal his past evasion, which went against the dictum of the Decalogue: *To volunteer for all sorts of sacrifices, requesting and wishing to be appointed to see the riskiest action and hardship.*

On Saint Valentine's Day, in 2008, Captain Vela, a single man, was strolling on the streets of his city under the rain. As a young officer, he had managed to obtain a teaching position and since then, he lives in Madrid. He taught Military Rules of Conduct and Civility to soldiers in the Military Reserve. Shy of six feet tall, he walked in his uniform, which he wore only on special occasions, smelling of Old Spice aftershave lotion and forcing himself to maintain his military composure. He fantasized the day's magic would lead him to meet a woman and fall in love. But in the evening, he was still alone, unlucky, and weary. Raindrops splashed on top of his umbrella, slid down its curve, dripped onto his boots, and pooled to the ground. "Monotony and loneliness," he murmured to himself.

At some point, his wandering took him near the *Casino Militar,* an elegant Officer's Club, which had served as a place where he could show that he knew how to behave like a gentleman. He would arrive in his uniform, a daper officer, play pool with his peers, and dance with some of the ladies who admired him. Conscious, though, of his popularity being lately at a low level there (although he couldn't see the reason for it) he stopped abruptly in the middle of the sidewalk; then he turned around and walked in the opposite direction. He moved fast under his umbrella, as someone propelled by fear, oblivious to the crowd moving along the sidewalk and the window displays of gifts for St. Valentine's. Something made him remember that the Café Paradise was nearby. He liked this café, always animated. He would often go in and enjoy a drink, sitting at the counter and watching the activity.

That evening, he entered the Café Paradise. The place was busy. A couple of ladies turned their heads to glance at him with a touch of admiration on their faces, and he felt gratified. As he looked around to find a seat, he saw a thin, serious man with a white goatee and a sullen appearance, wearing a light brown corduroy jacket, sitting alone at a table for two by a big window. It appeared that the only space available would be at his table, but Vela got the impression of something odd going on with the man occupying it. He hesitated to approach him and ask whether he would mind sharing his table; he looked like a wasted man. Not knowing what to do, he involuntarily shook his umbrella, which he was carrying half open, and a few drops of water scattered around; some reached the man's jacket.

"I'm sorry," Vela said.

The man made a gesture to indicate he didn't care at all.

"As a matter of fact," Vela ventured saying, "I meant to ask whether you would mind sharing your table." Vela became aware of an on-and-off beeping noise that seemed to come from the man's chest. Did it come from his lungs? Should he dare to share his table? He felt an impulse to run away.

"I am not a talker," said the man in a grave voice.

Vela hawked. "I see. I don't talk much either," he then said politely as he sat on the other chair with caution.

They exchanged a brief look at each other, and quickly, they turned their heads to look out the window as if expecting to spot someone in particular. Outside, it was getting dark. The street lights were not on yet.

A waiter hurried to their table.

"A cup of coffee, please," Vela ordered.

He noticed his tablemate was drinking coffee too.

The two men cast another quick look at each other. Vela estimated the man could be in his late fifties. But he looked so gaunt! For a while, they remained silent, both turning on and off their heads to view the outside. When the waiter came back with the coffee, they took a lengthier glance at each other.

"Are you married?" the man asked.

Luis Vela felt the impulse of getting up and leave, but instead, he said, "No."

Two young women sat three tables away. They talked and laughed loudly, drawing people's attention. One was petite, pale, with delicate carmine-red lips; the other, had a chubby body, round face with fleshy lips, and short, lemon-colored hair. Both wore colorful, low-cut blouses.

"Two hookers, I believe. Don't you think?" the man said, pointing to them.

"Maybe that's what they are," Vela replied.

"It's a shame. The women I meet don't put up with my problem," the man said abruptly.

Vela was taken aback.

"What do you mean?"

"I've got fibrosis of the lungs," said the man, looking at Vela directly.

For split second, Vela held his breath. Was it compassion or intrigue that he felt for the other?

"How long have you been sick?"

"As a young man, I worked as an apprentice electrician, but I had to quit due to shortness of breath."

They seemed to have forgotten that they had claimed not to be talkers. Vela clicked his tongue; then he took a sip of coffee.

"As a young man did you say?"

"Yes. I get a pension. I live alone. My name is Ramiro."

Vela let a touch of compassion settling in his chest.

"I'm pleased to meet you, Ramiro."

They shook hands. Vela fancied Ramiro as a wounded soldier, someone in need of his help. He took another sip of coffee, appreciating the warm feeling in his mouth.

"How do you handle things, you being sick, Ramiro?"

"I take walks." Ramiro did not hesitate.

A fit of laughter shook Vela's chest. Perhaps all this was a joke?

"You mean... You just walk around?"

"Yes."

They looked directly at each other. Vela read in Ramiro's face that he was serious about what he was saying.

"You would be surprised if I told you the kind of things one can see by strolling in the streets," Ramiro said.

What things might Ramiro meant, Vela couldn't imagine, for he had wandered the streets all day long, looking for love and finding nothing but loneliness. Bemused, he shifted his head away from Ramiro and looked around. A mature woman, wearing a hat, sat on a stool at the counter. At that moment, she lit a cigarette. Why is she alone? He turned back to his companion.

"Don't you get tired of walking, Ramiro?"

"I don't fatigue if I stop and rest once in a while."

"I see. Now, let me introduce myself. Luis Vela, an Army captain."

"Please to meet you. You wear your uniform with nobility, Captain."

Vela took the compliment as a matter of fact. "Thank you."

"Are you retired?" Ramiro asked.

"Not yet, but pretty close. Like you, I live alone. Would you like another cup of coffee?"

"I only drink one cup a day. Thank you."

Another moment of silence fell between them. Vela gazed again at the woman by the counter.

"Do you enjoy watching people, Captain?"

Luis Vela, feeling a little embarrassed, turned his attention back to his companion.

"I'm sorry, Ramiro. I got distracted. I was just wondering who could that lovely lady at the counter be?"

"I see. Who knows?"

Ramiro himself began to glance around.

"Captain, please, look at those two," he said, pointing to a young couple who sat at a table a few feet away from them.

Vela looked at the couple. He thought she was pretty, and he, a Navy officer in the uniform, seemed to have eyes only for her.

"What about them?"

"I wonder whether this is their first date."

"What makes you think so, Ramiro?"

"Well, she appears animated, and he composed—"

"In matters of love, some people are luckier than others," Vela cut him short.

The Decalogue indicated that one should feel glad about other officers' successes. But at that moment, noticing happiness in the Navy officer's countenance while he, Luis Vela, remained sitting there, across from a sick man, he felt as if he was the wounded soldier.

"By the way," Ramiro went on, "I wonder, Captain, why do you stay single?"

Luis Vela reflected for a short while. Years ago, he had married the daughter of a Portuguese military surgeon who at the time was living with his family in Madrid. He had met her at the Officer's Club and found her charming and elegant, always dressed like a princess. But she turned out to be a capricious woman, and he soon realized he had made a mistake by marrying her. He divorced her after four years of marriage. The Portuguese family went back to Lisbon, and he never heard about his ex-wife again.

"I was married for some time, although we had no children," he answered.

"Did your wife die?"

Vela set his elbows on the table and his chin on his intertwined fingers. "We divorced. It's all forgotten now. I was thirty-two when we got married."

But he silently acknowledged feeling lonely and being eager to make new acquaintances, to find love. Ramiro began to nervously play with his cup of coffee, rotating it to the left and the right over the saucer.

"How do you handle things, Captain?"

Vela caught Ramiro's sarcasm. Nevertheless, how was he handling his life?

"I don't do much. Occasionally, I go hunting the Quail with a few old friends."

"No girlfriend?" Ramiro looked askance at Vela, who drew a wry smile.

"Just women friends, no obligations. As I said, I live alone, not far from here. I come to this café once in a while and spend some time socializing."

"I see."

Now, Vela himself began playing with the coffee set in front of him, tinkling the spoon against the cup handle.

"Earlier this afternoon, I met Lola," Ramiro snapped.

Vela stopped playing with his cup. "Is she pretty?"

"I like women with wide hips."

Vela's eyes perked up. He called the waiter. "Two more coffees, please," he ordered. But Ramiro shook his head. "No more coffee for me, thank you.

"Lola is my type of woman, Captain," he went on. "She has a plump body, like a quail. Do you get it?"

Vela liked the comparison. "I love everything related to quails."

Both men exchanged a complicit glance.

"But the fibrosis in my lungs get in the way," Ramiro spoke again.

"Oh! I'm sorry."

Ramiro's fingers drummed on the table while Vela could hardly wait to hear the unfolding story.

"Lola landed in Madrid last fall from Colombia." Ramiro seemed to read Vela's mind.

"Why in Madrid?"

Ramiro appeared eager to share his story.

"She was a single mother, living with her mother some-where in rural Colombia. Both her mother and her child were killed by guerrilla militants in a random shooting while they were searching households because one of their members was missing. She found herself with no income or savings, and desperate to find a job. Through the Internet, she found a job opening with a house cleaning service here, and she came with a work permit."

Vela noticed Ramiro appeared fatigued at this point. To give him time to recoup, he turned to look at the two giggling women. The chubby one was retouching her fleshy lips with lipstick. He imagined Lola might look like her.

"Is she young?" he asked.

"About fifteen years younger than I am," Ramiro said. "She was doing fine until last month when she was laid off."

Ramiro's sharp nose, sucked cheeks, thin mouth, and long goatee triggered a feeling of estrangement on Vela.

"You can't help her?" he asked.

Ramiro shook his head. "Lola doesn't have any funds, not even to pay her rent."

"There you go! You could take her home, couldn't you?" Vela said and opened his arms in a gesture of benevolence.

Ramiro leaned back.

"I am a sick guy, but not a lecher," he said, his hands trembling. "I don't take advantage of homeless women!"

Vela realized there was energy left in his sick companion.

"I'm sorry. I didn't mean to offend," he said.

Ramiro brought his face forward, closer to Vela. "I'm disgusted at my condition," he whispered, and Vela heard the whistling from his chest more clearly than he had before.

Ramiro leaned back again.

"I spotted Lola in *Casa de Campo Park* near the entrance to the zoo," he said. "I suppose you know hookers hang around that area?"

Vela nodded.

"I approached her," Ramiro continued, "and realized that she was on the brink of becoming a hooker herself on this St. Valentine's Day. She desperately needed money."

"Did you help her?"

"I thought of bringing her home, as you have suggested, but it'd have been unfair."

Luis Vela mentally searched for a dictum in the Decalogue that related to the issue Ramiro was facing, but found none, which was disappointing for he had hitherto thought the book was thorough in matters of human conduct.

"This is a free country. You can enter any lawful deal," he said and took a deep breath, believing he had just come up with something righteous and profound.

"But I'm a sick man!" Ramiro shouted.

He is a wounded soldier. He should be excused from participating in combat, Vela mused to himself.

"Of course, you owe to consider the condition of your lungs before taking any action," he said.

"You hit the nail on the head, Captain. That's my dilemma. I know sex will worsen my condition, but, on the other hand, not acting like a man will hurt my feelings."

Vela felt a bit of admiration for him.

"How can I help?" he wondered.

"Well, Captain; my dilemma is my dilemma."

At that moment, the two happy women laughed loudly.

"Speaking of skirts," Vela shifted the course of their conversation to give Ramiro a respite, "between those two loudy women, which one do you like better?

"The same one as you do, Captain," Ramiro quickly answered.

"But you can't possibly know which one of the two I like better?"

"Yes I do. I read it on your face while I was describing Lola's features to you."

Vela had no choice but to admit his companion's keenness on that.

"However, I married a slim woman," he declared.

"Perhaps that's your dilemma, Captain. You married a slim woman, but you are attracted to the chubby type, like the one there, with dyed blond hair."

Vela didn't reply. He shifted in his chair as someone feeling uncomfortable. He checked his watch.

"I must go," he said.

He got up, grabbed his umbrella, flicked his cap under his arm, and checked his uniform was correctly buttoned.

"It's been a pleasure, Ramiro."

"Same here, Luis, I mean, Captain Vela." Ramiro made a gesture of getting up from his chair.

"Please don't trouble yourself," Vela pleaded.

They shook hands, and Vela walked toward the exit with his habitual composure. On his way out, he heard Ramiro calling his name.

"Please, Captain, remember me, in case I perish in combat as a good soldier."

Vela noticed Ramiro's eyes had become shadowed. "I left my phone number written on a paper napkin, in front of you," he said. "An Officer must always look after his soldiers."

Captain Vela stepped outside. It had stopped raining, yet streams of water ran along the curbs toward the street drains. Although a chilly evening, there were people everywhere: in and out shops, cafes, movie theaters, Metro. As he walked home, a short distance, he became conscious of a strange cacophony going on in his ears: Ramiro's lungs whistling, the two festive women laughing, and water drops splashing from the eaves down to the sidewalk. After a short while, though, these noises stopped, and a sense of loss came over him: he missed Ramiro's company. He wondered whether he had ever talked with anyone as intimately as he had just done with Ramiro. However, he also wondered whether he could ever have Ramiro as his friend. For Ramiro did nothing but wander through the streets. He was a sick fellow, a decayed man at the end of his rope, while he, Captain Luis Vela, was a healthy and well-mannered gentleman.

When he got home, he took his uniform off and put on his pajamas. He moved into the leaving room, served himself a shot of whiskey, and sat down in front of the TV. He hoped watching sports would distract him from thinking about Ramiro. All in vain, for the memory of Ramiro, with his difficulty breathing and his dilemma about Lola came back to haunt him. Unable to concentrate on anything else, he turned the TV off, served himself another drink, and, lying on the coach, gave himself to speculate about Ramiro and Lola until he fell asleep.

When he woke up next morning, Friday, it was past ten. He thought about Ramiro again and wished he would ring him. In fact, more than anything, he wished hearing about Lola from Ramiro. While trimming his mustache in front of the mirror, he fancied Lola with a short, robust body, shaped like a quail, and smelling of wood. He envisioned her as still young, with firm breasts, solid thighs and buttocks, and felt sexually aroused. He wished Ramiro would call him and introduce him to her. He made a cup of coffee for himself and sat down in the kitchen to plan his weekend. He thought of going to the military stables and spending some time horse riding. He started packing his pants and riding boots when the thought entered his mind that perhaps he could meet Ramiro wandering the streets. He got up in a hurry, changed into casual clothing, grabbed his coat and leather cap from the hook, and left home.

Outside, a warm winter sun bathed the buildings and pavement, which appeared cleaner than usual due to the prior day's rain. The streets were pretty empty at that hour. He walked slowly and aimlessly. His wandering took him to the Officer's Club. He felt tempted to go in and have a cup of coffee at the bar, but he quickly gave up this idea, afraid his presence there would trigger less of a wave of admiration than it once did. Instead, he kept on walking as he had done the day before, St. Valentine's.

At dusk, he found himself roaming in *Casa de Campo Park*, near the zoo. He was thinking of Lola, of the *Lola* he had forged in his imagination from Ramiro's description of the real person. From the corner of his eye, he glanced at each hooker he came across, hoping he would recognize Lola among them. He felt possessed by an overwhelming sense of responsibility, thinking he, an Army officer, had the obligation to save her from falling into a depraved lifestyle—*to have the determination to solve problems*, he remembered the Decalogue said. Suddenly, it dawned on him that Lola might have moved in with Ramiro the night before after he had left the Café Paradise. This thought exasperated him. Instinctively, he left the area, and rushing like someone who is late for an appointment, he flashed a taxi to Café Paradise.

Inside, he went to the same table he and Ramiro had occupied the day before, but, of course, Ramiro was not there. For a split second, he thought: he is dead. He looked around searching for some familiar faces, but he only recognized the waiter who had served his coffee. His presence, though, gave him confidence that people do not die as quickly as he had just thought Ramiro would have died. He was ready to leave when his eyes fell on a hunched, little figure, sitting at a table in a distant corner. He got closer to it.

"My good Lord, Ramiro. It's you!"

Ramiro's eyes were alert, and he seemed happy despite his distressing breathing.

"Luis, I mean Captain Vela, I'm glad to see you again. Would you join us for coffee?"

Vela was started. He took his hand onto his chest, feeling his heart suddenly pounding hard. "Is Lola here?" he asked in a weak voice.

"She'll be here shortly to pick me up. She moved in with me last night. I'm a happy guy, not wandering the streets anymore"

Vela wanted to run away, but his legs didn't obey him. He felt sick in his heart. In split second, he collapsed onto the floor. The same waiter called an ambulance, and the paramedics drove the captain to the nearest hospital.

Two weeks later, still convalescent from a heart attack, he continued ruminating, obsessed about Lola and Ramiro, waiting for him to call, waiting to hear more about her. One evening, when he had gone out for a walk in his neighborhood before dinner, his phone rang. He thought it would be Ramiro calling. It was Lola.

"Hello, I'm Lola. I'm calling to let you know that Ramiro died last night of a heart attack," she said point-blank. "Your number is on his phone."

Vela found himself overwhelmed by inexplicable guilt.

"I was expecting his call—"

"I know. He was going to call you today, but he died in his sleep."

They remained silent for a minute.

"I've been thinking a lot about you, Lola."

"I've met Ramiro's sister. She's good to me. His funeral is in two days."

"How can I help?"

Vela tried to regain his habitual demeanor, to block his guilty feeling.

"Ramiro spoke highly of you, Captain."

"Anything you wish, Lola—"

He couldn't talk. His heart was beating hard, his breathing accelerated.

"I'm thinking of my mother and my son and of doing justice."

"I'll do anything. I'll take you back to Colombia if that's what you want." He was talking fast, as in a whisper.

"Why?" she asked. "Why would you do that?"

Luis Vela held his breath for a few seconds.

"I think...I love you," he stuttered.

"You have never seen me!"

"Ramiro described your looks. I can imagine—"

"Would you help me to find those who kill my family?"

In Vela's ears, Lola's words sounded like a challenge.

"What do you mean?"

"I mean the two guerrillas who killed my mother and my son for no reason at all."

Vela felt trapped.

"I'm a man of principles," he managed to say, a bit angry.

"I know where to find and fight them," Lola added.

"I hate war." He thought about all the times he had in the past refused to volunteer to fight, and his teeth gnashed.

"Yet war is what we have in Colombia, Captain"

"I hate fighting," he said, and his voice sounded strange to himself.

"Then, Captain, you should follow your principles. I go by my instinct."

Suddenly, Captain Vela felt hopeless, perennially lonely. He stood on the sidewalk, near home, holding a silent phone in his trembling hands, grasping for air, aching in his heart, and losing his faith on the Decalogue, but having no clue of where to turn to find some satisfaction in his life.

A Beautiful Afternoon
in April

I hadn't heard from my brother Serafín since I left Madrid for Bilbao three months ago. Then while I was shaving, reassuring myself I looked good in the mirror, getting ready to meet my new girlfriend and go out to have fun, I heard the phone.

"Hello, Eugene. It's Melissa."

Her voice sounded weak.

"What's up?"

Melissa and Serafín had met in junior college and married three years ago when both were 20. She had been a runaway teen, and I can't help but feel distrustful of her as a wife. Her single mother raised her until she turned nine and her mother married an older widower, who, Serafín says, was critical of Melissa.

"Your brother—" I tapped on the speaker icon. "He's turning into a stranger."

"What do you mean?" I held my breath. I live with the apprehension that something might go wrong with my brother. Although I can't explain the rationale for my worry, Melissa's statement made my heart accelerate as if something emotionally familiar was forthcoming. As a child, I often woke up in the middle of the night to my parents' arguments and heard Serafín's crying. Full of apprehension, even then, I anticipated my brother would need my protection, and Serafín has always looked at me as an older friend.

"Can't explain it over the phone," she said. "Do you plan to come back soon?"

"Not soon," I said bluntly.

I am 27, single, a curator with the Spanish Alliance of Museums in a temporary assignment at the Guggenheim, and dating a girl I like a lot. So, no, I wasn't planning to return to my apartment in Madrid soon. Besides, as I say, Melissa and I had never got along; why would she now want to see me instead of explaining herself over the phone?

"Please come," she said in an unusually subdued voice.

Through my brother, I knew of Melissa's wild behavior she had exhibited when younger. Serafín found out she had had an abortion before they had married and took him pains to learn how to live with it. When they announced their plans to get married, I was shocked, but I could do nothing to stop it. Now, on the phone, she didn't say what the urgency was, which maddened me, guessing they might be in a marital mess and needed a savior.

After we hung up, my first impulse was to contact my brother. But on second thought, I decided to give Melissa, for once, the benefit of keeping her call confidential.

The next day in Madrid, I texted her: 'Let's meet at noonish in *Retiro Park*, beside the lake jetty.' It was a beautiful afternoon in April, and I figured strolling outdoors while we talked would be relaxing, or less conflictive if the issue she was ready to share with me affected my relationship with my brother than staying at home. Melissa, brunette, with a short hairstyle, long legs, and a somewhat ungainly gate can be easily identifiable at a distance.

"Thanks for coming," she said. "How was your trip?"

"Uneventful."

She made a move as if intending to give me a hug, but I instantly tilted my head slightly backward, not being ready to compromise without knowing what was at stake, and my gesture seemed to dissuade her from her intention.

"What's up?" I asked as we began strolling along the lakeshore.

"It's pleasant here."

She wore a grey cotton blouse, black Capri pants, and tennis shoes. We had the lake on our left, and trees, gardens, and pathways spread around us. A smell of wet grass lingered in the air.

"How's Serafín?" I felt impatient to hear her concerns. In contrast to my way of being, enjoying social gatherings and friendships, Serafín is a shy guy. He hates crowds and prefers to draw, surf the web, play video games, and ride his bicycle.

Melissa jerked her head toward the lake as if she had suddenly spotted a repulsive birthmark on my cheek she couldn't endure to face. A bunch of rowboats floated about.

"It's—" she started saying, when a bunch of kids ran out of a nearby playground and bumped into us, interrupting her statement. A couple of them apologized on the run.

"It's been going on for some time," she then said, and I thought, since they have lived together. Spurred by his wife, Serafín quit college to take a job as a draftsman with a company dedicated to the design of medical instruments. They had leased an apartment on the outskirts of the city and needed money to cover the expenses. I understood his move but told him to be careful not to curtail his college education and limit his future opportunities.

"For how long?" I asked, trying to sound impartial.

"About two months." She paused and looked at me as if intending to analyze my reaction. "One of his coworkers confided in me," she continued, "that Serafín was leaving his drawings unfinished, to his boss's astonishment."

My brother showed he had a hand for drawing since he was a kid. He loved it and wanted to be a professional designer. Hearing from Melissa that he had been neglecting his work sounded like something being out of sort.

"Why would he neglect his work?"

Melissa threw me a look as if I was someone living on another planet and had just landed on earth, which made me infer that she thought I should know better.

"He does the same thing at home," she said.

"What thing?"

Melissa glanced at me again with an expression of irritation.

"Serafín is turning into a stranger," she said.

When our father abandoned us, Mom tried to help us understand the situation. I was nine years old and thought that our father had left home because he was tired of us, but Serafín was only four, and he walked around the house crying and calling 'Dad, Dad' as if Dad was lost and he was looking for him.

"He may be under stress," I said and kicked a little rock down the pathway in frustration for my failure to figure out what could be going on with him. Two magpies, which were on the ground behind an acacia, suddenly flew away, which startled Melissa. It was then that I noticed her pallor and that she didn't have makeup on. A tiny leather bag hung from her shoulder, and she got a pack of Camels out of it and offered me a cigarette. I shook my head.

"I'm afraid Serafín is disturbed because I'm not the wife he expected me to be." She got a box of tissues out of her bag and dabbed her eyes. Her words revealed she believed that she was the cause of Serafín's distress. Was their marital mismatch showing up?

"That's too bad," I said.

Melissa went on venting while we kept strolling: Serafín ended up losing his job last week, and strangely enough, she said, he's unconcerned about it. I stopped walking and stood immobile in the place. That piece of news didn't click with the image I had of my brother, a loner but a conscientious guy.

"Has he talked to you about you not meeting his expectations?" I braced myself for the worse as we resumed walking.

"No. He lives preoccupied with something else, but he won't say what." As she talked, I glanced about; we were approaching the Rose Garden, and I took a deep breath to smell the fragrance and gather some insight. "At home," Melissa continued, "Serafín smokes incessantly."

Although my brother has inherited mostly our mother's traits, including gray eyes and blond, straight hair (I'm taller than he is, with dark eyes and curly hair), and quiet temperament, he can turn obsessive with some stuff, like smoking.

"Maybe he's on drugs," I said and thought of our dad, a gambler, and user.

"I don't think so," she quickly said. "Of course, we like to smoke a joint together once in a while, but I've searched his pockets and the drawers on his desk and found no traces of drugs."

I didn't doubt her words; in the past, she had probably been an expert on the use of them.

"I don't know what to think about what might be going on with him," I said. I had the impression that even the smallest understanding of the nature of Serafín's problem escaped both of us. "What else does he do at home?"

"Sometimes, he starts a drawing but leaves it unfinished. Often, he takes off after dinner and comes back late. If I ask where he's been, he gives non-sense answers, like saying that he counted houses in the neighborhood, which leaves me super-perplexed. Even during our intimate times, he suddenly gets distracted and—"

"No need to, Melissa." At that point, my resentment against her began to cease a little. "What's happening is sad and weird. I'll call my brother and see for myself."

She nodded. The sun was still high, and the shadows on the ground dense. We had passed the Rose Garden. Melissa gazed into space with a thoughtful look, and I respected her silence. After we left the park, she took the subway back home, and I walked to my Madrid apartment.

I called my brother the next morning, Sunday, and invited him to come to a soccer game in the afternoon; we both love soccer, so he accepted and said he would come on the bus.

I arrived early by Metro and walked to the nearby bus stop. The evening was warm. I had a light sweater tied to my waist in case in the stadium the temperature descended. I spotted my brother on the bus as it came to a stop. He wore a black coat with the hood over his head. When he came out of the bus, I went to him; however, he stood passively in place as if his shoes were glued to the pavement, his face inexpressive. I broadened my smile to compensate for his coolness and gave him a hug. He reciprocated sluggishly. His coat turned out to be a thick raincoat, even though there were no signs of any rain. A feeling of estrangement flashed over me, but I said nothing.

Serafín followed the game with interest. Maybe I'm making a mountain out of a molehill, I reflected, and looked around, hoping to find someone else wearing a raincoat. Nobody did. The game ended in a draw.

"Do you care for a beer before going home?" I asked. We had just exited the stadium.

"Sure."

My brother appeared to be in a fair mood.

"I know an Irish Pub two blocks away."

We walked there. The place was packed with people coming out of the game. Two empty stools were available at the counter, and we took them. Several TV screens showed a variety of sports broadcasted through different channels. We ordered a pint of Guinness each. While sipping beer, we glanced at one or another of the TV screens, at the people sitting next to us, at each other, and we chatted about the match we had seen. I was hesitant to abruptly shift our conversation to personal matters, but my brother did it for me.

"You've got a girlfriend?"

"Yes, in Bilbao. I wish you could meet her. She's the prettiest and smartest girl in the world," I said, but Serafín's demeanor had suddenly changed; he looked absentminded. He kept watching the TV screen and holding his mug of beer, unmoved. His lack of participation hurt my feelings.

"Did you hear me?" I asked.

"Yes," he said with indifference.

A wave of heat invaded my chest as I realized he became unreachable. I took a deep breath and a long sip of beer and for a while, we didn't talk.

"Do you like tropical fish?" He then asked.

"Tropical fish?" It sounded like a silly question.

"Yes. I draw colorful fish, and then I go to the aquarium to see them."

My stomach turned. What Serafín had said was laughable. Was he kidding me? He went on drinking his beer and watching golf on the TV screen with glassy eyes, unaware of his silliness. He searched his pockets and produced a crumpled pack of Camels. He took a cigarette out of it.

"You can't smoke here," I said.

He returned the squeezed pack to his pocket obediently.

"We better leave so that you can smoke outside."

We left the pub, and he lit his cigarette and started walking down the street as if he knew where we would be heading. I followed him and leveled up with his pace. Soon, I realized that he was heading towards a nearby Metro. When we reached the subway entrance, he kept going downstairs oblivious to my presence, and the overwhelming feeling of estrangement hit me again.

"Goodbye, Serafín. Take care," I said. What else could I tell him?

On my way home, I called Melissa and shared my impression with her. "Whatever is going on with Serafín is beyond logic," I said, and hearing my own words made me conscientious of a latent truth, that my brother had sadly turned into an unreachable, odd individual, set apart from the rest of us.

"It would be wise taking Serafín to see a psychologist, you think," she said.

I agreed, grateful for her taking the initiative.

When a few days later, after I had returned to Bilbao, Melissa called to let me know that the doctor had said the problem with Serafín was due to the insidious creeping of mental illness, a sense of uncertainty stirred my intestines. I couldn't pinpoint what it was about until Melissa said, 'It could happen to you too, you know.' I didn't reply but the apprehension I had always had that something might go wrong with Serafín returned; only now I also worried about my own sanity. 'Serafín is turning into a stranger,' Melissa had said, and now I felt guilty for having suspected that she was to blame for my brother's trouble; one can easily be wrong with presumptions. I felt deeply sorry for my brother. I wanted to share my worries with Melissa, but I could only manage to promise I would commit myself to help them the best I could.

After we hung up, I was confused, my mind filled with pressing questions. Who or what was to blame for my brother's insanity: our family dysfunction, my dad's craziness, Melissa's past behavioral instability? I obtained not even half-satisfactory answer on my own. I thought about my girlfriend, whether she had noticed a change in me, any incongruence in my train of thought or silliness in my utterances or…I'm still searching for answers a week after I came back.

Pietro's Dilemma

Pietro, a high school senior living with his parents, walks home this Thursday evening and walks into de kitchen moving fast and looking distracted.

"Where have you been?" his mother asks. She's feeding their two cocker spaniels when Pietro steps in and hurriedly opens the fridge and grabs a small bottle of water. "You look so jittery, Son."

An only child, Pietro dreams of becoming a professional soccer player. His father teaches P/E at the local community college and happily supports his goal. His mother, an Animal Control Officer with the Humane Society, tries to instill in him the idea of becoming a vet; two sets of values about which Pietro often vacillates, although overall, his dream of playing soccer professionally prevails over his mother's suggestion of him becoming a veterinarian.

"I'm tired, Mom. That's all," he says.

Pietro often comes home feeling tired after his soccer practice and gym exercises. On this occasion, though, he is also upset by what happened to him on the street. He gulps water from the bottle until it is empty, and then rushes to his room, closes the door, and throws himself on the bed with his head under the pillow, trying to keep images of the flames burning the man's flesh out of his mind. He tightens the pillow over his head until he finally falls asleep.

In the morning, while combing his hair in front of the mirror, the same imagery returns, but now it presents itself in slow motion, more plainly, as if his mind was a movie screen, which torments him and makes his hand shake. 'I didn't find the courage to get the man entirely out of the fire. I'm a fucking coward!' he speaks to his image in the mirror. He would have given everything he possessed if he knew the man was not seriously injured.

Before he leaves his room and walks into the kitchen, where he knows he'll most likely face his mother again—his father leaves earlier for work—he determines not to say a word about how he feels, hoping that the ghost of the incident will soon vanish from his memory.

"You looked edgy last night. What's going on, Son?"

Pietro remains cool and avoids coming near his mother, eating breakfast. "I told you, Mom. I was tired."

His mother throws him a look that he translates as meaning skepticism.

"Is there anything you are worrying about?" she insists.

"Mom!" He knows that she won't dig too deep into his affairs because she must leave for work.

She quits asking questions, drains her coffee, gets up from the table, grabs the purse she had left on the kitchen counter, and approaching her son, she touches the nape of his neck with her fingertips, 'take it easy,' she says, and goes.

Despite Pietro's will, the thought of being a coward nags him and makes him shiver with guilt. Throughout the entire day at school, he shies away from his friends, and when he gets home in the evening, he avoids communicating with his parents and goes straight to his room. Lying on his bed, his hands behind his head, he ruminates about the incident and tries in vain to rid himself of the voice of his consciousness saying he's a chicken until exhausted, he falls asleep.

A couple of hours later, Pietro wakes up startled by hearing a voice in his sleep shouting 'get him out.' Half-awake, he battles with the bedclothes as if trying to drag a fellow combatant out of some danger. Then, he sits up in his bed, swamped in sweat, and gazing to the space in front of him with widely opened eyes, he yells, 'Fire!' An instant later, he jumps out of bed, and although unsteady, he makes it to the shower. Under the cold water, he tries hard to figure out what's going on with him. He is aware, nevertheless, that he has just awoken from a dreadful nightmare, which revives in him the terror experienced during the fire incident of last evening. He also wonders whether his parents had heard his screaming.

When Pietro comes out, pretending he's fine, but still, the wringing of his hands speaking of his uneasiness, both his parents are eating breakfast, and like every Saturday morning, he takes a seat at the table. The family came to America from Italy when Pietro was a child of 10. Everything looked different in Los Angeles than it had looked in Trieste: the school, the teachers, the playground, the language. He grew up with the feeling of swinging between two cultures like a weathervane that turns around with the wind. In time, though, he felt comfortable about his cultural blending.

"Coffee?" Pietro asks and holds the pot suspended in the air, ready to pour coffee into his parents' cups, but he sees they are filled, and instead, he pours it into his.

As he returns the pot to the table, he senses his parents might have heard his yelling in the middle of the night, and this realization makes his face blush.

"What's going on, Pietro?"

"Nothing, Mom."

He avoids making eye contact with either parent, and crosses his feet under the chair in an effort to stay cool.

"It looks like something is going on, though," his father says.

Pietro smears butter on his toast, but hearing his father's words, freezes his action and remains silent.

"Please, Son, say what it is," his father insists.

Pietro gives him a fleeting look, but he says nothing and resumes spreading butter on the bread.

"You guys make me feel like a thief," he then says and bites on his toast.

His father doesn't reply, and his mother, still chewing a piece of melon, glances at him a little in awe.

"Please tell us," she says.

Pietro blushes. He wants to tell them everything but can't bring himself to admit that he's a coward. He would lose his father's favor to become a strong soccer player, and his mother might doubt his capacity to help anybody. He drags his feet further back under the chair and lifts a glass of water to his lips, but he chokes on the liquid and coughs violently. He covers his mouth with the napkin until the spell is over.

"I don't know," he then says, on the brink of tears.

A silence follows during which all three remain idle. Then, Pietro takes another sip of water and keeps his eyes cast down; he clears his throat. "I was riding on my skateboard—" he coughs again and drinks more water. "The man was there, under the freeway." He pauses and stares at the empty glass in front of him while his parents stare at him.

"Who was there?" His mother asks.

Pietro glances at his father across the table, enjoying his breakfast, and then at his mother, waiting for his response.

"The homeless man."

Both his parents nodded. A homeless man had lately camped under the freeway-bridge a few blocks away from their home.

"What happened?" asks his father.

"It was a chilly evening last Thursday if you remember. The man had started a bonfire, and wrapped in a worn-out blanket, he stood there on the edge of the flames, sipping wine from a bottle. As I passed him, I said, 'Hi,' and he replied, 'Hey.'" He pauses again.

"You passed him—"

"A few yards past him, I heard a thumping noise and a scream. I stopped and turned around to check—"

"The man fell into the bonfire?" his mother asks.

Pietro nods.

"He probably was drunk," said his father.

"I don't know. He cried, twisting his body." Now, Pietro speaks fast. "Wine poured out of the bottle, fueling the fire—"

"How terrifying," his mother says.

"I grabbed his feet to drag him out of the flames—"

"You did the right thing, Son," his father says.

Pietro wishes the whole thing ended here. "I slipped and fell," he continues in a subdued voice.

"Oh, Lord! Did you get burned?" his mother asks.

"No. I got up very quickly. But I panicked and ran away. I mean, I left him there defenseless. I'm a—" Silence follows. Pietro's feet quiver under the table, and this makes the table also shake. "I have bad dreams about it," he says.

His parents remain immobile in their seats, glancing at each other and then at their son.

"I think you're in shock, Son," His father breaks the silence.

Pietro drives his hands to hold his knees, making efforts to stop his trembling. "I don't know," he says. "I think I would feel better if I knew the guy was all right."

The table doesn't shake any longer. Pietro takes a furtive glance at his mother, looking for something, but he can't say what. She looks pensive.

"It's not your fault," she says.

Pietro silently appreciates her words, which he interprets as supportive, but wonders what she means that isn't his fault. He still thinks he's a coward and desperately wishes this feeling would go away. He turns his eyes to his father.

"Perhaps you were not strong enough to pull him completely out?" he says.

Pietro sank on his seat, motionless, hands on his knees, eyes lost in space. If he lacked the strength to drag a man out of a bonfire, could he still become a soccer player?

"The man has to be found somewhere, anyway," his father adds.

Hearing these words, Pietro's eyes brighten. "Excuse me," he says and gets up from his chair and runs out to his room. There, he checks the local news online—on a chilly evening, last Thursday, the police found a man lying on the street with several burns caused by a bonfire, still going on a few feet away, and they took him to the County Hospital. Without hesitation, Pietro leaves home and takes the Metro.

"We can't provide information about any patient," the hospital receptionist says. "It's confidential."

Pietro insists he must see the homeless injured man. The receptionist doesn't give in but suggests he talks to her manager. Pietro accepts and repeats his request to the manager, a middle-aged woman who looks like his mother and politely interrupts his explanation to make a phone call.

"All set," the manager then says. "This patient had no ID on him when the police brought him to the ER. He later said his name is Florindo. He knows who you are. Go ahead and visit, Room-21. But please make it brief."

Another, younger, patient shares the room-21 with Florindo, both lying in their own bed and gazing at Pietro when he walks in.

"Hi," Pietro says, addressing Florindo.

"Hey!"

Silence sets in. Florindo, with his black beard and eyes, might be his father's age, Pietro guesses. The other patient, in contrast, is of pale countenance, has blue eyes, and looks much younger. He reminds him of a soccer teammate player whom he hates because he's critical of his playing after their games, which angers him because the other player is taller and a bully, and Pietro barely can compete with him.

"You're alive!" says Pietro.

"You helped me."

Florindo gazes at him from his pillow. His hands are wrapped in bandages. Pietro wonders how he manages to eat and what other burns he has on his body.

"I'm sorry for what happened," he says.

"What happened?" the younger patient asks.

Not of your business, Pietro wants to respond. "He fell in a bonfire," he says instead.

"Boy! That's why he yells 'Fire' several times in the night, which wakes me up. Boy! He sits up in his bed, looking scared like a mouse facing a cat. Maybe you should take him home after he's out of the hospital, you know, like on paid vacation," the younger man says.

Pietro jaws clench. He hates sarcasm, but gets a hold of himself and does not respond. What this guy says about Florindo, his cries at night, however, resembles the problem he has. Has the accident affected them in the same way?

"You should take him home," the younger patient reiterates.

Pietro looks at him with disdain, but at the same time, he understands that he has nothing more to say or do there.

These people are not teachers or coaches. I don't know how to talk to or interact with them, although I feel the need to help Florindo in some way.

"Can you spare a couple of dollars?" the younger patient asks.

Even the guy's voice reminds Pietro of his teammate's timbre. He glances at the young patient's shoulders, which look broad, and wonders if he is as strong as his teammate. Could he make for a better soccer player than himself? He hates big-headed guys.

"Okay, Man. Take care," Pietro says, addressing Florindo and ignoring his roommate. "Maybe I'll see you again?"

"Maybe," the other guy mocks, "if you happen to swing by the spot where he camps."

Pietro turns a deaf ear to these challenging words one more time, biting his tongue, and leaves the room and then the hospital.

On the train, on his way back, Pietro realizes that Florindo and the other disgusting guy, along with others like them, are destitute people who coexist in the same society he lives in and he doesn't know how to relate to them. And the thought of it brings the memory of a speech delivered by a psychologist at his school. It was one of a series of presentations from career people that the principle had organized to help the students with their future choices. He had enjoyed the talk and had even given a thought to the role of a psychologist, but he had made up his mind he wanted to be a soccer player.

If I became a psychologist, though, he now guesses, I would be able to talk with people like Florindo and show them the way to find good food and decent shelter and stay active, and I wouldn't feel like a coward. Suddenly, it dawns on him that he has a dilemma, for the achievement of such a plan would take a long time and he would have to give up soccer. Why am I in such a mess? Is all this shit due to the fright the fire incident caused?

When Pietro gets out of the Metro station, he remembers that it is Saturday and his folks will be at home, but he isn't in the mood to face them yet. Not now, he needs to clear his mind first. I feel at odds with myself. I better amble around for a while.

After two hours of continuous walking and musing on his dilemma, he comes across a Subway, and feeling hungry and thirsty, he goes in and buys a sandwich and a coke. Then, he decides to sit on a bench in a nearby public park while he eats. Not five minutes go by, however, when a disheveled middle-aged man, pushing an old bicycle with a filthy bag tied to a stand behind the saddle, approaches him, begging. This individual has a surprising resemblance to Florindo.

"Here!" says Pietro, offering the rest of the sandwich to him.

"I'm not hungry," the stranger says. "Can you spare a couple of bucks? He stands with his ramshackle bike four or five feet away.

Florindo had never asked for money. What would he have done if Florindo had asked him for money? His own thoughts were causing him distress.

"Better a sip of coke? Pietro extends the can to the man. He wonders whether this guy has turned surly because of homelessness.

The man shakes his head. "Will you spare a couple of bucks?"

"What do you need the money for?"

"I'll buy meds." He scratches his head covered with abundant and filthy dark hair.

"Are you sick?" The man really doesn't look sick, although he looks much thinner than Florindo.

"Syphilis," the beggar claims and draws a smile that Pietro captures as filled with a mocking and hostile intention.

"Liar!"

The words Pietro wanted to say, he couldn't get them out fast enough. The guy only looked for money and tried to deceive him by playing the game of having contracted syphilis. He jumps up from the bench enraged and takes a step toward the beggar as if ready to punch him on the face. The man steps back, quickly goes up on his bicycle and pedals away. "You're a crazy man!" he yells as he rides off.

Enraged, Pietro throws the rest of his sandwich to the pigeons and the can of coke into a nearby trash container. 'Wow! You have to calm down,' he shouts and starts on his way out of the park. He doesn't doubt his sanity. I'm not crazy. I'm angry at myself for my failure to save Florindo from his burns, bitter at Dad for saying I'm not strong enough, and mad at the other two homeless guys for being assholes. It might happen, he ponders, that the incident of last Thursday has shocked me, as Dad said, that I'm having these sickening bad dreams and feeling so bad because of it. Perhaps the thought of giving up soccer for psychology might be due to my eagerness to redeem myself for feeling like a coward. Maybe panic blinded me and made me flee the scene. But, like Mom likes to say, one swallow doesn't make a summer.

Pietro decides to stride toward home, juggling his thoughts, trying to make sense out of what's happening. When he approaches the spot under the freeway-bridge where Florindo stood by the bonfire, the scene from the incident comes back to mind in a flash so real that makes his body shake. He again feels the impulse to run away, but presently there isn't a fire and no homeless people around. What does he fear? Although Pietro finds no answer, he notices that he calms down and his jogging slows down.

The thought of becoming a psychologist enters his mind anew. His wish to help Florindo and others like him persists, but he doesn't have to do it at the expense of giving up professional soccer. The thought of tackling both goals simultaneously filters into his consciousness. He had read about some athletes who had done the same. Why not him? Attempting to pursue this new goal would be like moving between two cultures, like he has always done. In this way, Pietro embraces such a challenge as the logical thing to do, as if he had for a long time considered doing it. I must double my commitment to become stronger, he determines. Dad says that at my age I can still grow and develop more muscle. When he arrives home, his dilemma begins to pale.

At the Gate

Sitting in front of a tiny brick-and-plaster house where she lives with her parents, a girl of six, with hazel eyes and curly dark hair, arranges little bouquets of wildflowers. A stone's throw from her house runs a river of narrow bed and fast current. From this river, the kids fish trout, and the locals call it *Il confine acquoso* (watery boundary) because its course divides the vast olive fields at which front the seasonal workers live in their humble dwellings from an urban zone where the wealthy reside. Several wooden bridges facilitate the transit between the two areas.

This girl loves wandering around, crossing over to the other bank and peeking into wealthy people's properties. She stands at a gate of a mansion and watches a little girl playing inside. She stands there, watching the other girl until the flight of a crow over her head makes her attention shift, and she leaves.

As she walks back home, she envisions being wealthy like the girl behind the gate. She wonders why she isn't and wishes everything showed clearly in the world, like the colors of the flowers she carries in her hand—white, red, and pink.

"Why we aren't rich?" she asks her parents.

"We came to this land when you didn't have teeth yet," her father says. "We work, stick in hand, shaking the branches in the trees and picking the olives, row by row, and day by day for as long as the weather remains warm. It takes time to get wealthy."

The little girl gazes at him with a look of perplexity. The mother seems to ponder what might be in her daughter's mind.

"We do what we can so we can live here, and you go to a nice school," she said.

The girl puts a distant look in her hazel eyes.

"Everyone has what they have," her father says.

The little girl turns to him with a frowning gesture. "But why we aren't rich?"

The parents produce no quick answer, and this delay bores the little girl. Without understanding, she walks out of the hut and sits near the door, grateful for the December pale sunshine after the cold of the previous night. She begins to put together the flowers she has picked up earlier to make a bouquet: pale cyclamens, resilience pansies, and perennial daisies.

The mother wakes her up the next morning and puts a rag doll that she has made in her daughter's arms.

"Babbo *Natale* (Santa Claus) left her on the window sill," she says. "Merry Christmas!"

A tender look of love and appreciation shows in the girl's eyes. She kisses and cradles the doll; she smiles at her mother and thinks of the wealthy girl of the mansion. From the kitchen table, her father observes them with contentment.

"If you go outdoors to play, make sure you wrap the doll with a kitchen cloth and don't venture to go too far," he says, and the little girl nods.

"It's snowing!" her mother says.

The little girl goes outside and plays with her doll all day long. The trees, the roofs, everything looks bulky and white.

Her eyes squint as sunshine hits the layers of snow and reflects on her face, but she doesn't want to miss any of the scenes around her. But it's getting dark, and she still wants to go and see the wealthy girl.

In spite of her father's warning, the little girl ventures to walk across the bridge. When she reaches the gate she knows, the view of a dispersed yellowish, mysterious light surprises her. It comes from a large wooden-framed lantern, with glass walls and a thick candle inside. A stake anchors the lamp, which wears a snow hat, into the white ground. She wonders who set it there. In this pool of yellowish light, the wealthy girl plays with fancy toys in the company of some friends. The whole scene reminds her of the fairy tales her mother reads to her before falling asleep. She stands there, but something inside tells her the wealthy girl won't come to the gate, and her feet are cold. "Everyone has what they have," she tells her doll as she takes off, and turning her head back to the gate, "We're happy too," she adds and hurries back home.

Marie

After Pierre and I got married in Pau, where we lived, we moved to Cerbère, at the extreme east of the Pyrenees, where he had taken a job as a park ranger. We fell in love with the village and enjoyed the beach. One evening, just before sunset, we discovered a cove between large, dark rocks that captivated us. People played in the water, and it soon became our favorite spot on the beach. A strange-looking old woman, dressed in a black robe, sat on the sand. I pointed her out to Pierre.

"Oh! She's the Vieux Cécile. I've read about her. Nobody knows how old she is.

Local people speculate that she dwells with the Eagle somewhere in the mountains. A legend—you know."

"Scary!"

"When something goes wrong in town, everybody blames the Vieux Cécile for it. She sits in the sun for hours on end and speaks to nobody."

One evening, three years later, while lying on the sand beside Pierre, I wondered whether we would ever have a child. The Old Woman sat not far from us, and I got the impression that she had said, 'you will have a gifted baby girl.'

"Have you said anything?" I asked Pierre.

"I've said nothing. Is it your imagination?"

126

Two mornings later, after Pierre had left for work, I came out of our little house to water the plants in the front yard when I saw a wicker basket beside the door. Hesitant, I looked inside. I became breathless: a babbling baby in diapers! Then, I heard a flapping: a black eagle flying away over the house. I didn't know what to think. My heart pounded in my chest. I grabbed the basket and carried it inside. I immediately phoned Pierre.

"She is a baby girl, Pierre. She may be a week old." Carefully, I lifted the baby and held her. "She is beautiful!"

"Call the doctor. I'm heading home."

The physician said the baby was healthy. Everybody in town expressed their amazement at the occurrence. The authorities launched a search to find the baby's parents. The parish priest baptized her—Marie—and a regional judge agreed for us to become her foster parents. After a year of an unsuccessful quest, I convinced Pierre we should adopt Marie.

With curly, black hair and vivacious hazel eyes, our daughter was growing into a fabulous little girl. Every time we three went to our favorite cove to play on the sand, anxiety shot up as I witnessed the Vieux Cécile, sitting there. What if—I would think, but say nothing.

Marie exhibited extraordinary vision. Once, I watched her while she sat in the middle of her room, facing the window, coloring a daisy on which she had drawn a bee.

"That's a beautiful bee," I said.

"It's still there." She pointed to the window.

I went to the window. Outside, a bee rested on a flower. I was amazed at Marie's visual power. Was she visually gifted? My memory of the Vieux Cécile popped up.

Marie started primary school in Argeles-sur-mer, a town a few miles north. On a morning of dense fog at ground level, some of us, parents, got on the school bus with the kids. About a mile from the school, the fog thickened even more. Unexpectedly, Marie yelled, 'A deer is on the road!' Wheels screeched, and the bus slowed down and stopped some twenty feet from a fawn, which stood in the middle of the road, dazzled by the vehicle's lights.

"Who yelled, 'a deer'?" the driver asked.

"She did!" a boy shouted, pointing to Marie.

"Phew! Girl, you've got an eagle eye!" the driver said.

We all looked out the windshield. I took a deep breath; the animal was alive. Quietly, it ran away beyond the side of the road, and a minute later, the bus continued on its way. I thought the fright has passed, but Marie sank in her seat for the rest of the trip and said nothing.

Each morning, after the fawn incident, I had to drag her to get on the school bus.

'What's wrong, eagle eye?' the driver would ask, but she wouldn't say. Instead, she remained downcast. Her teacher reported that Marie often looked distracted, like lost in thought, and recommended that she stay at home until we found out what her problem was. One night, she woke up screaming. Pierre and I ran to her room.

"What's wrong, sweetheart?" She was sitting on the bed, wringing her hands, eyes wide open. I hugged her.

"My eyes—I'm turning into an eagle!"

"Scary," I said and squeezed Pierre's hand with all my strength.

He left the room. A minute later, he came back, holding a mirror. "Look, Marie, dear!" She moved away from me to look.

"The Vieux Cécile!" I couldn't contain my sense of a bad omen.

"Honey, stop! That's just a legend. I think Marie is still in shock after the fawn incident and what the bus driver said to her."

"Your eyes are yours, not the eagle's eyes," he said to Marie, holding the mirror in front of her face. "Please tell her, Antoinette, that her eyes are only hers."

I wanted to believe his words with all my might. I got closer to Marie and looked at her image in the mirror from behind her shoulders. "Honey, you have beautiful eyes!" I said wholeheartedly, for I had never before experienced an instant of such clarity of mind as I had done then, splitting superstition from real life like a sieve separates gold nuggets from useless sediment. "And they are only yours," I added, totally convinced.

Marie turned to me. I repeated the words I had just said, and she smiled, nodded yes, and turned to us with her arms extended.

The Easel on the Beach

"Leave L.A., Audrey, and go to an exotic place to nourish your artistic talent," my friend Debbie said.

We were at a Community Building that the city had granted to local young artists for them to use it as a studio setting. Debbie was working on my portrait.

"Leave and go where?"

I admired her artistic talent to render my eyes with a happier expression and my hair a more glamorous appearance in the portrait than what I knew they looked like then. Would I ever acquire half that skill?

"Go to a tropical island."

Her small working space was crowded with boxes of brushes, palettes, the easel, and loose drawings spread all around. Some of her canvas hung on the walls that enclosed her niche. I glanced at them from the chair where I sat while posing for her—all beautiful. It had been months since I had even opened my case of paints. I wanted to paint, but I found no inspiration around or within me.

"I doubt I would get too far as a painter," I said.

"Who knows?" She eyed at my countenance under a late-afternoon light, filtered through a skylight, and proceeded to retouch some lines on her canvas. Then, she covered her production with a white cloth, full of blots of paint. "Just a few more details left. I'll show it to you when you're back."

What do I have to lose? I wondered. So, I collected some fresh oils, and following Debbie's advice, I flew at night, from Los Angeles to Puerto Plata, in the Dominican Republic, ready to look for my muse.

The ocean murmur, a gentle breeze, and the squawking of seagulls welcomed me in the morning. I stood barefoot on the sill of the opened balcony: A blue vastness extended throughout space, waves swayed in-and-out over the white sand, and in the background, the solemn *Pico Isabel de Torres*—Heavenly. Enticed by the scenery, I began sketching a few strokes, hoping to create an oil painting later. I had created just one worthy of being praised by Debbie since we had completed our Master's in Visual Arts, two years ago. She had obtained several awards for her work and even some money. Would I ever be capable of painting as well? I tried to imitate Debbie's way.

I set the easel and canvas on the balcony between the open shutters. I traced a line of blues and steeped back to check. Maybe this would work—I encouraged myself. As I mixed up a blob green and yellow to create a light brown for the mountains, my eyes fell on a slim young man about my age in a long white T-shirt and worn-out brown khakis. He stood barefoot on the sand in front of an easel between my room and the shore-line. There was something odd about him. I wasn't sure what—the way he leaned into the canvas a little too close, the way he lurched back so quickly to glance at the ocean and back to his work. Curious about his production and unhappy with my sketching, I couldn't help but go down there and have a peek at his work.

"Hi, I'm Audrey."

He looked at me through squinting eyes and inexpressive countenance as if he was seeing me at a distance.

"Amazing!" I said.

He had painted a sculptural naked female body riding upon a cresting wave. I took my eyes away from his canvas and shifted my gaze toward the sea: mellow waves, nobody surfing.

"What's your name?" I asked.

"Theophilus," he said, looking at the far-off.

Messy blond hair, blue eyes that avoided direct contact, anodyne attitude, and peculiar mannerisms, I recognized I had just met a weirdo. Fortunately, he understood English. Envious of his artistic talent and perplexed about his odd behavior, I stood by his side, convinced he would fail to acknowledge my presence: slim figure, curly, styled black hair, and rather pretty dark eyes.

"Congratulations," I then said and moved away.

Strolling along the shore, I found myself obsessing about his method of composition, thinking it would have never occurred to me to do anything like what he had done, and done it by memory, and so beautifully! Where did Theophilus get the inspiration from?

I was still lost in thought while eating lunch at the bar-restaurant of the hotel when I discerned Theophilus's ungainly gate. He was alone, wearing his T-shirt and shorts, and sat at a table set at the opposite corner from me, oblivious to anything else. I took this opportunity to attentively study his moves and gestures. He seemed such a loner. Yet I had the impression that now and then, he acted as if talking to someone else who invisibly sat at his table. Perhaps he's crazy, but quite an artist. I wished I would paint like him.

Three days later, at sunrise, with a calm ocean, and a spotless sky, I spotted Theophilus on the beach again, near the water, painting. He had a bottle of beer half-buried in the sand, and repeatedly, he glanced at this object and then added touches to his painting.

When I approached his easel and looked at his production, I was speechless, for the image on canvas was at odds with his subject model. He had painted a cluster of multi-color glass objects, which looked as if randomly dumped into some corner of a warehouse: pieces of bottles with big bellies, wine porrons, plates, and lamps. It struck me the careful distribution of tonalities and reflections of light. Suddenly, it occurred to me that I was looking at a still image like the ones seen through a kaleidoscope. I turned my head to look at the half-buried bottle: sunlight hitting the water reflected onto the bottleneck, and scintillation gave way to moments of an illusion of multiplication. Not only Theophilus was a great artist but also an imaginative guy. I again congratulated him on his artistic achievement. He mutely nodded his head, which I read as his way to say thank you, and I moved ahead.

Strolling along the seashore, I realized the beauty of my surroundings—the people on the beach, the ocean murmur, the water birds, the trees, and the proud Pico Isabel de Torres— yet I felt unable to find inspiration and create a painting like Debbie's and Theophilus's. What was wrong? That painting, the only one I'd had produced that Debbie praised, the green-and-orange-and-blue colored iguana, crawling on a thick bare branch of a tree, came to mind. I had painted it solely out of imagination, like Theophilus's wave female rider, like most of Debbie's paintings. Suddenly, an irresistible force led my steps into my room in the hotel. I opened the shutters, set the easel in the balcony sill, and started rough sketching, looking to the ocean. I worked until dusk, and the next morning I realized that I was drawing a portrait of Theophilus, himself painting on the beach.

I worked on it steady, day in and day out, until a month later, it was finished, and I experienced a sense of completeness.

I thought to find Theophilus somewhere on the beach and show it to him, but guessing he would simply nod his head made me desist of the idea. I decided to go back home. I was dying to see Debbie's work and show her my new painting.

Debbie's painting was outstanding, and she praised my work. "Who knows," she said, "You might get somewhere." I knew by then that, like for Theophilus, imagination is a source of inspiration.

The Bridge

In the summer prior to the new millennium, a seasoned Mexican architect, with a reputation as a bridge designer, was at the Benito Juárez International Airport on his way to Texas to participate in a meeting regarding a project to build a bridge across the Rio Grande.

At the gate, he joined the boarding line. A young Mayan woman with a colorful fabric satchel slanted on her shoulder aligned herself behind him. While waiting, the architect set his suitcase on the floor and wrote something in a pocket notebook. When he tried to pick it up, the suitcase had disappeared. No sign of it. He turned around and saw the Mayan lady holding his suitcase, the satchel slanted on her shoulder, and striding away. He started chasing her. When he was about to catch her, she sharply turned a corner and entered a solitary area of the airport, where two men, Mayan in appearance, were waiting. They immediately flanked the architect.

"This is a friendly kidnapping," one of the men said.

They were wearing white shirts and grey pants.

"Who are you?"

For an answer, the architect received a gentle push on his back to start moving. The woman with the suitcase followed behind. A Volkswagen van waited outside of the building with the driver at the wheel and the engine idling. The Mayan woman jumped onto the passenger seat, and the two men, with the architect in between them, occupied the back. One of the men covered his eyes with a bandana.

"It'll be a long trip. Have a drink!" The other man said as he picked up a bottle of mescal from a case left in the van and brought it to the architect's lips, forcing him to gulp down a long sip.

Soon, the architect fell asleep. At intervals, he woke up, only to feel the bottle of mezcal attached to his mouth, and the effect of the alcohol made him go back to sleep. When the vehicle reached the destination, the kidnappers stepped out and dragged the architect out, drunk as a barrel. They lifted and carried him like a flour bale onto a nearby small wattle and daub dwelling and flung him and his bag onto a mattress inside the place to sleep it off.

When the architect woke up the next day, the sun, along with shrieks from wild birds, conversations, and a smell of tortillas, coffee, and fried frijoles filtered in through an open window. He couldn't figure out his whereabouts. He was hungry and in need to urinate. Fortunately, in the dwelling, he found a tiny restroom with a toilet and running water. Then, he changed into a fresh shirt, taken from his suitcase, and stepped out of the shack. A group of people sitting on the ground gathered around a wood fire.

"Who are you?" he voiced.

"We are Tzotzil people," their boss answered in Spanish.

"And where is this place?"

"This is our territory, the Ocozocoautla municipality in Chiapas. We are part of the indigenous Council."

The architect realized he was in the rainforest. He stood in front of them silently until the chief gestured for him to join them and eat. He recognized his kidnappers among them. While he sipped coffee and ate tortillas and frijoles, the Tzotzil people continued their conversation in their language, giving him no participation. When he began to feel recomposed, the group stood, and the boss signaled for him to follow them. Whacking mosquitoes with his hand, he walked along with the group.

About a mile later, they stopped and stood forming a semicircle. The spectacle couldn't be more absurd. A very tall, white wooden ladder, with only one rail, stood in the midst of a small valley, surrounded by a dense mass of dark trees, the whiteness of its structure contrasting with the darkness of the place. The architect raised his eyes expecting to see something at the top of the ladder. But it ended stupidly and lonely under a natural vault formed by a cluster of pink clouds. Further on, lay a clear horizon. Then he saw a pipe, set near the base of the ladder, ejecting a stream of water onto an undefined, rocky ground.

The architect turned to face the group inquisitively.

"The Government provides us with water for irrigation. We control the output," said the outspoken man.

"That makes sense," the architect said, looking up again in wonder.

"The top of the ladder is our window to the world," the other said. "We brought you into our territory so you can check for yourself."

At that time, a man, who was wearing a rope tied around his waist, detached himself from the group, approached him, and in a blink of an eye, he passed part of the rope around his waist, leaving a length of about four feet between the two of them. Silently, the man pulled him to the ladder and both climbed up in tandem to the top. Afterward, they descended and released themselves from the rope.

"We want the Mexican Government to fund the building of a bridge across the wide river you've seen from the top of the ladder," the leader said.

The architect took a couple of steps toward the man with a humble expression on his face. "I see your point," he said.

"We want a bridge to facilitate trading with our brothers on the other side of the river," the chief reiterated.

The architect nodded. He took a deep breath. "I see your point," he repeated.

The outspoken man nodded.

"What do you expect from me?" the architect asked.

"We want you to go back to Mexico City and convince the Federal Government of building a bridge."

"I see your point," the architect said, and the Tzotzil man nodded.

No records of the architect's intervention at the Federal District exist, but the Chiapas Bridge was built at the exact point where the Tzotzils had wanted it.

The Deer

I wish somebody would tell these people I'm not crazy. I keep repeating my story over and over, but nobody believes me. A couple of hours ago, the police brought me to this mental institution on a *hold* under the suspicion of my being a danger to others.

I come from Montana, and in my family, we are all hunters, even my two older sisters. Last year, I got my license for the Big Game, and my father bought me this rifle. 'You'll be a good hunter, Son,' he said.

I love my rifle. My father put me in touch with a hunting guide here in New Mexico, where I'm in college. Before I got the rifle, my dream was to excel in basketball. I'm eighteen and 6' 4" tall. Some of my friends think I'm too skinny for the sport because I weigh a hundred and seventy pounds. So, I go to the gym to strengthen my muscles.

Since I got the rifle, though, I dream of killing a trophy deer. I wake up with this vivid image in my mind, and I get excited about the real possibility. So, yesterday, I called the guide. We agreed I would meet him at his camp high above Taos.

Early today, I dressed in my hunting clothes, put my rifle and backpack in my car and drove to meet the guide. I arrived around mid-morning. A thin layer of fresh snow covered the ground. The sky looked clear. A cool breeze held the smell of the pines. We began hiking south, and by noon we entered a zone filled with clusters of aspens scattered among big rocks, their leaves tinted an enchanting yellow. Wow! I suggested taking a break to enjoy the panorama. 'If you want to be a good Big Game Hunter, we should start scouting and going towards the valley.' The guide said, and we went on.

Some four miles later, I noticed the vegetation was greener than before. 'A stream flows nearby,' my guide said. I looked about, and it was then that I spotted a line of hoof prints on the trail. 'A thirsty lone elk is probably ambling to the stream,' the guide guessed. My heart skipped a beat. We tracked the row of prints until the trail split, and the prints became quite blurry. We agreed each of us would follow one of the two divisions.

I moved slowly, kept my breathing shallow and my rifle steady, ready to shoot as soon as my target made itself visible. The trouble was, however, many objects looked like a deer: a dark boulder, a fallen branch, a beam of light over the grass… Then, not farther than forty yards from me, standing among shrubs, this magnificent specimen of a heavily antlered deer appeared and quickly disappeared like a vision. I felt dazzled as if mesmerized. Worried that it would turn around and head uphill, I kept my eyes on its footprints and focused on the smell of its fur.

At a certain point, the lone deer took a sharp change of direction, and in my quest, I found myself stepping into a gully. I heard the noise of flowing water, perhaps the stream the guide had talked about. I then climbed the wall of the ditch, so I could position myself on the more even ground and catch sight of my target again. I raised my eyes over the upper edge and was astonished at the view of this spectacular, almost surreal head-and-neck figure of a deer that stood a few feet in front of me, a silhouette superimposed over the background of a vast horizon, loaded with dark clouds whirling in space. What a magnificent creature!

From my position, I didn't see anything else, except for a few treetops in the distance. I was not thinking, but I managed to aim the rifle where I guessed the deer's heart would be, and I pulled the trigger. 'Ahhhh!' I heard. Oh, my God, I've shot somebody. I froze. I pulled myself up out the gully. A middle-aged man lay on the grass, his hands tightly held around his left thigh. Anticipating the worst, I ran to him. Blood was oozing through the fabric of his jeans, and tears sliding down his cheeks. With my hunting knife, I tore the area of his pants that covered the wound, which looked superficial, and began helping him.

"I'll call an ambulance," I said.

"And I'll call the police," he replied.

We remained there, unable to properly communicate with each other. I sensed his anger. I said that I hadn't seen him, that I thought I was shooting at a deer, not him. He said I was crazy. I didn't like his assessment. Suddenly, I felt an urge to leave him and continue hunting. The noise of sirens, though, made me think twice about running away.

The police and the ambulance arrived at the same time. The officers asked a few questions. I heard the injured man was a photographer on assignment. He was taking a picture of the totem with the icon of a deer's head, the thing I had taken for a real one when I shot him. Then one of the officers turned to me. I told him my story, but from the start, I'd the impression the officer did not believe me. Then, things went fast: the ambulance took the photographer to an emergency room, and the patrol car brought me to this mental institution under the suspicion of being mentally disturbed and a danger to others.

I wish somebody would tell these people that I'm not crazy, only naïve about hunting experience, with a lot to learn from this incident. I hope they understand what I'm saying before my folks, my teachers, and my friends find out what happened and where I am and ruin my reputation.

The Hiker and the Hawk

When light and shade reach a high contrast, heat burns the weeds, and pebbles crackle under the sole of the boots, a young ornithologist, his face and arms tanned by a merciless sun, hikes on a bare trail. A couple of hours ago, he was walking along a canyon pass among plants of broad leaves and chestnut trees to track and, if opportunity presents itself, catch the Long-tailed Sylph, a unique species of hummingbird. How did he get off the path and find himself in this hot valley?

With the palm of his hand, the man wipes his sweaty forehead. He is enjoying the experience, though – the distant hills, the yellow fields, the green cacti with their fruit turned red, the sound of his steps. But how did he get here? *The Blue Skimmer did it!* In his mind, he sees again, emerging from a stream, right at the edge of the path, an unusually long blue insect. It turns around, and a white, doll-like face stares at him: "I'm a sylph, and in our world, we protect each other. Leave the little bird alone." The wind brings the words to his ears as the insect flaps its wings. At that moment, a jet of air blows his way, and he feels transported by it. And now, here he is, hiking on a dusty trail.

He is trying to find his way around when a big bird, standing on top of a solitary cactus, draws his attention. *It's a hawk.* The ornithologist walks closer to the bird. *What might a bird of prey see in me?* The hawk clenches its claws tightly. He appreciates the bird's elongated body, dark brown feathers, sharp hooked beak, and strong claws. Slowly, he advances ever closer to it, gripping the leather straps of his backpack, and he sees blood stains on its chest. He stops and stands on the edge of the trail, in front of the hawk, which now adopts a haughty and defiant pose. Its beak also appears to be blood-stained. He hates what he is seeing: the hawk has trapped a white dove, which is bleeding to death in its claws. The Blue Skimmer appears again, flapping in the air between him and the big bird: "Give up your hunt. Look what's happening to the dove." A gentle breeze brings these words to him.

Much to learn, the hiker reflects, feeling shaken, and appeals to his intuition to chart his course.

Feeding the Family

Taking the bus to work is more advantageous than driving since the bus stops close to my apartment and the hospital where I'm an assistant cook.

I'm 21. Most people on the bus are older than me. Rarely, anyone speaks; we exchange glances. In particular, a slim, elderly man — his hair, although white, is still abundant— catches my attention. He wears rimless, round glasses and has the air of a philosopher. He's always on the bus when I board.

Yesterday, a young woman, wrapped in a worn shawl, sat on the bench under the bus-stop canopy. The morning was sunny and warm. A boy of about 5, with messy, brownish hair falling down past his ears and eyes played with a terrier on the sidewalk. I stood to the right of the woman.

A bus arrived. It wasn't mine or theirs. It left. After it took off, I looked up and saw a heavyset man in a worn blue shirt and corduroy pants coming out of a McDonald's across the street. He stood beside his truck unwrapping an Egg McMuffin.

"Psst," the woman in the shawl whispered to the boy, jerking her chin towards the man.

The child commanded the dog, and they ran across the street, free of traffic at that moment. They lingered in the vicinity of the man briefly before the terrier jumped like an acrobat and snatched the sandwich out of the man's hand. The dog ran holding the sandwich between its teeth.

"I'll bring it back to you," the boy said, chasing behind the dog.

The man wiped his greasy fingers on his pants.

"Don't bother, kid, the dog has its tongue on it!" he yelled and walked back to the restaurant.

The terrier dropped his trophy at the woman's feet. She picked it up and divided it into three portions. My bus came, and I boarded. Trough the back windows, I saw the three of them on the bench enjoying the sandwich. Fascinating, I thought.

This morning, before taking the bus, for kicks, I went to the same McDonald's and bought a McMuffin. I went out and stood on the curb, unwrapping it. Like yesterday, the family was under the canopy, watching me. Before I blinked thrice, the boy and the terrier were beside me. Knowing what they were after, I offered my food to the boy. With a grimace of disgust, he rejected it, and the dog peed on my shoe. Frustrated, they went back to the woman.

The bus arrived. I crossed the street in time to catch it. The philosopher sat in the front seat. We glanced at each other. "You disrupted their method," he said. I was shocked. The man was reading Discourse on the Method, by René Descartes. "Enlightening," I said and walked to the back.

The Pot-Bellied Man

The pot-bellied man thinks he's a barrel. His belief comes from a repetitive dream he's had from years back. The man believes what he dreams. He hears the gurgle of liquid inside him when he moves. In his sleep, the barrel rolls over the edge of his bed, and knocks the tip of a boot or an empty bottle of booze before it crashes onto the floor. He hardly feels his wounds. Half asleep, he returns to bed and gets some rest. In the morning, he walks into the bathroom, stands in front of the toilet, opens the tap of the barrel, and pees. The man then goes into the kitchen and gulps down a can of beer to begin refilling the barrel. He pauses between cans of beer, and thinks of a time when he had a job, a wife, and a few friends. But he lost his job and the place in his heart he once had for his wife and friends. At the end of the day, the man feels his belly's tense, like the strings of a guitar. He fears the barrel might leak. Perhaps it could be reinforced? But when he goes back to sleep, he dreams the same dream.

A Gift of Love

As your birthday approached, bella signora, I went to the *Shop of the Inspiration*. I wanted to choose a gift that you would treasure. On the door I knocked, but it didn't open. I pushed it hard, but it didn't yield. This mishap threatened to harm my imagination. For I fancy you as I could never imagine any other woman. I dream of you, and in my dreams, you always look gracious, whether you appear floating in pink cloud or lying on a purple velvet couch.

From the *Shop of the Inspiration*, I went to the *Shop of the Ordinary*. I checked rings, necklaces, bracelets; everything seemed dull and boring. 'Why are you crying?' the saleswoman asked. I thought of you, your liveliness, and your angelical smile. I thought of the summer nights lying on the beach under the moonlight, the balm of your lips on my skin, the warmth of your soul in me, and seagulls, lovers of the moon, surrounding us.

'It might be the fluorescent light,' I said.

My imagination weary, my eyes stumbled on this pearl. Please, take it as my gift of love.

The Solitary Tree

The summer heat has burned the chaff on the field and turned the fallen leaves brown. Every morning he walks down to his barn. The sound of sand creaking under the soles of his shoes on the ground reminds him of a pair of combat boots that fit younger feet. He looks back. Perhaps he missed the pair of combat boots sitting on the porch? But only a span of dust rises inches behind him, whirls, and vanishes, leaving no trace. He moves on.

On the last day of the summer, before entering the barn, he pauses and listens to the twittering birds. The sound comes from nearby trees behind a stone wall that separates his farm from a public park. He fancies the birds are saying *look for him; don't give up*. Inside, a pile of logs, ready to feed the fire place when winter comes, lies in the corner behind the door; blocks of hay rest on shelves; rakes, wicker brooms, horses' harnesses; everything is in its place as it has always been. The long mirror with a thin metal frame hangs on the back door. He can't remember whose idea was to put it there. He stands in front of it: a tall man, sun-tanned skin, broad shoulders, and steady hands. Then, to let the breeze refresh the barn, he opens the door ajar. Good heavens! For a moment, the mirror reflects a soldier's portrait in battle uniform, wearing combat boots, and his face and body shape resembling his own. He squints to focus. "What's—" He turns to look outside: the mirror reflects the image of long intertwined and exposed to sight roots, which feed a small tree that dwells alone against the stone wall's surface. The image of the soldier fades away, and the farmer closes the door and his eyes. And when he opens them again, he sees himself in the mirror with the signs of grief in his eyes. He turns around and begins to work, emptying sacks of wheat into a corner of the barn.

The Mongrel Dog

During a visit to a local kennel, Elisa, standing in front of the bars that separated the public from the dogs' compartments, pointed to a gloomy mongrel that stood alone in a cubicle. Michael, her speech-therapist husband, who stood beside her, glanced at it, pouted his lips, and wrinkled his nose. Deplorable!

"Do you really care for this dog?"

"I like it," she said.

They had met through the Internet in January, 2014; they liked each other, and from then onwards, they dated steadily. Sex was good, both agreed, but would their personalities be compatible if they decided to go further in their relationship? To test their long-term mutual likeness, they decided to live together throughout the four seasons, and they leased a small house in the San Francisco Bay Area. The experiment was successful; in February 2015, they married. He was 40, not too tall, but well built, and looking healthy. She had passed the childbearing age; petite, with dark eyes and pale countenance looked like one of those old porcelain German dolls. None had been married before nor had children.

An employee, a young guy with big hands and dark complexity approached them. "Her name is Siba," he said referring to the same dog. "If you like," he continued, "I can take her out to the court-yard so you interact with her."

Elisa nodded, and the man walked Siba outside; they followed him. The idea of adopting a dog had emerged six months after they had married, more for their enjoyment, having it as a companion during their outdoor excursions, than as a watchdog.

"How old is this dog?" Michael asked.

The employee delayed his answering until he released Siba into the fenced yard and let her roam about. "She's ten years old, our vet estimates," he then said.

Hearing these words, Michael quickly turned to Elisa. "Dear, I thought we were looking for a greyhound puppy, not an old gawky dog." A few years ago, he had owned an Italian greyhound, slim and fast like the devil, a joy to watch him run.

"Oh, don't say that, Michael."

He gazed at the filthy, mournful dog more attentively—its coat was white with orange patches spread on its head, back, and legs. He put a face of disbelief. Was Elisa having a moment of mental fogginess?

"How can you like such a—"

Trotting awkwardly, Siba came over and stumbled on Michael's legs, interrupting his statement. He pushed her away with his foot with such energy that his action looked more like a kick than it did like a push. The dog whined for a moment, then peed on the grass, and then approached Elisa and merrily danced around her feet.

"Be gentle with the dog, please," she said to her husband.

Michael felt like saying that he disliked the dog entirely, but instead, he mumbled, "Damn dog!"

Siba, being playful with Elisa, produced a few friendly barks, and Michael noticed she was missing some teeth and others had turned yellow. He clicked his tongue.

"How can you fall for such a pitiful dog?"

"Well, you know, Michael, there is no accounting for taste."

Michael did not reply. He wondered whether their difference in the taste for dogs might be but one, like the first swallow in spring, among the existence of other unnoticed differences.

After the helper took Siba back into the kennel, Elisa walked straight to the adoption office, and Michael followed. A middle-aged male clerk with a black, thick mustache, and a friendly smile, stood behind the counter, and they approached him. Michael put his hands in his pockets and stood beside his wife, gazing at her in disbelief while she communicated her interest in adopting the dog. Suddenly, Michael felt like a wave of heat creeping up his spine and blinding him. He was ready to voice his exasperation when the clerk intervened: "This dog is not available for adoption," he said, and Michael thought his words sounded more like those uttered by a referee in a boxing match than words spoken by a kennel's employee.

Elisa took a deep breath, leaned on the counter, and thrust her chin to also look at the screen. "Why isn't she?" she asked.

"This is a sick dog," the man said after rechecking the info available to him.

Michael, meanwhile, struggled to remain calm and figure out what should his standing be during the unfolding conflictive situation; he found it appalling that his wife took an unilateral decision on adopting that sick dog against all logic.

"However," the employee said, "sometimes we allow people to take a sick dog home for a few days to check with a vet before adopting."

Elisa turned to glance at Michael with a mild smile, her dark eyes speaking of her intention of taking the clerk's advice.

"Honey," Michael hurried to say, "why such a whim? We're facing a sick dog!"

"I like this dog," she didn't hesitate.

"I see," said the clerk, shifting his eyes from one to the other as if they were two opponents in the boxing ring.

"I see," said Michael as well, although he felt uncertain of what it was that he saw.

In the end, on that summer evening, Michael and Elisa walked out of the kennel leading Siba on a short leash. While they advanced through the parking lot toward their car, the barking symphony from the dogs in the kennel gradually faded out, and Michael felt like he was a passenger on a ship that had left the dock to an unknown shore. They settled into their hatchback— Siba in the back, visibly uneasy—and Michael started the vehicle.

"We should stop at the nearest animal hospital," Elisa said and googled for addresses.

"O.K.," Michael said dryly, mistrustful of his power of assertiveness to confront his wife's absurd pretensions.

An animal emergency facility was located a couple of miles away. Michael drove there. The vet, Dr. Rosado, a middle-aged man, short and chubby, wearing light-green surgical scrubs came out to the entrance hall and greeted them. Standing in the room, Elisa dragged Siba to his feet while she explained the problem. Dr. Rosado listened attentively, and then guided them and Siba into the examining room.

"This dog has an abscess in the rectum," he said after he finished his checking.

Michael and Elisa looked at each other quizzically.

"It can be surgically removed," Dr. Rosado said while washing his hands at a basin in the room.

"How much would it cost?" Michael asked.

"About $1,500," he said while drying his hands.

Michael rubbed his palm over his forehead in a gesture of alarm. This expenditure was outrageous. Elisa had never challenged his level of tolerance to such an extent. Why would she presently push limits?

"Is it risky?" asked Elisa.

"All surgery carries a risk, but if successful, the dog will be cured," Dr. Rosado said.

Michael silently asserted himself that he didn't like that particular dog. "Would you mind Doctor if my wife and I talked it out before deciding?" he asked.

"Please, go ahead."

They left the room and walked back to the entrance hall.

"In my view," Michael said with energy, "adopting a sick dog makes no sense."

They stood in the middle of the hall. Elisa looked at her husband straight as if she had expected his comment. "There isn't any going back, Michael," she said in a whisper as if afraid of someone listening.

"What do you mean? Of course, there is a way out!" He couldn't believe she would hold on to such illogical reasoning. Perhaps there was something wrong in her way of thinking that he hadn't picked up?

"You witnessed," she said, "the demonstration of affection that Siba displayed toward me in the court-yard at the kennel, and—"

"That's nothing but sentimentalism!" At that point, he didn't mind showing anger. She apparently believed the dog had chosen her for its mistress.

"I'll cover the bill out of my savings," she said.

The statement took Michael a little by surprise. By Elisa paying the bill, she seemed to claim ownership for the dog, but he, Michael, still had to live under the same roof. What was going on in her mind?

"But, Elisa, it isn't only the money. It's—"

It dawned on him at that very moment that he was dealing not only with his wife's wishes but also with an established alliance, which he had witnessed developing, between her and the dog.

"Do as you wish," he conceded.

Back in the doctor's office, Elisa told him, to Michael's amazement, that her husband and she had agreed to Siba's surgery. Therefore, they left the dog admitted in the facility, and they went home.

That evening, Michael couldn't sleep a wink. He couldn't brush away the thought that adopting a sick dog was temerity. How would they take care of it? Throughout the night, he tossed and turned in bed so often that his fidgeting woke his wife. He then tried to convince her of the futility of her enterprise, but she wouldn't listen; instead, she quickly went back to sleep until the alarm went off. When they got up, she said that she would take some time off (she worked as a manager in an appliance store) to go pick up Siba and take care of her. Michael thought, but didn't say, she definitely had assumed ownership of the dog.

That day, contacted about Siba being ready for discharge, Elisa went to pick her up. An employee got the dog out into the reception room. It was wearing an E-collar. Elisa gazed at Siba with wide eyes, for the dog, wearing such a large plastic cone, looked like a creature from another planet. The helper said that according to the doctor, Siba was stable and ready to go home on antibiotics, but they should do follow up with their vet. Elisa agreed, then paid the bill, and walked out to the car. She set Siba, still drowsy, on a blanket in the back, and drove home.

Standing in the middle of her kitchen, staring at the dog, and the dog at her, it seemed Elisa didn't know what to do next. She phoned Michael at work.

"I wonder where the dog should sleep."

"You decide, Elisa. It's your dog."

"She's quite weak to sleep outdoors—"

"Whatever." He concluded.

Elisa risked leaving Siba alone in the kitchen for a short while, since the dog was still drowsy, and ran to a nearby pet shop to buy a dog bed, a collar, and a six-foot leash. When Michael came back from work, he found the dog's bed set in a corner of the kitchen and Siba on it. During the night, however, the dog wandered around. Elisa got up several times and tried to calm her down with little success. Michael sensed that the sick dog might alter not only their sleep pattern but also their intimacy.

The next day, Elisa made an appointment with the local animal clinic, and Siba's first outing was to visit the vet. She sniffed the threshold at the door from the outside and refused to go in until Eli encouraged her with sweet words. As they stepped into the waiting room, a space of about ten square feet, Siba's nose came in touch with that of a dark-coated bulldog, and they shoved each other like deer in a struggle until Elisa and the owner of the other dog, a middle-aged woman of humble appearance, managed to break the struggle. At that moment, the vet's assistant, a thin, young man called for the bulldog. Then it came the turn for Siba.

In a friendly manner, the vet's assistant lifted Siba onto the examining table, and the doctor, a healthy-looking man in his fifties, proceeded to examine the patient following his routine, his fingers sliding over the dog's coat like tentacles, focusing on the surgical scar.

"She'll be fine," he said in a Polish accent after he had finished the clinical examination. "In a couple more days you can take off the pet-collar."

"Thank you, Dr. Ku—"

"Kurboranowsky," he helped. "You can call me Dr. K."

"Thank you, Dr. K.," Elisa said and, a bit embarrassed, led Siba to the exit.

On her way home, Elisa swung by the pet shop and bought some dog toys to keep Siba entertained while she and Michael went to work. Soon it became evident, though, that Siba wasn't a playful dog. During the day, she ran around in the yard and barked at every living creature she encountered on her way. When tired, she lied down in the sun, leaning against a wall, and slept long siestas. Nights were problematic because she didn't like sleeping in her bed. Elisa tried to make it cozier by throwing in a blanket, but it didn't help either. The situation became a source of distress for both spouses, and Michael, with little resistance on the part of his wife, opted to sleep on the living room couch.

In the end, Elisa, perhaps out of concern about how badly things were going between Michael and her took Siba to the pet shop and allowed her to sniff the beds on the rack until her nose became glued to one of them made from a tartan fabric, and Elisa bought it. That fixed the problem at night, and Michel returned to sleep with his wife. Nevertheless, he became conscious that, because of the dog, something, which he couldn't or didn't dare put in words, was changing in their relationship.

One day in August, Elisa walked downtown to meet a couple of friends and took Siba, by now off the plastic collar, along. They all sat on a terrace for coffee. As a precaution, Elisa had tied the leash to the leg of her chair. Suddenly, she felt a jerk that pulled her out of her seat and onto the ground while Siba lashed out, dragging the chair behind, chasing a poodle across the street. Halfway on the run, the leash tangled with the legs of a woman, and she, the dog, and the chair together rolled over the asphalt. Passersby quickly came up and encircled them.

"My God!" the fallen lady said as she got up from the ground. "From where did this dog escape?"

The scene took a theatrical flavor.

"We were there—" One of the Elisa's two friends pointed to the terrace where they had been sitting. "The dog saw this poodle—"

"My husband and I," Elisa cut her short, "have recently rescued this dog from the pound. We're trying to get to know her better. I'm so sorry—"

"Well, it seems I'm not hurt," the woman said.

"I'm so sorry!" Elisa repeated, circling her arms as if encompassing everybody there.

After these words, onlookers began to disperse, Elisa took charge of Siba again, her two friends returned the chair to where it belonged, the poodle disappeared from the scene, and the show ended.

When Michael came back home that evening and heard from his wife at dinner about the incident, he couldn't flatten his arising anger.

"Frankly, Elisa, I'm fed up with the dog's behavior."

"That's the problem, Michael. Siba is not an impeccable dog. She has issues, and you cannot forgive that she has them."

Michael stirred on his chair. He dropped the utensils on the table, grabbed the glass of wine in front of him and drained it with a gulp.

"Why do I have to put up with this shit?" he mumbled, looking into space.

"It's up to you, Michael, how to value facts realistically and not let yourself become overwhelmed."

Michael stretched up his torso, dragged his feet under the chair and abruptly pushed it back. She's telling me that the problem doesn't fall on the dog but on me. He got up. "I'm not the one who adopted this damn dog!" He walked out of the dining room.

Since the argument at dinner, the spouses lived in a silent but tense state of resentment, and again stopped sleeping in the same bedroom, although they continued sharing outdoor excursions on weekends. Joaquin Miller Regional Park, located at a walking distance from their home in Oakland, became their main destination. On and off, Michael harbored hope that Siba would do well on those trails, but his expectations soon vanished when, over the next few occasions, he witnessed the dog's moving ungainly throughout. He wondered whether Siba would ever excel in anything.

On another day in October, while hiking on a narrow trail along a gorge at the bottom of which a stream ran, unexpectedly, Siba took off and went down the cliff until she got caught in the bramble. Elisa turned to her husband for help, but Michael reacted laggardly, and it was only with much struggle that they managed to recue Siba to safety.

"I don't think this is a *normal* dog," Michael snapped.

"Well, it's easier to see the mote in another eye—"

Michael didn't listen any longer. When it came to his feelings about the dog, his wife didn't give a damn, and any attempt of reconciliation looked like a lost battle. Nevertheless, they managed to regain their composure and keep on hiking. Siba, perhaps sensing his master's disenchantment, stayed on course at front for the rest of the excursion, sniffing at wet shrubs, and animal droppings. When they returned home, Michael felt exhausted, more so due to their confrontations than physical exercise. He wondered for how long they could go on with such a struggle without something in their marriage breaking down.

On another day at the park, Siba took off ahead of them in the pursuit of some prey. The tracking led her to the recent droppings of cow manure on which she rolled over from side to side, so when she came back to her masters, she stank.

"The dog is buttered in shit!" Michael put on a face of disgust.

"She's only an animal."

"That's Right. But why did you insist in adopting such a damn animal?"

Michael's face had turned red. Elisa took a few seconds before she replied. "What's done is done," she then said.

"No!" Michael kicked a rock in the direction of Siba and almost hit her. "What's done could be undone."

"Calm down. We'll give her a bath when we get home."

"Not me, dear, I won't touch her. Gross!"

When they returned to the car, Michael refused to allow the dog in; the stench would permeate everything inside, he said. Elisa, holding Siba by the leash, grudgingly tried to refute her husband's decision while she also attempted to get herself and the dog in the car. But Michael wouldn't yield. He got in first, shut the door, and drove off at all speed like a lost soul.

Being left alone in the park with the dog, Elisa had little choice but to walk Siba home. When she arrived, Michael was not there. She led Siba straight to the back yard and gave her a bath, shampooing and rubbing her coat repeatedly until she made sure no traces of cow droppings remained.

Once satisfied with the job, Elisa walked Siba inside the house and fed her. Then she stepped into the garage to check if the car was there; it wasn't. At that moment, her cellular rang. It was a freeway patrol officer calling to notify her that Michael was in a car accident at the level of the Bay Bridge. "Reckless driving," the officer said when Elisa asked what had happened, and he added that Michael had tried to change lanes at high speed but miscalculated the distance to another vehicle and ended up veering off so fast to his right to avoid a collision that the front of his car crashed against the freeway shoulder. An ambulance had transported him to the county hospital in San Francisco with a broken leg, and his car would be towed away. Did she have any preference for a car body-shop? "No," she replied.

After the shocking news she had just received over the phone, Elisa displayed a progressive fidgeting behavior. She made arrangements to leave Siba at a Day Care Center for dogs in the neighborhood, and next, she rented a car and took off to see Michael in the hospital.

The accident resulted in a fractured ankle, treated and wrapped in a cast. "Not a big deal," he said, but he had to do physical rehabilitation and be on sick leave for a while, he added. Elisa drove him home the next day; during the trip she said that she was ready to give up Siba. Michael replied they should, if she didn't mind, talk about it later because he felt tired and wanted to nap.

The back yard at home enclosed a porch of about forty by fifteen yards, layered with Mexican red-ochre tiles; a wooden fence set on the sides and the far back of the property marked its limits; a few camellia trees spread about completed the landscape. In this setting, Michael started his rehabilitation practices, following instructions from his therapist, while his wife was at work. It was the last week in October. On crutches, he would take tiny steps back and forth down the porch. Siba watched him from a corner and he purposely ignored her presence.

After a couple of days, though, the dog came closer and walked by his side. He let her, and soon it became like a game: On and off, Siba advanced faster a few steps ahead of her master, and Michael hurried his pace to catch up, and by carrying on this play, he realized his practicing rehabilitation became entertaining and it accelerated his improvement.

A week went by, and the two spouses hadn't brought up the issue of giving up Siba that Elisa had initiated while driving Michael back home from the hospital. However, they had managed to seamlessly patch up the hostility they held against each other.

"I think I'm on my way to finding a foster home for Siba," Elisa said one early evening at the beginning of November.

They sat around a little table on the porch with a glass of wine. The sun still shined behind the Oakland hills. Michael caught himself distractedly petting the dog for the first time.

"Which home?" he asked and consciously quit petting the dog. He grabbed an anchovy from a plate with appetizers that Elisa had prepared to accompany their drinks.

"A young man at the Day Care likes her. He says he wouldn't mind taking her home if we decide to give her up."

"What do you think?" He wondered what each of them had done wrong to let a dog disrupt their marriage.

"It's up to you, Michael. I'll be O.K. with your decision."

"I must say, Siba makes a good companion during my exercises. It seems she guesses what I'm doing. Let's wait for a while longer before deciding."

Elisa gave him a wide smile. She got up from her chair and headed inside the house. "I'll set the table for dinner," she said, brushing her husband's nape in passing.

About a week later, Michael got up in the morning to a cool but sunny day with a craving for walking outdoors. He was off the crutches and wished to check out how well he could do in nature. He wondered whether Siba would keep behaving like she had done so far on the porch, which had entertained and helped him.

Point Isabel is a tiny peninsula off the San Francisco Bay, harboring a large dog's park, easy-to-hike-on trails, and several recreational areas. Michael was familiarized with the zone. While Elisa was at work, he took Siba to the park. He started walking slowly on a marked pathway across an area of flat terrain towards the water. Siba heeled beside him like she had done at home, which pleased him. Golden retrievers busied themselves with catching tennis balls their masters threw from the edge of the moderately steep shore into a water channel below, which divided the peninsula in two halves.

When they were three or four yards from reaching the channel, Siba, apparently excited by the view of the retriever's action, ran to join them, but stumbled on the rocks at the edge of the cliff and fell into the water. It quickly became apparent that she didn't know how to swim; ineffectively, she tried to keep her nose afloat. Michael didn't know what to do. Suddenly, a young man dove into and dragged Siba to safety. Standing on the ground, soacked and trembling, Siba looked pitiful. Some of the people around brought their dogs to look at her.

"She doesn't know how to swim!" One of the onlookers yelled, laughing.

Michael felt his contempt for the dog re-emerging.

"You know," an elderly, bearded man said, "one can teach a dog how to swim."

It dawned on Michael that what the elderly man had said was true, that with appropriate training, dogs can learn a lot of things. He had trained the Italian greyhound; he could likewise train Siba. Little by little, he was accepting the point of view that he couldn't blame his wife for liking Siba. 'There is no accounting for taste,' she had said. That he tried to change his wife's taste for the dog was at the core of their disagreements. He realized that it is not possible to see every aspect of another person's character simply by living together throughout the four seasons; it takes longer to get to know someone better, and he wondered whether that was also true for dogs.

Without further interaction with the people at the park, he walked to the exit. Siba heeled beside him as if nothing had happened. The dog was not an impeccable one, as Elisa had put it, but that wasn't her fault. Why didn't it occur to him, throughout the four months they had Siba, to train her? He left the park and went home. He wanted to share his considerations with Elisa.

Winding Roads

I joined the Salk Institute in San Diego, California, from Toronto on a Fellowship in 1990. I was 30. Keylor Montes, from Buenos Aires, became my mentor. He was 50, and he had worked at the Salk for twenty years. We were both biologists, and since, we have done research together for twenty years.

When I first met Keylor, I thought he looked like Carlos Gardel, the legendary tango singer. 'Well,' he said when I brought up my comparison to his attention, 'I can't sing, but I used to play the clarinet.' Nevertheless, six-feet tall, slim, with straight-back black hair, dark eyes, and bushy eyebrows, he resembled, in my memory from pictures and movies, Gardel's looks, except for the singer's perennial smile, which in Keylor's case, an attentive and serene expression replaced it. In time, he gained weight, and his hair gradually turned gray, but his attentive and serene expression prevailed.

Right after his retirement at 70 in December 2010, Keylor and Marina, his wife of thirty-six years, went on a vacation trip, which included Argentina, and he texted me with pictures from some places they were visiting. I thought they were enjoying a well-deserved leisure time.

After they came back, they invited Laura, my dear Canadian wife for seventeen years, and me, Paul Gascony, to a soirée at their home in La Jolla. They wanted to share their experiences with us, and Keylor wished to catch up with what was happening in the lab.

"Nothing new there," I said. "Busy as usual. But we're dying to hear about your trip."

It was mid-February. We had arrived shortly before the sunset, and because the weather was warm, we sat around a table with appetizers and drinks on the porch. Laura and I hadn't been to Buenos Aires, so she asked about it.

"When in Boca, you know, the borough where Keylor was born and raised in Buenos Aires," Marina jumped in, "he said that maybe we should move there."

Keylor raised his eyes toward me apologetically as if he didn't have the right to move away from our lab. I meant to say that of course, it was natural he wanted to do so, when Laura took the lead: "Isn't it amazing? I mean how charming the place where we grew up can be!"

With little apparent conviction, Marina nodded yes. I searched inside myself to see if Laura's declaration applied to me as well, if I had at any time felt like moving back to Toronto after I retired, but I hadn't. Of course, the thought of retiring had not entered my mind.

"What would you do there?" I asked Keylor.

He poured wine into our glasses before answering.

"I guess I could find a part-time teaching job or something like that at the Biology Institute in Buenos Aires, where I worked before I came to California, to keep my mind occupied."

I hastened to reach for a bite-size sandwich filled with fried goat cheese to avoid speaking my mind by chewing, to stop myself from saying that what he had said made little sense, that he could obtain any teaching or administrative job in our Department, and maybe with a more advantageous deal than he could find it in Buenos Aires and free from the stress of moving abroad.

"For now, I don't worry about it, anyway," Keylor said, addressing me directly, so I thought he had read my mind.

We experienced a moment of silence until Laura broke it.

"What other places did you visit that you liked?"

Her question shifted the conversation. They talked about the places they had visited in Miami and New Orleans until the breeze turned colder, and Laura began to sneeze. By then, we had enjoyed the evening and thought it prudent to say goodbye and leave.

While driving back home, Laura asked whether I thought Keylor would come back to the Salk Institute and work in some capacity, or perhaps volunteer his time. I said that I was confident he would. 'Look at Marina,' I said, 'She's happy doing voluntary work at the Museum.' We were both well acquainted with Marina's volunteering activity with the Educational Programs at the Maritime Museum, which she had gladly started right after she retired a few years back.

About a month later, I heard from Keylor that they were leaving on another trip—this time to coastal Mexico. During their travels, he again kept in touch with us through texts and photos. On this occasion, however, I became aware of a subtle change in his way of speaking. 'Today,' he wrote, 'I sat on the beach at sunset. Marina went for a swim. Crepuscular light made the water appear mysterious and the sky golden.' These were words of a poet or an artist rather than a scientist.

When they came back, three weeks later, I invited Keylor to join me at a little restaurant near the lab, where we liked to eat lunch, and I mentioned my observation about the words he had used.

"While in Mexico, I realized that we don't remain the same person throughout our entire lives,' he said.

I missed him in the lab, and, really, I didn't see where he was leading me.

"What do you mean?"

"Well, living free of professional ties is a privilege."

I felt disappointed and at the same time uncertain about what to expect. Two months before he retired, Keylor went through significant health problems. He first suffered an episode of vertigo that took him to the hospital and deprived him of his balance, rendering him unable to walk on his own for many days. Upon returning to the lab, he had a stroke, which made his vision blurry and double, and he found out he also had high blood pleasure. Following the advice from his doctor, he retired in December 2010.

Before he fell sick, we had started a new research project on kittens' acquiring behaviors. I understood his reason for retiring, but deep down I hoped he would give me a hand with the work once he recovered.

"Perhaps you don't feel completely recovered?" I asked and glanced at him attentively from across the table, checking for observable physical changes. But I saw the same serene expression; if anything, the grey areas of his hair perhaps showed a little more extensive.

"Oh, I'm all right. It's simply that I desire to experiment with things I could not do while working."

But I knew Keylor had a competitive vein, and I couldn't imagine him exclusively committed to living a hedonistic lifestyle.

"Well, Keylor, you know better."

I've always respected Keylor's opinion, even if I disagree with him. But that day, our conversation during lunch filled me with the suspicion that perhaps he was going senile. Yet I immediately felt terrible for thinking that way, especially when he insisted on paying for the meal.

I didn't hear from Keylor for several weeks. I kept myself busy at work and returned home late at night. Coincidently, work was also keeping Laura quite busy, so we didn't see much of each other either. One evening, however, in March, while eating a late dinner, Laura said that Marina had called her about Keylor.

"Quel est son probleme?" I said distractedly.

We were speaking French; both our parents are French Canadian. We met at the Consulate in San Diego, where she still works as a coordinator of Canadian travelers associated with California business organizations. We married when we were both in our mid-thirties. As it's the case with the Montes, we have no children, but we all love our jobs.

"Marina said Keylor is getting depressed."

"What do you think she meant?" The news had caught my attention, and for a split second, the thought of Keylor's going senile re-entered my mind.

"Being idle, she believes, drives him crazy."

We were having grilled salmon and red potatoes. "Do you care for another piece of salmon? I offered her after I had served myself seconds.

"Yes, please."

I served her a fillet of fish and pour some more white wine into our glasses.

"That's surprising," I said. "Last time Keylor and I lunched together he felt quite optimistic about life."

"Not now. I think we should have them for tea."

I agreed.

They came one Sunday afternoon, and we had tea and dessert in the living room. Keylor and Marina sat on the couch, and Laura and I on armchairs, across from them; we all faced a coffee table on which Laura had set a tray with the teacups and saucers. Keylor appeared a little fidgety. At first he and I did some shoptalk while Laura and Marina chatted about their worlds. He gave me some input on how to proceed with an experiment I was stuck with, which I appreciated.

"And what's going on with you, Keylor? Laura then asked bluntly.

Keylor turned to her with an expression of having been taken aback.

"Why don't you tell her?" Marina encouraged him.

Keylor hesitated. He turned to look at me even if I wasn't the one asking. "What happens is that— staying idle is getting on my nerves."

"But I thought—" I stopped for a second; then I said, "that you wanted to take things easy and enjoy life as it comes."

"Yes, but doing just that is not fulfilling."

I felt disarmed. How could he be helped? Keylor got up from the couch and walked to the French window. "I must get involved in something meaningful," he said, looking out.

"Something useful to fill his days, he means," said Marina, still sitting on the couch, sipping tea.

"It seems to me the problem has an easy solution. He should come back to the lab!" I felt triumphant.

A silence fell among us during which Keylor down-crested returned to occupy his seat on the couch. Marina grabbed his hand as if he needed consolation.

"He'll find something on his own," said Laura in a conciliatory tone of voice.

When we resumed talking, we focused on exploring potential plans of action, but Keylor didn't participate. Nevertheless, after they left, I felt hopeful he would choose to come back to the lab and work with us, his team of researchers, 'in some capacity' as Laura had said back in February. After all, he had proved to possess a great ability to adapt and manage whatever matter he needed to, so he would reach his goal.

He didn't show up, though. A week or so passed, and worried about his state of sanity, I called him. His mind still whirled around the same issue of being idle and needing to find something meaningful to do. I again suggested he should swing by the lab. But he dismissed the idea: 'Maybe I should take things easy, travel around, and enjoy life as it comes.'

Marina tried to get her husband out of the dispirited state he had fallen into. She often phoned after work and shared her concerns with us.

"I can't for the love of God figure out what he's looking for," she said during one of her calls towards the end of May. "I know it's neither money nor prestige. None of that moves him currently."

The thought of Keylor's coming back to our Department haunted me, so I insisted on it through Marina.

"Let's clear the air, Paul," she said. "He isn't interested in that."

I took Marina's declaration as definitive, and after we switched off, I admitted to Laura that I felt disconcerted. Was Keylor going senile? Was he in search of a new identity? A bunch of questions popped up in my mind that evening. Only one answer presented itself clearly in my consciousness: Keylor's heading to a new phase in his life. But, in my eyes, he appeared so self-undefined that, being an old man, I was afraid he would run out of time. What should I do, I tried to put myself in his shoes, outside of my field of expertise? Anyway, by the time Laura and I were ready to go to bed, I noticed her uneasiness, hearing my divagation, and I quit talking. I swallowed a sleeping pill, and hoped to fall asleep.

Time went by without news from or about Keylor. At the beginning of the summer, he surprised us by announcing that he wanted to coach science-fiction writers. 'Helping writers grasp scientific concepts they can successfully apply in a story might quench my intellectual thirst,' he said. Such an out-of-the-blue decision resulted, at the least, intriguing. I saw his point, though, and so I agreed with his judgment. But his enthusiasm for the job didn't last. A month later, he confided in me his frustration with the task. 'I can't say this line of work is worth my time because the author is the creator, and I operate like a gauge—your protagonist's ideas are off the scientific range, or wrong, and so on,' he said.

Keylor quit the job. As I listened to him as he related his complaints to me, I also remembered that he had always approached new projects systematically; the spontaneity with which he operated on this occasion might have caused the failure. Right at that moment, I grasped that there is a cost for shifting one's identity, for attempting to redefine oneself.

On the surface, Keylor's quitting his new occupation looked like a minor deal, but Marina said that he again turned down-crested and spoke of wasting his life by not being engaged in something meaningful. I couldn't brush away the thought of Keylor's entering a vicious circle of starting and quitting new commitments. Why would he want to change the destiny of his life? What else could, other than his mastering of biology, bring personal success at his age? Marina also said that sitting under the trellis with grape-vine tangles across its roof in the backyard, playing the clarinet, perked him up a little. She wondered if by them going on another vacation would help, and I said that most likely it would.

The Montes left on vacation to Portugal. Marina was of Portuguese descent and she spoke the language. Keylor had met her at the library in our Department, where she worked as a database consultant until she retired. When they married, she had been divorced for several years. They made a happy couple, although she never had a child.

At their return from Portugal toward the end of July, they invited us again to a soirée, pretty much the same setting and environment as we had experienced back in mid-February when they had returned from Argentina. The weather was much warmer, however, and Laura and I stayed until midnight. Both of them appeared to be happy, and Keylor spoke at length of how much they had enjoyed listening to the Fado singers at the restaurants they went to and also about the pleasure of getting lost on purpose in old Lisbon.

Nevertheless, once back at home, Marina resumed her volunteer activities and Keylor his rumination about what to do with his life. For a while, he entertained the possibility of volunteering his time, 'maybe at a local museum, like Marina, or the Public Library.' For some reason, though, which he never shared with me, he failed to do so, and his quest for 'something meaningful' began to sound like a broken record; so much so that when in August he came up with the plan of using his time to translate Spanish articles on biological research into English, I took his declaration with a grain of salt. 'With little training, I suppose I could board the boat,' he said. On the other hand, I thought that this plan sounded more in tune with his background and showed optimism for his success. But Keylor didn't pursue that avenue either. He said that translation didn't allow much room for innovation, 'because the translator must remain faithful to the author who is the creative brain.'

Altogether, Keylor's interest in becoming a scientific translator died. At that point, I wondered when he would understand that for him to excel, which he so badly wanted, he should use his experience as a biologist. At his age, what else could he transform himself into? But he was, in my eyes, so focused on his current quest, to find 'something meaningful' to get involved in, that his past accomplishments, no matter how outstanding, he no longer considered.

Having lost all hope Keylor would at any time return to help us collecting data obtained through research, for the rest of the summer, I concentrated on finishing the research project we had designed together last year and pushed my worries about him aside. So, when at the beginning of the fall, Laura and I found out through Marina that Keylor dedicated most of his time at home to fervidly playing his clarinet, none of us made much of it. 'At least, playing music gives him something to do,' Laura said. But when, two weeks later, Marina further shared that they had attended a Mozart's clarinet concerto at the Performing Arts Theater and Keylor had listened to the clarinetist without blinking as though he had never heard that music before, I thought something obsessive might be going on with him. That from there on, Keylor spent hours on end practicing the clarinet was no surprise. But hearing that he was going out by himself and meeting other musicians in the community was something else. Then, Keylor himself called and said that he had joined a band.

Shortly before Christmas, Keylor sent Laura and me an invitation to attend a concert of pop music arrangements, interpreted by his band, at one of the Concerts-by-the-Sea music venues in town. The program included music from the Beatles and other pieces such as *Life in a Glass House*, by Radiohead, which required the performance from one or more clarinetists. We enjoyed the concert. When it ended, Keylor set his clarinet on his lap while he wiped the sweat off his forehead with a handkerchief he took out of his pocket. Then, he got up from his chair and joined the other musicians to take a bow before the audience. They received a big applause.

Later that evening, Keylor asked Laura and me to please join him and Marina for dinner at the restaurant *Boca,* in San

Diego, to celebrate the success of the show. Before we started eating, we toasted with champagne; then, in conversation, Laura and I expressed our admiration for his performance during the concert.

"How is it possible," I asked, "that you played so well after such a short time of practice?"

"Well, Paul, we need to ask ourselves what is possible."

"I agree. But with aging—"

"Despite aging or because of age."

The waiter brought a large tray with *parrillada* and set it in the middle of the table. Each of us picked and choose single morsels of meat and served ourselves.

"I see what you mean, Keylor," Laura intervened, "But playing the clarinet is something very different from doing research in biology."

I nodded my head in agreement with Laura's assessment.

"I've always enjoyed playing the clarinet," Keylor said, and I remembered he had said the same thing when we first met.

He reached for the bread basket on the table. Marina, holding the knife and fork ready to cut through a crispy pork chop, smiled at us, implying her husband was able to succeed on anything he focused on. I had often witnessed his displaying a strong desire to be successful in his work and enjoying the process for its own sake. But right at that moment, I thought we were comparing apples to oranges.

"However, Keylor," I said, "Biology is our field of specialization."

"Yes. But it doesn't speak of who I've been before."

I reflected on what he had said. I'd always wanted to be a biologist. But then, I remembered that as a young man, I developed a passion for track-and-field. Once, I won a gold medal in the 400-meters dash at a national event, which filled me with pride and the desire to repeat the accomplishment. Then, I saw myself as an athlete.

"The past is past," I said. "One should focus on the here-and-now."

"It depends," Keylor said and waved the waiter to come to the table.

"It depends on what?" Laura, who followed the conversation with much interest, asked.

"On—" The waiter approached. Keylor asked for a napkin because the one he was using was wet from spilled champagne.

"On whatever brings personal satisfaction in life," he concluded.

It dawned on me that Keylor's hunger for personal satisfaction, not money or prestige, as Marina so keenly had once pointed out, had been his quest since he retired.

"Assuming I agree with your judgment, Keylor," I said, "let me ask, why have you changed the source of your satisfaction?"

"Remember, Paul, I didn't choose when to retire."

Of course, I remembered it, I wanted to say so when Laura shot, "You could have gone back to the Institute and taught or something."

"I entertained that possibility for a while as you all know, but curiosity, the desire to seek something different, to imagine new ways to achieve, and finding inspiration from within myself drew me to catch up with music and improve my playing the clarinet."

We remained silent while finishing the dessert. "I was lucky to meet a group of fine musicians, join their band, and practice together," Keylor added.

The waiter came again to the table and asked whether we wished anything else. Keylor swept his eyes through each of us quizzically. "No, thank you," he said to the waiter.

"I believe Keylor could play in an orchestra," Marina said with candor while we were getting ready to leave.

'Well, dear, anxiety to excel often leads to the belief that one is better than what he is," Keylor hurried to say. "Besides, as I said, it wasn't prestige but something meaningful that I needed."

Outside, Laura and I congratulated Keylor again and then said goodbye to them.

"I guess is a trade-off," Laura said while we drove home.

"What Keylor has done, you mean?

"Yes. It takes courage. Would you do that when you retire?" She turned her head to look at me to see how I reacted.

I took a moment to reflect. "Hard you say," I responded. I certainly have learned a lot from his journey. But for now, I'm happy with what I do. What about you?"

"It's hard to say for me too. I guess we have to wait and see."

We left the issue there and remained silent until we got home, only five minutes later.

Grandpa's Old Neighborhood

Louis Montiel, the dog breeder, and the prospective buyer of his breeding business had exchanged texts and emails. That afternoon, however, the buyer called because he wanted to take a good look at the facility before making up his mind.

Anne, Louis Montiel's only daughter, and her 8-year-old son, Marcelo, had also come to visit.

The buyer took a close look at the setting, the accounting books, the hygiene precautions set in place, and the general environment. He took notes on the whelping boxes, the adult dogs, the puppies, and the stock of dog food. He and Louis Montiel discussed business.

After the potential buyer left, the family went to Louis's home, next door to his breeding installation in San Bernardino, California, and sat at a wooden table on the porch to chat and savor hot chocolate and biscuits.

"Is anything wrong, Dad? Anne had noticed her father's expression looked gloomy.

"Wrong? No. Only I can't decide if I should sell my business."

"All things considered, Dad, I think you should. You're almost eighty. Don't you think it is time to retire and make life easier?

"Grandpa, are you going to sell your puppies?" Marcelo asked.

The boy had shown curiosity about his grandpa's dogs ever since he was a baby.

Anne had brought a tray with a jar filled with hot chocolate, three mugs, and biscuits out to the table. Louis Montiel dunked a biscuit in the hot chocolate, something he and the boy loved to do. He raised his eyes and looked at his grandson as if considering his words before responding.

"Grandpa is a little tired from taking care of his puppies," Anne jumped in. She had sat beside her son and across from her father. "He has done it for many, many years," she added and glanced at her father's thin and scarce grey hair, and wrinkled forehead and hands.

Anne wanted to say, but she didn't say it because she judged Marcelo was too young to grasp, that her father had been an indefatigable dog breeder for over fifty years. She knew he had enjoyed his occupation thoroughly and made a decent living out of it. But over the last two years, since her mother passed away, after they had been married for so many years, she had witnessed him getting fatigued and losing enthusiasm for the business.

Meanwhile, Marcelo quizzically looked at his mother, and then at his grandpa, trying to guess what was going on.

"When I grow up, I'm gonna take care of your puppies, Grandpa," he said with self-confidence, "Don't sell them to that man who came to see you," he added, cupping his mug with chocolate and addressing his grandpa as if implying he meant business.

"Honey, what you say sounds lovely," Anne said, "and I know you mean it. But it's a long time until you grow up enough to take care of grandpa's dogs."

Marcelo put on a face of annoyance and rejected her mother's judgment as untrue.

"But, Mom, you and Dad say every month I'm growing up a bit."

"Well, that's true, but—"

It seemed his mother was going to counter challenge her son's argument when Louis intervened. "What your mother means is that after you learn everything that is to be learned at school and grow into a strong young man, we'll talk about it."

"I'm pretty strong. Look!" Marcelo flexed his right elbow and closed his hand to make a fist and show his grandpa a bumpy, tiny biceps.

Anne grew a little impatient with Marcelo's insistence on taking care of the dogs. She thought his probing made her father uncomfortable.

"Grandpa, you have your puppies since a long time ago?"

"Yes, since a long, long time ago."

"You go ahead and tell him." Anne addressed her father. She got up from her chair and made a move to going inside the house, and on her way in, she added that Santi, her husband, had to work till late, and she thought she should cook some dinner and eat there together before she and Marcelo went home.

Louis nodded. He knew his daughter had meant for him to tell the story of how he became a dog breeder, which he had recounted to family and friends many times. For a while, he remained silent, though. Marcelo stared at him expectantly.

"When I was about your age," Louis Montiel broke up the silence without further preamble, "I grew up in a neighborhood with many other children—"

"Like— they were your friends?"

"Well, we all played together after school."

Marcelo turned pensive. "Like— on a playground?"

Louis took a sip of chocolate. "If you ask me so many questions, I won't be able to finish my story before your mother calls us for dinner."

"I won't."

"OK, listen. This happened in the old country. We didn't play on a playground. Where we lived, we had plenty of open space to run about—"

"And animals?" The child couldn't resist the temptation of asking.

"Yes. We loved to catch crickets and grasshoppers and lizards—" Louis saw in his imagination the solid golden-stone apartment building where he lived as a child with his parents, surrounded by a vast wasteland, where they used to play soccer; and the dusty pathways leading through the orchards down to the river, where they used to fish. But he understood he should make the long story short. "And—"

"Dogs?"

"Well, the theme of dogs came about later."

"When?"

"I'll tell you if you promise not to interrupt."

"I won't." Marcelo felt excited by listening to his grandpa's account. He began to play with his mug nervously.

"When I was in Junior High, one of the kids, Danny, showed us something he had learned from a shepherd in the mountain village where his family passed the summers.

"What?"

"How to properly use a slingshot. Do you know what I'm talking about?

Although Marcelo was not sure, he nodded. Louis stared at his empty mug in front of him with a dreaming-like expression.

"I dreamt of getting better at it," he said in a low tone.

"Were you good at it, Grandpa?"

"Yes. I was capable of hitting a small birch from forty or fifty yards away. You know? those little trees with a white stem that you sometimes see in the parks."

"Wow!" Marcelo didn't have a clear idea of how a birch tree looked like, or how far of a distance forty of fifty yards meant to be, but he believed his grandpa and admired his dexterity.

"But one day, something happened," Louis continued in a more grave voice.

He expected a new question from Marcelo, but the child remained silent, waiting. The memory of the event, tough, saddened Louis. But he didn't want to let his daughter down, and he went on.

"'Hey!' I said to Danny. 'See that dog over there?'" Louis perked up again.

"'Sure,' Danny said.' The other kids had also seen the dog, small but strong, trotting across the field far away from us. I aimed at it, and Danny shouted, 'Don't! If you hit it on the head, you might kill it.'" Louis made a pause.

"Did you hit the dog?"

"The shot whacked its pee-pee."

Perplexity took over Marcelo's expression. He couldn't decide what to make out of what he had just heard. It sounded both funny and serious.

"Whacked the dog's pee-pee?" He needed reassurance so that he cleared his ambivalence.

Louis Montiel made himself aware of his grandson's confusion, caused by his words, and decided to lighten the drama. "The dog's name was Toby," he said in a cheery voice.

Marcelo reacted with a brighter face.

"Toby?"

"Yes. It belonged to some neighbors my folks knew."

"I like the name, Toby." Marcelo kneeled on his chair-seat and leaned his elbows on the table, eager to hear the rest of the story.

"Well, you'll see. I felt awful about what I had done. From then on, poor Toby had problems peeing. The other kids didn't say what had happened, and nobody found out. But I told Toby."

"You told the dog, Grandpa?" Marcelo had hard time to understand how that was possible.

"'Toby,' I whispered in his ears while caressing his ears, 'I'm the one who did it. I didn't mean to hurt you, only to scare you a little. I'm very sorry. I love you."

Marcelo listened with all his might, his eyes wet with incipient tears. "What did Toby say?"

"Well, he wagged his tail, filled with contentment. We became true friends. I told Toby that I would take care of him from thereon, and all the other dogs in the world."

Marcelo nodded.

"I want to take care of your dogs, Grandpa," he said whole-heartedly.

Louis Montiel got a white handkerchief out of his pocket. Surreptitiously, he wiped away a couple of tears that ran down his cheeks. Meanwhile, Anne returned to the porch; dinner was ready. Louis got up and walked straight inside the house.

"Mom, I told Grandpa I'm going to take care of his dogs," Marcelo told his mother on their way in. Silently, Anne caressed his black hair.

Bertha's House

In the spring of 1985, Bertha was 90 years old and a widow for fifteen years. At the time, most people living in Morondo, a village located in a flat, barren corner in the province of Castile, were elderly. They had worked in the fields, beyond the edge of the town, until they retired, and they lived their lives at a slow, unstressed pace.

Bertha lived alone in the same house she and her late husband had bought seven years after they married, a house built with brick and cement, with a fading out façade due to the passage of time and the effects of extreme weather. It had a corral at the back with a chicken coop, two pigs, three goats, and a bunch of rabbits.

Bertha and her husband had also worked in the fields for a salary, plotting, planting, and harvesting. They didn't have children, but being stoic, unspoiled people, attached to their obligations, traditions, superstitions, and territory, they had lived at ease with themselves and their surroundings.

"I can't cope anymore with everything," she said one morning in May of that year to William, her only brother, ten years her junior.

During his late school years, William had helped his parents in the fields. Sill, after he finished high school, eager to leave the village and find adventures, he enrolled in the army. Although poorly trained as a soldier, he volunteered to go to Morocco and fight in the Rif War. A year-and-a-half later, he was injured in combat, not by enemy fire but his own malfunctioning rifle. He lost his left forearm. Although he received an honorable discharge and granted a modest pension, the on-and-off occurrence of phantom pain tormented him—he never fully understood why a missing limb could still ache—and limited his ability to make a decent living.

"I'll help you," he said.

Standing beside the outer side of the house door while Bertha watered the small tomato and onion plots she grew in the front yard, he cast his eyes to the wide ploughland that extended all around and that belonged to either the Government or landowners. The workers' dwellings were scattered along winding narrow roads. The view brought memories of his struggle to work that land with only one arm and saddened him.

"You are busy enough caring for your wife," Bertha said.

At his return to Morondo from the war in the African colony, William married a peasant woman, Sarah, of the same age, knowing she had diabetes. Both adapted to live a simple life, and over the years, Bertha and her husband helped them as much as they could. Although they have managed to live independently in their small, humble house, Sarah was going blind from the diabetes and needed a lot of help to get by. Her husband was her only caregiver.

"What can you do, then?"

He knew Bertha was not well either. Although short, she had a sturdy body and steady hand. But cold winters and burning summers had bitten on her bones, and she had contracted arthritis, which, along with aging, and too-much-to-do to keep up with the property, had worn out her natural energy and limited her movements.

She offered no answer. When she finished watering, she turned off the faucet that protruded from the façade wall and coiled the hose on the stand. "There," she said. "The watering is done. Feeding the chickens comes next."

She walked towards the back of the house. Midway through, she got a bucket half-filled with grains out of the shed and carried it slanted on her waist to the chicken coop. William followed her steps.

"It's the house chores that tire me the most," she said and scattered grains among the chickens.

"You'll need somebody to help."

Since her husband died, Bertha had been self-sufficient. Recently, though, she acknowledged her limitations, and William would often bring up the issue of him and Sarah's selling their modest house and moving in with her. He could help with the domestic chores and the care of the animals. But Bertha disagreed, and he would not insist. If someone contradicted her about any particular subject matter, which she held based on intuition more so than actual knowledge, she could turn arrogant and dismissive. Still, he assumed that should Bertha go before him, the property would pass to be his by genetic hierarchy.

"Like who?" She turned to him.

William didn't say. The chickens' cackling fascinated him. He silently stared at them while Bertha emptied the bucket.

"Like who?" she repeated.

Absent-minded, William tried to decode the chickens' vocalizations.

"Sorry! What? Oh, yes," he remembered. "You'll need somebody to help with housekeeping."

She shook her head and rolled her eyes, a gesture that William interpreted as a rejection of his suggestion. She started to walk back towards the house, and he did so beside her. They stopped at the shed for a moment to return the bucket.

"You know," she said, "Amanda helps a little."

"She is our cousin. I don't mean that!"

William didn't doubt Amanda would help Bertha with minor chores, but that was not the kind of help he meant; it wouldn't be enough. As a child, Amanda's laziness had prevented her from learning at school, and at 75, gluttonous and chubby, she moved and walked slowly. She's good for nothing, he thought, and a sense of powerlessness came over him. Notwithstanding, he went on trying to convince Bertha she needed more help.

"Will you stay for lunch?" She impatiently cut him short when they reached the door.

"No, thank you. Sarah needs me. I should leave."

Amanda was wholly Morondo-local. An only child, she never married and lived with her parents. After her father, who had been sick for years, died, she continued living with her mother until she also died. Afterward, Amanda began visiting Bertha, and a year after her mother passed, the local authorities ordered the demolition of her family house due to an unsafe condition. Lacking sufficient income and skills to live independently, in that spring of 1985, Amanda ended up moving in with Bertha.

"Amanda is a saint," the neighbors would say to William. "She'll be of much help to Bertha."

Aside from her family, Father James, the parish priest, a handful of neighbors, and frequent churchgoers, all over sixty,

Amanda had but few other social contacts. It had always been that way for her. Her parents pushed her to work in the fields at some point in her youth, but she showed little motivation and worked only for a few years under low pay employment. Malicious tongues spread the rumor that she had never had a romantic experience.

"We'll see," William used to reply to those opinions. "I know our cousin. She loves to be indulged, and—"

"You have your wife," the neighbors would cut him short. "Living alone in the old age can be tough."

For William, Amanda, lazy, selfish, and clumsy, was far from being a saint. On the other hand, he couldn't figure out why he was resisting an arrangement so naturally initiated by the two women.

Towards the end of summer, during his visits to his sister, William perceived the house looked filthy, the dishes piled up unwashed, and a layer of dust covered the furniture. He realized that his sister's overall ability to keep up with housekeeping was in quick decline, but what about that of Amanda? On a warm and dry afternoon, William had come to show Amanda how to feed the animals and keep the corral clean so that Bertha didn't have to do it and risk a fall. Then, the three of them gathered in the kitchen and made sandwiches.

"Don't you see, Amanda, this house is dirty?" William dared say.

"I don't see what the big deal is," Amanda replied.

"Well, you might welcome some help with the house-keeping. Sarah and I happen to know of a Hispanic woman—"

"No! These foreigners come, get whatever they can, and go back to their countries. People talk about it at church."

William remembered a comment one of the neighbors had made a few days before, stating that Amanda wasn't a gadabout, and he dropped the issue. But why did she reject the extra help? They finished eating their sandwiches, and he left.

Throughout the autumn, William witnessed a further deterioration in Bertha's house. He still felt at a loss about why Amanda refused the extra help he offered. Bertha didn't help either, her overall awareness going downhill. He didn't know what to do. Although not religiously inclined—after he lost his arm he also lost his faith—he preserved the local traditions, and checking with the parish priest was something people in town did when they were in trouble.

Father James was a tall, lean, red-haired man born in Castile of an Irish immigrant father and a Castilian mother. As a young man, he entered the Seminary in the Capital of the province, and after ordained, he accepted an assignment to the Morondo Parish Church. He earned the trust of the congregation for his dedication and effort to solve others' problems, and he was always alert to the eventualities of the town. Then in his fifties, he maintained most of his physical looks and eagerness. He received William in his office, annexed to the sacristy.

"Father James," William said, "What should I do to bring hygiene and common sense into my sister's home? Amanda doesn't lift a finger to improve the situation."

"Is Bertha happy with Amanda?" Father James tore envelops open from a pile of correspondence set on his desk.

"I'm not sure."

"What could go wrong?" said the priest. He pointed with his letter opener to a chair across his desk for William to sit down.

"Perhaps—" the latter said after he sat, "you could persuade Amanda to change her behavior."

Father James stopped tearing envelopes open. He raised his eyes. "Amanda has no malice or worldly interests," he said.

William agreed that Amanda had no mundane vices, but his sister's house was filthy and stinking since she had moved in. If that state of affairs wasn't due to vice, what was it due to? "I don't know what could go wrong," he said, "but I know something is not right now."

Father James slowly pushed his correspondence aside and grabbed a wooden tobacco box that lay on his desk.

"A cigar?" He showed William the box with the cigars.

"No, thank you."

The priest lit and exhaled with delight. "I'll see what I can do to make things better for your family," he said and took a second puff on the cigar. "Meanwhile—" He switched the conversation to talking about his church and ongoing town events.

After he left the place, William thought that the priest had shown a wishy-washy attitude toward his issue. In vain, he persisted in his purpose of changing Amanda's behavior so that she would turn more active at home. However, the situation was getting worse. Dirt had reached even the slots of the doors; rivulets of dry food stained the walls; fluff accumulated under the beds, and so on. Amanda's parsimony enervated him. She responded to his suggestions about how to improve her performance in a simplistic, imprecise way, which led him to conclude she was an unreliable and untruthful woman. Furthermore, Amanda was not taking care of herself, either. She often complained of multiple ailments. William wanted her to understand the importance of seeing the doctor and following his recommendations, but she neither showed initiative to do it, nor did she stop complaining. He foresaw that with Bertha drifting into a sick passivity and unawareness of her surroundings, the house would soon be a pigpen.

Near Christmas, Father James did a yearly round of visits to those in the congregation who were sick or needed some help. During these visits, he learned about ongoing happenings in the community. Thus, for example, he found out that a late-teen parish-girl was pregnant, but nobody *knew* who the father was. He had occasionally seen the girl in church, who had impressed him as a devoted youngster. Gossiping, however, had shifted her reputation by insinuating lust.

This teen's pregnancy and its consequences occupied Father James's mind when he arrived at Bertha's place. As he stepped in, a strong smell of urine knocked him over and made him shift his attention from the teen's circumstances to Bertha's and Amanda's. He looked around and saw that the place was filthy. He remembered William's visit to his office; presently, he had evidence of what he had tried to convey to him. Returning to his church on foot, the priest reviewed in his mind the sins he had counted among the parishioners.

For Christmas Eve services, the church appeared packed. Bertha, weak as a finch by then, couldn't make it, but Amanda was present. Father James spoke during the sermon about lust, and it seemed everybody understood whom he had in mind. Then, subtly, he addressed laziness. "To neglect the care we owe to our loved ones is a sin," he said. William observed that one of Bertha's neighbors, sitting beside Amanda, turned toward her with a puzzling expression.

Sarah, having sensed the environment in church more so than seen it—by then, she was as blind as a bat—said to her husband when they stepped out of church: "I'm sure you realize some of the priest's comments referred to your family."

"The question is whether Amanda has also grasped it," he replied. Holding her hand, he guided his wife back home.

At the beginning of the New Year, whether due to sin or mere laziness, William assessed his sister's house remained in the status quo. The idea of seeking legal advice to put an end to the situation crossed his mind. A freezing January afternoon, he got the news, via a neighbor, that Bertha was sick. When he arrived at the house, he found his sister was in bed, confused, moaning, and breathing forcefully. Amanda, sitting beside her, occupied herself in ceremoniously wiping out Bertha's perspiration from her forehead with a flannel. A stench permeated the entire room.

"For how long has she been sick? William asked.

"She started with diarrhea, three days ago."

William reflected on her words. "Have you called the doctor?"

"She doesn't want to see the doctor." Amanda kept her eyes on Bertha's face.

From the other side of the bed, William took a step forward, bent over, gently pushed the flannel away from his sister's forehead, and looked closely at her face. Bertha's struggle to breathe and the expressionless look in her eyes scared him.

"I think she's very sick," he said as he moved upward. "But let's hope she gets well on her own. Isn't that what you're waiting for?" he added in a sarcastic tone.

"I do what I can," Amanda said.

William walked towards the door, but he turned his head before he stepped out: "Please, ask some of the neighbors whether they don't mind helping you change the bed sheets and spread some deodorizer in the room. It stinks. I'll bring the doctor."

At nightfall, William returned with Dr. Benitez, the town's physician, a stocky, medium height man in his fifties with a fat belly and large hands. Two women neighbors who had helped Amanda change the bed and curb the foul odor respectfully left the room as the physician walked in. Without further words, he proceeded to check Berta's pulse and skin turgidity. He then took his stethoscope out of his leather bag, slid the bell under the patient's nightgown, and listened to her lungs and belly. When he finished the examination, he shook his head and smacked his lips. He returned the stethoscope into the bag and applied a disinfectant on his hands. "Not good news," he said.

Amanda sighed and started weeping.

"Please—" William made a gesture to leave the room. She did. "What can I do?" he turned to Dr. Benitez.

"Not much. She has pneumonia and dehydration. At her age, those problems make her be confused. I'll make arrangements to transfer her to the hospital."

William knew Dr. Benítez referred to the nearest hospital, located in a town twenty miles away.

"I don't expect an ambulance to arrive in less than three hours. The staff is busy admitting other sick people from the region," Dr. Benítez said. "Meanwhile, call me if you see a change for the worse."

After the physician left, Amanda and the two women who had helped her with the cleaning entered the room. While waiting for the ambulance to arrive, Bertha's breathing worsened. It happened so fast that she expired after five agonizing minutes. The three women moved around the room stealthily as if Bertha was just asleep. They smoothed out the bedding and delicately touched Bertha's feet through the sheets, glancing at her face to make sure she was indeed dead. They moaned. One of the women said to William with a level voice that the deceased had had a golden heart.

Dr. Benitez, once notified of the demise, returned at dawn but limited his act to sign the death certificate, and he left. At sunrise, William went home, and soon after, he came back with Sarah, and everybody got ready for the wake. The news that Bertha had died was in the townspeople's mouths. Neighbors and friends arrived in twos and threes to pay respects to the deceased and express their condolences to the family. William went to the mortuary to pick out a coffin and flowers. Father James helped with the arrangements for the burial in the grave-yard behind the church.

During the funeral, the church was lit with thick candles and the chandelier in dim light. Guillermo, standing behind a makeshift podium, next to the coffin, adorned with wreaths of flowers, praised Berta's virtues while she was alive. As he spoke, he noticed that Amanda, kneeling on the bench, was whimpering and looking dejected. A wave of compassion nested in his heart, and he had the impression that Father James, who stood near the podium as well, noticed his swift reaction.

After the funeral, people began to leave the church through the gates that led to the attached cemetery. William asked Sarah to hold his arm and walk beside him because he wanted to catch pace with Amanda. And as they leveled up with her, he said, "I imagine this loss is hard. If it helps, know that you may stay in our home for a while."

"Thank you," Amanda hurried to answer. "But Berta's house is now my home."

A chill ran up William's spine. He wanted to slap Amanda with his only hand. But a squeeze on his arm from his wife made him cool off his intention and slow down their pace.

"I didn't think Amanda capable of such boldness," he said, upset.

"To her, that's her home, though," Sarah replied.

"It's outrageous!"

"Drop it. We're here to bury your sister."

William understood that the moment was not the right one to discuss issues of property. They had reached the ground where the family's grave lay. Father James, wearing a black cassock and golden chasuble, standing beside the locked coffin, read a prayer from a devotion book he held opened in his hands. When the casket was in the grave, a burial assistant passed a shovel to William, who grabbed it with his only hand, and helped by this employee, he, following the local ritual, tossed the first shovelful of dirt into the grave.

Following Bertha's death, William felt further diminished as a person, as if he had again been mutilated. Although Berta's temperament was different from his, the two had got along reasonably well. She and her husband had helped him and Sarah to get on with their own lives, which he had appreciated immensely and will never forget. Beyond the comfort of moving in and taking care of the house, which he considered his right, he felt a moral obligation to preserve his sister's and her husband's only legacy.

Throughout the winter, he dropped daily by his late sister's house, to Amanda's displeasing attitude, and turning a blind eye to the accumulating filthiness, he walked to the corral and fed the animals, which he loved to do. On the occasions when he ran into his cousin, their brief and rude interactions convinced him that she was adamant about keeping the house. He was going to need legal action to get her out of there. He cursed the day he enlisted himself as a volunteer in the army and went to war in the colonies. If he had remained in the village instead, he would now be a complete man with both hands to work, no fear and no bitterness. He realized he was getting old, growing weaker, and he worried about his and his wife's fate. These worries were tearing him apart. Sarah's input wasn't very encouraging either. He decided to share his concerns with Father James again.

"Please, serve yourself more soup. Matilde, my new house-keeping lady, is an excellent cook." Father James said. He had invited William to lunch with him.

While enjoying the soup, Guillermo, sitting at across from the priest, was giving free rein to speak of his anguish. Presently, he zoomed in his concern on the issue of his late sister's house.

"I should look for an attorney," he said and checked on his host's reaction, whose red hair, blue eyes, and measured table manners gave him a trusting appearance.

"That could take an eternity," the priest said. He held a spoonful of soup up in the air while glancing at his guest. "Besides," he added, "where will you get the money from?"

"Aha! Man of little faith," William ventured to saying. He drew a mild smile and added in a serious tone, "Bertha's bank savings were passed on to me. Not much money, but I want to invest it in rescuing her house."

A silence ensued during which Matilde, the plump and elderly housekeeper, brought a casserole with stew to the table. Father James had been unsure whether William, single-handed, would be able to handle the knife and fork simultaneously, and he had asked Matilde to please cut the meat into small morsels before cooking. When she left the room, Father James grabbed the serving spoon and helped first his guest and then him, delighting with the seasoning aroma. William felt grateful he didn't have to use the knife. He enjoyed eating the stew at ease.

"A noble thought," Father James said.

Encouraged by this response, William went on. "Perhaps you could convince Amanda to leave the house before I start with that."

"Perhaps we should leave the matter in God's hands."

"What do you mean?"

Father James took a minute to pour water in their glasses before answering.

"I could say a mass and you could pray a novena."

William had a sip of water. "I've no faith." He said and returned the glass onto the table in front of his plate.

Father James reached for his glass of water too.

"I've no right to push Amanda out of the house without a backup plan," he said.

Silence fell between the two men while they kept on eating. A sense of powerless invaded William's soul again. At his age, he didn't have that much time to wait for Faith's return before finding a resolution for his problem.

"We'll see," he said.

They kept talking, but Father James managed to switch the conversation to other community issues.

William had enjoyed the food at Father James's place, but felt disappointed at their meeting outcome. The priest had wanted to drag him into worship in the church before committing himself to help him. Loneliness, grief, and resentment towards his cousin afflicted him. He felt abandoned by heaven and earth, incapable of taking action.

He didn't go to Bertha's house for several days until the thought that the animals in the corral would be hungry gnawed his consciousness, and one morning, he went there unannounced. His heart sank at the view of the accumulated filthiness spread throughout. Subsequently, when Amanda went out to church, he would polish the full-length wall mirror in the hall, wash dishes in the kitchen, inspect the pantry shelves, dust out the old walnut dining table, and so on. He also watered the plants, took care of the animals, and swept the corral. He hoped that his commitment to sprucing up his sister's house would stimulate Amanda to become more diligent. But after a month of his labor without her having lifted a finger, he decided to look for legal advice. He was ready to spend Bertha's savings in the pursuit of his goal.

Luckily, Dr. Benitez put him in touch with an attorney with an office located in the same town where the hospital was, and William took the bus there.

"If a will exists in which your sister bequeathed to you the usufruct of her property, there'll be no problem," the attorney, a well-built man of about forty, said.

In William's ears, these were big words. He understood *will* and *usufruct*. "Bequeathed?" he asked.

The lawyer drew an apologetic smile. "It means if she passed you the house," he said.

Sitting face to face with the lawyer across his mahogany work table, Guillermo looked at him with narrowed eyes, pondering. "I don't know about a will but have no doubt Bertha wanted me to move into her house after her death," he said.

"Can you prove it?" asked the attorney in a somewhat challenging tone of voice.

William lowered his gaze.

"Prove?"

"Yes. Look for the original will or a copy of it."

William knew he had run out of arguments and questions. He agreed to look for the document, and the consultation was over.

It took a month for William to request another meeting with his legal counsel. He had little to add to what they had discussed the first time since he never found any copy of Bertha's testament anywhere in Morondo.

"Intrusion to somebody's property without permission is a crime," said the attorney. "Assuming the evidence of ownership shows up, it still takes a long time to resolve these cases because the other party has the right to challenge the Court decision."

William had never participated in or witnessed a trial. This was summer. Did the attorney mean to resolve the problem by the autumn or later? Sarah's blindness was progressively getting worse, and he wished to move her out of the tiny, ruinous home they lived in and move her into Bertha's where she could roam around more safely.

"And throughout this process, the defendant, Amanda, will be allowed to remain in the house," the attorney spoke again.

"Without the will, how long would it take? William asked.

"It'd take much longer. I can't tell you exactly."

"I'll keep looking for the will." William became conscious he had had an impulsive reaction, but he also realized he had no reason to retract. If Bertha had authorized the bank to transfer her savings to him, you would expect her to have done the same with the house. Trusting his luck, he decided to retain the lawyer and follow his advice. After his tragedy in the Rif War, this would be the most challenging fight he was about to undertake. He felt fully committed to fighting. And he battled throughout the autumn and the winter and the whole of the next year. He fought against Amanda's stubbornness not to give up her occupancy of Bertha's house. He quarreled with the neighbors' siding with his cousin and against Father James ambivalent attitude. With all his might he struggled with everybody who opposed his legal cause to the point of exhaustion, until the phantom ache in his missing arm returned. But he trusted his attorney.

During the winter of 1988, a trial finally took place in the Court House at the attorneys' town. A public counselor took Amanda's claim because she qualified for the status of an indigent person. Dr. Benitez and Father James and some of the neighbors were called to declare as witnesses. In the end, the verdict favored William and sentenced Amanda to vacate the property. But her attorney filed an appeal against the sentence before the same Court, and the process went on.

"Without that damn will, our chance of winning against the appeal is slight," the lawyer said.

"We'll see," William replied.

In the belief that he would win the legal ordeal, and afraid of running out of money before the process had ended, he sold Bertha's goats, and two months later, he did so with the pigs and the rabbits. But he didn't have the guts to sell the chickens. His attorney had advised he could do things like that because Amanda didn't pay for the household expenses. In William's eyes, Amanda hadn't changed a bit since Bertha passed away. She went to church and to the store but did a minimum of the domestic chores. She had always depended on others for her livelihood. She had learned to assume the victim role and craft stories that seem real and trigger a feeling of compassion and guilt in others.

In his mind, he imagined Sarah and him living at his late sister's house; there, Sara moved around more freely—she had refused to use a guide cane for the blind—and he listened to the chickens' clucking. Maybe he could learn how to decipher what they said. He dreamt of these scenes.

Six months later, the attorney summed William to his office. The Court had reviewed the appeal.

"The judge found no evidence to support Amanda's claim that she has the right to permanently live in the house after Bertha's death," the lawyer said.

William's face illuminated. He saw his chance. Heaven was opened. In his opinion, Bertha's house belonged to him merely by next of kin.

"Not without proof of ownership," his lawyer said.

For a moment, William's lungs stopped breathing, and his heart skipped a beat. "What do you mean?" he said.

"Of course, we could go that path—"

William couldn't concentrate. Suddenly, his war injury scene flashed in his mind, and the phantom pain shot up like a kite to the sky on a windy day. "Which path do you mean?" he asked.

"Naturally—"

But William didn't hear the attorney's words any longer. "We'll see," he mumbled. He got up from his seat across the attorney's mahogany desk, and respectfully left the office.

Father James had followed William vs. Amanda litigation with impartiality. Sarah said that that was his role as a pastor, but William believed the priest had a bit of a Pharisee. In any case, William didn't mind that Father James helped Amanda, when she was evicted, to settle in the only nursing home available for the poor people of Morondo. He and Dr. Benitez had cut a deal with the administrator of a nursing home in the vicinity to the hospital to admit the Morondo elderly who couldn't care for themselves due to lack of resources.

Near Christmas, William received the news from his lawyer that based on the rule of inheritance succession the judge had granted him and his wife the right to usufruct his late sister's house. However, they couldn't sell the property unless he possessed a will from the deceased prior owner, authorizing the selling.

William told Sarah to please get ready to make a move. Suddenly, she panicked. Each time he brought up the issue, she became uncontrollably scared and claimed to be unable to get a hold of herself. She feared to leave her home.

William drew strength from his insides and went to the house every day. He swept the floor, dusted out the furniture, cleaned the corral, and watched the chickens. As time went on, however, his going to the house became less and less frequent. He ended up selling the chickens, and finally, one day, he locked all doors and windows and stopped going there. He couldn't prove ownership; therefore, the house ceased to exist for him.

The house ceased to exist for everybody else in town. It stood there abandoned, the windows cracked, the roof collapsed, and the corral filled with debris. People referred to it variously as *Bertha's House*, *Amanda's House*, *William's House*, and *the House without an owner*. They couldn't believe why the Court remained irresolute, letting the property fall into such a ruin. But as far as memory goes, nobody lifted a finger to find a solution.

TRANSICIONES

Transiciones

Veinticuatro Relatos Bilingües

por

JOSÉ L RECIO

Adelaide Books
New York / Lisbon
2021

Prefacio

Durante los últimos cinco años, he escrito esta colección de relatos en inglés y los he publicado en diferentes revistas americanas y europeas; una vez publicados, los he traducido al español (mi lengua materna). ¿Por qué no procedí a la inversa? Para explicarlo he de acceder a un breve desvío biográfico.

Independientemente de la edad cronológica, a medida que avanzamos en años, somos conscientes de que periódicamente entramos en nuevas fases de la vida que requieren ajustes. El grado de satisfacción personal, a medida que nos hacemos mayores, depende en parte de una adaptación exitosa obtenida a través de cada periodo de transición.

Cuando debido a problemas de salud me vi obligado a jubilarme, después de una larga carrera como médico, me di cuenta de que, además de tratar de recuperar mi salud, entraba en una nueva fase de mi vida en la que tenía que resolver la incógnita de qué hacer durante el periodo de jubilación. La solución no llegó de una vez. Al principio, solo pensaba en recuperar mi salud y volver a trabajar en el campo de la medicina, la única alternativa que parecía lógica, a pesar de los consejos en contra, basados en mi todavía frágil salud, de amigos y familiares. Después de dos años de indagaciones e intentos fallidos, por fin, abandoné la idea de continuar trabajando en medicina. Para entonces, ya había, en gran parte, recobrado la salud.

La idea de hacerme traductor médico vino a suplantar el anterior plan. Después de terminar un Máster en traducción de un año de duración en preparación para el cometido, abandoné esa idea por considerarla insatisfactoria para mis expectativas. Fue en ese momento cuando me di cuenta de que lo que quería hacer era escribir. ¿Por qué escribir? Yo creo que nacemos con la tendencia innata para ser creativos, y el ser creativo es una parte esencial de mi vida; siempre lo ha sido. Escribo como una forma de expresarme artísticamente. La escritura es la herramienta a mi disposición para usarla con propósito creativo.

Después que me jubilé, en California (diciembre de 2008), mi mujer y yo nos trasladamos a vivir a España, y fue allí que comencé a escribir en español. Nuevas circunstancias, sin embargo, hicieron que, en el verano del 2012, volviéramos a California.

Yo tenía treinta y pocos años cuando vine a California la primera vez desde España y puedo atestiguar que el proceso de absorción de la lengua y cultura —es decir, adaptación— es gradual y largo. Si uno nace y crece en un país y después se cambia a vivir en otro, el proceso de adaptación requiere no solo la adquisición de la lengua, sino también la integración de dos culturas. Desde un punto de vista pragmático, sin embargo, es la cultura popular, incluyendo el lenguaje, la que domina la actividad social diaria de un país. La aceptación de tal realidad, y el estímulo recibido por parte de mi mujer americana, hizo que yo permutara el idioma y comenzara a escribir en inglés.

La mayor parte de los relatos en esta colección pertenecen a la categoría de ficción convencional, y los personajes reflejan aspectos autobiográficos, aunque ficcionales, y de fases de transición en sus vidas. Como dice uno de los personajes en el relato titulado "Nunca es demasiado tarde": 'Nadie está completamente solo en la vida', y el escribir un libro, cualquier libro, no se puede llevar a cabo en completo aislamiento; el autor necesita consejos de editores, críticos y lectores en general. Mi agradecimiento va para todas aquellas personas, familiares, profesionales de la escritura y compañeros escritores, que me han ayudado a alcanzar mi objetivo; demasiados nombres para enumerarlos aquí.

José L Recio
Pasadena, California, 2020

Un antiguo cementerio

En los últimos pocos años, Angélica ha vivido un calvario: su padre falleció, y ella se casó con su novio de la escuela secundaria, un mequetrefe que no servía para nada, y que resultó incapaz de bregar con las consecuencias de un aborto espontáneo que ella tuvo después de que se casaron y la divorció. Ella se fue a vivir con su madre otra vez porque, a los veintitrés años, no tenía otro lugar donde ir. Ahora Angélica está de vacaciones en Guadalajara, México, y comienza a revivir.

—Tienes que hacer algo para salir del pozo negro en el que te encuentras —Le había dicho su madre.

¿Pero a dónde podría ella ir? Sería mejor si estuviera muerta. No más intentos y fallos.

—¿Como qué? —preguntó.

—Pues como… ¿irte de vacaciones?

Se encontraban en la habitación de Angélica; ésta estaba tumbada en la cama y su madre de pie cerca de la puerta.

—No tengo dónde ir, Mamá —dijo y levantó la cabeza un poco.

—Podrías ir a Guadalajara. Yo pagaría tus gastos.

A Angélica se le entrecortó la respiración.

—¿La ciudad en la que tú y papá os conocisteis?

Yo estaba allí de vacaciones cuando conocí a tu padre. ¿Qué hay de malo en ello? — dijo su madre. —Al principio fuimos felices —añadió.

Angélica enderezó su torso y se sentó en la cama.

—Tú te has reprochado a menudo el haberle traído a Los Ángeles y haberte casado con él —dijo.

—Y todavía lo lamento. Pero yo no sabía en aquel entonces que el ser adicto al alcohol es una enfermedad.

Angélica se volvió pensativa. Su padre fue un borracho. Llegaba a casa ebrio después del trabajo y exigía que se le sirviera la cena a las 8:00 pm, la botella de vino sobre la mesa, el periódico a su lado, y tráeme esto, y lleva este plato a la cocina. Ella (Angélica) había perdido la oportunidad de disfrutar con sus amigas debido a las exigencias de su padre.

—Mamá, no veo por qué intentas justificar las conductas de Papá.

La madre reflexionó antes de hablar.

—Todos cometemos errores, Angélica —dijo entonces —. A menudo me pregunto cómo sería tu vida ahora si te hubieras casado con un hombre más sensato. Se acercó a la cama, se inclinó y besó a su hija en la frente. —Yo solo deseo lo mejor para ti, querida —añadió y salió de la habitación.

En el transcurso del mes siguiente, Angélica permaneció en su habitación por largas horas, tumbada en la cama o sentada en una silla cerca de la ventana, rumiando sobre su futuro, y gimiendo. En algún momento durante aquel periodo, sin embargo, comenzó a percatarse de su propio enfado y tristeza. ¿Quién era ella (Angélica) para reprochar a su madre el haberse casado con el hombre de su elección? ¿Qué decir de sus propias decisiones?

—Mamá, he estado pensando acerca de tu recomendación —le dijo a su madre un día en el que las dos se sentaron
a la mesa para cenar—. Me refiero a tomarme unas vacaciones.

—Yo te ayudaré con los gastos para dos semanas. No quiero
que uses tus ahorros, y yo no tengo mejor manera de emplear
mi dinero —dijo la madre y sus ojos resplandecieron.

—Agradezco tu generosidad, pero aceptaré tu ayuda solo
por una semana.

Angélica comía la sopa con un buen apetito, y su madre
la miraba y parecía estar contenta.

— He decidido ir a Guadalajara —Angélica dijo.

—Pero, yo pensé que…

—Ahora veo las cosas de un modo diferente —Angélica la
interrumpió—. No es tu culpa ni la mia el que elegimos mal
nuestros maridos. Estoy contenta de tener esta oportunidad
para visitar la ciudad donde vivió mi padre —Angélica hizo
una pausa—. El único problema que yo veo es que temo encontrarme allí con alguien de su familia.

—A tu padre le quedaban dos hermanas vivas, pero no sé
dónde residen ahora.

Angélica levantó los ojos del plato. —Gracias, Mamá, por
la cena tan exquisita.

—De nada.

Las dos terminaron de cenar.

Una semana después, Angélica voló a Guadalajara. Había
reservado una habitación en un hotel del centro de la ciudad.
Llegó allí a media mañana y se registró. Luego deshizo la maleta,
se duchó, se puso ropa cómoda —pantalones de lino, blusa de
algodón y playeras —y salió del hotel dispuesta a explorar la
parte histórica de la ciudad.

Cuando salió a la calle, sintió que una oleada de felicidad surgía dentro de ella. Comenzó a caminar confundiéndose entre la gente y mirando a su alrededor: los edificios famosos, las tiendas llenas de objetos, la Catedral… Entró en el templo. Unos cuantos turistas circulaban por los pasillos de las naves, mientras que algunos lugareños se arrodillaban en los bancos. Angélica se entretenía admirando las artísticas figuras religiosas, el repulgado púlpito y las vidrieras. Le gustaba los arreglos florares que alguien había colocado alrededor del altar. También ella se arrodilló en un reclinatorio para rezar, pero su mente se vio invadida por pensamientos inoportunos. ¿Había olvidado la pena causada por el aborto, el divorcio y las exigencias de su padre?

Durante el resto del día, Angélica trató de mantener su mente abierta para absorber cuanto de novedoso veía, pero al llegar la noche, ya en el hotel, su felicidad se mezclaba con tristeza, y su entusiasmo por absorber lo nuevo con pesadumbre por las pérdidas del pasado. No obstante, determinó levantarse temprano a la mañana siguiente para visitar un antiguo cementerio.

Cuando llegó, todo lo que encontró fue una larga pared de piedra, construida a lo largo de la acera de una calle estrecha, y una verja de hierro que daba acceso al campo santo. Un hombre vestido con camisa azul y pantalones kaki estaba parado cerca de la entrada.

—El próximo *tour* comienza a las 11:30 —dijo. El hombre sostenía un talego de tela gris en la mano que, distraídamente, columpiaba.

¿Será un mendigo?

—¿El próximo turno, dijo?

—Sí —respondió él, apuntando con su barbilla hacia una hoja de papel que estaba pegado en la puerta de entrada.

—Oh!, ya veo. Gracias.

Ella no lo vio exactamente, sin embargo, porque su pensamiento estaba todavía fijo en el hombre; algo en él le resultaba atrayente. Leyó la nota en el papel, estaba escrita a mano y especificaba las horas de visitas guiadas al cementerio.

—Tiene usted razón —dijo—. Quedan veinte minutos hasta la próxima visita.

Él se apartó unos pasos de ella y se sentó en una de dos rocas grandes colocadas allí como adorno, una al lado de la otra, en frente de la puerta de entrada. Ella decidió esperar hasta el próximo tour y fue y se sentó en la otra roca.

—¿Le interesan las leyendas acerca de este cementerio? —peguntó el hombre.

—¿A qué leyendas se refiere usted?

Él abrió el talego y sacó un panfleto. Angélica observó sus movimientos, su cara morena, su pelo rizado… ¿Pero le falta un ojo?

—Usted puede leer todo lo referente a las leyendas aquí —dijo él, sacudiendo el panfleto enfrente de ella.

Ella no puso atención a su ademán, solo le interesaba saber qué pasó con su ojo izquierdo.

—No, gracias —dijo.

El hombre, que parecía tener algo más de treinta años, volvió a meter el panfleto en el talego. Ella se le quedó mirando.

—Esto —él dijo de repente— me pasó durante una pelea. —Abrió los parpados del ojo izquierdo con los dedos pulgar e índice para mostrárselo—. Ella inclinó su cabeza hacia adelante para mirar y vio un ojo vacío con una membrana blanquecina en el fondo.

—¡Qué horrible! —dijo y se cubrió la cara con sus manos. —¿Ve usted bien con el otro ojo? —añadió.

—Veo, pero si me esfuerzo para leer me dan fuertes dolores de cabeza. ¡Soy como un cadáver viviente!

—Cuánto lo siento —dijo ella y apartó su cara de él.

—Por favor, discúlpeme si he herido su sensibilidad sin querer —el hombre dijo en un tono cortés.

Era aparente que en él había un toque de distinción, y Angélica se empeñaba en identificar de qué se trataba.

—Disculpe mi sensiblería —ella volvió su cara hacia él de nuevo—. Me llamo Angélica. Vivo en Los Ángeles.

—Encantado de conocerle. Soy Rodolfo.

A ella le gustó la forma en que él le dio la mano para saludar: una ligera presión y una leve reverencia.

—Usted habla español muy bien —dijo Rodolfo.

—Mi padre era de esta ciudad. Él siempre me habló en español —Angélica intentaba mirarle solo a su único ojo.

—¿Dijo usted *era* al referirse a su padre?

—Mi padre murió hace unos años. Yo soy hija única.

—Lo siento —dijo Rodolfo al tiempo que se persignaba.

Angelica interpretó el gesto como señal de respeto por el fallecido. ¿Alguna vez había ella mostrado respeto por su padre? Se encerró en sí misma. Mientras tanto, Rodolfo se fijó en su pelo largo y rizado, y el azul de sus ojos.

—¿Es su madre americana? —Rodolfo rompió el silencio.

—Sí.

Dos mujeres jóvenes llegaron a la verja, y Angélica oyó que hablaban en inglés. Comprobó la hora en su móvil.

—Es tiempo de unirme al tour —dijo.

—Siento lo de su padre —dijo Rodolfo—. Pero ella ya se había unido a las dos mujeres de camino a iniciar el tour.

El cementerio era un lugar pequeño. El joven guía mexicano explicaba en inglés los detalles del mismo, pero sus palabras no lograban despertar el interés de Angélica. Para ella, se trataba de un camposanto antiguo pero mal mantenido. Las

otras dos jóvenes en el tour no hacían más que preguntas estú-
pidas. Era frustrante. El guía les condujo a una esquina donde
había un grueso roble que estaba rodeado de una pared hecha
de ladrillo de poco menos de un metro de alta.

—Debajo de este árbol, según la leyenda, vive un vampiro.
Mucha gente cree…

—Discúlpeme —Angélica le interrumpió—. Yo no sabía
que estas visitas guiadas se realizan bajo un horario, pero el
tiempo de espera hasta que ésta empezó ocasiona que mis planes
para el día de hoy se retrasen, así que debo irme ahora.

Dio una propina al guía y se fue caminando hasta la puerta
de salida. Las dos mujeres y el guía le siguieron con la vista.

Cuando llegó a la verja vio que Rodolfo estaba todavía
sentado en la misma piedra. Este podre hombre no parece que
venda muchos panfletos. Abrió su monedero y sacó un billete
de cien pesos.

—No estoy interesada en las leyendas de sus panfletos, pero
acepte por favor mi contribución para su causa —dijo.

—Gracias. ¿A qué causa se refiere usted?

—No sé. Me apena la pérdida de su ojo.

Él se levantó y comenzó a oscilar el talego como si fuera
un péndulo. ¿Se habría entristecido?

—Le agradezco sus buenos sentimientos hacia mí —dijo
Rodolfo—. Sería un placer si me diera la oportunidad de co-
nocerla mejor.

—No puedo quedarme aquí por más tiempo. He com-
prado una entrada para un espectáculo en el centro de la ciudad.

—¿Puedo verla mañana? La estaré esperando junto a la
glorieta que está en frente de la Catedral a las 6:00 pm.

Aquella noche, Angélica apenas pudo dormir. Había muchas cosas que a ella le gustaban de Rodolfo, tales como el

bigote, las patillas largas, el modo de comportarse. ¿Pero qué buscaba él en ella?

A la mañana siguiente, al finalizar un tour de a pie por el centro de la ciudad al que ella se había unido, se volvió al hotel. Todavía pensando en Rodolfo, se bañó y cepilló su pelo. Luego se puso una blusa blanca, una falda roja, unos zapatos negros, y salió para encontrarse con Rodolfo. Éste se paseaba alrededor de la glorieta y parecía estar ansioso. Llevaba la misma ropa que en el día anterior más una chaqueta negra. Había algo que le faltaba, sin embargo. ¡Ah! No tenía el talego. Pero se le veía más elegante sin él. Cuando Rodolfo la vio, se acercó enseguida a ella saludando con la mano. Ambos se mantuvieron discretos y comenzaron a caminar por la avenida como si estuvieran acostumbrados a salir juntos. Él dijo que quería invitarla a cenar y ella aceptó la invitación. Así que fueron a un bonito restaurante en la avenida de Chapultepec.

—En este restaurante actúa un grupo mariachi —dijo él al entrar al lugar.

A Angélica le gustó la atmósfera y la vista del sitio.

— Esto te va a costar una fortuna —dijo.

—No te preocupes —dijo él mientras el ayudante de mesero les conducía a una mesa—. Tengo algunos ahorros de cuando trabajé. La venta de libretos frente al cementerio es solo para mantenerme ocupado.

—¿En qué trabajaste? —preguntó ella una vez que ocuparon la mesa.

—Antes de la pelea yo era dueño de una pequeña tienda, una librería —contestó con cara alegre.

Uno de los camareros se acercó a su mesa. *Pierna de cordero con mole y ensalada mixta*, ambos eligieron lo mismo.

—Yo pago por el vino —dijo Angélica.

—Mejor bebemos limonada.

El ayudante de mesero trajo una jarra de limonada a la mesa, y Rodolfo comenzó a servir el refresco con manos temblorosas. Levantó su vaso. —Por nosotros —brindó.

Chocaron sus vasos y Angélica le sonrió. En ese momento el camarero volvió con los platillos y comenzaron a comer.

—Yo he sido un alcohólico, pero ya no lo soy —dijo él— (una declaración que Angélica ya había oído decir por boca de otros alcohólicos, y ella sabía que para la mayoría de ellos se comprobaba que no era cierto).

—Pero yo he aprendido en los grupos de alcohólicos anónimos que…

—¡Mierda! —gritó él.

Ella se sobresaltó. El enfado de Rodolfo, sin embargo, se mostraba mezclado con una expresión de firmeza y determinación que a Angélica le gustaba.

—¿Cuál es tu opinión, entonces? —ella preguntó.

—Las personas alcohólicas no están hechas todas del mismo patrón. Yo sé de algunos que asisten a los grupos de alcohólicos anónimos, pero enseguida recaen en la bebida. En cambio, yo no voy a ningún grupo y, sin embargo, me mantengo sobrio por más de un año. Ya no soy un alcohólico —dijo y volvió a ocuparse de masticar otro pedazo de *cordero con mole* y beber limonada.

Después de un tiempo, el camarero se acercó a ellos de nuevo.

—¿Van a tomar postre? —preguntó, pero ellos negaron.

—Rodolfo, por favor, vamos a calmarnos. Después de todo, no estamos haciendo más que empezar a conocernos. Tal vez sea mejor salir del restaurante ahora y respirar el aire puro —dijo Angélica cuando terminaron de cenar.

—Bien, te acompaño al hotel —replicó Rodolfo todavía un poco contrariado.

Rodolfo pagó la cuenta. Según salían, Angélica echó una última mirada a los mariachis. Le encantaba los trajes de colores que vestían y los sombreros de ala ancha. Una vez afuera, comenzaron a caminar despacio. No se hablaban mucho pero se sonreían con frecuencia el uno al otro. De vez en cuando, sus cuerpos se juntaban debido al atropello de la multitud que se movía en todas direcciones, y entonces Rodolfo le abrazaba la cintura a propósito. Ella disfrutaba de ese contacto, que le recordaba el tiempo de recién casada.

—¿Puedo verte mañana? —Rodolfo preguntó cuando llegaron al hotel.

Angélica había anticipado que él le pediría salir juntos otra vez.

—Me puedes dejar un mensaje. Estoy en la habitación número trece —dijo y entró al hotel.

Al día siguiente se encontraron otra vez en la glorieta. Rodolfo la llevó a conocer el barrio donde él nació y se crió. Anduvieron por las calles y le enseñó el edificio de su antigua escuela y el parque dónde jugó al futbol. En su compañía, ella se sentía como una niña feliz, algo que raramente había experimentado con su ex marido.

—¿Dónde tenías la librería? —preguntó.

—Estaba localizada cerca del restaurante donde cenamos ayer. Podemos tomar el autobús hasta allí y te lo muestro.

Cuando se bajaron del autobús, él la condujo hacia una zona de calles estrechas con pequeñas tiendas alineadas todo a lo largo.

—Esta tienda que ves aquí, en su tiempo, fue la "Librería de Rodolfo".

Se habían parado en frene de una tienda con un escaparate lleno de trajes de quinceañeras de todos los colores. Una nube de tristeza invadió el único ojo de Rodolfo.

—Vamos a tomar un café —Angélica propuso.

Cruzaron la calle y entraron en el *Café Galeria*. Allí, Rodolfo habló con nostalgia acerca de su tienda que perdió y de su pasión por los libros y amor a la lectura.

—¿Te gusta leer? —preguntó

Angélica no había leído una novela desde hacía mucho tiempo y de momento se sintió disminuida en frente de él.

—Debería leer más —dijo—. Después de terminar la enseñanza secundaria me propuse hacerme maestra, pero me casé, y cesé en el empeño.

—¿Estás casada?

A Rodolfo se le veía conmocionado.

—No, quise decir que estuve casada. Nos conocimos en la escuela secundaria y nos enamoramos. Ahora estamos divorciados.

Angélica se moría por saber algo más de la vida privada de Rodolfo, pero no quería parecer intrusiva y empezar a preguntar.

—¿Tomas otro café? —preguntó Rodolfo ya más relajado.

—No, gracias. Mejor nos vamos.

Salieron del café y comenzaron a caminar hacia el hotel. Cuando ella iba a entrar, Rodolfo la besó. Ánglica sintió que su pecho se llenaba de satisfacción. Aquella noche, antes de quedarse dormida, pensó que ambos comenzaban a conocerse un poco mejor. Ella había disfrutado de su compañía.

El siguiente día era domingo, y Rodolfo la telefoneó temprano. Quería llevarla a un mercado indio que quedaba a una hora en autobús. —En la mañana el mercado está más animado —dijo.

El lugar, instalado a lo largo de la calle principal del pueblo, consistía en puestos de mercancías alineados en la acera de ambos lados. Una masa humana se movía entre las hileras de las casetas. Inmersos en un mar de cuerpos y artículos, Roberto le pasó su mano sobre los hombros, y Angélica se sintió contenta.

Al regreso, en el autobús, empezó a llover con ganas. Gruesas gotas resbalaban en los cristales de las ventanillas y velaban la vista del exterior. Dentro del vehículo, sin embargo, Angélica se sentía cómoda sentada al lado de Rodolfo. Él tomó su mano y la atrajo un poco más próxima.

—No puedo imaginar por qué tu ex marido optaría divorciarse de ti —le dijo al oído.

—Los dos éramos jóvenes y sin experiencia. Unos meses después de casados, yo tuve un aborto espontáneo. Mi ex marido no supo cómo copar con ello.

Ella se dio cuenta de que estaba revelando cosas íntimas. Incómoda, se puso a mirar afuera, pero todo aparecía opaco.

—¿Y qué me cuentas de ti? ¿Estás casado? —preguntó de repente, volviendo su cara hacia él.

—No. Por varios años viví con mi novia hasta que ella me dejó después de que yo tuve la pelea en el bar.

¿Pero por qué, se preguntaba Angélica, una mujer va abandonar a su novio en un momento de crisis?

—Yo tomaba mucho —dijo él, como si le hubiera leído la mente.

—¡Ah!, ya veo.

La parada del autobús quedaba a tiro de piedra del hotel, y se bajaron. La lluvia había cesado. Cuando entraron al vestíbulo, Angélica dijo que se sentía cansada, y Rodolfo le dio un beso de despedida y se marchó.

Al día siguiente, que era el último en Guadalajara para Angélica, ella invitó a Rodolfo a cenar. Será un placer, le dijo. Había visto un pequeño pero atractivo restaurante un par de días antes durante sus rondas turísticas. Durante la cena, la conversación se centró otra vez sobre ellos mismos.

—¿Vives solo? —ella preguntó.

—Después de que mi novia y yo rompimos, yo me fui a vivir con mi madre. Mi padre murió hace cinco años. Fue un alcohólico. Yo soy hijo único, como tú.

Angélica, al oír estas palabras, soltó el tenedor sobre la mesa y bebió un sorbo de agua con gas.

—Un montón de coincidencias en nuestras vidas —dijo.

Ambos se sonrieron con aire de complicidad. ¿Qué pensaría su madre, Angélica se preguntaba, si ella le dijera que había conocido a un atractivo mejicano?

—Solo por curiosidad, Rodolfo, ¿Cuáles son tus planes para el futuro? —le preguntó.

El tragó el último bocado de bistec que había llevado a su boca y se le quedó mirando.

—Con toda honestidad —dijo después— ahora que te he conocido y que ya no tomo, me siento con ganas de volver a mi negocio.

—Pero dijiste que te produce dolor de cabeza…

—Es verdad —dijo, cortándole la palabra—. Mira, Angélica, tú me gustas mucho. Yo creo que los dos podríamos entrar en negocio juntos. Lo que quiero decir —añadió con júbilo— es que tú harías la parte de la lectura y yo llevaría la administración.

—Eres un cielo, Rodolfo. Yo también siento afecto por ti. Desgraciadamente, ya me voy mañana.

El parecía sorprendido, y entonces ella cayó en la cuenta de que hasta ese momento no le había dicho que ella ya se iba mañana.

—¿Volverás pronto? Te estaré esperando.

—Necesito tiempo para recuperarme, Rodolfo. Emocionalmente, esta semana ha sido para mí como ir en la montaña rusa. Te enviaré mis noticias. Lo prometo.

Cuando salieron del restaurante, notaron que la brisa era fría; sin embargo, ellos prefirieron caminar hasta el hotel. El iba cabizbajo, como derrotado. Pero ella había aprendido en las reuniones de AA que las personas alcohólicas a menudo esperan que alguien llegue para rescatarles de sus recaídas. ¿Por qué Rodolfo odiaba AA? Ella se acordó de que su padre, después de asistir a su primera y única reunión de AA, salió de ella odiando estos encuentros, pero nunca llegó a mantenerse sobrio por sí mismo. ¿Sería Rodolfo capaz de ello?

—Pienso que deberías ir a las reuniones de los AA —dijo.

—Ya hemos hablado de eso. Tú ya sabes lo que yo pienso de esas reuniones.

Angélica no sabía qué pensar, a quién creer, qué hacer. Necesitaba tiempo para reflexionar. Por el momento, le dijo a Rodolfo, ellos deberían dejar las cosas como estaban, es decir, quedar como amigos.

De vuelta en Los Ángeles, Angélica le contó a su madre acerca de Rodolfo mientras tomaban té en la cocina. Su madre mostró sorpresa de que su hija se hubiera interesado por un hombre a quien le faltaba un ojo.

—Él asegura que nunca va a recaer de nuevo en la bebida —Angélica dijo.

—¿Tiene a alguien que lo apadrine?

—No. Él se siente capaz de conseguirlo por sí mismo —Angélica dijo en voz queda—pero quiere que yo vuelva a Guadalajara.

Su madre puso un gesto que Angélica leyó como de escepticismo.

—¿Tú crees, Mamá, que Rodolfo será capaz de mantenerse sobrio?

Su madre tomó un sorbo del té antes de contestar.

—No sabría decirte, pero sí te diré que amar a un hombre que es un borracho es algo muy difícil de conseguir.

El silencio reinó por algún tiempo. Entonces Angélica se retiró a su habitación, que su madre le reservaba, y trató de relajarse y dormirse, pero su mente se mantenía activa, llena de recuerdos e impresiones de la semana que había estado en Guadalajara con Rodolfo. Por un largo tiempo se debatió acerca de qué hacer hasta que al filo de la madrugada se quedó dormida. Al amanecer, se despertó sobresaltada, tapándose un ojo con las manos. ¡Estoy ciega!, exclamó. Enseguida se levantó de la cama y, todavía tapándose el ojo, corrió a la ventana. Temblorosa, retiró sus manos: un sol naciente se reflejó en su cara. He estado ciega durante toda mi vida, dijo en voz alta y siguió hablando: herida debido a la tiranía de mi padre y el ofuscamiento de mi ex marido y ahora me siento impresionada porque a Rodolfo le falta un ojo y confundida de su falso optimismo y su búsqueda por alguien que lo rescate. My madre, recapacitó, me ayudó a salir del pozo negro en el que me encontraba y no debo volver a caer. ¡Basta!.

El conflicto de Ernestina

De niña yo pasaba mucho tiempo con mi abuela (todos la llamábamos Ernestina) mientas mis padres iban a sus trabajos. Ella iba a buscarme al salir del colegio y me llevaba al parque, o a ver películas para niños o de música; lo pasábamos muy bien, y yo la quería mucho.

El día en que empecé la escuela primaria, Ernestina me llevó al colegio, que caía cerca de casa, en San Francisco. De camino, ella me preguntó si yo sabía dónde estaba Boston.

—Pues claro que sé —contesté.

En verdad, en el año 2001, yo no sabía donde exactamente estaba Boston situado en el mapa, pero había oído a mi papá hablar acerca de esa ciudad cuando se refería a mis abuelos.

—¿De verdad que sabes dónde está Boston, Martina?

—Mi papá dice que está muy lejos de aquí, pero que es un sitio muy bonito.

—Tu papá tiene razón. Boston es una ciudad hermosa.

Entonces, mi abuela me dijo que ella y el abuelo Arturo tenían la misma edad y que los dos se criaron en Boston, pero vinieron a California cuando tenían veintiocho años, y aquí nació mi papá. Por supuesto, yo no me acuerdo de las palabras exactas con las que ella me habló entonces, pero sé que esto fue lo que quiso decir. Yo hice unas pocas cuentas de memoria.

—Abuelita —dije— ¿Es verdad que tú eres sesenta años mayor que yo?

—¿Qué? Déjame ver…Pues sí, porque yo nací en el año 1931, y tú naciste en…

—Pues claro, abuelita, tú tienes sesenta años más que yo.

Yo no podía imaginarme creciendo lo suficientemente rápido como para alcanzar su edad. Pregunté a mi padre cuantos años tenía, y me dijo que treinta y ocho. Yo lo miré primero a él y luego a mamá, que dijo que tenía un año menos que papá, y todavía no podía yo imaginarme cómo iba a alcanzarlos. Pensé que tenía que haber alguien más en la familia que fueran mayores que yo pero más jóvenes que mis padres, o algo así. Yo tenía una vaga idea de que nuestra familia no era muy grande. Conocía a los abuelos por parte de mamá solo en fotos, porque ellos murieron antes de que yo naciera. Vivían en Boston, Massachusetts. Su hermano y dos sobrinas también viven en la Costa Este, pero solo en raras ocasiones los vemos.

Yo me ponía muy contenta cada vez que mi abuelita venía a buscarme al salir del colegio. Ella siempre contestaba a todas mis preguntas. Mis amiguitas de entonces también les gustaban estar con Ernestina cuando nos juntábamos porque ella escuchaba lo que decíamos y se notaba que era una persona justa.

En otra ocasión, me contó que ella era la más joven de tres hermanas y que tenían un hermano. Sus papás y las hermanas murieron de problemas debidos a la bebida, pero ella y su hermano, Teodoro, que estaba casado y tenía dos hijas, no bebían. Teodoro vivía en la costa este de los Estados Unidos y era el único miembro de la familia con la que ella se mantenía en contacto. Me dijo que a ella y al abuelo Arturo nunca les gustó la bebida y que por eso decidieron venir a California. Cuando vivían en Boston, dijo, ambos trabajaban en diferentes compañías de seguros, y cuando llegaron a San Francisco encontraron un empleo muy parecido, aunque Ernestina se jubiló antes de que yo naciera.

Unos años más tarde, tendría yo unos nueve o diez, empecé a oír comentarios acerca de que el abuelo Arturo, que acababa de jubilarse, se mostraba raro. Aunque yo no pasaba tanto tiempo con él como lo hacía con Ernestina —el abuelo Arturo todavía trabajaba cuando Ernestina iba a buscarme a la salida de la escuela—, una vez que él se jubiló yo le veía más a menudo y me gustaba que a veces me llevaba a tomar un helado, o él venía a verme jugar al fútbol. Por eso, cada vez que oía decir que se comportaba de forma extraña, yo no me lo creía, porque para mí él era una persona normal. Sin embargo, un día le pillé haciendo pis contra la fachada de la casa.

—Abuelito, ¿qué estás haciendo?

Él ni se inmutó.

—Echando una meada —dijo.

—¿Por qué no vas a casa y lo haces en el cuarto de baño?

—Porque las ratas mean en el retrete.

Me quedé perpleja, aunque debo admitir que también encontré la escena divertida. Entré corriendo en la casa. La abuela Ernestina se preguntaba dónde estaría el abuelo; le conté lo que acababa de ver. "¡Ay, Martina!, el abuelo Arturo se está poniendo mal de la cabeza, y lo veo peor cada día que pasa", me dijo.

Ese día comprendí que al abuelo le pasaba algo raro y que sus manías iban en aumento, lo cual traía a la familia en jaque. Aún hoy en día (escribo estas notas en el año 2014) me asombro al recordar el cambio de personalidad tan dramático que le ocurrió por entonces. Sin ton ni son, gritaba palabrotas e insultos contra la abuela, o salía a la calle desnudo y perseguía a las mujeres que veía, para escándalo de los vecinos. "Un calvario", se quejaba Ernestina. Finalmente, los médicos le diagnosticaron un tumor cerebral. Descartaron la cirugía debido a la localización, algo referente a los lóbulos frontales, según dijeron, a favor de radiación, pero mi abuelo no mejoró y poco después murió.

Después de fallecido, yo comprendí que las rarezas de su conducta se debieron a los efectos del tumor, lo cual hizo que sintiera pena por él y vergüenza ajena por que se le criticó duramente. Estaba agradecida por los regalos que me hizo y los sitios a los que me llevó al comienzo de su jubilación; pensando en todo ello, me ponía triste. Pero había muchas cosas que estaban cambiando en mi vida. Mis padres me cambiaron de escuela, que quedaba a más distancia. Ernestina ya no era quien me llevaba o traía, sino que ahora iba y venía en coche con uno u otro de mis padres, y lo mismo pasaba con las prácticas de fútbol y otras actividades fuera de casa y de la escuela.

Echaba de menos el tiempo que antes pasaba con mi abuela. Mi madre iba a verla con frecuencia y algunas veces me llevaba con ella. Uno de esos días, Dorotea, que era muy amiga de Ernestina, estaba con ella, ambas sentadas en la mesa de la cocina, tomando té y hablando bajo, tratando de consolarla. Cuando mi abuela me vio entrar abrió sus brazos, y yo corrí hacia ella, y me dio un abrazo y un beso. Luego saludó a mamá y enseguida se aquietó. No hizo ninguna pregunta de cómo estábamos, si a mí me gustaba el nuevo colegio, nada de nada. Yo me aparté y me puse a leer uno de los cuentos que mantenía en su casa, pero mis oídos seguían lo que ellas hablaban. Dorotea decía que Ernestina apenas probaba bocado. Yo miré de reojo y noté sus pómulos chupados. Me entristecía verla tan demacrada. Me parecía que debería suceder al revés: ahora que el abuelo Arturo no estaba presente, la paz debería reinar en la casa. Por supuesto, yo omitía en mis cavilaciones el hecho de que mi abuelo se había ido para siempre, una omisión que la abuela validó un

minuto después al declarar que no podía conciliar el sueño en
la noche porque "Arturo entra en la habitación, se sienta en
el borde de la cama y me llama puta."—Dijo "puta". Aquella
noche, cuando me acosté, lloré mucho. Trataba de entender por
qué le iba tan mal a Ernestina y por qué todo tenía que resultar
tan confuso; yo quería entenderlo.

A medida que pasaba el tiempo, Ernestina se volvía más
solitaria. Yo me acostumbré a verla decaída, pero me dolía el
alma cada vez que iba a verla.

—¿Qué le pasa a Ernestina? —le pregunté a mi mamá.

—Está de luto —dijo—. Echa de menos a tu abuelo. Bueno,
también está un poco confundida sobre qué pensar. Como tú
sabes, el abuelo Arturo se comportó de una forma tan rara en
los últimos tiempos que ella no sabe a qué atenerse.

—¿Está papá de luto también?

—Sí, también. Todos estamos en duelo, pero cada uno lo
expresamos de forma diferente —contestó.

Pensé que mi tristeza tenía que ver más con que veía a
Ernestina sufrir. Mis padres pensaban que ella iba a necesitar
más ayuda. Nosotros le echábamos una mano en los menesteres
de la casa, pero no parecía ser suficiente para que Ernestina se
mantuviera limpia y sana. Así que mamá contrató a Amelia a
través de los Servicios Sociales, una muchacha guatemalteca,
de veinte y pocos años, dotada de una gran sensibilidad para
el cuidado de los mayores. A mí, Amelia me cayó bien desde
el primer momento. Yo soy rubia, de ojos azules y piel muy
blanca, pero cuando vi a Amelia, envidié el brillo de su piel
morena, sus chispeantes ojos negros y su pelo liso, negro como
el carbón. Me encantó cómo hablaba inglés, con un acento
que yo nunca había oido antes. Sus padres eran inmigrantes,
y ella era una niña cuando vinieron a California. Amelia fue a
la escuela y también ayudó a sus padres con su negocio, pues

creaban artefactos guatemaltecos que vendían en los mercados callejeros.

A veces pensaba que Ernestina ya no iba a ser la misma persona que cuando yo era más joven, y ese pensamiento me llenaba de miedo. Amelia se percató de ello, y me ayudó a mantener mi equilibrio emocional. Si pasaba tiempo sin tener noticias de Ernestina, yo llamaba a Amelia y le preguntaba cómo iba mi abuela. No obstante, antes de terminar la educación primaria, cuando iba a cumplir doce años, sentí como una obligación moral el comenzar a tomar nota de lo que sucedía.

Revisando después mis notas de entonces me vino la idea de dar forma al presente escrito. Durante un año más o menos, mis entradas se limitaron a describir hechos negativos acerca de la condición de Ernestina, como que no se alimentaba lo suficiente, que no dormía lo necesario, que no hablaba con la gente, que permanecía en su cuarto, casi en la oscuridad, por horas, y cosas similares. Luego vino la primera nota más positiva, pues escribí: "Ernestina quiere venir a mi escuela para ver mi actuación en la obra que vamos a representar en el teatro".

Ernestina fue a ver nuestra actuación, que era de ballet, y yo me puse muy contenta, más de lo que había estado en mucho tiempo. Pensé que la actitud de mi abuela había cambiado. Yo no podía decir cuándo tuvo lugar tal cambio, pero no me importaba porque lo importante era que cambió, y, desde aquel día, reanudó algunas de sus previas actividades. Me pareció un milagro. Pero una vez que recuperó su estima y confianza, dijo a Amelia que ya no necesitaba de sus servicios, lo cual me pareció un error.

No obstante, mi abuela comenzó de nuevo a vivir su vida, ahora como viuda, sin ningún problema, hasta que en septiembre del año 2007 recibió la noticia de que Teodoro había sufrido un ataque al corazón y falleció. Una de las hijas le llamó por teléfono desde Boston para comunicárselo. Teodoro estaba divorciado y vivía solo. Ernestina, a su vez, llamó a mis padres y ellos a mí. Así que cuando salimos al recreo, llamé a Ernestina.

—Siento mucho lo que ha pasado —dije.

—Gracias, querida. El que Teodoro se haya ido….

Ernestina se quedó en silencio.

—¿Te encuentras bien? —pregunté, pues la oí gimotear.

Por momentos no dijo ni que sí ni que no. Y luego declaro:

—No me siento con ganas de vivir.

¿Cómo podía yo consolarla?

—Todos te vamos a ayudar a superar estos malos tiempos —dije.

—Gracias, Martina, mi niña —contestó, y estuvimos de acuerdo en terminar la conversación.

Mis padres acompañaron a Ernestina a Boston para que estuviera presente en el funeral de su hermano. Cuando regresaron, unos días más tarde, yo noté un cambio en la expresión de Ernestina, pero no me podía figurar de qué se trataba. Después que descansó del viaje, la invité a tomar té y postre a una cafería que yo sabía le gustaba. Ernestina iba vestida toda de negro, lo que ensalzaba el azul de sus ojos y el pelo blanco. Se había puesto un collar de oro que destacaba sobre el vestido. Pero se la veía muy pálida, y entonces recordé que mi padre siempre dijo que mi abuela de joven era muy delgada, con pecas, de brazos y piernas largos, y que a veces se la veía muy pálida.

—Siento mucho lo que ha pasado —le repetí.

—Gracias. El que Teodoro se haya ido… —volvió a decir y se calló.

Permaneció en silencio, mirando fijamente a la taza de té sobre la mesa sin pestañear, las manos caídas sobre el regazo y la expresión desvanecida. Me puse triste, y entonces comprendí que el cambio que yo había observado en la cara de Ernestina cuando volvió del funeral se debía a la tristeza.

—¿Te ocurre algo? —pregunté.

Se asustó, y en aquel momento, se le saltaron las lágrimas. Temblorosa, se las apañó para sacar un pequeño pañuelo de su bolso y se secó las mejillas.

—Nada en este mundo podrá ya hacerme feliz —dijo.

Me levanté de la silla y, rodeando la mesa, me acerqué a ella y la abracé. Lloramos juntas, y cuando se nos fue el hipo y pudimos hablar otra vez, nos referimos a otros temas tales como mis planes de estudio para el futuro, el lustre del collar que ella llevaba, el cual, me dijo, lo había heredado de su madre y otras pequeñeces. Pero mientras charlábamos yo me di cuenta de que la tristeza que la infligía era profunda y me parecía que, como ella dijo, ya no se iba a recuperar de su desazón. Después que nos fuimos, ya en casa, me arranqué a llorar incontrolablemente.

Aunque se la veía desconsolada, Ernestina trató, sin embargo, de recuperarse, pero se quejaba de dolor en la espalda. El Dr. Morgan, su médico, un hombre de entrada edad, alto y delgado, de buenas maneras, a quién yo conocí en una ocasión en que me encontraba en casa de mi abuela y él vino a verla, dijo que el dolor de espalda se debía a una debilidad de las vertebras por osteoporosis, y advirtió del peligro de sufrir caídas.

Eso hizo que mis padres se preocuparan de que Ernestina viviera sola. Cuando mis abuelos llegaron a San Francisco, rentaron un apartamento hasta que ahorraron lo suficiente como para comprar una casa, la misma en la que Ernestina todavía vivía en aquel momento. Mi abuela argumentaba que ella era capaz de cuidar de sí misma, e, incluso, quería trabajar como voluntaria en el hospital. En efecto, poco después, Ernestina comenzó a trabajar por unas horas al día, tres días a la semana. Su cometido consistía en servir comidas a los enfermos, procurarles el periódico y algunas revistas, y darles ánimo. Pronto se la conoció, según ella misma nos dijo, como "la señora del pastel de calabaza" porque con frecuencia les llevaba hogazas de pan de calabacín que ella horneaba. Un quehacer con otro, Ernestina estaba ocupada, y yo creía que se había recuperado. Lejos estábamos todos de anticipar que una noche, en el invierno del 2008, Ernestina sentiría dolor de pecho y la ambulancia la llevó al hospital, donde los médicos le diagnosticaron un infarto al corazón. Alguien del hospital contactó a mi padre para informarle de lo sucedido y obtener su visto bueno antes de proceder con una cirugía de derivación.

Después de la operación, el cirujano recomendó que Ernestina no viviera sola. Yo estaba presente cuando el médico hizo esa recomendación porque había acompañado a mis padres cuando fuimos a recoger a mi abuela del hospital. A Ernestina se la veía débil, y, a poco, mi madre llamó a Amelia para que volviera a casa con ella. A pesar de la ayuda prestada, un mes más tarde, Ernestina se calló. Amelia nos contó que antes de sentarse para comer, mi abuela fue al cuarto de baño, y un momento después, se oyó un golpe sordo. Amelia se apresuró a ir y ver qué pasaba y cuando vio que Ernestina estaba en el suelo, confusa, enseguida llamó a una ambulancia.

Yo acompañé a mis padres otra vez a visitar a mi abuela en el hospital al que le habían ingresado. Mi madre, quien trabaja en la oficina de un grupo de médicos, habló con el facultativo al cargo del cuidado de Ernestina y luego nos dijo que, de acuerdo con la opinión del médico, Ernestina se había fracturado dos vertebras y se quejaba de dolor de espalda. Al parecer, para resolver el problema necesitarían operarla.

Después de la operación, el cirujano recomendó que Ernestina fuera desde el hospital a un centro de rehabilitación. Yo a veces fui con mis padres o con Dorotea a visitarla allí. Pasaron semanas de incertidumbre acerca del nivel de recuperación que Ernestina podía alcanzar, y cuando regresó, por fin, a casa, tuvo que usar un andador provisto de tres patas y todavía se quejaba de dolor. Me pareció que había envejecido y se la veía deprimida. Todos tratamos de levantarle el ánimo, y, algunas veces, yo la llevé a pasear al parque.

En la primavera del 2008, yo me encontraba cerca de terminar mis estudios de educción secundaria y guardaba la esperanza de que Ernestina asistiera a la ceremonia de fin de curso. Una tarde, poco antes de la fecha asignada, sin embargo, mientras veía la tele sentada en el sofá, Ernestina dijo sentirse mareada y, antes de que Amelia pudiera percatarse del problema, su cuerpo se desvió hacia un lado y ella se calló al suelo. Amelia llamó a mi padre, quien llamó al servicio de ambulancia para que la transportaran a la sala de urgencias. Allí, los médicos diagnosticaron una hemiplejia izquierda debido a un "ictus cerebral". Ernestina se quejaba de dolor y quemazón en el hombre y brazo izquierdos.

Cuatro días después, Ernestina salió del hospital en silla de ruedas con recetas e instrucciones para hacer terapia física. El Dr. Morgan le hizo una visita a domicilio. Dijo que él se había mantenido en comunicación con los médicos que la atendieron en el hospital y le confirmaron el diagnostico y la secuela actual. "Ernestina va a necesitar cuidados y reposo", advirtió.

—Yo no quiero vivir así —Ernestina dijo una vez que el Dr. Morgan se fue.

Estaba acostada en la cama cubierta con un camisón de lino porque no podía aguantar el picazón que las mantas le producía.

—Con la ayuda de todos, te vas a mejorar, ya lo verás —dije.

—Me parece que no va a ser así, querida. Creo que me voy a convertir en una carga para todos vosotros.

—Papá dice que va a contratar a una enfermera para que te cuide.

—Yo no creo que pueda aguantar estas molestias por mucho tiempo. Quiero que tú me lleves a ver al padre Damián.

El párroco es un poco más joven que Ernestina, tiene una buena reputación entre los miembros de la parroquia; ellos se conocieron a través de la iglesia, años atrás.

—De acuerdo —dije— te llevaré a verle.

Mi madre tenía un nuevo coche y me regaló su viejo Toyota. Así que a la mañana siguiente, con la ayuda de Amelia, pusimos la silla de ruedas y el bastón en el maletero del coche, y conduje a Ernestina hasta la iglesia. Le pedí a Amelia que nos acompañara, pero mi abuela lo negó con la cabeza.

Cuando llegamos a la iglesia parroquial, el padre Damián salió y empujó la silla, con Ernestina en ella, dentro de la iglesia, atravesó la sacristía y nos llevó a una sala donde se recibían a los feligreses que deseaban ver al sacerdote. Allí ayudamos a Ernestina a bajar de la silla, ella con su bastón, y tomar un asiento alrededor de una mesa redonda cercana a una ventana. En la mesa había una bandeja que contenía una tetera y galletas, junto con algunos libros de devoción. Yo me dispuse a salir para dejar que hablaran ellos solos, pero Ernestina me detuvo. "Quédate", dijo. Así que me senté en una silla a su lado y enfrente del padre, que se sentó más cerca de la ventana.

—Padre Damián, yo no quiero seguir viviendo de esta manera —empezó diciendo Ernestina.

El padre puso cara de sorpresa.

—¿Te encuentras deprimida, Ernestina?

—Me duelen los huesos, estoy inválida y no quiero convertirme en una carga inútil para mi familia. Pido a Dos que me lleve de este mundo.

El cura sirvió el té, y él y yo cogimos una galleta.

—Me temo —dijo— que el Señor no va a escuchar tu plegaria.

Yo bajé los ojos y sumergí la galleta en la taza de té, y él hizo lo propio en la suya.

—¿Por qué lo dice, Padre? —intervino Ernestina.

El párroco pareció dudar por unos instantes antes de hablar.

—Lo que tú pides a nuestro Señor es que cambie los planes que Él tiene para ti.

Yo me di cuenta de que Ernestina se estaba impacientando y suspiraba como si el dolor fuera en aumento.

—Me resulta difícil aceptar su opinión —dijo ella en tono sarcástico.

El sacerdote parecía estar anonadado.

—¿Qué esperas de mí, Ernestina?

—Que me ayude a morir dignamente —dijo con firmeza.

—¡Eso equivaldría a eutanasia!

El padre Damián puso sus ojos en mí como diciendo, por favor échame una mano en este asunto. Yo, sin saber bien a qué atenerme, me acerqué más a mi abuela y le agarré la mano izquierda; se la noté muy fría. Su expresión era de desacuerdo, y me acordé de que ella no toleraba que se le tocara la parte izquierda de su cuerpo. Así que enseguida le solté la mano y ella produjo un suspiro de alivio.

—Recuperemos la calma —dijo el sacerdote, y añadió, dirigiéndose a Ernestina—: ¿Te apetece una galleta?

Él extendió la mano para agarrar una de las galletas, pero Ernestina negó con la cabeza.

—Tienes un problema de fe —dijo él entonces de manera vehemente.

Ernestina levantó el bastón y lo ondeó brevemente en el aire. Se la notaba fatigada. Me miró con una expresión que indicaba claramente su deseo de salir de allí. Yo pensé que ya no le quedaban argumentos. Desde que tuvo el ictus no se concentraba bien y no le salían las palabras que quería decir, todo lo cual, la irritaba. El padre Damián pareció entender la situación y permaneció en silencio, mirando afuera de la ventana, como si tratara de encontrar una solución al problema hasta que, por fin, nos despedimos y regresamos a casa.

Yo le confié a mi madre lo que estaba pasando con Ernestina, y ella decidió emplear a una enfermera vocacional licenciada para que la ayudara. El Dr. Morgan hizo arreglos para que se instalara una cama de hospital en la habitación de Ernestina. A pesar de los cuidados, pasado un mes desde la visita al padre Damián, ella sufrió otro accidente vascular cerebral. Parecía cosa del diablo, porque ahora se quedó casi ciega. Yo no podía mirarla sin romper a llorar. El doctor Morgan se presentó en la casa para reconocerla y los dos hablaron en privado mientras mis padres y yo esperábamos en la sala de estar. Cuando el doctor salió de la habitación parecía estar preocupado.

—Ella quiere morirse —nos dijo, y un segundo después añadió—: Aunque yo quisiera ayudarla, no puedo.

Mi madre le ofreció una taza de café y le invitó a sentarse con nosotros.

—A mí me ha pedido también que la ayude a morir. Cuando me lo pidió, yo no supe qué contestar —dijo mi padre.

—Por supuesto —replicó Dr. Morgan—. ¿Quién pude decir dónde acaba la vida?

Esa última pregunta me sonó a misterio. ¿Qué tipo de ayuda era la que Ernestina necesitaba realmente? Sentí el impulso de levantarme, entrar en la habitación de mi abuela y preguntarle a ella directamente. La encontré despierta, pero antes de que yo le hiciera la pregunta, ella se adelantó para explicarme brevemente lo que ella esperaba de alguien. Lo que quería era que alguien le inyectara algún poderoso narcótico directamente en la vena. Yo la escuché asombrada. Ahora ya sabía lo que ella quería exactamente. ¿Por qué ninguno de nosotros se atrevía a ejecutarlo?

—El padre Damián y el Dr. Morgan me han decepcionado —añadió.

Se me saltaron las lágrimas. No encontraba palabras que a ella le sonaran justas; así que no dije nada, solo le acaricié la frente.

A partir de entonces, Ernestina se puso peor. Ya no podía ni erguirse en la cama, y se quejaba de dolor. Una vez unos y otra vez otros, entre todos tratamos de mantenerla limpia, disponer de los residuos, cuidar de que no se deshidratara y de administrarle las medicinas. Hasta que entró en coma y en menos de dos semanas las uñas y los labios se volvieron morados, dio un último suspiro, y expiró.

Después del entierro, los recuerdos del tiempo que pasé con mi abuela se me amontonaron en la mente sin orden cronológico: las imágenes de su angustia en el último suspiro se mezclaban con las de los momentos felices en el parque, ella empujando el columpio y yo disfrutando de mi atrevimiento infantil. Aún en la actualidad, cuando ya estoy en la universidad, en los momentos de quietud mientras escribo estas líneas, los recuerdos se apilan en mi cabeza. Ernestina anticipó cómo iba a ser el final de sus días; no quiso ni convertirse en una carga para la familia ni cometer suicidio. Apeló a la familia, su párroco, su médico para que la ayudaran a morir con dignidad, pero no consiguió la ayuda que ella buscaba. Me pregunto qué piensan otros médicos, sacerdotes y personas sabias de la sociedad en general acerca del dilema que surge en algunas personas cuando al final de sus días están entre la vida y la muerte y, como Ernestina, sufren física y moralmente. Y también, ¿qué hice yo para ayudarla? ¿Qué le diría si la pudiera ver de nuevo? ¿Diría, tal vez, perdóname, Ernestina, que no supe cómo ayudarte. Yo te quiero mucho, te echo mucho de menos y no te olvido? Adiós, abuelita.

Lucas Parra

Es el año 2010, y Lucas Parra no ve el momento de encontrarse ya allí. Está listo para regresar a su vieja ciudad en España, donde nació y se crió. Sus padres emigraron a América cuando él tenía diez años y se establecieron en California.

En el tren, después de que el avión en el que viajó aterrizara en el aeropuerto de Madrid, Lucas ocupa un asiento de ventana y observa el paisaje al amanecer. Es el final del verano, y los campos aparecen desprovistos de cereales. De vez en cuando, una bandada de pájaros cruza el cielo, y algún que otro pueblito solitario se ve en la distancia. Cuando el tren entra en la estación de destino, Lucas se baja y toma un taxi hasta el hotel en el que tiene reserva.

—Bienvenido, señor Parra —el joven recepcionista dice. Prendida en la solapa lleva una etiqueta con su nombre: Armando. El estilo del corte de pelo, las puntas del bigote curvadas hacia arriba y los botones dorados de su uniforme van de acuerdo con la apariencia del hotel, un edificio de dos pisos, cuyo interior denota un toque de corte italiano.

—Gracias.

El botones le conduce a la habitación. Lucas comienza a deshacer la maleta y colocar sus prendas en el armario. Cuando saca un suéter azul, de cuello de tortuga, se acuerda de Patricia, su difunta mujer, que, como él, fue hija de españoles inmigrantes. Se habían conocido en la universidad. Hace seis meses que ella falleció, de cáncer, y él la echa mucho de menos. Por fin, Lucas saca un último par de calcetines de la maleta y la empuja debajo del maletero. Se ducha, se cambia de ropa y, hacia el mediodía, sale del hotel.

Camina por una avenida ancha, con edificios altos de oficinas y apartamentos, alineados a lo largo de ambas aceras y pequeños jardines distribuidos a los lados de la calzada. El sonido de campanas que le llega desde una vieja iglesia aprisionada entre dos edificios acapara su atención. Así que él mira hacia arriba, a la torreta, comienza a llover, y una gruesa gota de lluvia le cae en el ojo. Lucas va vestido con chaqueta marrón y zapatos negros, ambos de cuero, pero no lleva paraguas; se apura a andar deprisa. Piensa en Patricia y desea que ella estuviera a su lado, pero ella ya no existe, y él ha de llevar a cabo los planes que los dos hicieron antes de que ella muriera. Estuvieron de acuerdo que regresarían a España. Será magnífico, ella había dicho.

En su apresuramiento, se resbaló en el pavimento humedecido y su cuerpo salió impulsado hacia adelante hasta chocar con un hombre joven que llevaba un poncho amarillo y que estaba barriendo los charcos acumulados en la acera con un escobón de mimbres.

—!Eh!, Anciano, mire por dónde anda —el barrendero dijo— Y añadió—: A su edad, una caída significa la cadera rota. Yo he visto que eso pasa cuando llueve.

—Lo siento —Lucas dijo, y disminuyó su marcha.

Anciano, se dijo Lucas mentalmente. La palabra le aguijoneó un punto débil. Cuando él anunció su decisión de jubilarse, el director de la compañía de residencias para ancianos, dónde Lucas trabajó por muchos años, usó el mismo término: Usted, Lucas, le dijo, ha contribuido en gran medida a mantener la calidad de esta institución. Ahora que usted es ya un anciano, debería considerar la posibilidad de cambiarse a vivir en una de nuestras residencias. Gracias, Lucas contestó, pero por ahora tengo otros planes.

Apresurándose de nuevo bajo la lluvia, Lucas se siente optimista. Por supuesto, no es posible borrar las patitas de gallo que asoman alrededor de los ojos, ni hacer que las canas desaparezcan para siempre, pero él se siente sano, y la mente le funciona bien. Su vista ya no es tan aguda como antes había sido, pero el choque contra el barrendero fue un puro accidente. ¿A qué viene el cuento de llamarle *Anciano*? Según va caminado, lleva la cabeza un poco inclinada hacia abajo para evitar que las gotas de lluvia empañen sus lentes. Hecho una sopa de cabeza a pies, llega a la Plaza Central, justamente cuando el reloj del ayuntamiento marca las doce del día y, coincidentemente, deja de llover y sale el sol. Ahora Lucas se encuentra en un amplio espacio urbano, rodeado de oficinas, boutiques y restaurantes. Se dirige a una de las terrazas y ocupa una mesa próxima a otra donde se sienta un joven, en cuya mesa hay un plato con un bocadillo, una taza de café y una botella de agua. El joven lee un periódico, que aparta ligeramente para mirar al recién llegado.

—No esperaba que lloviera —dice Lucas—. Y se sacude el agua del pelo.

—Pero ha estado nublado toda la mañana —el joven replica.

Lucas sacude las solapas de su chaqueta. —Tiene razón —dice.

—Usted no es de aquí, ¿verdad? —El hombre dobla el periódico y lo pone sobre la mesa.

—¿Por qué…

El camarero se acerca a Lucas. —¿Qué desea tomar?

—Un bocadillo de jamón, un café solo y un vaso de agua, por favor —contesta Lucas.

Enseguida vuelve a la conversación. —¿Por qué lo dice?

—Por como habla usted.

—Bueno, yo he vivido fuera por muchos años.

—Me lo imagino —dice su vecino de mesa, y sigue comiendo el bocadillo.

—¿Qué quiere usted decir con que se lo imagina?

—Que usted debe ser uno de esos retornados.

Lucas se mantiene en silencio.

—Todos vuelven —sigue diciendo el joven—. Algunos de los que vuelven tienen la esperanza de hacer grandes cosas aquí. Es cómico. Yo mismo estoy buscando empleo. Eso es por lo que compro el periódico. Aquí no se encuentran muchos trabajos.

El camarero vuelve con la consumición, y Lucas espera hasta que se va antes de hablar otra vez.

—Es duro —dice entonces.

—Muy duro. Pero, por favor, permita que me presente. Me llamo Marco, y soy administrador de negocios.

—Yo soy Lucas Parra, contable y jubilado.

—Bueno, es usted un anciano respetable. Sea bienvenido —Marco dice, y coge el periódico de la mesa.

—Gracias.

Lucas sigue comiendo el bocadillo y tomando sorbos de café mientras ojea la actividad en la Plaza. Se imagina Patricia y él paseando y familiarizándose con la gente. Después de un tiempo, le entra sueño y piensa que probablemente se debe al cambio de horario debido al viaje. Llama al camarero, paga el importe, sonríe a Marco y se va derecho al hotel para descansar.

Al día siguiente, y por al menos dos semanas más, Lucas se dedica a explorar partes de la ciudad a pie, y va de una oficina a otra en su empeño por formalizar su residencia en el país. En algún momento en el transcurso de estas excursiones urbanas entra por casualidad en un parque público, y enseguida lo reconoce: es el mismo parque en el que él solía jugar de niño. Desafortunadamente, no le encuentra el encanto que, recuerda, una vez tuvo, pues ahora se ven menos pájaros revoloteando en los árboles, y hay menos patos en el estanque y más gente alrededor. Este parque fue punto de reunión para los amigos. Desde aquí se encaminaban hacia el rio siguiendo las lindes de las huertas. Lucas tiene nostalgia de aquellos tiempos y decide caminar hasta allí.

Tres muchachos están pescando. Redes de pesca, cañas de bambú y otros aparejos se ven repartidos por la orilla. Lucas observa a los tres jóvenes pescadores. Le gustaría tener nietos, pero Oscar, su único hijo, y su mujer china, Sue, no tienen descendencia. Ellos se fueron a vivir a Hong Kong después de que se casaron. La última vez que Lucas los vio fue en el funeral de Patricia; Sue parecía estar enferma. Ellos pasan por apuros económicos, pero nunca han aceptado ayuda. Lucas se acerca a la orilla del agua.

—¡Eh!, muchachos, ¿hay suerte?

—Acabamos de llegar —uno de ellos dice.

—¿Qué estáis usando como cebo?

Otro de los muchachos se vuelve hacia él. —Moscas artificiales, por supuesto —dijo.

—¡Oh!, ya veo. Cuando yo tenía vuestra edad, los amigos cavábamos justo a la orilla del rio para encontrar lombrices.

—Ahora hay nuevos inventos, abuelo —voceó el tercer mozuelo, quien era más alto y fuerte que los otros dos.

Lucas no dijo nada, se quedó inmóvil. ¿Piensa este muchacho que yo soy menos hombre porque soy viejo? Lentamente, se aparta de ellos. Un agente inmobiliario le espera en su oficina localizada en el centro de la ciudad. Patricia había planeado el alquilar un apartamento hasta que vendieran la casa en California. Hacía un día soleado, era agradable andar por el campo y a él no le gustaba subirse en los autobuses o tomar un taxi, así que volvió a la ciudad andando.

El agente de inmobiliaria, un hombre que aparenta estar en los cuarenta, vestido con chaqueta gris y corbata azul, y que habla con acento argentino, le sugiere ir a pie a ver un piso que a él le parece que cumple con las condiciones que Lucas desea. El apartamento se ubica en un edificio de tres pisos, que se encuentra localizado en un área tranquila, y tiene dos dormitorios, dos baños, comedor y sala de estar con puertaventanas que dan a un parque.

—El apartamento está en inmejorable condición —el agente enfatizó.

—Muy bonito. —Lucas está de pie en frente del balcón y, mirando hacia el parque, añade—: ¿Cuales son los términos de la renta?

—Antes de firmar el contrato —responde el agente— la compañía dueña del edificio requiere que el futuro inquilino haga un depósito.

—¿Un depósito? —Lucas se rasca la cabeza al tiempo que se vuelve hacia su interlocutor.

—Me va usted a disculpar, señor Parra, pero ese es el requisito de la compañía, además de pagar un porcentaje al agente inmobiliario, una cuota de comunidad, dos meses de renta por adelantado y…

—¿De verdad? Yo nunca he oído de tal ristra de obligaciones.

—Verá usted, al edificio se le considera de importancia histórica.

Lucas traga saliva y se vuelve para mirar afuera de nuevo. Ve un sauce en el parque que empieza a interesarle más que el apartamento. Trata de ver si hay un estanque cerca del árbol, pues sabe que al sauce le gusta el agua.

—Algo de menos pretensión —dice, aun mirando afuera.

—Tal vez debería haberle advertido…

—No es su culpa —Lucas le interrumpe, volviéndose hacia él, y añade—: Soy viudo. Trato de seguir los deseos de mi difunta esposa. Ella nunca dijo que deberíamos vivir en un edificio de importancia histórica —concluyó con una sonrisa.

—Sin duda, señor Parra, yo puedo enseñarle otros pisos. Pero, si me lo permite, usted, siendo ya un respetable anciano, quizá debería considerar…

—¡Una residencia de mayores! —Lucas dice y va derecho a la puerta.

—Una vivienda en comunidad de mayores, señor Lucas.

—Bueno, me lo pensaré —Lucas dice, y añade con una sonrisa—: De cualquier modo le agradezco el que me haya enseñado este apartamento, pero ahora debo irme.

Afuera, el sol del atardecer tiñe las calles de púrpura; a lo lejos se ven nubarrones densos que se aproximan. Lucas se dirige a su hotel. Le gustaría estar ya asentado en su ciudad; a este respecto, ha respondido a un anuncio de una compañía que dispone de empleos a tiempo parcial para consejeros de finanzas.

Cuando Lucas llega al hotel, Armando le pasa una hoja de papel con un mensaje. Él lee: El señor Miranda desea entrevistarle a las 11 de la mañana. Lucas entiende que se trata del anuncio de trabajo al que ha respondido. Cena en el restaurante del hotel y después va a su habitación.

A la mañana siguiente, Lucas se dispone a acudir a la oficina del señor Miranda, cuya dirección se encuentra a poco menos de un kilómetro del hotel. La mañana huele a lluvia, pero en esta ocasión Lucas se apropia del paraguas. Cuando llega al lugar se da cuenta de que el edificio tiene una apariencia clásica. ¡Oh, no. Otro edificio de corte histórico! Se acerca al número de la oficina y toca el timbre. Una mujer, vestida con chaqueta y falda azul oscuro, abre la puerta.

—Hola, señor Parra. Por favor, pase. El señor Miranda le recibirá muy pronto.

—Gracias.

En la antecámara, Lucas deposita el paraguas en un contendor cilíndrico, colocado cerca de la puerta de entrada para tal propósito, y toma asiento. Coge un número de la revista Forbes de una mesita auxiliar y comienza a hojearla, pero enseguida vuelve la secretaria, que el señor Miranda ya está disponible, le dice, y le conduce hasta la oficina. Lucas esperaba encontrar un lujoso espacio, pero el lugar, aunque amplio y bien iluminado, está amueblado de forma modesta. Después de saludarse mutuamente, el señor Miranda se sienta detrás de su mesa de trabajo e invita con un gesto a que Lucas tome asiento enfrente de él. No pasan ni quince minutos cuando Lucas ya ha resumido sus credenciales.

—Su experiencia como contable se ajusta a nuestras necesidades —el señor Miranda dice, y añade—: Sin embargo, el puesto que ofrecemos requiere tener que viajar muy a menudo, tanto nacional como internacionalmente.

Lucas se muestra como un cachorro al que su dueño le acaba de dar un comando.

—Yo no tengo ningún problema en tener que viajar —dice.

—Bueno, verá, es la capacidad de recuperación lo que nos preocupa —dice el señor Miranda.

Lucas pasea su mirada por las fotos familiares distribuidas por el pupitre, yendo de una a otra, intentando disimular su decepción.

—¿La capacidad de recuperación? —pregunta.

—Por favor, no me lo tome a mal, señor Parra. La edad de una persona, en sí mismo, no es, por supuesto, un factor descalificable.

—¿Hay otro factor descalificable? —Lucas levanta la barbilla y mira a su interlocutor con curiosidad.

—Lo que importa es la realidad de las circunstancias.

Abatido, Lucas se echa para atrás sobre el respaldo de su asiento. Se siente herido en su orgullo por las palabras del señor Miranda; herido, como pasó con el director de su compañía en América, y el barrendero en la calle, y Marco, y los muchachos que pescaban en el rio, y el agente inmobiliario… También está enfadado y a punto de explotar. De repente, da un puñetazo sobre la mesa de despacho que tumba los marcos con las fotos.

—¡Ya entiendo! —grita, y añade—: lo que dice de la realidad.

El señor Miranda levanta sus ojos hacia él.

—Bien, pues le dejaremos saber el resultado de esta entrevista tan pronto como sea posible —dice.

Se dan la mano otra vez. Lucas se siente extrañamente relajado. El señor Miranda levanta el teléfono y llama a la secretaria para decirle que la entrevista ha terminado, y Lucas sale de la oficina a la antesala. Al recoger su paraguas, nota la presencia de un hombre joven, sentado en el mismo sitio donde él se había acomodado antes.

—¿Marco? —Lucas pregunta.

—Sí, y usted es…

—Lucas Parra

—¡Ah!, sí, claro. ¿Cómo está?

—Pues me siento curiosamente relajado. Escucha, Marco, se da la coincidencia de que ambos hemos contestado a la llamada para el mismo trabajo. Yo creo que a mí no me lo van a dar, pero si tú lo consigues, llámame, por favor (aquí Lucas le pasa el número del hotel) y lo celebraremos juntos.

—Así lo haré.

Afuera, está lloviendo. Lucas abre el paraguas y comienza a caminar hacia el hotel. Mientras camina, reflexiona acerca de los muchos cambios por los que él ha pasado en su vida: el reemplazo de los discos de vinilo por los discos compactos, la máquina de escribir por el ordenador personal... Sin darse cuenta, se dice asimismo, uno pasa de una a otra realidad. Absorto en sus ideas, apenas si percibió la presencia del mismo barrendero con el que se había chocado, cubierto con el poncho amarillo y barriendo los charcos afuera de las aceras.

—¡Eh!, Abuelo —grita el joven del poncho— Gusto en verle de nuevo. Ya veo que ha aprendido la lección y lleva paraguas para protegerse de la lluvia.

—Esa es la realdad, Joven —responde Lucas según sigue su camino.

Cuando llega al hotel, Armando le saluda.

—Hola, señor Parra. Tiene otro mensaje —Con una sonrisa, Armando arranca una hoja de un cuaderno de notas del hotel y se la pasa.

Lucas sostiene el papel entre dos dedos mientras observa a Armando con las puntas del bigote curvadas hacia arriba y su uniforme con los botones dorados como personaje de novela.

—Me pregunto, Armando —le dice— si después que sales del trabajo encuentras difícil el cambiar de realidad.

—No. Yo paso rápidamente de una a otra realidad.

—¿Quieres decir que tú cambias de realidad como los turistas que visitan lugares yendo y viniendo en el mismo autobús?

—Pues, no lo había pensado así, pero, la verdad: sí, es más o menos así.

Lucas se sonríe y se aleja de la recepción. Cuando llega a la puerta de su habitación, se lleva el papel con el mensaje a la boca y lo sujeta entre los labios mientras busca la tarjeta-llave en sus bolsillos y después abre la puerta. Una vez dentro, se para frente a la ventana y con la mirada perdida en la calle reflexiona sobre las experiencias por las que ha pasado durante las últimas semanas. Para el señor Miranda, se dice, la edad dicta el nivel de resistencia que la persona tenga para desarrollar un trabajo; para Marco, la posibilidad de encontrar empleo; para el agente de inmobiliaria, el tipo de vivienda; para… Un avión de propulsión que cruza el espacio dejando una cola de humo corta sus pensamientos. Agarra la hoja de papel que sujeta entre los labios y lee el mensaje: "Conseguí el trabajo. Lo vamos a celebrar en el bar del Gran Hotel, esta tarde a las seis. Acude, por favor. Marco."

A las seis y cuarto Lucas se presenta en la entrada del Gran Hotel y enseguida atisba a Marco en el bar, está de pie junto al mostrador y rodeado de media docena de amigos, todos hombres. Lucas cruza el hall de entrada, entre los sofás de cuero italiano, pisando en alfombra roja, y se une al grupo. "Este señor es mi amigo Lucas, contable jubilado", Marco dice a los otros a modo de presentación.

A Lucas le agrada el que Marco se refiera a él como "mi amigo" y muestra una sonrisa de satisfacción. Alguien le pone un vaso de Bourbon-on-the-rocks en la mano y él lo levanta, mirando a Marco, en actitud de brindis. "¡Ah!" —exclama después que lo prueba. Marco pide otra ronda de bebida y aperitivos, y todos charlan de empleos y aventuras amorosas; Lucas sonríe y escucha.

—Yo también soy contable —alguien le cuchichea al oído—. Me llamo Rubén.

Lucas se vuelve para ver al que le habla: hombre de baja estatura y piel cetrina, de cuarenta y tantos años.

—Usted es el primer contable con el que topo en este país —dice—. Mucho gusto en conocerle.

Rubén se sonríe. Lucas se siente contento de encontrar amigos.

Cuando termina la celebración y se despiden, Lucas se vuelve al hotel. Se siente un poco borracho, pero exaltado. Entra en su habitación y enciende todas las luces. Anda de un rincón al otro como si estuviera buscando algo. Son las diez de la noche. ¿Debo acostarme? ¿Darme una ducha? ¿Ver una película? ¿Tomar otro trago? Echa una mirada al mini-bar. "¡No!", dice para sí. Se sienta al borde de la cama y saca dos tarjetas de visita del bolsillo de la camisa, coge el teléfono y marca el número impreso en una de ellas.

—¿Diga? —una voz como distante pregunta.

—¿Es Marco?

—Sí.

—Marco, soy Lucas, llamo para…

—Lo siento, pero tengo compañía.

—¡Oh! Yo solo llamaba para agradecerte de nuevo…

—No hay por qué.

Marco cuelga el teléfono. Bueno, que se le va a hacer. Piensa en Patricia; le gustaría compartir con ella lo bien que lo ha pasado con Marco y sus amigos. Se levanta y vuelve a caminar por la habitación hasta que se cansa y comienza a desvestirse. Se pone el pijama y se sienta en el medio de la cama. Pero antes de echarse a dormir hace otra llamada, esta vez al número que hay en la otra tarjeta.

—¿Diga?

Esta vez Lucas reconoce la voz de Rubén.

—Hola, Rubén, soy Lucas. Espero que no le llame en un momento inoportuno. Me doy cuenta que es tarde y…

—No se preocupe, Lucas, mi mujer y yo nos acostamos tarde. ¿Qué pasa?

Lucas se siente más relajado y dice:

—Llamo para agradecerle.…

—No hay necesidad de ello. Para mí es un placer. Si le puedo ayudar en cualquier cosa… Después de todo, usted acaba de llegar a este país, como quién dice, y…

—Así es. Hace un poco más de un mes —Lucas acomoda las almohadas y vuelve a recostarse en ellas.

—¿Vive solo? —pregunta Rubén.

Lucas cruza los pies sobre la cama.

—Mi mujer falleció hace seis meses —De repente, se da cuenta de que se siente muy solo.

—Le puedo preguntar por qué ha venido a este país?

Lucas percibe que no hay asomo de reproche en la pregunta de Rubén y, de forma sucinta, le cuenta su historia.

—¡Increíble! ¿Cuál es su próximo plan?

—No sé bien. Por ahora estoy hospedado en un hotel. Claro, me gustaría…

—Entiendo. Bueno, yo trabajo para una compañía que maneja complejos residenciales para mayores. Tal vez a usted…

—Qué coincidencia. Resulta que un agente de inmobiliaria me aconsejó que yo visitara ese tipo de vivienda.

—Pues…Escuche: yo puedo hablar con el administrador, es una mujer, conocida por todos como María. Ella le puede llamar y quizá a usted le guste visitar el complejo. ¿Qué me dice?

—Creo que eso estaría muy bien.

—Bueno, pues ya veremos. Buenas noches.

—Buenas noches, Rubén, y gracias por todo.

Lucas recibe la llamada de María y, aunque un tanto escéptico, acepta ir a visitar el complejo. Decide ir andando en la soleada mañana de otoño. Cuando llega al lugar, nota que la verja de hierro que da entrada al jardín interior está entreabierta y decide pasar y echar una ojeada. Una fuente redonda situada en el centro del jardín, con una estatua del Ángel Caído en el centro, le cautiva; chorros de agua se proyectan hacia arriba intermitentemente. Ve cómo los gorriones se bañan en la fuente y luego extienden las alas al sol. A su alrededor se esparcen áreas ajardinadas de diferente tamaños y diseños, muy bien cuidadas. Lucas se imagina rosas, pensamientos, y camelias creciendo en la primavera y dando color a estas zonas.

—Dígame, caballero, ¿puedo ayudarle en algo? —una voz masculina pregunta.

Lucas se vuelve para verle. Es el jardinero.

—Tengo una cita para ver a la administradora.

—Pues venga por aquí, caballero —el jardinero le guía.

Una vez llegado a la oficina de la administración, Lucas se presenta a María, mujer de pelo negro, con reflejos ámbar, en melena corta, ojos negros y unos dientes blancos como la nieve que hacen juego con su vestido. Lucas no se esperaba que ella fuera una mujer negra y de una presencia tan placentera, una mujer madura pero de buen ver.

—Siéntese, por favor —dice María y señala un par de sillas gemelas, colocadas alrededor de una pequeña mesa auxiliar que está en el centro del despacho.

—Una fuente muy bonita —Lucas dice y señala el jardín con el dedo—. Supongo que en la primavera las flores ofrecerán un colorido paisaje.

—Desde luego, y también una exquisita fragancia. Pero, por favor, permítame que le informe brevemente acerca de nuestro complejo.

María le explica que los edificios de viviendas son tres y forman un rectángulo sobre una extensión de tantos metros cuadrados, que hay tantos apartamentos por edificio y las ventanas dan o al patio central, donde él vio la fuente, o a la calle.

El rectángulo se cierra por una pared blanca con la verja de hierro repulgado.

—¿Le gustaría ver los apartamentos disponibles? —pregunta María.

—Sí, por favor. Supongo que Rubén le ha dicho que yo estoy viudo y que…

—Sí, Rubén me dijo. Siento mucho lo de su mujer, señor Parra. Rubén también mencionó que usted se está reincorporando a nuestro país.

—Así es — dice él, esbozando una leve sonrisa—. De vuelta en mi viejo país, entrado en mi tercera edad.

Lucas se siente a gusto con María. Ella parece ser acomodadiza, y la oficina de buena estética. Encima de la mesa de despacho hay un vaso con lilas blancas, y cuadros de paisajes colgados en las paredes. María ha colocado un juego de té en la mesita donde se sientan.

—Voy a llamar a alguien de nuestra oficina para que le dé un tour por el edificio antes de presentarle a nuestro agente inmobiliario para que le enseñe las unidades. Espero que le gusten.

María se levanta, va a su mesa de trabajo y usa el teléfono. Después vuelve a donde está Lucas.

—Todo arreglado —dice—. Por favor, si tiene alguna pregunta déjenos saber en cualquier momento.

—Gracias.

Una mujer proveniente de la oficina de relaciones públicas guía a Lucas a través de las distintas dependencias del edificio, explicando el uso de las mismas, hasta que oyen los altavoces llamando su nombre. Entonces vuelven a la oficina de la administración y conoce al agente inmobiliario, Ángel, un hombre joven, pelirrojo, con pecas.

—¿Es su nombre Ángel, como el de la estatua del Ángel Caído de la fuente? —Lucas intenta parecer chistoso.

El agente inmobiliario, hombre amable y de habla calmosa, se sonríe. Al cabo, le enseña tres apartamentos amueblados, a cual más confortable. A Lucas le gusta lo que le ve, y cuando regresan a la oficina de administración, firma un contrato de renta por un año. Cuando sale de la oficina se vuelve a pie, disfrutando del sol de la tarde, pero siente el estómago vacío y decide parar en un bar-restaurante a comer un bocado antes de llegar al hotel.

Una vez en su habitación, se tumba en la cama y piensa lo agradable que sería si pudiera hablar con Patricia. Y entonces, hace un esfuerzo para imaginar la presencia de su difunta mujer y evocar su voz.

—Es maravilloso hablar contigo, Patricia —dice en voz alta—. Te echo mucho de menos.

—Espero que te encuentres bien —se dice así mismo, evocando la voz de su mujer.

—Sí, estoy bien —contesta con voz natural.

—¿Y cómo están Oscar y Sue? —continua simulando la voz de Patricia.

—Oscar está bien, pero su mujer continúa teniendo recaídas de su enfermedad.

Vas a tener que ayudarles, piensa que dice Patricia.

—Estaré listo si ellos me necesitan —Lucas dice en voz alta, y añade: —Patricia, tengo un montón de cosas que contarte.

En este punto, Lucas para de hablar consigo mismo; está llorando. Se da cuenta de lo inútil de su intento: Patricia ya no existe, y él está solo en la vida. Se quita los lentes y se dispone a dormir. Al amanecer se despierta sobresaltado y con prisa, como si tuviera que desempeñar alguna obligación. ¡Ah, la mudanza! De eso es de lo que yo quise hablar con Patricia. Va al cuarto de baño y se ducha; luego se viste, sale, y camina hasta el complejo para mayores. Cuando llega allí, ve que la verja del jardín está otra vez entreabierta. La empuja para abrirla del todo, y pasa.

—¿Desea algo el señor? —una voz familiar pregunta.

Es el jardinero que está regando las plantas unos metros más allá.

—Ah, hola —dice Lucas—. Usted ya me enseñó el camino al edificio de la administración. ¿Se acuerda?

—Sí, señor, ahora me doy cuenta.

—Gracias, de cualquier modo.

Una vez dentro del edificio, Lucas se llega hasta la ventanilla de la recepción y pide ver a María, la administradora. La recepcionista marca la extensión y transmite el mensaje. Luego dice—: Estará disponible en unos minutos.

—Gracias.

Lucas espera impaciente hasta que la recepcionista le dice que la administradora ya está lista para recibirle; entonces él se dirige a la oficina. María le invita a que se siente. Lucas intenta explicarse, pero no le salen las palabras.

—Tal vez sea mejor si hace una lista —María dice y le pasa un cuaderno.

Lucas escribe algunas palabras.

—Tengo una sugerencia —vuelve a hablar María—. Aquí hay gente que se ofrecen voluntariamente a ayudar a los nuevos residentes.

Una semana más tarde, Lucas se siente feliz en su apartamento, sentado en el sofá de la sala de estar, tomándose un café y mirando al jardín por la ventana. Los chorros de agua suben y caen de forma coordinada, y él piensa que ha tenido mucha suerte en la elección de vivienda.

Al aproximarse el invierno, Lucas se divierte caminando en la nieve, oyendo el crujido bajo las suelas de sus zapatos, y contemplando las torretas de campanas cubiertas con un manto blanco. Pero al llegar diciembre, sin embargo, se siente solo, y un día llama a María.

—¿Hola?

Lucas guarda silencio por un tiempo y luego dice: —Habla Lucas.

—Ah, sí, hola. ¿Algún problema?

—No. No sé cómo expresarme... Me gustaría conocer a más gente de por aquí.

—Pues organice una fiesta.

—Perdone, ¿cómo dice?

María entonces le comenta que en el complejo hay un grupo de voluntarios que están encantados de organizar fiestas de bienvenida para los nuevos inquilinos. Lucas se pone muy contento.

Unos días después. María conduce a Lucas a través de uno de los salones de recreo, abriéndose camino por entre las mesas y sillas dispuestas para la ocasión, y le presenta a otros residentes. Lucas teme que no va a recordar los nombres de muchos de los que va conociendo y lucha por retener detalles de sus fisiognomías. Al cabo, pregunta a María si no le importa que se sienten por un tiempo. Se sientan a una mesa en la que hay aperitivos y una botella de vino. Mientras charlan, se sirven unas lonchas de embutido y una copa de rosé. Lucas oye de María que es divorciada desde hace diez años y no tiene hijos. Y él le cuenta a María acerca de Patricia, que en paz descanse, de Oscar y de Sue; le dice también que él, Lucas, no entiende por qué los hijos permanecen tan alejados. Mientras conversan, miran alrededor, y Lucas ve que Rubén y su mujer, Iris, ocupan una mesa cercana. Lucas se disculpa, se levanta y va a saludarlos. Un minuto después vuelve con ellos a la mesa donde está María y entran en conversación. Iris dice a Lucas que ella es una de las voluntarias que cooperan en la organización de eventos en el complejo y que necesitan de alguien que se haga cargo de la contabilidad, y pregunta si Lucas no estaría interesado. Otros invitados se paran a saludarles y algunos entran en conversación. Lucas se divierte enormemente.

Cuando termina la celebración, Lucas se siente satisfecho. Al salir, camina despacio hacia su apartamento a través del jardín. Al llegar a la fuente, se para y respira hondo para dejar que la brisa refrescante entre en su pulmones. "Es tiempo de ir a casa" se dice al reanudar su camino.

Durante los días siguientes a la fiesta de bienvenida, Lucas recibe llamadas y tarjetas de felicitación de muchos de los asistentes. María le invita a una recepción en su casa para celebrar la Navidad, e Iris le escribe animándole a participar como voluntario para llevar los números en la organización de los eventos venideros. Tales demostraciones de afecto hacen que Lucas sienta que es bien aceptado en el complejo para mayores que ha elegido para vivir.

Hoy, sin embargo, solo halla una carta en el buzón. Es de Oscar. Lucas la coge, entra a su casa, va a la cocina y la pone sobre la mesa mientras él se prepara un café. Luego se sienta y mira fijo al sobre como galgo a su presa. Toma un sorbo de café, echa mano del abridor de cartas y rasga el sobre. Lee dos líneas y no sigue: Sue ha fallecido. De repente, le entra zumbido de oídos y sus manos se vuelven temblorosas, pero con un gran esfuerzo para calmarse consigue reanudar la lectura. Sue murió en el hospital debido a una exacerbación grave de la enfermedad de sangre que padecía. Oscar escribe de su profundo abatimiento. Se siente muy solo en Hong-Kong (la familia de Sue vive en Beijing), quiere volver a California, dice que necesita a su padre y le ruega que él también regrese. Cuando acaba de leer la carta la arroja sobre la mesa como si fuera un pedazo de plomo. El zumbido de oídos se hace más gravoso; Lucas no puede pensar con claridad. Se levanta de la mesa, va al armario, coge el abrigo y sale de su casa.

En la calle, de manera automática, se dirige al parque de su infancia y desde allí vuelve a caminar hasta el rio. Luego se vuelve y anda hasta el centro de la ciudad. Entra en la terraza del restaurante donde conoció a Marco el primer día que llegó. Pero Marco ahora está ocupado con su trabajo. Lucas sale de la terraza y regresa a casa. Se quita el abrigo y los zapatos y se recuesta en la cama mirando al techo, pensando en Patricia, hasta que se queda dormido.

Por la mañana, Lucas se despierta sintiéndose intranquilo. Está convencido de que Patricia le ha hablado mientras dormía. Se viste y sale para ir derecho a la oficina de la administración a hablar con María.

—Lo siento, María, pero he de volver a California —dice.

La administradora lo mira con sorpresa.

—¿Lo dice en serio?

Ambos están de pie en el medio de la oficina, mirándose el uno al otro, como confundidos. María hace un gesto para que Lucas tome asiento, pero él dice que no.

—Sue, la mujer de mi hijo, ha fallecido. Oscar se vuelve a California. Me necesita. Prometí a mi mujer que si me necesitaba yo estaría dispuesto a ayudar.

—Le acompaño en el sentimiento —María dice, y entre ellos, se interpone un breve silencio, hasta que ella añade—: Romper el contrato que ha firmado va a llevar algún tiempo, sin embargo.

—Lo sé.

—Quizá le convenga dejar algo de dinero en la cuenta del banco para pagar una o dos mensualidades de la renta en caso de que la realidad en su vida lo traiga de nuevo a nosotros.

Lucas reflexiona por unos momentos.

—Tal vez haga así —dice—. A veces las circunstancias determinan nuestro destino, como el viento el movimiento de la veleta.

María afirma con la cabeza. Se le acerca, y ambos se dan un abrazo en una despedida cargada de emociones.

Nunca es demasiado tarde

Durante la última borrachera, instintivamente, ella terminó llamando a su puerta. Ambos habían sido compañeros de juergas y luego amantes. Pero de todo ello hacía ya mucho tiempo.

Con los pocos arrestos que le quedaban, y el peso de sus setenta años a la espalda, se sentó a la mesa de la cocina enfrente de él.

—¿Qué queda de ti a parte de tus huesos y una pizca de espíritu reflejado en tus ojos? —Preguntó él, con miedo de apagar un último aliento de esperanza.

—Con el tiempo, se adquieren hábitos, algunos nos traen goce, mientras que otros nos hacen llorar —dijo ella, con voz temblorosa.

—Te veo consumida por el alcohol. Pero tú no lo aceptas, ¿no es así?

Después de estas palabras, él trató de apaciguarse cuando vio lo patético de su cara. —Quizá sea éste mi último puerto. Aquí echo el ancla.

Le entró un golpe de tos. Luego, encendió un cigarrillo.

—Por supuesto —dijo él— Imagino que a continuación vas a hacer anillitos de humo y contarme historias de años pasados.

—¿Por qué iba a hacerlo? —Ella exhaló el humo del cigarrillo a través de sus labios puestos en hocico para formar aros y añadió—: Tu sabes todas mis patrañas acerca del alcohol, la nicotina, el juego…

—Es verdad que yo conozco tus alegrías y tus tristezas.

Ella le echó una mirada ávida a través de los aros de humo.

—Tal vez deberíamos rezar para romper esos malos hábitos.

—Dudo que desaparezcan solo con oraciones. Yo mismo tengo que luchar cada día para mantenerme sobrio.

Ella le ofreció un cigarrillo. Él dijo que no con la cabeza. Luego se levantó y trajo una botella de agua y dos vasos a la mesa.

—Por favor —Ella empujó uno de los vasos para que él le sirviera agua. —Así que ahora, sobrio, estás contento —añadió—. Para ti llegó la primavera y se acabó el invierno.

Él se sirvió agua en el otro vaso —Te escucho —dijo.

Ella bebió su vaso de agua.

—Quiero parar de tomar —dijo con voz firme.

Él se dio cuenta de que algo en ella revivía. —Tu decidiste irte de mi lado —dijo, tratando de amortiguar cualquier tono de reproche en su voz— y ahora vuelves a mi casa hecha polvo y pidiendo compasión.

Ella aplastó la colilla dentro del vaso de agua vacio. —Sin la bebida, temo que mi vida se vuelva sombría —dijo.

Él tamborileó la mesa con sus dedos —Y yo temo que tus vicios pronto acabarán contigo.

Ella levantó los ojos para mirarle cara a cara. Las facciones de su cara se ablandaron y se le saltaron las lágrimas. —Tengo miedo de enfrentarme a la vida por mí misma.

—Nadie camina completamente solo por la vida.

Sobrevino el silencio. Ella trató de ganar su compostura. —Necesito ayuda —dijo, secándose las lágrimas. —Necesito tu guía.

—¿Mi guía? Los grupos de alcohólicos anónimos deberían servirte de guía. Yo solo puedo animarte a que asistas a sus reuniones lo antes posible.

—Empezaré mañana.

—¿Y por qué no el mes próximo? —él preguntó con ironía.

Ella dudó por un momento —Hoy mismo —dijo al fin.

—Ahora mismo —dijo él.

Ella afirmó con la cabeza. Entonces ambos se levantaron de la mesa y salieron juntos.

Palmiro

—¡Estoy harta de tu desidia! —Silvia dice y sale del apartamento dando un portazo.

Palmiro, sintiéndose instigado, salta de la cama y va al baño; odia que ella le despierte de madrugada. Minutos después, se pone la sudadera, cuelga un Marlboro de los labios y sale de estampida a la calle en el Centro de Madrid. "I'll light your cigarette…" —Oye la canción a través de los auriculares y enciende el cigarrillo.

Palmiro, uno noventa de estatura, delgado y pálido, camina sin rumbo. Cuando le entra hambre, se tienta el bolsillo —tiene algún dinero— da una última chupada a su tercer Marlboro en la mañana y entra en un café que está situado en la esquina de dos calles estrechas. Un par de parroquianos se sientan a una de las mesas disponibles, pero Palmiro prefiere el mostrador.

—Un café solo, sin azúcar, y una tostada —comanda a la camarera con cara de ángel que está detrás de la barra. —¡Hija de la gran…! —masculle entre dientes.

—Disculpa, ¿te estás refiriendo a mí? —La camarera, que parece ser de su misma edad, de unos veinte años, le corta la palabra con cara de asombro.

—Lo que digo es que pronto compondré una canción de éxito, y ella va a saber quién soy yo —dice Palmiro.

La camarera relaja sus hombros y se atusa el pelo, corto y negro, con la yema de los dedos.

—¿Eres músico? —pregunta llena de expectación.

—Compongo canciones.

Ella sonríe y se aparta para preparar la tostada y servir el café.

—¿Y quién es *ella*? —pregunta cuando regresa.

—Es mi novia. Se parece a ti, delgada y grácil, solo que ella es rubia con ojos azules. Por alguna razón, esta mañana se despertó refunfuñada y se largó del apartamento dando un portazo.

—Sus razones tendrá —dice la camarera.

—Lo que ella quiere es que yo busque trabajo y me deje de soñar —Palmiro sacude su cabeza en señal negativa.

—¿Y cuál es tu sueño?

Yo soy un artista, piensa pero no dice. En lugar de responder, se da prisa a terminar el desayuno y pagar.

—Pronto sabrás quien soy yo, encanto —le grita a la camarera según sale.

Afuera, un sol vivo de primavera le ciega; se olvidó las gafas de sol. Cruza la calle y prosigue andando despacio por la otra acera, sombreada, ajustándose los auriculares: "You don't bring me anything, but down…" —dice la canción. Continúa caminando hacia la Puerta del Sol y cuando llega allí, entra en la boca del Metro. En el vagón, siente bochorno, suda profusamente, y se limpia el sudor de la frente con la manga. "Un hombre mata a su novia con un hacha". —Palmiro lee en un periódico que uno de los pasajeros sostiene abierto delante de sus ojos. Desvía la cabeza a un lado para evitar el tener que vomitar. Se apea en la segunda siguiente parada.

Sale del Metro en la Calle Fuencarral, respira profundo un par de veces y comienza a andar en busca de un determinado edificio de tres pisos. Cuando lo encuentra, entra, sube las escaleras hasta el segundo y se para en frente de uno de los apartamentos, cuya puerta está pintada de un rojo intenso. Apaga el móvil y toca el timbre. Silvia abre la puerta.

—¿Cómo te atreves a venir al apartamento de mi hermana? —le espeta.

—No puedes romper conmigo de esa manera, Silvia.

—¿Quién me lo va a impedir? —Ella endereza los hombros.

—Yo te quiero y…

—No, Palmiro. Tú te quieres a ti mismo. Por dos años, yo estoy yendo a trabajar…

—Ya sabes que yo no sirvo para mantener un empleo —le corta.

—¡Ese es tu problema! Estoy cansada de oír tus excusas —se lleva las palmas de las manos a su vientre como si tuviera dolor.

—¡Yo soy un artista! —dice Palmiro.

—¡Y yo estoy embarazada! Vas a ser padre. —Ella le mira directamente a los ojos.

Aturdido, Palmiro empuja la puerta, pero Silvia la cierra de golpe. ¡Maldita sea! Está embarazada. Voy a ser padre. ¿Qué quiere decir todo esto? Palmiro permanece de pie frente a la puerta, como paralizado, hasta que el reflejo del color rojo le borra la vista. Entonces, se pone un cigarrillo en la boca y se da la media vuelta. La noticia de que Silvia está embarazada hace que le tiemble el estómago. ¿Qué se supone que él debe hacer? —Pronto voy a componer una canción de éxito y entonces… —balbucea según sale del edificio.

No sabe a dónde dirigirse. De repente, le viene a la mente el recuerdo de la camarera del café donde había entrado antes y decide volver allí. Ahora el local está lleno de gente, Palmiro, nervioso, se dirige a la barra y se sienta en uno de los taburetes que está libre.

—¡Oye guapa! —dice a la camarera— dame una cerveza.

A pesar de su bravata, su estómago tiembla y su corazón se agita. El parroquiano sentado a su derecha, un hombre de bastante edad, le mira con cara de pocos amigos. La camarera se le acerca.

—¿Es que alguien te ha zarandeado? —pregunta.

—Lo que pasa es que no sé a qué mundo pertenezco —dice.

Ella le mira con compasión.

—Me llamo Mónica —dice con una sonrisa.

—Yo soy Palmiro.

—¿Qué clase de cerveza quieres?

—Dame una caña.

La persona a su izquierda, una mujer de edad media, un poco calva, le mira y hace una mueca de desdén.

—¡Soy artista! —grita Palmiro.

Nadie hace el menor comentario. Mónica le sirve la caña y con mucha calma pregunta cuál es su problema.

—No puedo mantener ningún trabajo, ¡carajo! —grita y aprieta el vaso de cerveza con tal fuerza que le tiembla el brazo.

Se crea tensión en el ambiente. Palmiro se da cuenta de que está siendo el foco de atención por parte de todos y se coloca los auriculares con gesto de indiferencia. Con cautela, Mónica se le acerca y golpea con los nudillos en el área del mostrador de madera enfrente de él como si llamara a la puerta de su casa. Palmiro se quita el auricular del oído izquierdo.

—Nosotros, los artistas —dice ella en voz baja— también somos capaces de trabajar.

Palmiro, turbado, se le queda mirando. Sus oídos paran de oír la música que el móvil transmite.

—Me falta poco para convertirme en bailarina —Mónica continua con cara de satisfacción— pero si no trabajara aquí, no podría afrontar los gastos de mi preparación.

La declaración de Mónica hace que la calma regrese entre los presentes, pero Palmiro sigue intranquilo.

—¿Qué te debo? —pregunta.

—Invita la Casa.

—Gracias —Se marcha cabizbajo.

Distraídamente, otra vez deambula por las calles pero ya no escucha la música. Al dar la vuelta a una esquina, sus ojos tropiezan con la inscripción del nombre de la calle. Se trata de una placa de baldosines blancos, adosada a la fachada de un edificio, con la inscripción *Calle del Clavel* y un dibujo de un grande clavel rojo en el centro rodeado de varios otros más pequeños. Algo en la composición de la lámina llama su atención. De repente, los claveles se mueven por sí mismos en frente de sus ojos y se redistribuyen en forma de palabras: *Haz algo práctico*, Palmiro lee. ¡Qué cosa tan extraña!

Palmiro sacude la cabeza y emerge del trance sintiendo miedo, pero también determinado a tomar acción. He de hacer algo, piensa. Duda si volver al café y agradecer a Mónica sus palabras de aliento o retornar a ver a Silvia y compartir con ella su determinación de buscar trabajo.

Tres pájaros negros

Al amanecer, Ana, Carolina, y yo nos dispusimos a marchar por senderos empinados desde la falda del Pico de las Espadas hasta alcanzar la cima de ese monte aragonés.

Cuando finalicé mis estudios de medicina, comencé a trabajar en la Sala de Urgencias del hospital público. Ana también trabajaba allí, y el Director del Departamento determinó que yo me uniera a su turno. Pronto me di cuenta de que Ana tenía gran capacidad de trabajo, lo cual yo admiraba. Cuando ella me habló de su afición al alpinismo, pensé que su entereza física quizá se debía a la práctica de ese deporte.

—¿Te interesa el alpinismo? —preguntó.

Yo no sabía mucho acerca de ello. Me prestó un pequeño libro sobre el tema, que ella había publicado, y lo encontré interesante.

—Me gustaría intentarlo —dije después de leerlo.

De ese modo conocí a Carolina, estudiante de Arte. Cuando Ana me la presentó, enseguida noté que era una chica de naturaleza sensible. Carolina y yo comenzamos a salir juntos, y ella sugirió que nos uniéramos a Ana en sus excursiones pirenaicas. Aunque yo no podía imaginarme a Carolina —menuda y pálida— capaz de marchar por senderos empinados, la idea de hacer ejercicio al aire libre me resultó atractiva.

Juntos, los tres nos embarcamos a menudo en aventuras excursionistas. Se notaba que Ana poseía una gran aptitud para enseñar cómo luchar contra las adversidades atmosféricas y del terreno. Yo admiraba a Ana, pero Carolina me atraía más. También me di cuenta de que entre estas dos mujeres existía un fuerte lazo de unión.

Así, pues, al amanecer de hoy, los tres comenzamos a caminar por senderos en cuesta arriba, determinados a alcanzar la cima. Ana marcando el paso, Carolina en el centro y luego yo, no tan alto como Ana pero en buena forma. Habríamos andado unas dos horas cuando comencé a notar que mi mochila se hacía más pesada sobre mi espalda, y quise saber si Carolina también lo estaría notando.

—¿Estás cansada? —le pregunté.

Afirmó con la cabeza pero no se quejó. Deduje que Ana le habría enseñado a desarrollar resistencia. Ana procuraba que nosotros nos mantuviéramos fuera de peligro todo el tiempo. Ella tenía confianza en sí misma y era consciente de su responsabilidad como líder. Carolina, sin embargo, necesitaba palabras de aliento de vez en cuando.

Hacia la mitad del camino, nos tomamos un descanso. Nos sentamos en una roca aplanada que yacía al lado del sendero, comimos algún piscolabis que llevábamos en la mochila, y bebimos agua de nuestras cantimploras. Ana notó la presencia de nubes allí dónde antes el cielo había aparecido despejado.

—Huele a lluvia —dijo—. Debemos darnos un poco más de prisa.

Reanudamos la marcha. Se levantó una brisa más fría, y en el aire flotaba un olor a ozono como si se avecinara una tormenta. Yo confiaba en la pericia de Ana. Ella apresuró el paso y tiró de nosotros en el último trecho hasta que al filo del mediodía coronamos la cima, sudorosos pero satisfechos. El sol se ocultaba entre nubes gruesas, y la atmósfera era gris y opresiva. Sentí que no podía respirar bien, y Carolina dijo que se notaba mareada.

—Escuchad un ruido que retumba a lo lejos. Es el viento —Ana advirtió—. Hemos de permanecer fuertes.

El viento aullador parecía galopar hacia nosotros, remolinándose entre las rocas. Momentos después, unas nubes densas se rasgaron, resonaron truenos, y una serpentina de fuego cruzó el espacio. Tres grandes pájaros negros que volaban justo por encima de nosotros recibieron una violenta sacudida, perdieron su rumbo, y antes de que los restos sin vida de uno de ellos cayera a nuestros pies, otro latigazo de fuego se enredó entre el cuerpo de Ana, y ella se derrumbó sobre el suelo rocoso. Al instante, me acerqué a su lado y le tomé el pulso.

—El latido es muy débil —dije.

Carolina se había puesto en cuclillas a dos metros de nosotros. Temblando, nos miró como si se tratara de una aparición, como si Ana y yo fuéramos habitantes de otro mundo, un mundo desconocido para ella. Le apliqué a Ana respiración boca a boca, tomando el pulso con frecuencia, hasta que comprendí que su corazón había parado de latir para siempre.

Me aparté de su cuerpo inerte y me acerqué a Carolina, quien daba la impresión de estar pasando por un trance: los dientes le castañeaban, las manos le temblaban, y los ojos los mantenía muy abiertos. El ventarrón seguía arremolinándose a nuestro alrededor. Con cuidado, atraje a Carolina primero hacia mí y enseguida hacia abajo para tumbarnos en el suelo; ella no opuso resistencia. Ambos yacimos inmóviles sobre el terreno, conmocionados, hasta que una lluvia torrencial nos sacó del sopor. La oscuridad reinaba por todas partes; era como si el sol hubiera huido de nuestras vidas.

—Ana ha muerto —dije—. Debemos dar parte a la policía.

Apenas podía mantenerme en pie. Agarré mi teléfono móvil para llamar, pero no había señal de recepción. Pedí a Carolina me dejara usar el suyo. Con mano temblorosa me lo pasó. Tampoco había señal de recepción.

—Volvamos al valle —dije—. Necesitamos ayuda.

Con mucha dificultad, Carolina se las apañó para sacar de su mochila una mantita que me la pasó mientras apuntaba con su mirada hacia el cuerpo de Ana. Yo agarré la manta, me dirigí hacia donde yacía el cadáver y, sin tocar nada, lo tapé.

Carolina y yo iniciamos la bajada tratando de seguir el mismo camino por el que habíamos subido, pero el viento y la lluvia habían borrado las marcas de los senderos. Ella siguiéndome, y yo lleno de miedo de que perdiéramos la ruta, librando obstáculos, descendimos al valle y llegamos a la casita que los tres habíamos alquilado el día antes. Lleno de aprehensión, entré yo primero; Carolina me siguió. En ese mismo momento, la cruda realidad hizo que me estremeciera: los tres habíamos ocupado la casita el día antes, pero ahora solo éramos dos. Me sentí abrumado, indeciso acerca de qué hacer, qué pensar, qué decir a Carolina.

—Te quiero —dije, y mis palabras sonaron como dichas a destiempo.

—Ana ya no está con nosotros —respondió Carolina con voz de ultratumba, y sus palabras me sonaron como el anuncio del fin de un viaje, la estación terminal.

Agotado, me senté en el sofá de la sala de estar mientras que Carolina se retiró a descansar en el dormitorio. Yo llamé a la policía. Cuando comencé a describir lo que había pasado, me vino a la memoria el recuerdo de un empleado público que llegó en ambulancia a la Sala de Urgencias de nuestro hospital dos noches antes. Estaba cerca de la muerte debido a una descarga eléctrica que había recibido mientras trabajaba en una instalación. Ana se encargó del caso. Aplicó el desfibrilador sobre el pecho del paciente y lo reanimó.

"No la pude salvar", dije automáticamente al oficial al otro lado del teléfono. El policía me aseguró de que ellos despacharían inmediatamente un helicóptero hacia el lugar. También me pidió que Carolina y yo permaneciéramos donde estábamos hasta que los agentes de la policía llegaran para entrevistarnos.

Cuando terminamos de hablar por teléfono, me recosté en el sofá y traté de relajarme, pero no encontraba paz porque mi mente no se libraba del recuerdo del fatal suceso. ¿Sobrevivirían los dos pájaros negros que perdieron en vuelo a su otro compañero? ¿Habíamos nosotros perdido Ana para siempre?, me preguntaba, hasta que me quedé dormido.

He despertado hace solo un rato. Son las dos de la mañana. Por unos instantes, no estuve seguro de lo que había sucedido hasta que recordé que Carolina estaba descansando en el dormitorio. No nos habíamos comunicado desde que llegamos a la casa. Fui a la habitación. Ella estaba despierta. "Ayer perdimos a Ana, que los dos amábamos", dijo con voz distante.

Dejé que descansara, y me volví al salón, donde me encuentro ahora, sentado en el sofá, esperando a que llegue la policía y preguntándome si Carolina y yo seremos capaces de amarnos sin Ana.

El Teso Pueblo

Hacía cuarenta y siete años que el padre Lionel Guzmán era el párroco de la iglesia de La Santa Cruz y se sentía viejo para continuar el ejercicio de su ministerio. Tenía el pelo canoso y los músculos doloridos, a pesar de que su estilo de vida campestre le había ayudado a mantenerse en buena forma física. Él era ladino, descendiente de colonos europeos, más alto que la mayor parte de los lugareños. No usaba la sotana más que en contadas ocasiones y cuando impartía los servicios religiosos, pero siempre llevaba un crucifijo de buen tamaño sujeto a una fina cadena que colgaba de la cintura. En el pasado, con frecuencia andaba varios kilómetros a través de caminos polvorientos para asistir a las bodas, consolar a los enfermos graves o visitar a familias que necesitaban su ayuda. Hacía un par de años que, en una noche de truenos y relámpagos, pasada ya la media noche, alguien aporreó su puerta.

—¡Padre Guzmán!

Una voz femenina le llamaba. Se puso la camisa y los pantalones sobre el pijama.

—¿Quién llama?

—Soy yo, Irma. Ulil, mi marido, salió al monte a la caída del sol para recoger mimbre y no ha regresado. Tengo un mal presentimiento. ¡Ayúdeme!, por favor.

Hacía cuatro meses que Irma y Ulil se habían casado y ella estaba embarazada.

El padre Guzmán abrió la puerta. Irma, una joven Maya, vestía con güipil de color rojo oscuro y nagua de tela blanca y se cubría los hombros con una mantilla verde. Se le notaba aprehensiva y venía empapada.

—Ayúdeme, por favor —dijo.

El sacerdote no estaba seguro si él no estaría soñando.

—Espera un momento para que me ponga las botas y agarre un par de linternas.

Anduvieron a prisa por la ladera del monte, el uno junto al otro, en silencio, tensos, alumbrando el camino con sus linternas. Ella conocía bien la zona en la que estaban porque con frecuencia acompañaba a su marido a recoger mimbre con que tejían cestos y esteras. "Ulil, Ulil", gritaba Irma, y el padre Guzmán también gritaba el nombre. Pero no obtenían repuesta, solo se oía el sonido del viento y la lluvia sobre las hojas de los árboles. De repente, el cura se tropezó con un bulto oscuro y grande que yacía entre un montón de agujas de pino. Pensó que se trataba del troco de un árbol quemado y derribado. Pero Irma, a su lado, se desmayó, y entonces él comprendió que a Ulil lo alcanzó un rayo y lo mató.

Al Padre Guzmán le llevó semanas para recuperarse del trauma. Lentamente, sin embargo, volvió a ocuparse de su misión: ganarle el terreno a los protestantes en favor de los católicos. Los evangelistas habían construido una iglesia, lo que le traía martirizado. Estaba convencido de que el rito y la iconografía católicos les iba mejor a los nativos que la liturgia protestante y, al comienzo de 1981, mantenía el entusiasmo por su cometido. Pero eran tiempos difíciles, pues una parte del país estaba en guerra: los militares defendían el Gobierno de Guatemala contra grupos de guerrilleros rebeldes que surgían en distintas localidades incluyendo las zonas montañosas, cuna de la Civilización Maya. Aunque el conflicto armado no había llegado al poblado de El Teso, la gente se inquietaba a medida que se filtraban las noticias sobre las atrocidades cometidas no muy lejos de allí.

El Padre Guzmán había hecho una petición por escrito al Obispo para que la Diócesis enviara otro sacerdote a la parroquia de La Santa Cruz, que lo necesitaba. Pero la Diócesis contestó que no era posible conceder tal petición debido a la escasez de sacerdotes y la urgente necesidad de servicios religiosos en las zonas de guerra, que se llevaban a cabo por los pocos sacerdotes disponibles. No obstante, el párroco insistió, y después de su tercera petición, recibió contestación en marzo, unos días antes de la fiesta anual del pueblo. Se ajustó las gafas para leer: "… se hace ahora posible el atender a su petición y proveer a su parroquia con la ayuda necesaria…"

Leía la carta a Ismael, el mestizo que ejercía de administrador de la parroquia.

"… El Padre Francisco Palenque, un joven jesuita con una clara vocación de dar ayuda espiritual al humilde y necesitado, en breve se presentará en su iglesia parroquial de La Santa Cruz".

La carta estaba firmada por el secretario personal del Obispo. Mientras el Padre Guzmán la leía, las manos le temblaban. El anciano sacerdote se quedó pasmado cuando Ismael se lo dijo—: Sus manos están temblorosas.

—¿No crees, Ismael, que tú mismo temblarías de alegría si estuvieras tan contento como yo lo estoy ahora?

Se encontraban en la sacristía, que también la usaban a veces para asuntos de oficina. El cura estaba de pie junto a la mesa de trabajo, mientras que el empleado se ocupaba en limpiar un candelabro que colgaba del techo, cerca de la puerta que daba a la iglesia. En aquel momento, el cura soltó la carta sobre la mesa y se sentó en su silla en silencio; se le notaba cansado. Se acordó de que Ismael también había notado su temblor mientras elevaba la Hostia para su Consagración durante la misa. Incluso Indalecia, la mujer Maya que trabajaba como cocinera y ama de casa desde hacía tantos años, le había notado el temblor. "Le tiemblan las mano, Padre", le dijo un día cuando, comiendo la sopa, él se llevó la cuchara a la boca. Se preguntaba cuantos otros habrían notado su tembleque. Cabía en lo posible que Irma, quien ya estaría cercana dar a luz, también se hubiera percatado de ello. Se preguntaba si el temblor se convertiría en un problema, porque él necesitaba mantenerse firme para llevar a cabo su misión. Miró afuera de la ventana, hacia el gran volcán. Pero enseguida se levantó como con prisa y dijo: "Hay mucho que hacer, Ismael. Mejor pongámonos a trabajar".

La gente del pueblo se ocupaba en preparar los puestos para el mercado y adornar las calles con vistas a celebrar la fiesta anual que generalmente coincidía con días calurosos. En el pueblo vivían unas dos mil personas, la mayor parte eran descendientes de los maya y trabajaban como agricultores, tejedores y artesanos. El Teso Pueblo había visto días más prósperos cuando la capital de Guatemala estaba en el Valle del Panchoy y se construyeron magníficos edificios en la ciudad y en los pueblos del valle. Todavía contaba con un antiguo puente y un puñado de edificios coloniales, uno de ellos se utilizaba como la sede del ayuntamiento, y otro era el juzgado, ambos localizados en la Plaza Central. Las estrechas calles de adoquines que rodeaban la Plaza eran las que se estaban adornando.

Durante aquellos días en los que la gente se ocupaba de los preparativos para la fiesta, Francisco Palenque llegó al pueblo. Una mañana llamó a la puerta de la casa del párroco, adjunta a la iglesia. Indalecia la abrió y los dos permanecieron en silencio durante unos segundos, mirándose, hasta que él dijo:

—Soy el padre Palenque.

—¿Padre…? —Indalecia dudó, como si no hubiera oído bien el nombre.

—Francisco Palenque. Acabo de llegar en el autobús. —Él habló en Kaqchiquel, la lengua indígena del lugar.

Indalecia estaba en presencia de un joven Maya.

—¡Ah, claro! Sea bienvenido, Padre Palenque. Me llamo Indalecia. Soy ama de casa del Padre Guzmán. —Ella habló en español.

—Perdone que no le haya dejado saber la hora exacta de mi llegada por anticipado —dijo él, también en español.

El joven cura vestía una camisa azul oscuro con las mangas remangadas, pantalones de pana y botas de estilo militar, llenas de polvo. Como equipaje traía una bolsa de cuero, arrugada, colgada al hombro.

—El Padre Guzmán sabe que usted llegaría en cualquier momento —dijo Indalecia.

En efecto, Lionel Guzmán se sentía ansioso de conocer a su nuevo ayudante. Pero en el hall de la entrada, de pie en frente de Francisco Palenque —delgado y más bien bajo de estatura, de pelo negro y ojos oscuros— se sintió envejecido. ¡Francisco parecía un chaval!

—¿Usted entraría al seminario de muy joven, calculo? —dijo Lionel.

—No recuerdo que alguna vez quise hacer algo diferente.

El padre Guzmán asintió con la cabeza y dijo—: Yo soy Franciscano, soldado de Cristo.

Se miraron en silencio.

—Pero, déjeme darle la bienvenida a El Teso Pueblo —dijo Lionel, y acto seguido añadió—: Indalecia, mi ama de casa le acompañará a sus cuartos. Supongo que quiere descansar por algún tiempo.

Además de la casa del párroco, la parroquia disponía de un pequeño edificio adosado a la iglesia, donde Francisco Palenque se alojó.

A Francisco le gustó la iglesia, un edificio sólido, construido con cemento y piedra, aunque sin tener las características de ningún estilo arquitectónico en particular. Estaba localizado en la Calle Primera, a unos cien metros de distancia de la Plaza Central, y se alzaba en la mitad de un llano, desde donde se divisaban estupendas vistas del Gran Volcán.

—Esta iglesia se construyó algún tiempo antes de la independencia de Guatemala —dijo el Padre Guzmán mientras se dirigían al interior del edificio.

—¿Qué había aquí antes de que se construyera? —preguntó Palenque con los ojos puestos en una gran figura de Cristo en la Cruz, tallado en madera y colgado de la pared al fondo del altar principal.

El Padre Guzmán no sabía la respuesta, y, en lugar de ello, apuntó con el dedo hacia el Cristo. —¿Es impresionante, no? —dijo.

—Desde luego —dijo Palenque.

Después de recorrer el total de la iglesia, Lionel Guzmán condujo Francisco Palenque a la sacristía donde el sacristán estaba trabajando.

—Ismael ayuda con todo, desde bodas a funerales, y, además, es nuestro administrador —Lionel le dijo a Francisco a modo de introducción.

—Muy bien —dijo Francisco y enseguida—: Mucho gusto en conocerle.

Se dieron la mano. Ismael, unos años más joven que el párroco, era un hombre fornido, de apariencia sana, que estaba siempre bien atildado. Vivía con su mujer, no lejos de la iglesia. No tenían hijos. El Padre Guzmán intervino de nuevo—: El Padre Palenque pregunta qué había en el lugar de la iglesia antes de que se construyera.

—Hasta donde yo sé —dijo Ismael— nadie ha oído decir que antes de la iglesia hubiera nada de importancia en esa parcela.

—La pregunta es válida, sin embargo —argumentó Lionel Guzmán, dirigiéndose a Ismael— Mira lo que está pasando ahora con el Puente Antiguo.

Se sentaron en sillas de mimbre alrededor de una mesita situada en medio de la sacristía.

—Indalecia nos va a servir café enseguida —dijo Guzmán.

Francisco estiró las piernas al frente y cruzó las manos sobre su vientre al tiempo que preguntó—: ¿Qué está pasando con el Puente Antiguo?

El párroco también estiró sus piernas y se reclinó en el respaldo de la silla.

—Un par de arqueólogos —dijo— vinieron hace dos meses, lo inspeccionaron y dijeron que el puente tiene más de mil años.

—Interesante —dijo Francisco, pero Lionel Guzmán guardó silencio.

Entonces intervino Ismael—: Parece que los americanos han prestado dinero al Gobierno para que lo inviertan en proyectos a realizar en este valle. Uno de esos proyectos consiste en la recanalización del agua del rio que fluye por debajo del puente para dar paso a parte de una nueva carretera.

—¿Se piensa derribar el puente? —preguntó Palenque.

—Así es. Pero muchos se oponen a derribar un puente con una historia tan antigua. Además, hay mucha gente que piensa que la construcción de una nueva carretera que pase por el pueblo va a facilitar la llegada de soldados. Lo cual les asusta —dijo Ismael.

—No me extraña —dijo Palenque.

En ese momento entró Indalecia con una bandeja conteniendo el café y unas pastas. El Padre Guzmán cortó un pedazo de pan dulce y se sirvió una taza de café.

—El asunto presenta dos caras —dijo— Por un lado, la gente del pueblo ve que el Gobierno ha aceptado el que se les prive del agua de regadío que necesitan para cultivar el maíz. Por otro lado, la construcción de una carretera que pase por aquí, a la larga, les va a beneficiar.

—¿Dónde se sitúa la Iglesia en ello? —preguntó Palenque.

—La gente dice que el rio les pertenece a ellos —dijo el párroco.

—¿No es eso verdad? —dijo Palenque.

El Padre Guzmán mojó otro bizcocho en el café y se lo llevó a la boca con cuidado para evitar que su mano temblara. Ismael retomó el hilo de la conversación.

—Nuestra parroquia de la Santa Cruz no es la única implicada en el proyecto —dijo— Piedras Blancas también se ve afectada por el mismo plan.

—Ya me doy cuenta —dijo Palenque.

Los tres continuaron charlando por un tiempo mientras se tomaban el café.

A la mañana siguiente Francisco Palenque volvió solo a la iglesia. A aquella hora temprana, dentro había más claridad. Un grupo de mujeres indígenas se ocupaban en fregar los suelos, colocar floreros, limpiar los candelabros de alrededor del altar y sacudir el polvo de repulgados reclinatorios. Tenían todas las luces encendidas. Francisco les sonrió a la vez que se presentó a sí mismo—: Yo soy el Padre Palenque, vuestro nuevo sacerdote —dijo, y preguntó—: ¿Quién usa los reclinatorios?

—Se reservan para la gente importante —contestó una de las mujeres.

—¿Dónde están los reclinatorios para el resto de la gente? —volvió a preguntar con la sonrisa en los labios.

La mujer lo miró con cara de sorpresa, como diciendo: debería usted, señor cura, estar mejor informado.

—Usan los bancos —dijo.

—Oh, ya me doy cuenta —el joven cura afirmó y les dijo adiós con la mano al tiempo que continuó su visita a la iglesia por sí mismo.

Una vez al año, el padre Guzmán decía una misa solemne a las doce del día para honrar al santo patrón del pueblo. Ataviado con casulla de colores vivos, encabezaba una procesión, avanzando a paso lento desde el portón de entrada a la iglesia hasta el altar mayor, por el pasillo central. Aquel año, el padre Palenque, vestido de sotana negra y sosteniendo una cruz grande, metálica, pero de peso ligero, iba detrás de él. Seis niños, vestidos con túnicas blancas, les seguían, esparciendo incienso por el aire. La gente del pueblo miraban al padre Guzmán con ojos abiertos, llenos de admiración, como si fuese un dios, y él se mostraba contento de ver su iglesia llena a tope. Vio a Irma, de pie a la entrada —ya a punto de dar a luz—. También distinguió al Dr. Julián Bruno, médico, que pasaba ya de los cincuenta, que vivía en Piedra Blancas, a unos diez kilómetros de distancia, pero que cada año venía al El Teso para asistir a la misa solemne. Lionel Guzmán también hacía gestos de saludo a los que ocupaban los reclinatorios. Cuando llegó al pie del altar, hizo una genuflexión y se concentró en los asuntos de Dios. Cuando terminó la misa, bendijo a los feligreses: "Que el Señor abra las puertas de la Fe para todos", dijo.

Aquel día el mercado estaba abarrotado de gente y presentaba un cúmulo de mercancías de distinta índole y colores, y un olor mezcla de chiles, tortillas de maíz, aguardiente y café. El padre Guzmán se acercó al mercado al comienzo de la tarde. Para él, el moverse cada año entre tantos puestos y gente era como un recordatorio del paso del tiempo. El porquero vendía los cerdos como cada año, solo que en el presente se le notaba más viejo: cargado de espaldas, y con más arrugas en la cara. Lionel Guzmán pensó que él mismo también estaba envejeciendo, cuando oyó una voz que lo llamaba. Era Irma; estaba parada, de pie, unos metros más allá. De los hombros le colgaban cestos de varias formas y colores. Ella le estaba indicando que se moviera hacia la Calle Primera, y él lo hizo, preguntándose qué era lo que Irma querría que él viese.

Primero vio que un malabarista, rodeado de un círculo de espectadores, ejercía sus habilidades. Después se encontró con otro círculo de gente rodeando a un hombre que les hablaba. Se acercó y enseguida reconoció que se trataba de Francisco Palenque. "Yo vengo de las sierras y os puedo asegurar que allí no hay compasión para la gente pobre", decía. Lionel comprendió que aquello era lo que Irma quiso que viera. Le pareció que lo que Francisco estaba diciendo tenía sentido, que tarde o temprano todo el mundo en el pueblo tendría que aceptar los hechos. No había más que escuchar la radio clandestina que emitía desde Cuba para comprender que el conflicto armado no era entre cristianos y paganos sino entre el poderoso y el oprimido. Francisco Palenque no perdía su tiempo y se comunicaba bien con la gente del pueblo. Decidió que lo más prudente en aquel momento sería no interferir, y se alejó de allí.

En abril comenzó la temporada de lluvias. Y con los primeros chaparrones, también llegó a El Teso el Teniente Atilano, un joven ladino, de poco más de treinta años de edad, alto y rubio, con una voz potente. Venía a supervisar la orden de servicio miliar obligatorio decretado por el Presidente de la República.

Las lluvias torrenciales no cesaban, de modo que a finales de mayo, las calles estaban embarradas y los campos del cultivo de la milpa encharcados. El alcalde del pueblo, Ulmil Zunc, hombre maya de unos cuarenta y tantos años que se daba aires de ser un político ambicioso, publicó un edicto para notificar a la población de la urgencia de juntarse y discutir un plan de acción para afrontar los efectos de la inundación. Convocó una reunion a celebrarse en el ayutamiento. El techo artesanal de la sala de reunión atrajo miradas de admiración por parte de los concurrentes.

—Lo primero que hay que hacer es poner remedio para prevenir cualquier deslizamiento de tierra —dijo el militar a la audiencia.

El alcalde, el jefe de la policía y el teniente ocupaban asientos sobre una plataforma al frente, a un nivel más alto que el resto de la gente. Ulmil Zunk sacó un bolígrafo de su bolsillo y escribió algo en una libreta.

—Con mis respetos, Teniente, lo que necesitamos son más recursos —dijo Zoilo, un hombre maya, menudo, que estaba allí en representación de los agricultores.

—¿Qué necesitan ustedes? —preguntó el teniente.

Todos callaron. Solo se oía el batir de las gotas de lluvia sobre los cristales de las ventanas.

—Con los desagües obstruidos —dijo el médico por fin— temo que surja un brote de disentería.

—Si se da el caso, el ejército ayudará a evacuar a los enfermos —dijo el teniente.

Ulmil escribió algo más en su cuaderno.

—Señor —dijo Zoilo con actitud humilde— La milpa es nuestra fuente de ingresos.

—No se asusten —el oficial dijo— La nueva carretera, una vez construida, va a facilitarles el desarrollo económico.

Los presentes entendieron que el comisario se refería a los planes del Gobierno de recanalizar el curso del rio para construir una nueva carretera, para lo cual se necesitaba derribar el antiguo puente; carretera que se uniría a la Vía Panamericana y que, supuestamente, traería comercio al pueblo. Ulmil añadió otra nota en sus escritos, el Dr. Bruno se mantenía atento para captar las noticias que favorecían a su causa, y el padre Guzmán, sus dedos cruzados para evitar el temblor, soñaba con rellenar los huecos de la fachada de la iglesia donde en otro tiempo existieron esculturas de santos labradas en piedra.

—Si se me permite —el médico dijo, levantando la mano para hacerse ver— yo quiero añadir que también necesitamos más ambulancias y por lo menos otro médico.

Sus palabras levantaron un murmullo de aprobación por parte de los asistentes, incluyendo el curandero y la comadrona. Un buen número de gente del pueblo, cuando se encontraban indispuestos, acudía primero al curandero y solo en el caso de que no mejoraran buscaban acudir al Dr. Bruno.

—Nuestra iglesia… —comenzó a decir el padre Guzmán— Bueno, los nichos en la fachada frontal están vacíos. Antes de que yo tomara cargo como párroco contenían esculturas labradas en piedra. Pero ahora, ahora… Con el padre Palenque incorporado a la iglesia, pensamos que se podrían tallar nuevas esculturas para rellenarlos.

Su voz se apagaba. Ismael, sentado a su lado, le agarró la mano con discreción para evitar que le temblara, y Francisco hizo un gesto de aprobación. El teniente Atilano miró el reloj de pared en la sala —había pasado casi una hora— y gesticuló al alcalde para que terminara la reunión. "Aquí concluye la discusión", dijo Ulmil y añadió: "Muchas gracias a todos por su participación".

Los asistentes se levantaron, recogieron sus ponchos de los percheros a los lados de la sala de reunión y se marcharon. Afuera, Ismael cobijó al anciano párroco bajo su paraguas. Mientras caminaban juntos a casa, Ismael se percató de que el padre Guzmán iba encorvado hacia adelante y andaba con paso incierto.

—Espero que este militar nos traiga el bien —dijo Lionel Guzmán.

—Dijo que el Gobierno nos ayudará —afirmó Ismael y pateó una piel de plátano fuera del camino.

—Gracias por apartar la cáscara del plátano —dijo Guzmán y añadió—: Queda mucho por hacer.

Llegados a su casa, abrió la puerta, se despidió de Ismael y entró.

En Junio, los trabajadores agrícolas se reunieron en los campos de maíz para celebrar su tradicional ritual bajo la luz de la luna llena en preparación para la cosecha. Había parado de llover, pero los trabajadores seguían compungidos a causa de los daños causados por las recientes inundaciones, lo que significaba una disminución en el volumen de la recolección de cereales. Pero allí estaban, los hombres con máscaras alegóricas y las mujeres ataviadas con sus güipiles bordados con figuras de animales y plantas. Se encontraban al puno de iniciar el tradicional baile en honor de *Maximon,* deidad de su devoción, y suplicar a la Madre Tierra se mostrara fertil, cuando vieron un helicoptero que aterrizaba no muy lejos de ellos. Fueron testigo de una escena de desembarco de hombres, la mayoría de ellos en unifrome militar, que enseguida corrieron hacia el boscaje.

Al día siguiente, la escena del helicoptero, junto con el recién nacido bebé de Irma, se convirtieron en la comidilla del pueblo. La aparición del helicoptero desencadenó diversas opiniones. Hubo quienes sospechaban que en el pueblo había grupos comunistas clandestinos y mantenían que los soldados que llegaron en el aparato venían para erradicarlos. En cambio, otros entendían que los soldados habían venido para ayudar a las autoridades locales a implementar la orden del servicio militar obligatorio y aseguraban que entre la gente que desembarcó había también agentes del Gobierno vestidos de civiles. Y un puñado de gente opinaba que El Teso Pueblo se había convertido en zona de paso y lugar clave para el Gobierno, aunque no se sabía la razón de ello. Pero quizás el alcalde lo sabía.

Ulmil informó al pueblo de que los civiles que descendieron del helicoptero eran canadienses expertos en materia de la localización de petroleo crudo. El Gobierno había expandido la exploración de posibles areas petroleras que abarcaban el Valle del Panchoy, incluyendo El Teso Pueblo. En cuanto a los soldados, ellos estaban en el pueblo solamente en función de ayudar al teniente a cumplimentar el alistamiento militar obligatorio.

El Padre Guzmán convocó a Francisco Palenque e Ismael a la sacristía para hablar de los planes de mejora de la iglesia. Coincidió que fue en uno de esos días de lluvia torrencial y ellos oian el tamborileo de las gotas cayendo sobre el tejado. Indalecia les trajo café y pastas. Lionel Guzmán se llevó la taza a los labios con mucho cuidado, agarrandola con ambas manos para evitar verter el líquido debido al temblor.

—Es mucho lo que tenemos que hacer —dijo y añadió—: Traer una nueva pila bautismal, un nuevo altar de mármol, encargar las estatuas para los nichos de la fachada…

—Escuelas, más agua potable, un montón de cosas necesitamos —Francisco Palenque le interrumpió— Me imagino —añadió— que es cuestión de establecer prioridades.

—¿Cuál sería su prioridad? —Ismael le preguntó.

—Expresarnos con una sola voz —Palenque contestó.

El párroco y el sacristán intercambiaron una mirada inquisitiva.

—Hablando de unidad —dijo el párroco después de unos momentos— Julián y yo pensamos escribir al Obispado detallando lo que necesitamos para nuestra iglesia y sus pacientes.

—Me imagino que sería mejor que escribieran al Gobierno —dijo Ismael.

El párroco hizo un gesto como si se sintiera incómodo. Trató de cruzar las piernas, pero enseguida desistió al notarse torpe en la realización de los movimientos.

—El Presidente de la República y el obispo comen juntos con frecuencia —dijo y añadió—: En relación a la unidad de la que hablas, Francisco, encuentro que el concepto es complejo y difícil de explicar en una carta.

Después de esas palabras, y no teniendo más asuntos que discutir, dieron la reunión por terminada.

Entre tanto, un grupo de reclutas disidentes escaparon a las montañas después de rehusar enlistarse al servicio militar obligatorio. No obstante, había gente en el pueblo que vio una oportunidad de prosperar económicamente cobijados bajo las alas del Gobierno. Bajo una generalizada atmósfera de incertidumbres, sin embargo, se organizó una protesta pública.

Zoilo se las apañó para convencer a medio centenar de trabajadores agrícolas a acudir al Puente Antiguo en la mañana del día designado para su demolición. Alineados alrededor del puente, formando una cadena cogidos de la mano, manifestaron su oposición al derribo. El teniente, el alcalde, el jefe de policía y un buen número de curiosos, incluyendo los dos curas, estaban presentes en la escena. El teniente y Zoilo se hablaron a distancia para tratar de llegar a un acuerdo.

—El teniente reconoce vuestro interés por evitar que el puente se derribe —Ulmil anunció al público hablando a través de un megáfono, y poco después la gente se dispersó de forma pacífica.

Por coincidencia, aquel mismo día, la hija de Ulmil se casó con un diplomático en la iglesia de La Santa Cruz. El padre Guzmán llevó a cabo la ceremonia religiosa y luego asistió a la recepción de la boda en la casa del alcalde. Para la fiesta, se colocaron mesas y sillas en el jardín, y la gente circulaba por todas partes, charlando, riéndose, comiendo y bebiendo. La banda del pueblo tocó marimba. Cuando llegó el padre Guzmán se dirigió a la primera mesa bajo la sombra que vio, pero el Dr. Bruno le interceptó en su camino.

—Lionel —le llamó— Tengo buenas noticias para ti.

En privado el médico y el cura se tuteaban.

—Vamos a sentarnos primero, Julián —dijo Lionel, señalando la mesa bajo la sombra.

—¿Te traigo algo para tomar? —preguntó el médico.

—Sí, por favor, un ponche de ginebra.

El padre Guzmán fue a ocupar la mesa mientas el médico fue al rincón del jardín, donde se había instalado un bar provisional, y se hizo con la bebida. Dos personas habían ya ocupado la misma mesa; saludaron al párroco con una sonrisa, pero él no les habló. Cuando el médico se acercó a la mesa con la bebida, el padre Guzmán le preguntó de qué se trataba la notica. Las otras dos personas se levantaron, inclinaron sus cabezas a modo de reverencia y se alejaron.

—El Gobierno ha aprobado todo lo que le pedimos en la carta al Obispo —dijo el médico.

—¿Sí? Me cuesta trabajo creer que…

—No solo eso, sino que también quieren facilitarte un jardín en la explanada de la iglesia.

El párroco se le quedó mirando con ojos muy abiertos.

—Pero yo no pedí ningún jardín —dijo.

—Es un regalo del gobierno.

Lionel Guzmán se disponía a añadir algo más cuando vio a Irma que llegaba inesperadamente a la mesa.

—Yo no me esperaba que ese hombre estuviera aquí en la boda —dijo Irma.

—¿A qué hombre te refieres? —preguntó el doctor.

—Al teniente.

—¿Qué hay de malo en ello? —Lionel preguntó.

—Ayer, fui a mi puesto en el Mercado —respondió Irma, con los ojos puestos en el párroco, y siguió—: El teniente me miró con ojos de lujuria —sacudió la cabeza hacia un lado para expresar disgusto y luego añadió—: Soy viuda y madre de este bebé. Odio a ese teniente. —A este punto comenzó a llorar.

La presencia de Irma, con el bebé a horcajadas sobre la cadera, los pechos maternales balanceándose sobre el agitado pecho, todo cuanto ella representaba, desencadenó en el sacerdote el deseo sexual. Se puso a rezar en silencio, sujetando el crucifijo con fuerza entre sus manos.

—Zoilo y el padre Palenque —Irma continuó hablando— piensan que el teniente y los otros extranjeros han venido aquí a oprimir al pobre y ensalzar al rico.

Con una mano se enjugó las mejillas. El padre Guzmán la miraba fijamente con la boca abierta y el labio inferior temblando; solamente los ojos expresaban su asombro. En aquel momento, los recién casados, junto al teniente y algunos invitados más, se les acercaron. "Por el próspero futuro de El Teso", brindó el teniente.

Irma apenas si pudo contener su ira. Se llevó la mano a la cabeza como para ajustarse la gruesa trenza de pelo negro que le caía por detrás del cuello y, apretando al bebé sobre su cuerpo, se alejó. La tensión que se había creado se disipó, y la fiesta siguió.

Cuando el padre Guzmán se disponía a despedirse de los anfitriones e irse de la fiesta, sin embargo, no se sintió bien. Había sido un largo y emocional día. Primero vino la protesta contra la demolición del Puente Antiguo por la mañana, luego la boda en la iglesia al mediodía y, finalmente, la celebración de la fiesta de recepción y la escena de conflicto entre Irma y el teniente. Trató de levantarse de la silla, pero los músculos se le acalambraron y sus piernas permanecieron rígidas.

—Te llevaré a casa —dijo el médico, y añadió—: Debes descansar, y pronto te sentirás mejor.

El doctor Julián Bruno había llegado a Piedras Blancas unos quince años antes de que el padre Lionel Guzmán empezara su misión en la parroquia de El Teso, y los dos hombres pronto se hicieron amigos. Para ver a sus enfermos, el médico iba de un lado para el otro en bicicleta hasta que compró una motocicleta Honda, que todavía la conservaba, y, más tarde, un Volkswagen Beetle de color negro.

Como el médico lo había anticipado en la boda de la hija de Ulmil, el anciano párroco mejoró en poco tiempo. Quería saber qué le pasó, pero no se atrevía a peguntar al médico. No se trataba de que le tuviera miedo a la muerte, sino más bien a quedarse inválido y, por consiguiente, incapaz de llevar a cabo los planes que tenía para la iglesia. El templo de la Santa Cruz, o su visión de una iglesia remodelada tanto en el interior como el exterior, representaba para él el símbolo de su legado como sacerdote del pueblo. "Mis manos tiemblan, Francisco, pero no me atrevo a consultar con Julián Bruno", le confió al joven sacerdote cuando éste vino a verle durante el tiempo que estuvo haciendo reposo en casa.

La casa del párroco era una modesta vivienda que consistía en un dormitorio, cuarto de baño, sala de estar, comedor, cocina y una sala que el cura usaba como despacho. Cuando Francisco vino a verle, los dos se sentaron en la sala de estar cerca de la ventana a través de la cual podían ver el volcán a lo lejos.

—¿Una copita de brandy? —preguntó el anciano cura.

—No, gracias.

—Yo lo probaré —dijo e hizo sonar una campanilla para llamar a su ama de casa y pedirle trajera la botella de brandy.

—¿Por qué no consultas con el curandero entonces? —Francis preguntó.

—¿Qué puedo alegar como motivo de mi consulta?

Francisco Palenque estiró sus piernas enfrente de él.

—Pues, pegúntale si sabe de alguna pócima que te pueda ayudar con el temblor —dijo.

—Preguntaré a Julián cuando me sienta más animado.

Indalecia volvió con la botella de brandy y dos copas en una bandeja, y Francisco sirvió una copa a Lionel Guzmán.

—Necesito unas manos más firmes que las mías para bregar con los asuntos de estos tiempos —dijo el párroco.

—Yo estoy aquí para ayudar.

—Parece que estos asuntos son más complicados de lo que uno pudiera anticipar.

—Las cosas nunca son cristalinas en tiempos de guerra —dijo Francisco con una sonrisa benevolente.

—Me doy cuenta de ello, pero lo que a mí me preocupa es la seguridad de nuestra comunidad.

Era ya de noche, y en la sala, que daba al norte, comenzaba a dar frio. El padre Guzmán hizo sonar la campanilla de nuevo para pedir a Indalecia que le trajera una manta.

—¿Cuál es el problema? —preguntó Francisco.

—Irma habla de que la gente tiene opiniones dispares cuando se trata de interpretar lo que está aconteciendo en el pueblo.

—Bueno, por supuesto, la división de opiniones es inevitable en estos casos.

Indalecia volvió a entrar en la sala trayendo una manta de lana.

—Ninguno de nosotros debe volverse político —dijo Lionel Guzmán, visiblemente más confortable con la manta sobre su vientre y el brandy en el cuerpo.

—Pero debemos comprometernos de alguna manera.

El padre Guzmán le miró con cara de preocupación.

—¿Tú no eres comunista, verdad? —le espetó.

Francisco no se inmutó. Se inclinó para coger la botella de brandy y sirvió otra copa a su máster.

—Irma habla de los "oprimidos" —insistió el párroco.

Francisco dejó la botella de brandy sobre la mesa. En público, él se había identificado así mismo como perteneciente a la clase pobre, nacido en el seno de una familia de labradores de las tierras altas.

—Hablemos con claridad —enfatizó, y añadió—: Nosotros, la gente maya, somos chapines de agudo instinto. En este país, las autoridades impiden nuestro progreso porque si progresamos no nos pueden manipular.

El anciano sacerdote se echó para atrás sobre el respaldo de la silla, cruzó los brazos sobre el pecho y dijo—: Espero que no te vuelvas político.

—Yo soy simplemente un catequista.

El padre Guzmán le sonrió con gesto de tolerancia.

—Lo que yo deseo es que nuestra iglesia luzca bien, como corresponde a la Casa de Dios —dijo en tono conclusivo.

Francisco Palenque se dedicó a enseñar el catecismo con todo ardor. Convenció a Dr. Bruno para que le vendiera la motocicleta Honda, ya que averiguó que el médico la usaba solo en raras ocasiones después que se compró el coche. En la moto, se aventuró a viajar por las tierras altas—Sololá, Cobán, Petén— donde el conflicto armado tomó raiz. Como consecuencia, el padre Guzmán notó un aumento en el número de feligreses, lo que le liberaba de la obligación de predicar para convertir a los paganos y le daba la oportunidad de concentrarse en acelerar el plan de mejora de la iglesia. La creación de un jardín en la explanada ya estaba en marcha, pero no los otros proyectos, ya que la Diócesis declaró que la implementación de los mismos iba a llevar algún tiempo.

Francisco Palenque se dio cuenta de la importancia de difundir la palabra adecuada entre todos aquellos que deseaban escuchar y, de este modo, promover la unificación. Entendió el concepto de economizar energía y se convirtió en defensor del pobre y oprimido. "Lo que necesitamos es de un lugar donde yo pueda enseñar a la gente a hablar con una sola voz", dijo al padre Guzmán.

El párroco escribió de nuevo al obispo, pidiendo autorización para explorar la posibilidad que Francisco apuntaba y, muy pronto, recibió el visto bueno para habilitar un edificio que estaba abandonado cerca de la autopista Panamericana y que se convirtió en el Centro de enseñanza del catecismo.

—¿De qué parte de la Biblia hablas a tu gente, Francisco? —Padre Guzmán quiso saber.

Los dos sacerdotes se paseaban en el casi finalizado jardín en la explanada de la iglesia una templada mañana al comienzo de noviembre. Querían familiarizarse con los nombres de los árboles y plantas que ya crecían allí.

—Sobre todo, les hablo del respeto que se debe al prójimo.

—Palo de jiote.

—¿Perdón?

—¡Oh! Estoy leyendo el nombre de este árbol escrito en el rótulo pegado al tronco.

Francisco puso atención al árbol que señalaba su maestro: estaba arrugado y carecía de hojas.

—Ya veo —dijo.

—Va a crecer como un árbol tortuoso —respondió el párroco en tanto echó a andar de nuevo. Pero pronto se detuvo y preguntó—: ¿Sabias eso?

—¿A qué se refiere?

—A que las ramas del palo de jiote crecen entrelazadas unas a las otras.

—Sí, lo sabía.

Se acercaron a otro árbol joven.

—Este es un ciprés —apuntó Guzmán y añadió: —Va a crecer bien derecho.

Francisco asintió con la cabeza.

—Antes te referiste… —El párroco se cortó hasta encontrar las palabras exactas—. Respeto al prójimo, dijiste.

Se pararon simultáneamente para observarse el uno al otro.

—Quise decir justicia y unión —replicó Francisco.

—Esos conceptos son difíciles de explicar.

Los dos se sonrieron amablemente y continuaron su paseo.

—¿Quiere decir que suenan a política? —dijo Palenque.

—Quiero decir que el teniente puede estar en desacuerdo con el modo en que tú enseñas el catecismo. Es algo…

—¿Tortuoso?

—No es derecho como el ciprés.

Francisco se separó de su compañero y, según caminaba, comenzó a hablar a las flores de forma enfática y como si fueran su audiencia: "El Amor, según enseña Cristo, consiste en romperse el lomo si es preciso con tal de ayudar al prójimo, y ello sin pedir nada a cambio".

—Eso es hablar bien, en cristiano —asintió Guzmán.

—Lo sé. Por algo soy jesuita. Pero no estoy convencido de que todo lo que se dice que Jesucristo enseñó sea verdad.

En aquel momento, oyeron la voz de Indalecia que, de pie a la puerta de la casa del párroco, le llamaba:

—Le llaman al teléfono —dijo.

El párroco se detuvo por un instante y luego dijo—: Lo siento, Francisco, pero debo volver a casa. Continuaremos el paseo por el jardín en otra ocasión.

A continuación se dio la vuelta y, arrastrando un poco los pies, fue a contestar el teléfono, mientras que Francisco continuó explorando el nuevo jardín.

Los cambios que acontecían en el pueblo no se sucedían de un modo suave. No todo el mundo se beneficiaba de las mejoras introducidas, o no en la misma medida, en particular los trabajadores agrícolas. Los celos y el deseo de venganza proliferaban en el renaciente El Teso Pueblo. Las familias cuyos hijos tuvieron que aceptar el patrullar las calles como civiles, apartados de los campos de cultivo, notaron la disminución en el volumen de producción de los cereales. También se produjeron hechos inesperados. Irma, por ejemplo, se fue a vivir con el teniente. Bajo su protección, ella se convirtió en líder de un grupo de mujeres bordadoras y tejedoras de cestos que ella unificó para formar una cooperativa y facilitar el comercio de exportación de sus trabajos. El padre Guzmán vio la conducta de Irma como una traición y rehusó rezar por ella, según su sacristán declaró, más tarde, que había dicho.

En medio de este panorama de cambios, el padre Guzmán se despertó en la noche del once de diciembre sobresaltado al oír a gente que gritaba y aporreaba a su puerta. Le recordó la sensación de urgencia que Irma le transmitió la noche en que murió su marido. Trató de levantarse para ver de qué se trataba, pero su cuerpo se resistió a obedecer cualquier movimiento. La gente acumulada afuera de su puerta, sin embargo, no esperó a que él la abriera; la derribaron a golpes.

Julián Bruno, Ismael, Indalecia y un buen número de vecinos entraron en torbellino a su casa y en su habitación. Le ayudaron a levantarse y lo llevaron hasta la ventana, y entonces vio, bajo una luna llena, que su iglesia estaba en llamas; ardía por los cuatro costados. Él nunca había visto un fuego más espectacular. Le impresionó. "¿Por qué —murmuró— tiene que pasar eso?, ¿ese infierno?, ¿por qué?" Sintió opresión en el pecho, como si tuviera un torniquete apretándole el corazón, y, de repente, sus ojos cesaron de ver; se volvió ciego para cuanto le rodeaba. En su lugar, con los ojos de la mente vio una procesión de eventos ocurridos en su vida desfilar enfrente de él. ¿Estaba Dios enojado con él debido a la actitud pecaminosa que había adoptado frente a Irma? No obstante, él era consciente de que, a pesar de sus debilidades, nunca se había pasado de límites. Aunque durante su vida de sacerdote había tenido que combatir momentos de lujuria, el echar mano del crucifijo que siempre llevaba consigo le salvó de caer en la tentación. Hubo veces en las que dudó de su vocación religiosa, pero siempre se sometió a la voluntad de Dios. ¿A qué venía entonces este castigo de ver su iglesia en llamas?

—El Centro de catequesis del padre Palenque también está en llamas —dijo Julián Bruno, y sus palabras sacaron al párroco de su estado de confusión y volvió a ver la iglesia en llamas.

—¿Dónde se halla Francisco? —Lionel Guzmán preguntó.

—Los guerrilleros lo aprehendieron.

El anciano sacerdote se sintió traicionado. Pensó que Francisco había prendido los fuegos a propósito porque él —Lionel Guzmán— no le facilitaba toda la ayuda que necesitaba para llevar a cabo su cruzada contra los que oprimen al humilde y al pobre. De repente, dio un puñetazo al cristal de la ventana con fuerza inesperada.

—¿Es Francisco comunista? —preguntó enfadado, con sus ojos fijos en el fuego.

—Cálmese, Padre, por favor —Ismael dijo y añadió—: No, no lo es.

Al oir estas palabras, el padre Guzmán se calmó.

—¿Por qué entonces… —parecía no estar seguro de lo que quería saber.

—Es un defensor del Nuevo Cristo —le cuchicheó Ismael al oído.

El párroco se volvió hacia él por un instante, su cara enrojecida debido al reflejo de las llamas a través de la ventana, y volviendo a mirar afuera preguntó—: ¿A qué te refieres?

El fuego crecía a marcha agigantada. Ese era el edificio de su iglesia, símbolo de su dedicación a la causa de Dios, su única finalidad en la vida, y de su entrega a hacer de su parroquia en el Teso Pueblo un modelo de obediencia al Señor. Tal destrucción constituía una pérdida indescriptible para él.

Las motas de ceniza flotaban en el aire y sus siluetas, iluminadas por la luz de la luna, se asemejaban a bandadas de pájaros de mal agüero que la brisa empujaba hacia el nuevo jardín en la explanada.

—Han acusado a Francisco de pertenecer al ejército guerrillero de los pobres —declaró el doctor Bruno.

—¿Es él, de verdad, un guerrillero? —el párroco preguntó, sus ojos todavía en las llamas y las cenizas.

—No —contestó el médico, y añadió—: Él es un catequista.

Lionel Guzmán, sus manos temblorosas, se retiró de la ventana e hizo intención de acercarse a Julián Bruno.

—¿Crees que el Ejército lo va a ejecutar? —preguntó.

—Sus enseñanzas implican que los pobres pueden y deben tener acceso al poder —dijo Julián y añadió—: Esa es la razón por la que los militares, en venganza, están quemando iglesias y lugares donde se enseña el catecismo y deteniendo a los que allí predican, desde las tierras altas hasta El Teso.

Mientras el médico hablaba, entró más gente en la casa del párroco. Lionel Guzmán creyó ver a Irma entre los recién llegados y se le aceleró el pulso, pero se equivocó. Se preguntó a qué bando ella se inclinaba. Entonces, se volvió otra vez hacia el médico y, de sopetón, dijo—: Julián, ¿cuál es mi mal?

—Tú tienes la enfermedad de Parkinson.

El padre Guzmán asintió con la cabeza como indicando que él sabía todo acerca de esa enfermedad.

—Indalecia! —llamó a su ama de casa y dijo—: Ayúdeme, por favor, a volver a mi cama.

Indalecia le ayudó a acostarse y, en poco tiempo, se quedó dormido con el crucifijo entre sus temblorosos dedos.

El Paseante

Luis Vela había adoptado el Decálogo de cadetes del ejército de su país como su modelo de conducta y etiqueta.

"Algún día, vas a superar a tu padre en rango", su madre había proclamado cuando Luis, a los dieciocho años, ingresó en la Academia general militar. Después de graduarse como alférez, sin embargo, declinó la oportunidad de desplazarse voluntariamente al Sahara Occidental para defender las colonias españolas de la invasión Marroquí. Él mismo se hizo consciente, entonces, de que le gustaba todo lo militar excepto ir a la guerra. Su padre, antes de fallecer, había alcanzado el rango de Coronel, pero Luis, hijo único, a los cincuenta y ocho años, llevaba en las hombreras de su uniforme el emblema de Capitán. Ya no había mucho tiempo para ascender, todo lo que él podía hacer era olvidar su pasado de eludir un deber moral que, así lo entendía, iba en contra del dictum en el Decálogo: Ser voluntario para todo tipo de sacrificios, solicitando y deseando ser nombrado para entrar en acción y afrontar las situaciones más arriesgadas.

El día de San Valentín, en el año 2008, el Capitán Vela, hombre soltero, paseaba por las calles de la ciudad bajo la lluvia. Cuando era un joven oficial, se las había apañado para ob-tener un puesto en la enseñanza militar y quedarse en Madrid;

enseñaba las Reglas militares de conducta y urbanidad a soldados alistados en la Reserva. De alrededor de un metro noventa
de estatura, en su uniforme, que se lo ponía solo en ocasiones
especiales, caminaba manteniendo la compostura de buen militar, oliendo a loción Old Spice y, llevado por la magia del
día, imaginándose encontrar la mujer de sus sueños y enamo-
rarse de ella. Pero al anochecer, aún caminando en solitario, sin
suerte, se sintió cansado. Gruesas gotas de agua se estrellaban
en su paraguas abierto, resbalaban por la curvatura, salpicaban
sus botas y caían al pavimento. "Monotonía y aburrimiento",
murmuró para sí.

Luis Vela siguió caminando y, después de un tiempo, se
encontró en la proximidad del Casino Militar, un elegante club
de oficiales, el cual siempre le servía de campo de experimenta-
ción para exhibirse y mostrar sus nobles cualidades. Le gustaba
llegar vestido con su uniforme, acicalado, y jugar al billar con
sus compañeros oficiales o bailar con algunas de las señoritas
que frecuentaban el club y le admiraban. Era consciente, sin
embargo, de que últimamente, entrado ya en los cincuenta,
su popularidad en el club estaba decayendo (aunque no veía
la razón). De repente, se paró en seco en medio de la acera, se
dio la media vuelta y se alejó. Apretó su marcha bajo el paraguas, como alguien que huye del diablo, sin prestar atención a
la gente con la que se cruzaba o los escaparates con toda clase
de regalos para el día de San Valentín. No obstante, aunque
distraído, algo que vio le hizo acordarse del Café Paraíso, que
quedaba no lejos de donde él se encontraba. Le gustaba este
café, siempre tan animado. A menudo iba allí, se sentaba en un
taburete cerca del mostrador y observaba a la gente que había.

Aquella noche, Luis también fue al Café Paraíso. El lugar
estaba animadísimo. Se dio cuenta de que, al entrar, un par
de mujeres jóvenes se volvieron para mirarle con gesto de

admiración y se sintió satisfecho de su pose. Echó una mirada a su alrededor para ver si había algún sitio libre cuando sus ojos se tropezaron con la presencia de un hombre delgado, de facciones serias, con barba de chivo, vestido con chaqueta de pana marrón, que estaba sentado solo en una mesa para dos, situada cerca de la ventana. Notó que el único hueco libre estaba allí, al lado de aquel hombre. Pero a Luis Vela le dio la impresión de que había algo raro en el individuo que la ocupaba. Dudó si aproximarse a él y preguntar si podía compartir su mesa, pues el hombre parecía un esqueleto. Indeciso, sacudió su paraguas, que sostenía semiabierto, de forma refleja, y las gotas de agua salpicaron a su alrededor y en parte alcanzaron a mojar la chaqueta del individuo en cuestión.

—Perdone —se excusó Vela.

El hombre hizo un gesto de indiferencia como indicando que a él las gotas de agua le traían sin cuidado.

—En realidad —se arrancó Vela a decir— yo venía a preguntar si no le importa que compartamos la mesa.

Luis Vela oyó un pitido intermitente que parecía se originaba dentro del pecho del hombre allí sentado, ¿sus pulmones? No le pareció prudente sentarse a su lado y le entró el deseo de huir.

—No soy muy hablador —dijo el hombre con voz grave.

Luis Vela carraspeó.

—Pues, yo tampoco soy muy hablador, que digamos —dijo con cortesía y se sentó en la otra silla con precaución.

Intercambiaron una breve mirada y enseguida ambos se pusieron a mirar a través de la ventana como si esperaran ver pasar a alguien conocido. Afuera, ya era de noche, aunque todavía no se habían encendido las luces. Uno de los camareros se aproximó a la mesa con prisas.

—Un café, por favor —dijo Luis Vela, después de percatarse que su acompañante también estaba tomando café.

Los dos hombres se echaron una mirada otra vez. Vela calculó que el otro tendría unos cincuenta y tantos años. ¡Pero estaba tan demacrado! Por algún tiempo, ambos se mantuvieron en silencio, cada cual girando la cabeza de vez en cuando para mirar por la ventana. Pero cuando el camarero regresó con el café, ellos aprovecharon el momento para mirarse con más detenimiento.

—¿Está usted casado? —preguntó el hombre extraño.

Luis Vela sintió el deseo de levantarse e irse de allí, pero se contuvo y dijo—: No.

A tres mesas de distancia se sentaban dos mujeres jóvenes. Hablaban en voz alta y se reían a carcajadas, llamando la atención de mucha gente. Una era de constitución menuda, pálida, con un delicado toque de carmín en los labios. La otra era regordeta, con cara de pan y labios carnosos, y tenía el pelo teñido del color del limón. Ambas llevaban blusas de colores chillones, muy escotadas.

—Dos rameras, ¿no cree? —el hombre preguntó, apuntando a las dos mujeres.

—Eso parecen.

—Es una pena que las mujeres que conozco no toleren mi problema —dijo el hombre de forma tajante.

Luis Vela se sorprendió.

—¿Qué quiere usted decir?

—Yo padezco de fibrosis pulmonar —dijo el otro y clavó sus ojos en Vela.

Éste detuvo la respiración. ¿Era compasión o curiosidad lo que sentía por aquel individuo?

—¿Cuánto tiempo lleva usted enfermo?

—De joven, trabajé como aprendiz de electricista, pero tuve que dejarlo porque me entraba fatiga y me quedaba corto de aire.

Al parecer ambos hombres se olvidaron de que habían dicho que no eran habladores. Luis chasqueó la lengua, y luego tomó un sorbo de café.

—¿De joven, dice usted?

—Así es. Hasta la fecha, vengo cobrando una pensión. Claro, vivo solo, y eso ayuda. Me llamo Ramiro.

Ahora Vela entendió que sentía compasión más que curiosidad por el pobre diablo.

—Mucho gusto en conocerle, Ramiro.

Se dieron la mano. Luis Vela se imaginó que Ramiro era como un soldado herido, alguien que necesitaba ayuda. Tomó otro sorbo de café, y el calorcito en la boca le confortó.

—¿Cómo se las arregla, Ramiro, para salir adelante, estando enfermo?

—Me doy paseos.

Luis Vela no pudo contener la risa. ¿Estaba Ramiro de broma?

—¿Quiere decir que todo lo que hace es andar de aquí para allá paseando?

—Eso mismo.

Se miraron de frente. Vela leyó en la cara de Ramiro que lo que decía iba en serio. Entonces, Ramiro añadió—: Le sorprendería saber, si le dijera, cuantos chismes se oyen mientras uno deambula por las calles.

A qué clase de chismes se refería Ramiro, Vela no se lo imaginaba. Pues él mismo se había pasado el día paseando por las calles, antes de entrar en el café, con la esperanza de encontrar el amor, pero hallando nada sino soledad. Perplejo, desvió su atención de Ramiro y miró a su alrededor. Una mujer de mediana edad, que llevaba un sombrerito, estaba sentada en un taburete, tomando algo en el bar. En aquel mismo momento la mujer encendió un cigarrillo. ¿Por qué estará sola? Después de una pausa volvió a poner su atención en su compañero.

—¿No se cansa, Ramiro, de andar paseando por las calles todo el día?

—No, si hago pausas para descansar.

—Ya veo. Bueno, déjeme que me presente: Me llamo Luis Vela, Capitán del ejército de tierra.

—Pues mucho gusto en conocerle. Me he dado cuenta de que usted lleva su uniforme con mucha clase, Capitán.

Vela aceptó el cumplido de manera natural.

—Gracias —dijo.

—¿Está usted en activo?

—Sí, por ahora, pero ya estoy pensando en jubilarme. Como usted, yo también vivo solo.

Se hizo un silencio, y luego Luis Vela añadió—: ¿Se toma otro café?

—Muchas gracias, pero solo tomo un café al día.

Sobrevino otro momento de silencio. Vela dirigió su mirada de nuevo a la mujer sentada en el bar. Ramiro rompió el silencio—: ¿Le gusta observar a la gente, Capitán?

Eso hizo que Vela volviera a entrar en la conversación—: Perdone, Ramiro, me distraje un poco. Me estaba preguntando quién puede ser la mujer tan encantadora que está allí sentada, en el bar.

—¿De veras? ¿Y quién sabe?

Ramiro comenzó también a ojear a su alrededor.

—Capitán, mire por favor a aquella pareja —dijo y apuntó en la dirección de una mesa cercana donde se sentaban un oficial y una mujer.

Vela los miró. Pensó que la mujer era bonita y que el oficial de marina parecía tener ojos solo para ella.

—¿Qué le ve a esa pareja de extraordinario? —preguntó Vela.

—Nada. Solo me pregunto si hoy salen juntos por primera vez.

—¿Qué le hace pensar eso, Ramiro?

—Bueno, pues el ver la atención que ella le pone y lo compuesto que él se mantiene, y…

—En asuntos de amor. Algunos tienen más suerte que otros —tajó Luis Vela.

El Decálogo señalaba que uno debería ponerse contento de los éxitos alcanzados por otros oficiales. Pero en aquel momento, al ver la felicidad reflejada en la cara del oficial de marina mientras que él, el Capitán Vela, permanecía sentado allí, enfrente de aquel hombre enfermo, se sintió como si él fuera el soldado herido.

—A propósito —dijo Ramiro—, me pregunto, Capitán, por qué sigue soltero.

Luis Vela se quedó pensativo. Algunos años antes estuvo casado con la hija de un portugués, cirujano militar, que vivían en Madrid. Se conocieron en el Club de Oficiales; le pareció que ella era una mujer encantadora y elegante, vestida siempre como una princesa. Pero con el tiempo resultó ser una mujer antojadiza, y él comprendió que había cometido un error al casarse con ella. A los cuatro años de casados, se divorciaron. La familia portuguesa regresó a Lisboa, y él nunca más supo de su ex mujer.

—Yo estuve casado por unos años, aunque no tuvimos hijos —contestó.

—¿Es que su mujer falleció?

Luis Vela puso los codos sobre la mesa y la barbilla entre las manos.

—Nos divorciamos. Ya todo está olvidado. Yo tenía treinta y dos años cuando nos casamos —contestó, y al pronunciar estas palabras sintió soledad, ansiedad de hacer nuevos amigos, de encontrar el amor.

Ramiro comenzó a rotar su taza de café sobre el platillo.

—¿Cómo se las apaña viviendo solo, Capitán?

Vela notó el sarcasmo en la pregunta. Pero, ciertamente, ¿cómo le iba viviendo solo?

—No tengo muchas obligaciones. De vez en cuando, voy con algún otro aficionado a la caza de la perdiz.

—¿No tiene novia?

Ramiro miró de reojo a Vela, y éste insinuó una sonrisa.

—No, solo un puñado de amigas, sin compromiso. Como le digo, vivo solo, no muy lejos de aquí. A menudo vengo a este café y trato de conocer a gente.

—Entiendo.

Luis Vela empezó a rotar también su taza de café y a campanillear tocando el mango con la cucharilla del azúcar.

—Esta tarde, hace unas horas, conocí a una mujer que se llama Lola —soltó Ramiro de improviso.

Vela paró de juguetear con la taza.

—¿Es bonita?

—Bueno, a mí me gustan las mujeres de cadera ancha —contestó Ramiro.

Los ojos de Luis Vela se avivaron. Hizo una seña al camarero para que se acercara.

—Otros dos cafés, por favor —pidió cuando el camarero se acercó a la mesa.

Ramiro, sin embargo, movió la cabeza en sentido negativo.

—No más café para mí, gracias —dijo y enseguida volvió al tema de la conversación—: Lola es mi tipo de mujer, Capitán. Tiene un cuerpo regordete como el de una perdiz. No sé si me entiende.

A Luis Vela le gustó la comparación.

—A mí me gusta todo lo relacionado con la perdiz —dijo.

Los dos hombres intercambiaron una mirada de cómplices.

—Pero la dichosa fibrosis se interpone en mi camino —Ramiro continuó.

—¡Ah, claro! Lo siento.

Ramiro comenzó a tamborilear en la mesa con los dedos mientras Luis se esforzaba en ocultar su ansiedad por oír la historia de Lola.

—Lola aterrizó en Madrid desde Colombia —dijo Ramiro como si leyera la mente de su compañero de mesa.

—¿Por qué vino a Madrid?

Ramiro parecía animado a contar su historia.

—En Colombia era una madre soltera y vivía con su propia madre en algún pueblito. Pero tanto la madre como el hijo murieron en una refriega urbana. Los guerrilleros empezaron a tiros, sin miramientos, mientras buscaban en las casas a uno de sus compañeros que había desaparecido. Después de la tragedia, Lola se encontró con que no tenía ahorros, ni ingresos. Estaba desesperada por encontrar algún trabajo, y a través del Internet halló una oferta para trabajar en limpiar casas aquí, en Madrid. Consiguió un permiso de trabajo y vino.

Vela percibió que Ramiro parecía fatigado y para darle tiempo a que se recuperara, él se puso a mirar en silencio a las dos jóvenes y risueñas mujeres. La regordeta se retocaba los labios con una barra de carmín. Él se imaginó a Lola en el cuerpo de aquella mujer.

—¿Es Lola joven? —preguntó.

—Probablemente ella sea unos quince años más joven que yo —calculó Ramiro y añadió—: A ella le ha ido bien en Madrid hasta el mes pasado en que se quedó sin trabajo.

Vela observó más detenidamente la cara de Ramiro: la nariz aguileña, los pómulos hundidos, los labios finos y la barba de chivo le causaban una impresión de fantasma.

—¿Puede usted ayudarla? —preguntó.

Ramiro sacudió la cabeza negativamente.

—Lola no tiene dinero suficiente ni para pagar la renta de su habitación.

—¡Ahí está! Puede llevarla a vivir en su casa, ¿no? —dijo Vela y abrió sus brazos en gesto de acogimiento.

Ramiro se echó para atrás en la silla.

—Estoy enfermo, pero no soy un aprovechao —dijo con vehemencia y añadió—: Yo no sangro a las mujeres sin techo.

Vela notó que las manos le temblaban a Ramiro, aunque mostraba tener algo de energía en reserva.

—Lo siento, Ramiro, no quise ofenderle.

Ramiro entonces se inclinó hacia adelante sobre la mesa y se acercó a Vela.

—Yo estoy cabreado debido a mi condición —le susurró, y Vela oyó ahora el pitido de su pecho más claramente.

Ramiro volvió a reclinarse sobre el respaldo de la silla.

—Yo vislumbré a Lola en la Casa de Campo, cerca de la entrada al zoológico —continuó—. Me imagino que usted sabe que por allí rondan las putas.

Luis Vela asintió con la cabeza, y Ramiro prosiguió—: Me acerqué a ella. Me pareció que estaba a punto de convertirse ella misma en puta, en este día de San Valentín. Me dijo que necesitaba dinero urgentemente.

—¿Y qué hizo usted?

—Pensé llevármela a casa, como usted ha sugerido, pero no habría sido honesto.

Vela trató de recordar alguno de los puntos del Decálogo que se relacionara con lo que Ramiro decía, pero nada le vino a la memoria, lo cual le disgustó, pues hasta entonces había pensado que el contenido del Decálogo abarcaba todos los aspectos de la conducta.

—Bueno, vivimos en un país libre, en el que usted puede hacer lo que crea conveniente, siempre y cuando se atenga a la ley —dijo y respiró hondo, convencido de que acababa de decir algo profundo y justo.

—¡Pero yo estoy enfermo, demonios!

Luis Vela reflexionó: en verdad que Ramiro es un soldado herido y se le debe excusar de participar en combate.

—Por supuesto, usted debe de tener siempre en cuenta la condición de sus pulmones antes de entrar en acción —dijo.

—Acaba de dar en el clavo, Capitán. Ese es mi dilema. Yo entiendo que la excitación que acompaña a las relaciones sexuales puede empeorar mi condición, pero, por otro lado, el quedarse pasivo, no actuar como hombre, hiere mis sentimientos.

En aquel momento, Vela sintió admiración por Ramiro.

—¿Cree usted que yo le puedo ayudar?

—Bien visto, Capitán, mi dilema es mi dilema.

En aquel momento se oyó una risa estrepitosa que venía de las dos mujeres alegres.

—Y, hablando de faldas, —Vela cambió de conversación para dar a Ramiro un respiro— ¿Cuál de aquellas dos mujeres le es más atractiva?

—La misma que lo es para usted, Capitán —Ramiro contestó enseguida.

—Pero usted no puede saber cuál de las dos me gusta más.

—Oh, sí, claro que lo sé. Lo leí en la expresión de su cara mientras yo le describía el cuerpo de Lola.

A Vela no le quedó otra alternativa sino aceptar el hecho de que su compañero poseía un olfato muy fino.

—No obstante, yo me casé con una mujer delgada —dijo.

—Tal vez ese sea su dilema, Capitán. Se casó con una mujer delgada, pero a usted le gustan las mujeres regordetas, como aquella de allí, la que lleva el pelo teñido de amarillo.

Vela no respondió. Cambió de postura en la silla como si se sintiera incómodo. Miró la hora.

—Perdone, Ramiro, pero debo irme.

Se levantó, se echó el paraguas bajo el brazo y se cercioró de que su unirme estaba correctamente abotonado.

—Un placer conocerle, Ramiro.

—Lo mismo digo, Luis, perdón, Capitán Vela —al hablar, Ramiro hizo un gesto como de levantarse por cortesía.

—No, por favor —Vela dijo—, no se moleste usted.

Se dieron la mano. Vela, manteniendo su compostura, se alejó hacia la salida, pero antes de salir oyó la voz de Ramiro que le llamaba.

—Capitán, espero que no se olvide de mí en caso de que perezca en la contienda como un buen soldado.

Aún a la distancia, Vela notó tristeza en los ojos de Ramiro.

—He dejado el número de mi teléfono escrito en la servilleta de papel, sobre la mesa. Un oficial siempre debe velar por sus soldados, Ramiro.

El Capitán Vela abandonó el Café Paraíso. Afuera había cesado de llover, pero los regatos de agua todavía corrían a lo largo de las calzadas hacia las cloacas. Hacía frio, pero por dondequiera se veía gente que entraban y salían de los comercios, los cafés, los cines y el Metro. A medida que caminaba, Vela notó una cacofonía en sus oídos: el pitido de los pulmones de Ramiro, las risotadas de las dos mujeres festivas e incluso las gotas de agua que aún caían de los aleros al pavimento. Al cabo, estos ruidos cesaron, y entonces sintió que algo le faltaba, que echaba de menos la compañía de Ramiro. Se preguntaba si alguna vez él había hablado a alguien más con tanta sinceridad como lo acababa de hacer con Ramiro. No obstante dudaba si Ramiro y él podrían hacerse amigos íntimos. Ramiro no tenía más ocupación que deambular por las calles, era un hombre decrépito que parecía estar al final de sus días, mientras que él, el Capitán Luis Vela, era un hombre importante, sano y de buenas maneras.

Cuando llegó a su casa, se quitó el uniforme y se puso el pijama. Entró en el salón, se sirvió un whiskey y se sentó enfrente de la tele. Esperaba entretenerse mirando los deportes y parar de pensar en Ramiro. Pero fue en vano, pues la visión del hombre enfermo, con su respiración ruidosa y su dilema acerca de qué hacer con Lola, le atormentaba. Sin poder concentrarse en nada más, apagó la tele, se sirvió otro whiskey y, tumbado en el sofá, dejó que su mente especulara sobre Ramiro y Lola hasta que, rendido, se durmió.

Cuando despertó a la mañana siguiente, viernes, eran pasadas las diez. Otra vez pensó en Ramiro y deseó que le telefoneara. Pero más que nada, deseaba saber más acerca de Lola. Mientras se arreglaba el bigote en frente del espejo, se la imaginó: más bien bajita, de cuerpo macizo como el de una perdiz y oliendo a bosque. Se la imaginaba joven, de pechos firmes, muslos sólidos y nalgas… Se excitó. Guardaba la esperanza de que Ramiro le llamara para presentarle a Lola.

Se preparó un café y se sentó a la mesa de la cocina a hacer planes para el fin de semana. Pensó en ir a los establos militares y montar a caballo. Comenzó a poner en una bolsa el pantalón y las botas de montar cuando de repente se le ocurrió que tal vez podría encontrarse con Ramiro paseando por las calles. Entonces, aprisa, se puso ropa cómoda, agarró el abrigo y una visera de cuero del perchero, y salió a la calle.

Un sol de invierno caldeaba los edificios y el pavimento, que aparecía más limpio que de costumbre debido a la lluvia de la noche anterior. A esa hora, las calles estaban casi vacías de gente. Se echó a andar despacio y sin rumbo. Su deambular le llevó hasta el Club de Oficiales. Sintió la tentación de entrar a tomar un Martini en el bar, pero enseguida desistió de su propia idea, temeroso de que su presencia no despertara la admiración de otros tiempos. Siguió andando, como lo había hecho el día anterior, el día de San Valentín, bajo la lluvia.

Al anochecer se encontró, sin haberse percatado de ello, en el Parque de la Casa de Campo, cerca del zoológico. Pensaba en Lola, en la Lola que se había forjado en la imaginación a partir de las descripciones que Ramiro había hecho de la Lola real. Miraba de reojo a toda mujer con la que se cruzaba y que tenía pinta de ser una prostituta con la esperanza de divisar a Lola entre ellas. Estaba poseído de un alto sentido del deber, deduciendo que, como Oficial del ejército, tenía la obligación de salvar a Lola de hundirse en una vida depravada. Recordó lo que el Decálogo dictaba a ese respecto: tener la determinación de resolver problemas. De repente, se le ocurrió que tal vez Ramiro se había llevado a Lola a su casa la noche anterior, después de que saliera del café Paraíso e, instintivamente, se fue del parque con mucha prisa, como alguien que teme llegar tarde a una cita importante, y tomó un taxi hasta el Café Paraíso.

Dentro del café, se dirigió al sitio dónde Ramiro y él se habían sentado la noche anterior, pero Ramiro no estaba allí. Durante un segundo pensó que a lo mejor se había muerto. Miró a su alrededor buscando otras caras conocidas, pero solo reconoció al camarero que les había servido. Su presencia, sin embargo, lo tranquilizó, comprobando que la gente no se muere tan de un repente como él se había figurado respecto a Ramiro. Se disponía a salir cuando se fijó en un hombre todo arrugado que ocupaba una mesa en un rincón. Algo hizo que se acercará a él.

—¡Válgame Dios!

Era Ramiro, quien, a pesar de mostrar una muy penosa respiración, parecía estar contento.

—¡Luis!, digo, Capitán Vela, me alegro de verle. ¿Quiere sentarse con nosotros y tomar un café?

Vela se sobresaltó. Se llevó la mano al pecho porque temía que su corazón se le salía.

—¿Está Lola en el Café? —preguntó asustado, con una voz débil.

—Va a llegar enseguida para recogerme. Desde anoche vive conmigo. Estoy feliz, ya no tengo deseos de pasear por las calles.

A Vela le entraron deseos de salir corriendo, pero las piernas no le obedecieron. Le dolía el pecho. En un abrir y cerrar de ojos, se desplomó al suelo. El camarero llamó a una ambulancia y los paramédicos condujeron al oficial al hospital más próximo.

Dos semanas después, cuando aún se encontraba convaleciente después de sufrir un infarto, seguía rumiando, obsesionado con Lola y Ramiro, esperando que él le llamara, deseoso de saber de Lola. Una noche en que salió a pasear por las calles de su barrio antes de cenar, su teléfono móvil sonó. Esperaba que fuera Ramiro quien le llamaba, pero fue Lola.

—¿Hola? Soy Lola. Llamo para informarle de que Ramiro falleció anoche de un ataque al corazón —dijo sin preámbulos y añadió—: El número de su teléfono estaba en el suyo.

Luis Vela se sintió anonadado y lleno de remordimiento.

—Yo estaba esperando que Ramiro me llamara.

—Lo sé. Él iba a llamarle por la mañana, pero murió mientras dormía.

Hubo un silencio y luego Vela volvió a hablar—: He pensado mucho en usted, Lola.

—Ramiro me presentó a su hermana —dijo ella— Son buena gente. En dos días será el funeral.

—¿Puedo ayudarla en algo? —Vela intentaba recuperar su compostura, bloquear cualquier sentimiento de culpa.

—Ramiro le apreciaba, Capitán.

—Lo que usted necesite, Lola…

No pudo terminar su frase; el corazón le latía con fuerza y la respiración se le aceleró.

—Yo solo quiero que se haga justicia para con mi madre y mi hijo.

—Yo haré lo que usted me pida, Lola. Puedo llevarle de vuelta a Colombia si eso es lo que desea —Vela habló rápido, como en un susurro.

—¿Por qué razón? —Lola preguntó y repitió la pregunta—: ¿Por qué razón lo haría usted?

Vela hizo una pausa, reteniendo su respiración.

—Yo creo…Yo creo que la amo —musitó.

—¡Pero si usted ni siquiera me ha visto!

—Me basta con lo que Ramiro me dijo de usted. El resto yo puedo imaginarlo…

—¿Me ayudaría usted a encontrar los asesinos de mi familia?

A Vela la pregunta le sonó a reto.

—¿Qué insinúa?

—No insinuó, me refiero a los guerrilleros que mataron a mi madre y a mi hijo sin razón alguna.

Luis Vela se vio acorralado.

—Soy hombre de principios —dijo en tono energético.

—Pues, bien, Capitán, yo sé dónde encontrar a esos canallas y cómo combatirles.

—Odio la guerra —afirmó Vela.

Se acordó de las veces que había declinado el ir de voluntario a luchar por una causa y sus dientes le rechinaron.

—Y a pesar de todo, Capitán, guerra es lo que tenemos en Colombia.

—Odio la guerra —repitió Vela— y esta vez su voz le resultó a él mismo extraña.

—Si así es, Capitán, usted debe guiarse por sus principios y yo por los míos de mujer.

El Capitán Vela se sintió indefenso, muy solo. Se paró inmóvil en medio de la acera, cerca de casa, con el móvil en la mano temblorosa, procurando regular su respiración, con dolor en su corazón y perdida la fe en el Decálogo, pero sin idea de a quién acudir para encontrar alguna satisfacción en su vida.

Una hermosa tarde en abril

No sabía de mi hermano Serafín desde que salí de Madrid para Bilbao hacía tres meses. Un día, mientras me afeitaba, satisfecho de mi imagen en el espejo, acicalándome antes de salir para encontrarme con mi nueva novia y divertirnos, sonó el teléfono.

—Hola, Eugenio, soy Melisa.

Hablaba con voz debil.

—¿Qué pasa?

Melisa y Serafín se conocieron en el primer año de universidad y se casaron tres años más tarde, cuando ambos tenían veinte años. Melisa se había comportado como una adolescente rebelde, y yo no podía evitar el desconfiar de ella como esposa. Fue hija de madre soltera, quién la crió como hija única hasta los nueve años y luego se casó con un viejo viudo, quien, según Serafín, era muy crítico de Melisa.

—Se trata de tu hermano…

Pulsé el ícono del altavoz. Ella siguió—: Se está volviendo una persona muy extraña.

—¿Qué quieres decir?

Contuve mi respiración. Siempre he vivido con la aprehensión de que algo malo le iba a ocurrir a mi hermano. Aunque no sabría cómo justificar mi ansiedad al respecto, las palabras de Melisa hicieron que mi corazón se acelerara como cuando uno anticipa un mal augurio. De niño, con frecuencia me despertaba a media noche sobresaltado por las voces de mis padres que reñían, y entonces oía a Serafín, que lloraba. Lleno de ansiedad, aún en aquel entonces, yo pensaba que mi hermano iba a necesitar que yo le protegiera en el futuro. Y Serafín siempre me ha visto como si yo fuera un viejo amigo.

—No te lo puedo explicar por teléfono —dijo ella— Y añadió—: ¿Piensas volver a Madrid pronto?

—No, no pronto —contesté con aplomo.

Tengo veintisiete años, estoy soltero, trabajo de conservador con La Alianza Española de museos, ahora en Bilbao cumpliendo una tarea temporal en el Guggenheim, y estoy saliendo con una chica que me gusta un montón. Así que, no, no tenía planes de regresar a mi apartamento de Madrid en fecha próxima. Además, como digo, Melisa y yo nunca nos hemos llevado bien. ¿A santo de qué ella quería verme en lugar de hablar al teléfono?

—Por favor, ven —ella dijo con voz apagada.

Mi hermano me había contado algunas de las bravatas de Melisa cuando ella era más joven. En una ocasión, Serafín se enteró de que ella había tenido un aborto, antes de que se casaran, y a él le costó mucho el asimilarlo y vivir con el hecho. Cuando anunciaron que se iban a casar, yo me quedé pasmado de la noticia, pero no podía hacer nada para impedirlo. Y ahora, al teléfono, Melisa se niega a explicar cuál es la urgencia, lo que me irrita mucho, pues me imagino que se trate de algún problema de matrimonio y ella busque alguien que se lo resuelva.

Tan pronto como nos desconectamos del teléfono, mi primer impulso fue llamar a mi hermano. Pero pensándolo mejor, decidí conceder a Melisa, por una vez, el beneficio de la duda y mantener la privacidad de su llamada.

Al día siguiente, en Madrid, envié un mensaje a Melisa: "Nos podemos encontrar en el parque del Retiro, al lado del embarcadero". Era una hermosa tarde de abril, y me pareció que pasear al aire libre mientras hablábamos resultaría más relajante o menos conflictivo, en el caso de que lo que iba a decirme podría afectar mi relación con mi hermano, que si nos viéramos en casa. Melisa, morena, de pelo negro y melena corta, piernas largas y andar un tanto desgarbado, es fácil de identificar a distancia.

—Gracias por venir —dijo ella. Y enseguida—: ¿Cómo fue tu viaje?

—Sin ningún problema.

Melisa hizo un gesto como para darme un abrazo, pero yo instintivamente incliné un poco la cabeza hacia atrás porque no me encontraba dispuesto a aceptar su muestra de afecto sin saber antes lo que estaba en juego, y mi acción la disuadió de llevar a cabo su intención.

—¿Qué pasa? —pregunté al tiempo que comenzábamos a pasear a lo largo del lago.

—Pasear en El Retiro es siempre agradable.

Melisa llevaba una blusa gris de algodón, pantalones Capri y zapatos de tenis. Teníamos el lago a nuestra izquierda, y los jardines, arboles y senderos todo alrededor. En el aire se percibía un olor a hierba fresca.

—¿Cómo está Serafín? —Yo estaba impaciente por escuchar sus quejas. En contraste con mi modo de ser, dado a las reuniones sociales y a los amigos, Serafín es un tipo retraído. No le gustan las multitudes y prefiere actividades que se pueden hacer en solitario: navegar por el Internet, participar en juegos de videos y montar en su bicicleta.

Melisa giró su cabeza bruscamente hacia el lago como si de repente hubiera descubierto algún repulsivo lunar en mi mejilla, cuya presencia ella no pudiera soportar; dispersas en el lago flotaban algunas barcas de remo.

—El problema…—comenzó a decir, pero se calló porque un puñado de niños se nos cruzaron corriendo desde el área de juegos y la interrumpieron. Un par de ellos se disculparon mientras corrían.

—El Problema comenzó hace algún tiempo —continuó.

Y yo pensé, probablemente desde que se casaron. Un poco empujado por su mujer, Serafín dejó sus estudios para coger un empleo como dibujante en una compañía dedicada a diseñar instrumentos médicos. Habían alquilado un apartamento en un suburbio y necesitaban dinero para cubrir los gastos. Yo, entonces, entendí la urgencia económica, pero le advertí que tuviera cuidado no cortar sus estudios por mucho tiempo y arriesgar su futuro.

—¿Cuánto tiempo hace? —pregunté, tratando de aparentar mi neutralidad.

—Unos dos meses —dijo y se volvió hacia mí como queriendo analizar mi reacción. Y añadió—: Uno de sus compañeros en el trabajo me confió que Serafín estaba dejando sus dibujos sin terminar, para asombro de su jefe.

A mi hermano siempre se le dio bien el dibujo, desde niño. Le gustaba mucho y soñaba con hacerse diseñador profesional. Así que las palabras de Melisa, que él dejaba su trabajo sin terminar, me sonaron a algo fuera de lo normal.

—¿Por qué ha de hacer tal cosa?

Melisa me echó una mirada como si yo acabara de aterrizar desde otro planeta, lo que me hizo recapacitar de que yo debería estar mejor informado.

—Hace lo mismo en casa —dijo ella.

—¿Qué hace?

Melisa me miró con expresión de irritación.

—Serafín se está volviendo una persona muy extraña —dijo.

Después de que nuestro padre nos abandonó, mi madre trató de hacernos entender la situación. Yo tenía nueve años y me parecía que nuestro padre se había ido de casa porque estaba cansado de nosotros, pero Serafín tenía solo cuatro años, y le dio por andar por toda la casa llorando y gritando, Papá, Papá, como si su papá estuviera perdido y él tratara de encontrarlo.

—A lo mejor está estresado —dije, y, frustrado por no ser capaz de ver cuál sería el problema de mi hermano, di una patada a una piedra que rodó a lo largo del sendero. Dos urracas, que se habían posado en la arena detrás de una acacia, levantaron el vuelo, lo que hizo que Melisa se asustara. Fue en ese momento cuando noté que estaba pálida y que no llevaba maquillaje. Un pequeño bolso de cuero le colgaba del hombro, del cual ella sacó un paquete de Camel y me ofreció un cigarrillo. Yo lo rechacé diciendo que no con la cabeza.

—Me temo que Serafín esta alterado por mí, porque ve que yo no soy la esposa que él esperaba de mí —dijo.

Melisa sacó una caja de pañuelitos de papel de su bolso y se secó las lágrimas. Yo interpreté sus palabras como una declaración de que ella era la causa de los problemas de mi hermano. ¿Se estaba revelando el desajuste matrimonial?

—Eso no pinta bien —dije.

Entonces Melisa comenzó a destaparse mientras caminábamos. Serafín acabó por perder el trabajo hacía una semana y, sorprendentemente, añadió, no parecía que le importase. Yo me paré en seco. Esa noticia no me encajaba con la imagen que yo tenía de mi hermano, un tipo solitario, de acuerdo, pero también responsable.

—¿Te ha dicho él que tú no eres la esposa que él esperaba fueras?

Me preparé para oír lo peor mientras seguíamos andando.

—No —me dijo— Él está afectado por algo, pero no dice qué.

Mientras ella hablaba, yo miraba a mi alrededor; nos acercábamos al Jardín de las rosas, y yo respiré hondo para captar la fragancia y reflexionar.

—En casa —continuó Melisa— Serafín fuma sin cesar.

Aunque mi hermano ha heredado muchos de los rasgos de nuestra madre, incluyendo sus ojos claros, su pelo rubio y liso (yo soy más alto que él y tengo ojos oscuros y pelo rizado) y su temperamento tranquilo, a veces se comporta de una forma obsesiva, como en el caso de fumar excesivamente.

—A lo mejor está enganchado a la droga —dije, y pensé en nuestro padre, jugador y drogadicto.

—No creo —dijo ella enseguida— Por supuesto, a los dos nos gusta fumar un porro de vez en cuando, pero yo he revisado sus bolsillos y los cajoncillos en su pupitre y no he encontrado rastro de drogas.

No dudé de su palabra; en el pasado, ella probablemente había sido una experta en el uso de drogas.

—No se me ocurre qué puede ser lo que le pasa —dije.

Yo tenía la impresión de que ninguno de los dos teníamos ni la más mínima idea de qué era lo que le pasaba a Serafín.

—¿Qué más hace en casa? —pregunté.

—A veces empieza un dibujo, pero lo abandona enseguida. A menudo, sale por la noche, después de cenar, y vuelve muy tarde. Si le pregunto dónde ha estado, me da respuestas que no tienen sentido, como por ejemplo decir que ha estado contando casas en el barrio, lo cual me deja perpleja. Incluso durante nuestros momentos más íntimos, de repente se vuelve distraído y...

—No hay necesidad de que sigas contando esas cosas, Melisa —dije— En aquel momento mi antipatía por ella comenzó a hacerse más leve. —Lo que os está pasando —añadí— es triste y extraño. Voy a llamar a mi hermano y averiguar por mí mismo.

Ella movió la cabeza afirmativamente. El sol estaba todavía alto, y nuestras sombras se veían densas en el suelo. Habíamos pasado el Jardín de las rosas. Melisa miraba al espacio, pensativa, y yo respeté su silencio. Cuando salimos del parque, ella tomó el Metro, y yo volví a mi apartamento a pie.

A la mañana siguiente, domingo, llamé a mi hermano y le invité a ver un partido de futbol aquella misma tarde; a los dos nos gusta el futbol, así que él enseguida aceptó y dijo que llegaría en autobús. Yo fui en Metro, llegué antes y caminé hasta la parada del autobús. Hacía muy buena temperatura, pero yo llevaba un suéter de tejido fino atado a la cintura por si acaso en el campo bajaba la temperatura. El autobús hizo la parada y mi hermano descendió de él. Llevaba una chamarra negra con la capucha sobre su cabeza. Yo me acerqué a él, pero se quedó parado inmóvil en la acera como si las suelas de sus zapatos se le hubieran pegado al pavimento, inexpresivo. Entonces, yo exageré mi sonrisa para compensar por su frialdad emocional y le di un abrazo, que él recibió sin mostrar entusiasmo. Noté que la chamarra era gruesa y resistente al agua, aunque no había predicción de lluvia. Un sentimiento como de estar en presencia de algo extraño recorrió mi espinazo, pero no dije nada.

Serafín, no obstante, siguió el partido con interés. Tal vez yo esté haciendo una montaña de un grano de arena, reflexioné, y miré a mi alrededor con la esperanza de ver a alguien que llevara alguna prenda de vestir tipo gabardina, como la de mi hermano, pero no vi a nadie con ella.

El partido terminó en empate.

—¿Te apetece una cerveza antes de volver a casa? —pregunté a Serafín al salir del estadio.

—Sí.

Parecía estar de buen humor.

—Hay un Irish Pub cerca de aquí.

Fuimos allí. El bar estaba lleno de gente que, como nosotros, llegaban del campo de futbol. Vimos dos taburetes libres cerca del mostrador y los ocupamos. Varias pantallas de televisión transmitían diversos deportes por canales diferentes. Nosotros pedimos una jarra de Guinness para cada uno. Mientras nos tomábamos la cerveza, mirábamos a una u otra de las pantallas de TV, a las personas que estaban alrededor nuestro, y charlábamos acerca del partido que acabábamos de ver. Yo no me atrevía a cambiar de conversación de forma abrupta para hablar de asuntos personales, pero mi hermano lo hizo por mí.

—¿Tienes novia? —me preguntó.

—Sí, en Bilbao. Me gustaría que la conocieras. Es la chica más lista y guapa del mundo —dije— Pero la expresión de Serafín cambió de repente; se le veía como ausente, mirando la TV embobado mientras sostenía la jarra de cerveza en la mano sin moverse. Su pasividad me dolió.

—¿Me has oído? —le pregunté.

—Sí —dijo con indiferencia.

Una onda de bochorno me invadió el pecho al darme cuenta de que mi hermano estaba ido. Respiré profundamente, tomé un largo trago de cerveza y por largo tiempo permanecimos en silencio.

—¿Te gustan los peces tropicales? —preguntó al cabo.

—¿Peces tropicales, dices?

Me pareció una pregunta estúpida.

—Sí —dijo— Yo los dibujo y luego voy al acuario para verlos.

Sentí que mi estómago se revolvía. Lo que Serafín acababa de decir no tenía sentido, era irrisorio. ¿Estaría bromeando? Pero él seguía mostrándose indiferente, bebiendo cerveza y mirando golf en la TV con ojos vidriosos, sin que aparentemente se percatara de su indiferencia. Luego rebuscó en sus bolsillos y sacó un paquete de Camel, todo arrugado. Se llevó un cigarrillo a la boca.

—No se puede fumar aquí —le advertí, y volvió a meter el cigarrillo en el paquete de forma obediente— Y entonces dije—: Mejor nos vamos para que puedas fumar afuera.

Salimos del pub. Serafín encendió el cigarrillo y se echo a andar calle adelante como si supiera a dónde nos debíamos dirigir. Yo le seguí, haciendo esfuerzos por mantenerme a su nivel. Al rato, calculé que se dirigía a la entrada del Metro más próxima, y, efectivamente, cuando llegamos a la boca del Metro, Serafín siguió escalera abajo, inconsciente de mi presencia, lo que me produjo de nuevo ese presentimiento de que algo extraño le estaba ocurriendo a mi hermano.

—Adiós, Serafín, que te vaya bien —dije. ¿Qué otra cosa podría decir?

De regreso a casa, llamé a Melisa y le conté mis impresiones.

—Lo que quiera que sea que le pasa a Serafín está más allá de la lógica —le dije. Y mis propias palabras me hicieron recapacitar sobre una verdad latente: mi hermano se había vuelto emocionalmente inalcanzable, una persona rara, al margen de los demás.

—¿Tú crees que sería prudente consultar con un psicólogo? —Melisa preguntó. Y yo estuve de acuerdo y agradecido de que ella tomara la iniciativa.

Cuando unos días más tarde, yo ya de vuelta en Bilbao, Melisa llamó para decirme que el sicólogo había dicho que el problema de Serafín se debía al insidioso comienzo de una enfermedad mental, una sensación de incertidumbre agitó mis intestinos. No acerté a puntualizar de qué se trataba hasta que Melisa dijo: Lo mismo podría pasarte a ti, ¿te das cuenta? Yo no respondí, pero aquella aprehensión que yo siempre he tenido, que algo inesperado iba a pasarle a mi hermano, me atacó de nuevo, pero ahora afectaba también a mi propia cordura. Recordé que Melisa también había dicho que mi hermano se estaba volviendo una persona extraña, y ahora me entró un sentimiento de culpabilidad por haber sospechado de ella como causa de todo lo malo que estaba sucediendo, y comprendí lo fácil que es errar cuando uno se guía por supuestos. Me dio mucha pena mi hermano. Quise compartir mis emociones con Melisa, pero solamente fui capaz de prometer que trataría de ayudarles lo mejor que pudiera.

Después que Melisa y yo nos desconectamos del teléfono, yo me quedé confuso, mi cabeza llena de preguntas urgentes. ¿A qué o a quién era dado culpar por la locura de mi hermano: a nuestros previos problemas familiares, a la extravagancia de nuestro padre, a la pasada mala conducta de Melisa? No encontraba respuesta a ninguna de mis preguntas. Entonces pensé en mi novia, si ella habría notado algún cambio en mí, algo incongruente en mi modo de pensar o alguna estupidez en mi hablar, o… Aún estoy tratando de encontrar una respuesta coherente y ya ha pasado más de una semana desde que volví a Bilbao.

El dilema de Pietro

Pietro, quien vive con sus padres y está próximo a terminar la enseñanza secundaria, llega a casa en este jueves por la noche y entra en la cocina mostrándose acelerado y distraído.

—¿De dónde vienes? —su madre le pregunta.

Ella se ocupa en echarle de comer a los dos cocker spaniels que tienen cuando Pietro irrumpe en la cocina como un torbellino, abre la puerta del frigorífico precipitadamente y saca una pequeña botella de agua.

—Te veo muy agitado, Hijo —dice su madre.

Pietro es hijo único y sueña con hacerse un futbolista profesional. Su padre, quien es instructor de educación física en un colegio del barrio, ve con buenos ojos la decisión de su hijo. Su madre, quien trabaja como gerente en la Sociedad para la protección de animales, trata de inculcar en él la idea de hacerse veterinario. Pietro vacila a menudo entre estos dos puntos de vista, aunque en general el deseo de hacerse futbolista predomina sobre el de estudiar para veterinario.

—Estoy cansado, Mamá. Eso es todo —dice.

Con frecuencia, Pietro vuelve a casa cansado después de un partido de futbol o de sus sesiones de entrenamiento en el gimnasio. Pero en esta ocasión, sin embargo, está también alterado por lo que le pasó en la calle. Bebe el agua de la botella de un trago y se apresura a entrar en su habitación. Cierra la puerta tras de sí, se tumba en la cama y mete la cabeza debajo de la almohada. Quiere borrar de su mente las imágenes del fuego quemando la piel del hombre. Aprieta la almohada contra la cabeza hasta que el cansancio le rinde y se queda dormido.

Por la mañana, mientas se peina frente al espejo, esas mismas imágenes le vuelven, solo que ahora las percibe en cámara lenta, más plenamente, como si su mente fuera una pantalla de cine, lo que le atormenta y hace que sus manos tiemblen. "No tuve el coraje para sacar al hombre del fuego. ¡Soy un cobarde!", dice para sí entre dientes, mirándose al espejo. Daría todo lo que posee si supiera que el hombre se salvó.

Antes de salir de su habitación e ir a la cocina, donde sabe que se va a encontrar con su madre otra vez —su padre sale de casa para ir a trabajar más temprano— se promete no decir ni una palabra de lo que le está pasando, con la esperanza de que el fantasma del incidente pronto desaparezca de su memoria.

—Te vi nervioso anoche, Hijo, ¿qué pasa?

Pietro mantiene su calma y evita acercarse a su madre, quien está desayunando.

—Ya te dije, Mamá, que estaba cansado.

Su madre le lanza una mirada que él interpreta como diciendo que ella no se cree lo que le dice.

—¿Hay algo que te preocupa? —insiste su madre.

—¡Mamá, por favor!

El sabe que su madre no puede ahondar mucho en su situación porque tiene que irse a trabajar. Y en efecto, ella deja de hacerle preguntas, se toma el café y enseguida se levanta de la mesa, coge su bolso, que lo había dejado en la encimera de la cocina, acaricia con sus dedos la nuca de su hijo, "tranquilo", le dice, y se va.

A pesar de la buena voluntad de Pietro, el pensar que es un cobarde le fastidia y le trae un sentimiento de culpabilidad. Durante el día, en la escuela trata de alejarse de sus amigos y cuando regresa a casa en la noche evita el hablar con sus padres y se mete en su cuarto. Tumbado boca arriba en la cama, con las manos detrás del cuello, le da vueltas a lo que pasó y, en vano, trata de acallar la voz de la conciencia que le dice que es gallina, hasta que, exhausto, se queda dormido.

Un par de horas más tarde, Pietro se despierta sobresaltado al oír, mientras dormía, una voz que le gritaba: "¡Sácalo del fuego!" Medio dormido, lucha con las mantas como si tratara de salvar a algún compañero de batalla de un apuro. Luego, se sienta en la cama, empapado en sudor, y, mirando al vacio con ojos muy abiertos, grita: ¡"Fuego!" Un momento después, salta de la cama y, aunque tambaleándose, consigue llegar a la ducha. Bajo el agua fría tata de entender qué es lo que le está pasando. Es consciente, sin embargo, de que despertó debido a un mal sueño que, sin que el sepa cómo, le reaviva el terror que sintió durante el accidente del fuego de la noche anterior. Pero también se pregunta si sus padres le habrían odio gritar.

Cuando sale de su habitación, pretendiendo que no pasa nada, aunque el retorcimiento de sus manos indica que está nervioso, se encuentra con que sus padres están desayunando, y, como cada sábado por la mañana, él también se sienta a la mesa. Su familia es italiana. Sus padres vinieron a América cuando él tenía diez años. Comparado con Trieste, al principio, todo le resultó extraño en Los Ángeles: la escuela, los maestros, los juegos, el idioma… Creció con la sensación de oscilar entre dos culturas, como veleta que gira con el viento. Al cabo, sin embargo, consiguió vivir a gusto con su mezcla cultural.

—¿Café? —pregunta y mantiene la cafetera suspendida en el aire en espera de servir a sus padres, pero se da cuenta de que ellos ya se han servido. Entonces, se sirve el mismo.

Cuando termina de servirse y se dispone a dejar la cafetera sobre la mesa, tiene la sensación de que sus padres le han oído gritar en mitad de la noche, y ello hace que se sonroje.

—¿Qué te pasa, Pietro?

—No me pasa nada, Mamá.

Intenta por todos los medios evitar el contacto visual con cualquiera de sus padres y cruza las piernas por debajo de la mesa para controlar los nervios.

—Pues parece que algo te pasa —dice su padre.

Pietro comienza a untar una tostada con mantequilla, pero el comentario de su padre le paraliza la acción, y él se mantiene callado.

—Por favor, dinos qué te pasa —insiste su padre.

Pietro mira a su padre de reojo, y, callado, vuelve a untar el pan con mantequilla.

—Hacéis que me sienta como si fuera un ladrón —finalmente dijo y mordió un pedazo de la tostada.

Su padre no respondió, y su madre, que acababa de llevarse a la boca un trozo de melón, le miró como asombrada y, después de tragar la fruta, dijo:

—Habla, por favor.

Pietro se sonroja otra vez. Él desea contarles todo, pero no puede avenirse a tener que confesar que es un cobarde. Si lo suelta, piensa que va a perder la ayuda de su padre para convertirse en futbolista de primera, y en tocante a su madre, cree que a ella le entrarían dudas de si él tiene la capacidad para ayudar a nadie. Arrastra sus pies más atrás por debajo de la silla y se lleva un vaso de agua a los labios, pero se atraganta al beber y tose de forma violenta. Se cubre la boca con la servilleta hasta que se le pasa el ataque de tos.

—Yo no sé —dijo, a punto de llorar.

Se establece un silencio durante el cual nadie se mueve. Pietro bebe un sorbo de agua y mira al suelo; se aclara la garganta y dice—: Iba montado en mi patineta, cuando... —le entra la tos otra vez, bebe más agua y continúa—: El hombre estaba allí, debajo del puente de la carretera.

Se para de hablar y pone su mirada fija en el vaso de agua vacío en frente de él, mientas que sus padres se quedan mirándole.

—¿Quién estaba allí? —pregunta su madre.

Pietro mira a su padre a través de la mesa, que parece disfrutar del desayuno, y luego de vuelta a su madre, que espera una respuesta.

—El de sin techo.

Ambos padres movieron la cabeza afirmativamente para indicar que sabían de quién se trataba. Recientemente, un vagabundo acampaba debajo del puente que cruza la carretera, a poca distancia de su casa.

—¿Qué pasó? —pregunta su padre.

—El jueves fue un día frio, como recordareis. El hombre había encendido una hoguera y estaba de pie cerca del fuego, envuelto en una manta vieja y bebiendo vino por una botella. Al pasar yo dije hola, y él contestó ¿qué hay?

Pietro para de contar.

—¿Y bien? —su padre le anima a seguir hablando.

—Pocos metros más adelante, después de pasarle, oí un ruido sordo y un grito. Me paré y me volví para ver qué era.

—¿El hombre se calló al fuego? —su madre interviene.

Pietro afirma con la cabeza.

—Probablemente estaba borracho —dice el padre.

—No sé. Solo sé que lloraba y se retorcía —dice Pietro, hablando rápido, y añade—: El fuego se avivaba más debido al vino que se vertía de la botella, y...

—¡Terrible! —le interrumpió su madre.

—Yo le agarré por los pies —continúa Pietro—para arrastrarle fuera del fuego.

—Hiciste lo correcto, Hijo —dice su padre.

A Pietro le gustaría que la cosa terminara aquí.

—Me resbalé y me caí —continuó, hablando con voz apagada.

—¡Dios mío! ¿Te alcanzó el fuego? —pregunta su madre.

—No, porque me levanté enseguida. Pero me entró el pánico y eché a correr. Lo que quiero decir es que abandoné al hombre allí, sin defensa. Soy un…

Se hace un silencio. A Pietro le tiemblan los pies, lo cual hace que la mesa también tiemble.

—Sueño con ello —concluyó.

Sus padres permanecen callados, quietos en sus asientos. Intercambian una mirada y luego ambos ponen los ojos en Pietro.

—Yo creo que estás en estado de shock, Hijo —su padre rompió el silencio.

Pietro se lleva las manos a las rodillas en un esfuerzo por parar el temblor.

—No sé —dice y añade—: Yo creo que me sentiría mejor si supiera que el vagabundo está bien.

La mesa deja de temblar. Pietro mira de reojo a su madre sin decir nada, como esperando algo. A ella se la ve pensativa, pero un segundo después dice a su hijo : —Tú no tienes la culpa.

En silencio, Pietro hace un gesto de agradecimiento por sus palabras, pero, al mismo tiempo, se pregunta qué quiere decir con que no es su culpa. Él todavía piensa que es un cobarde, aunque trata desesperadamente de desembarazarse de tal pensamiento. Vuelve la cara hacia su padre al oírle decir que tal vez no fue lo suficientemente fuerte como para sacar al hombre completamente fuera del fuego. Pietro se hunde en el asiento, como si estuviera paralizado, con las manos en las rodillas y los ojos perdidos en el espacio. Si carece de fuerza para arrastrar un hombre fuera de una hoguera, ¿puede entonces convertirse en un futbolista poderoso?

—De cualquier manera —dice el padre— pienso que podemos encontrar al vagabundo en alguna parte.

Después de oír estas palabras, Pietro se siente reavivar.

—Disculparme —dice al tiempo que se levanta y sale precipitadamente hacia su habitación. Allí, cierra la puerta tras de sí y se concentra en la pantalla del ordenador, en las noticias locales, y lee: *En la fría noche del pasado jueves, la policía encontró un hombre, caído en la calle, que presentaba quemaduras producidas por una hoguera, todavía llameante a pocos metros de donde el hombre estaba, y lo llevaron al hospital público.* Sin más preámbulo, Pietro sale de su casa y toma el Metro hasta el hospital.

—No podemos facilitar información acerca de ninguno de nuestros pacientes ingresados porque es confidencial —la recepcionista en el hospital advierte.

Pietro insiste en que tiene que ver al vagabundo con las quemaduras. La recepcionista no cede en su opinión, pero le sugiere que hable con la encargada de la sala. Pietro acepta y repite su solicitud a la encargada, una mujer de mediana edad que le recuerda a su madre y quién, de forma amable, le interrumpe para hacer una llamada al teléfono.

—Todo arreglado —dice la encargada después de hablar por teléfono, y añade—: Este paciente no llevaba ninguna documentación cuando la policía lo trajo al hospital, pero más tarde dijo que se llama Florindo. Él asegura que sabe quién es usted, así que puede ir y visitarle, está en la habitación número 21, pero, por favor, sea breve.

En la habitación número 21 hay también otro paciente, cada uno acostado en una cama; ambos miran a Pietro detenidamente cuando éste entra.

—Hola —dice Pietro, dirigiéndose al que reconoció ser Florindo.

—¿Qué hay?

Al saludo le sucede un silencio. Florindo, con su barba negra y ojos oscuros, debe tener la edad de su padre, calcula Pietro. Su vecino, en cambio, está pálido, tiene ojos azules y es más joven. Este individuo le recuerda a uno de sus compañeros del equipo de futbol, a quién no puede ver ni en pintura porque se muestra muy crítico de su juego durante los partidos, lo cual le llena de ira porque el otro jugador es más alto y fuerte que él y más agresivo, de modo que Pietro no se atreve a competir con él.

—Estás vivo —Pietro le dice a Florindo.

—Tú me ayudaste.

Florindo le observa desde la almohada. Tiene las manos vendadas. Pietro se pregunta cómo se las apañará para comer y si tendrá otras quemaduras en el cuerpo.

—Siento mucho lo que pasó —dice.

—¿Qué Pasó? —el otro paciente pregunta.

Pietro quiere responder que no es de su incumbencia, pero, en cambio, dice—: Se cayó a una hoguera.

—¡Cielos! Eso es por lo que se pasa la noche gritando ¡fuego! y me despierta. ¡Cielos!

El joven paciente se incorpora para sentarse en la cama y mira a Pietro fijamente como el ratón al gato.

—Lo mejor que puedes hacer —dice el joven paciente, dirigiéndose a Pietro— es llevártelo a tu casa cuando salga del hospital, ¿sabes?, de vacaciones pagadas.

Pietro aprieta las mandíbulas. Detesta el sarcasmo, pero se controla y no responde. Lo que este individuo dice acerca de Florindo, sus gritos en la noche, se parece al problema que él tiene. ¿Es posible que el accidente les haya afectado a ambos de forma similar?

—Deberías llevártelo a tu casa —el joven repite.

Pietro le mira con desdén, pero al mismo tiempo comprende que él no tiene nada más que decir o hacer allí. Esta gente no son maestros o entrenadores. No sé cómo hablarles o relacionarme con ellos, aunque siento la necesidad de ayudar a Florindo de alguna manera.

—¿Puedes desprenderte de un par de dólares? — pregunta el joven paciente.

Incluso la voz le recuerda a Pietro la de su compañero de equipo. Le mira los hombros, que los ve anchos, y le parece que el otro es tan fuerte como su compañero. Si lo intentara, ¿podría llegar a ser mejor futbolista que él mismo? Odia ese tipo de gente.

—Está bien, hombre, cuídate —Pietro dice a Florindo, y añade—: Tal vez nos veamos de nevo.

—Tal vez —dice el otro paciente en guasa, y añade—: Si sucede que tu pasas por el lugar donde éste acampa.

Pietro presta oidos sordos a estas palabras de reto, se muerde la lengua y sale de la habitación y, poco después, del hospital.

De vuelta, viajando en el Metro, Pietro cae en la cuenta de que Florindo y su compañero de habitación, junto con otros muchos de su misma clase, son gente destituida que coexiste en la misma sociedad en la que él también vive, pero que no sabe cómo tratarlos. Su cavilación le trae a la memoria una presentación que un psicólogo hizo en su clase como parte de una serie de charlas, dadas por profesionales, que el director de la escuela organizó para ayudar a los estudiantes con sus elecciones futuras. A él le gustó aquella presentación, e incluso pensó en elegir la carrera de psicólogo, pero ya había tomado la decisión de hacerse futbolista. Pero si me decidiera a hacerme un psicólogo, reflexiona ahora, sería capaz de relacionarme con gente como Florindo. Les enseñaría a consumir alimentos sanos, a encontrar un cobijo adecuado y a mantenerse activos. No me sentiría como un cobarde. Se le ocurre pensar que es víctima de un dilema, ya que para llevar a cabo tal plan necesitaría mucho tiempo y no podría jugar al futbol de forma regular. ¿Por qué me pasan estas cosas? ¿Es toda esta mierda resultado del susto que me llevé el jueves?

Cuando Pietro sale del Metro se da cuenta de que es sábado y sus padres estarán en casa, pero él no está con el ánimo de verlos. No tan pronto, antes tiene que despejar su mente, encontrarse más a gusto consigo mismo. Será mejor pasear por un rato.

Después de ambular durante dos horas sin parar, rumiando acerca de su dilema, siente sed y hambre, y cuando ve una tienda donde venden bocadillos, entra y compra uno y una Coca-Cola. Después decide entrar en un cercano parque público y sentarse en un banco mientas come el bocadillo. No pasan ni cinco minutos, sin embargo, cuando un hombre de mediana edad, haraposo, que andaba empujando una vieja bicicleta, a cuyo sillín llevaba atada una bolsa muy sucia, se le acerca, mendigando. Para Pietro, este individuo tiene un sorprendente parecido con Florindo.

—Toma —dice Pietro y le ofrece el resto de su bocadillo.

—No tengo hambre —contesta el mendigo y añade—: ¿Podrías darme un par de dólares?

El hombre está parado, sujetando la destartalada bicicleta, a unos dos metros enfrente de Pietro, quien piensa que Florindo nunca le pidió dinero. ¿Qué habría hecho él si Florindo le hubiera pedido dinero? Sus propios pensamientos le estaban causando ansiedad.

—¿Tal vez le venga mejor un traguito de Coca-Cola? —dice al tiempo que le ofrece la lata con el refresco y se pregunta si el tipo se habrá vuelto hosco debido a su condición de mendigo.

El hombre rechaza la oferta, negando con la cabeza.

—¿Me puede dar un par de dólares?

—¿Para qué necesitas el dinero?

—Para compra medicinas —dice el mendigo y se rasca la cabeza, llena de abundante y sucio pelo.

—¿Estás enfermo?

Para Pietro, el hombre no parece que esté enfermo, aunque se le ve más flaco que Florindo.

—Sífilis —dice el mendicante y pone una sonrisa que Pietro interpreta como llena de sarcasmo y broma.

—¡Mentiroso!

Pietro no encontraba palabras para añadir otros epítetos. Al individuo solo le interesaba conseguir dinero y trataba de confundirle adoptando el papel de estar enfermo de sífilis. Se levanta del banco de un salto, enfurecido, y avanza hacia el vagabundo con la intención de darle un puñetazo en la cara. El hombre se echa para atrás y enseguida se monta en la bicicleta y pedalea para alejarse de allí, enfadado y gritando—: Estás loco.

Encolerizado, Pietro tira el resto del bocadillo al suelo para que se lo coman las palomas y la lata de Coca-cola al contenedor de basura. ¡Cálmate hombre!, dice para sí y comienza a caminar para salir del parque. Él no duda de su cordura: yo no estoy loco, se dice, estoy enfadado conmigo mismo porque no fui capaz de sacar a Florindo del fuego, descontento con papá por decir que no tuve la fuerza suficiente para hacerlo y cabreado con los vagabundos por comportarse como gilipollas. Puede ser, reflexiona, que el incidente del jueves pasado me haya impresionado, como dijo papá, y que las pesadillas que tengo y mi enfado sea debido a ello. Quién sabe, quizás la idea de dejar el fútbol para hacerme un psicólogo sea una forma de expiar mi culpa. Tal vez el pánico me cegó e hizo que saliera corriendo de allí. Pero, como dice mamá: no hay que tomar las cosas a pie de letra.

Pietro decide caminar hacia casa, tratando de ordenar sus pensamientos, de encontrarle sentido a lo que le está pasando. Cuando pasa por el lugar de debajo del puente donde Florindo se calentaba a la hoguera el pasado jueves, la escena del incidente vuelve a su memoria rápidamente y con tal exactitud que le hace temblar de cuerpo entero. Y otra vez siente el impulso de salir corriendo, pero se da cuenta de que ahora no hay ninguna hoguera encendida ni vagabundos alrededor. ¿A qué viene el pánico? Aunque Pietro no encuentra respuesta, nota que se va calmando y disminuye el trote.

La idea de hacerse psicólogo vuelve a su mente. El deseo de ayudar a Florindo y a otros como él persiste, pero ahora entiende que no hay por qué hacerlo a expensas de abandonar el plan de hacerse un futbolista profesional. El pensamiento de que puede conseguir ambas metas simultáneamente entra en su conciencia. Sabía de algunos atletas que lo habían conseguido. ¿Por qué no intentarlo también él? Tal intento habría de ser como el navegar entre dos culturas, lo cual él siempre ha hecho. De esta guisa, Pietro acepta el reto como lo lógico a hacer, como si hubiera contemplado el hacerlo desde hacía mucho tiempo. Determina el doblar su esfuerzo para hacerse más fuerte. Papá dice que a mi edad todavía puedo crecer y desarrollar más músculo. Cuando Pietro llega a casa, su dilema empieza a palidecer.

La verja del jardín

Al final de los años 40, los braceros que algunos terratenientes italianos empleaban para la recolección de la aceituna llegaban desde países lejanos, de lugares empobrecidos por las guerras. Llegaban en tren, viajando en compartimentos de tercera clase —algunas familias traían a sus hijos— y retornaban a sus lugares de origen con las primeras heladas. En ocasiones, alguna familia se quedaba.

Sentada en frente de una casita de ladrillo y yeso, donde vive con sus padres, una niña de 6 años, de ojos almendrados y pelo negro rizado, se entretiene haciendo ramitos de flores silvestres. A corta distancia de su casa corre un riachuelo de corriente rápida. Este estrecho rio, donde los niños gustan de pescar la trucha, es conocido por la gente del lugar como *Il confine acquoso* porque su curso limita los anchos olivares, donde los temporeros trabajan y viven en sus humildes estancias, de la zona urbana donde los ricos tienen sus residencias. Varios pequeños puentes de madera facilitan el tránsito entre estas dos zonas limítrofes.

A esta niña le gusta deambular, le encanta sobre todo cruzar el rio y husmear en las casas de los ricos. En este momento, ella está parada afuera de la verja de una mansión, en cuyo jardín de adentro hay otra niña que está jugando. Debemos ser de la misma edad, la niña de los ojos almendrados calcula. Ella sigue allí de pie, mirando a la otra niña hasta que algo—el vuelo de un grajo o una ráfaga de viento—hace que la distraiga, y se marcha.

Andando de vuelta a casa, la niña de los ojos almendrados se imagina que es rica como la niña del otro lado de la verja. Se pregunta por qué ella no lo es, pero la respuesta le elude como el lagarto que ahora corre sobre el sendero y enseguida desaparece. A ella le gustaría que todas las cosas se mostraran plenamente, como el ramillete de flores que lleva en la mano: flores blancas, rojas y rosáceas.

— ¿Por qué nosotros no somos ricos? —le pregunta a sus padres.

—Tu madre y yo vinimos a estas tierras cuando tú todavía tenías los dientes de leche —dice su padre— Trabajamos, varilla en mano, sacudiendo las ramas de los olivos y recogiendo las aceitunas que caen, surco a surco y día a día durante la temporada de calor. El hacerse rico lleva mucho tiempo.

La niña se queda mirando a su padre con cara de no entender muy bien lo que le está diciendo, mientras que la madre parece reflexionar sobre qué estará su hija pensando.

—Nosotros hacemos lo que podemos para seguir viviendo aquí y que tú puedas ir a una buena escuela —dice.

La niña pone una mirada distante en sus ojos almendrados.

—Cada cual posee lo que posee —dice el padre.

La niña mira a su padre con cara de curiosidad.

—¿Pero por qué no somos ricos?

Los padres tardan en darle una respuesta y ese retraso hace que la niña pierda interés.

Sin entender mucho de qué va la cosa, sale de la casuca y se sienta afuera de la puerta, agradecida por el calorcillo de un pálido sol de diciembre después del frio de la noche, y comienza a formar ramilletes con las flores que había recogido: flores de ciclamen, pensamientos y margaritas.

Cuando la madre despierta a su hija a la mañana siguiente, pone una muñeca de trapo, que ella ha confeccionado, en sus brazos.

—*Babbo Natale* dejó esta muñeca en la chimenea para ti. Feliz navidad! —dice.

Una expresión de ternura y cariño asoma en los ojos de la niña, quien besa y acuna a la muñeca, y sonríe a su madre, y piensa en la niña rica de la mansión. El padre observa la escena desde la mesa de la cocina con alegría.

— Si sacas la muñeca a la calle para jugar, procura arroparla con alguno de los paños de cocina y no te alejes mucho de la casa —le dice, y la niña afirma con la cabeza.

—Está nevando —dice la madre con una sonrisa.

La niña sale a la calle y juega con su muñeca todo el día. Los árboles, los tejados, el paisaje, todo aparece blanco y voluminoso. Sus ojos se entrecierran cuando el reflejo del sol en la nieve alcanza su cara, pero ella no quiere perderse nada de lo que ve a su alrededor. Cuando se da cuenta de que pronto va a oscurecer, decide ir a visitar a la niña adinerada.

A pesar del consejo de su padre, ella se aventura a cruzar el puente. Cuando llega a la verja del jardín, se sorprende de ver que éste se ve envuelto en una luz amarillenta y misteriosa que se desprende de un farol de madera con paredes de cristal y que dentro contiene un velón. El farol tiene un sombrero de nieve y está anclado al suelo por medio de una estaca; se pregunta quién lo habrá colocado allí. En esta luz amarillenta la niña adinerada y sus amiguitos juegan con juguetes lujosos. La escena le recuerda los cuentos de hadas que su mamá le lee antes de dormir. Ella observa, allí parada de pie, pero siente que la niña rica no se va a acercar a la verja, y los pies se le están quedando fríos.

—Cada cual posee lo que posee —le dice a su muñeca y se apresura a volver a su casa.

Marie

Después de casados, Pierre y yo nos trasladamos de Pau, donde vivíamos, a Cerbère, donde le habían ofrecido un trabajo de guarda parques. El pueblito donde nos instalamos, situado entre el mar y el extremo este del pirineo francés, nos encantó a primera vista, y disfrutamos de nuestros paseos por la playa. Un atardecer, al comienzo del ocaso, descubrimos una cala escondida entre rocas grandes y oscuras que nos encantó. Algunas familias con niños se bañaban y salpicaban el agua. Cuando yo miré a mi alrededor, sin embargo, me sorprendió la presencia de una mujer mayor, de apariencia extraña, vestida de negro de pies a cabeza. Estaba sentada en la arena de espaldas al agua. Hice que Pierre la viera también.

—¡Oh! —dijo él—. Debe ser la *Vieux Cécile*. Yo he leído algo acerca de ella. Nadie sabe cuántos años tiene. La gente de aquí especula que duerme donde las águilas rondan en la montaña. Ya sabes. Es una leyenda.

—Da miedo.

—Es verdad. Cuando algo malo pasa en el pueblo, todo el mundo culpa a la *Vieux Cécile* por ello. Durante el día, se sienta en esta cala a pleno sol durante horas sin hablar con nadie.

La cala escondida se convirtió en nuestro lugar de preferencia en la playa. Un atardecer, tres años más tarde, mientras

Pierre y yo tomábamos el sol tumbados en la arena, yo me preguntaba si alguna vez llegaríamos a tener un hijo. La anciana mujer se sentaba no lejos de nosotros, y tuve la impresión de que ella habló: "Vas a tener una niña dotada".

—¿Dijiste algo? —Pregunté a Pierre.

— Yo no he dicho nada. ¿No será tu imaginación?

Dos días más tarde, de mañana, después de que Pierre se había ido al trabajo, salí para regar las plantas del pequeño jardín enfrente de la casa cuando vi una canasta de paja junto a la puerta. Con precaución, miré dentro de ella. Se me cortó la respiración: ¡Un bebé balbuciente y en pañales! Entonces, oí un batir de alas: un águila negra se levantó en vuelo sobre el tejado. No supe qué pensar. Mi corazón latía con fuerza. Agarré la cesta y la llevé a casa. Inmediatamente telefoneé a Pierre.

—¡Es niña! Pierre, y puede que solo tenga una semana.

Con mucho cuidado, alcé al bebé y le sostuve en los brazos.

— Es preciosa —dije.

— Llama al médico. Ahora mismo regreso a casa.

El médico dijo que la bebé estaba sana. En el pueblo, todo el mundo expresó asombro acerca de lo ocurrido. Las autoridades emprendieron una operación de búsqueda para encontrar a los padres de la bebé. El párroco la bautizó con el nombre de Marie. Mientras tanto, el juez de la región autorizó que, por el momento, Pierre y yo actuáramos como padres adoptivos. Cuando pasó un año sin que la búsqueda diera resultado alguno, yo convencí a mi marido para que adoptáramos a Marie de forma definitiva.

Nuestra hija, de pelo negro y ojos verdosos y vivaces, iba creciendo y transformándose en una niña fabulosa. Pero cuando los tres íbamos a la cava favorita a jugar en la arena y bañarnos, me invadía una ola de aprehensión cada vez que veía a la *Vieux Cécile* sentada allí. Y si esta mujer…, yo pensaba, pero no decía nada.

Con el tiempo, comencé a notar que Marie poseía una extraordinaria visión. En cierta ocasión, yo la observé mientras ella estaba sentada en el suelo en el medio de su habitación, de cara a la ventana, con el cuaderno de dibujo, coloreando una margarita sobre la cual ella había dibujado una avispa.

—Tu dibujo es muy realístico —dije.

— La avispa está todavía posada en la flor —me contestó, apuntando a la ventana.

Me acerqué a la ventana y vi que afuera, en el jardín, una avispa estaba posada en una de las flores. Me quedé pasmada de la capacidad visual de Marie. ¿Sería una niña visualmente dotada? Me acordé de la *Vieux Cécile*.

Marie comenzó la escuela primaria en Argeles-sur-mer, una pequeña ciudad situada algunos kilómetros al norte de nosotros. Una mañana de densa niebla, en la que no se veía ni los pies, algunos padres subimos al autobús escolar para acompañar a los niños. Cuando faltaba poco más de un kilómetro para llegar al colegio, la niebla se hizo todavía más densa. De repente, Marie exclamó: ¡Hay un ciervo en la carretera!

Rechinaron las ruedas, y el autobús disminuyó la velocidad y se paró a unos metros enfrente de un cervatillo que estaba parado en medio de la carretera, deslumbrado por las luces del vehículo.

— ¿Quién dijo "hay un ciervo en la carretera? —Preguntó el conductor.

— Ella lo dijo —gritó uno de los niños y señaló a Marie.

—¡Uf! Niña, tú tienes ojo de águila —dijo el conductor.

El ciervo se arrancó corriendo hacia los árboles de afuera de la carretera. El autobús reanudó la marcha. Marie se sentó hundida en su asiento durante el resto del viaje sin decir una palabra.

Cada mañana, después de aquel incidente, yo tenía que empujar a Marie para que subiera al autobús escolar. ¿Qué pasa, Ojo de Águila?, el conductor le preguntaba, pero ella no decía nada, sino que permanecía cabizbaja. La maestra nos dijo que Marie se lo pasaba mirando a las musarañas y recomendó que se quedara en casa hasta que supiéramos cual era su problema. Nosotros la veíamos distraída. Una noche, se despertó dando gritos. Pierre y yo fuimos corriendo a su habitación.

—¿Qué te pasa, mi niña?

Marie estaba sentada en la cama, retorciéndose las manos y con los ojos muy abiertos. Yo la abracé.

—¡Mis ojos…Me estoy volviendo un águila!

Me entró miedo. Mientras abrazaba a Marie, me las apañé para agarrar la mano de Pierre, suplicante. Él se soltó y salió de la habitación. Pero un minuto después volvió con un espejo.

—Mirate en este espejo, Marie —dijo, y ella se separó un poco de mí para mirarse.

— La *Vieux Cécile*! —exclamé, y apreté la mano de Pierre con todas mis fuerzas.

—¡Antoinette, cariño, cálla! Eso no es más que una leyenda. Yo creo que Marie está todavía asustada tras el suceso del cervatillo y lo que el conductor le dijo. Ella lo toma literalmente.

— Esos son tus ojos, Marie, no son los de ningún águila —le dijo Pierre mientras sostenía el espejo enfrente de ella, y añadió—: Antoinette, dile que sus ojos son preciosos y son solo suyos.

Yo quería con toda mi alma creer en sus palabras. Me acerqué más a Marie y miré su cara en el espejo.

— Cariño, tus ojos son preciosos —Dije de todo corazón, pues nunca antes había experimentado un instante de tanta claridad mental, separando la superstición de la vida real como un tamiz que separa las pepitas de oro del sedimento inútil, e insistí, totalmente convencida—: Y tus ojos son solo tuyos.

Marie volvió su cara hacia mí. Entonces repetí lo que acababa de decir y ella se sonrió, movió la cabeza afirmativamente y extendió sus brazos para abrazarnos.

El caballete en la playa

— Sal de Los Ángeles, Audrey, y ve a algún lugar exótico donde alimentar tu talento artistic —mi amiga Debbie dijo.

Nos encontrábamos en el Edificio Comunitario que la ciudad había cedido a los jóvenes artistas locales como lugar de trabajo. Debbie estaba pintando mi retrato.

—¿Salir para ir a dónde?

Yo admiraba la habilidad artística de Debbie que le permitía pintar mis ojos con expresión más alegre y mi cabello con más brillo de lo que, en realidad, eran por entonces. ¿Llegaría yo algún día a desarrollar tal destreza?

—Vete a alguna isla tropical.

El reducido espacio en el que Debbie trabajaba estaba lleno de cajas con pinceles y paletas, el caballete, y cuadros esparcidos todo alrededor. Algunos de sus lienzos colgaban de las paredes que limitaban su estudio. Yo los contemplaba desde el taburete donde me sentaba mientras posaba para ella; todos ellos eran hermosos. Hacía meses que yo no tocaba mis pinceles. Aunque yo quería volver a pintar, no encontraba inspiración ni dentro ni fuera de mí.

— Dudo que yo vaya a llegar muy lejos como pintora —dije.

—¿Quién sabe?

Debbie contempló mi rostro de nuevo bajo la tenue luz del atardecer que se filtraba a través del tragaluz en el techo y procedió a retocar algunas líneas sobre el lienzo. Luego cubrió el montaje con una sábana blanca llena de manchas de pintura.

—Unos pocos detalles más y lo termino. Te lo mostraré cuando vuelvas de tus vacaciones —dijo.

¿Qué puedo yo perder? Me pregunté. Así que reuní algunos botes de pintura fresca y me dispuse a seguir el consejo de Debbie. Volé de noche desde Los Ángeles a Puerto Plata, en la República Dominicana, dispuesta a reencontrarme con mi musa.

Al amanecer, el murmullo del mar, una suave brisa, y los chillidos de las gaviotas me dieron la bienvenida. Me paré descalza sobre el suelo del balcón abierto: un azul inmenso se extendía a través del espacio, un continuo vaivén de las olas sobre la blanca arena, y a lo lejos el solemne Pico Isabel de Torres; todos estos elementos formaban un paisaje majestuoso. Encantada por la belleza escénica, comencé a esbozar un dibujo con la ilusión de completar una pintura al oleo más tarde. Desde que Debbie y yo terminamos el máster en Artes Visuales hacía dos años, solo una de mis pinturas al oleo había obtenido el visto bueno de ella. Mientras que por su parte, había obtenido varios premios por sus pinturas e incluso había vendido algunas. ¿Llegaría yo algún día a pintar tan bien como ella?

Monté el lienzo en el caballete, que instalé en el balcón abierto. Tracé unas líneas de azul y me retiré para ver el efecto. Tal vez esta vez lo consiga, me dije. Cuando me dispuse a mezclar los colores verde y amarillo para obtener un beige con que pintar las montañas, mis ojos se fijaron en la figura de un hombre joven y delgado de aproximadamente mi edad que vestía un niqui y pantalones kaki desgastados. Estaba descalzo, de pie sobre la arena, frente a su caballete, entre mi hotel y la línea de la costa. Se notaba algo extraño en su apariencia, aunque no estaba segura qué. Pero tenía que ver con la forma en que se inclinaba sobre el caballete y la maniobra brusca con la que se retiraba para mirar el océano y de nuevo el lienzo. Sentí curiosidad por ver su trabajo y, sin poder contener mi deseo, salí del hotel y me acerqué para echar una ojeada a su producción.

—Hola, me llamo Audrey.

Él me miró con ojos entreabiertos y gesto inexpresivo como si me estuviera viendo a alguna distancia.

—¡Impresionante! —dije. Pues había pintado una escultural mujer desnuda cabalgando sobre una ola. Desvié mis ojos de la pintura para mirar el océano: olas suaves y nadie surfeando.

— ¿Cómo se llama? —le pregunté.

—Teófilo —dijo, mirando el horizonte.

Pelo rubio estropajoso, ojos azules que evitan el contacto directo, actitud anodina y muecas extrañas, me di cuenta de que acababa de conocer un ser peculiar. Por suerte hablaba inglés. Envidiosa de su talento artístico y confundida acerca de la rareza de su comportamiento, me mantuve de pie a su lado, convencida de que él ni siquiera se daría cuenta de mi presencia, de mi menudo talle, mi pelo corto, negro y rizado y mis ojos oscuros.

—Enhorabuena —dije por fin y me retiré.

Mientras paseaba a lo largo de la costa, me sorprendí a mí misma obsesionada acerca del método de composición de Teófilo, pensando que a mí nunca se me habría ocurrido intentar algo como lo que él hizo, y que lo hizo de memoria, y tan bien hecho. ¿De dónde le venía a Teófilo la inspiración?

Estaba todavía absorta en mis propios pensamientos mientras almorzaba en el bar-restaurante del hotel cuando reconocí el desgarbado caminar de Teófilo. Iba solo y llevaba el mismo niqui y pantalones. Fue hasta una mesa situada en un rincón del restaurante opuesto a donde yo me encontraba y se sentó, ajeno a cualquier otra cosa. Aproveché la ocasión para observar más atentamente sus movimientos y gestos. Parecía ser un hombre tan solitario. Sin embargo, me daba la impresión de que, de vez en cuando, actuaba como si estuviera hablando con alguien que invisiblemente se sentara también a su mesa. Quizá esté loco, pensé, pero es un gran artista. Ya me gustaría a mí pintar como él lo hace.

Tres días después, a la salida del sol, en un día con el cielo despejado y el mar en calma, atisbé a Teófilo en la playa, cerca del agua, pintando. Tenía una botella de cerveza medio enterrada en la arena y una y otra vez la miraba y enseguida procedía a añadir toques a su pintura.

Me acerqué a su caballete para echar una mirada a su trabajo y me quedé sin habla, pues la imagen en el lienzo tenía poco que ver directamente con la botella en la arena que le servía de modelo. En su pintura se veían pedazos de cristales de colores que parecía como si alguien los hubiera tirado al azar en un rincón de algún bazar: botellas hechas añicos, porrones rotos, platos y pedazos de lámparas. Me llamó la atención, sin embargo, la delicada distribución de tonalidades y reflejos de luz. De repente me percaté de que la pintura era como la representación de una imagen aislada vista a través de un caleidoscopio. Me volví para mirar otra vez la botella enterrada en la arena, y en ese momento los rayos solares, reflejados en el agua, se proyectaban sobre el cuello de la botella y el centelleo de luz producía la ilusión de multiplicación del objeto. Teófilo no solo era un gran artista sino también un ilusionista. Le felicité por su trabajo; él movió la cabeza afirmativamente como para darme las gracias, y yo continué mi camino.

Caminando al borde del agua, me hice consciente de la belleza del lugar: la gente disfrutando en la playa, el juguetear de las olas, el corretear de las aves en la arena, y más lejos, las zonas verdes y el Pico Isabel de Torres. Y sin embargo, yo no era capaz de encontrar inspiración y pintar como lo hacían Debbie y Teófilo. ¿Por qué no? Me acordé de la única pintura mía que fuera del agrado de Debbie, una iguana de colores azul, verde y anaranjado caminando sobre una rama seca en un árbol. Lo pinté de memoria, como Teófilo pintó la mujer desnuda cabalgando sobre una ola encrespada, y como la mayoría de los cuadros que pinta Debbie. De repente sentí un irresistible impulso que me llevó directamente al hotel. En mi habitación, abrí el balcón, coloqué el caballete sobre el alféizar y observando el mar comencé a esbozar un dibujo. Trabajé hasta el anochecer, y a la mañana siguiente me asombré de mi propia ejecución: mi cuadro mostraba a Teófilo, él mismo pintando en la playa.

Trabajé de firme, todos los días, durante un mes hasta finalizar mi obra, y cuando la terminé, experimenté una sensación de integridad y perfección. Pensé que debería encontrar a Teófilo y enseñarle mi cuadro, pero supuse que él se limitaría a mover su cabeza sin decir una palabra y desistí de mi propósito. Decidí volver a casa. Me moría por ver mi propio retrato que Debbie había terminado y también por enseñarle mi nueva pintura.

El retrato que Debbie hizo de mí me pareció una obra extraordinaria, y ella me felicitó por mi trabajo. Quién sabe, Audrey, dijo, tú puedes llegar muy lejos como pintora. Para entonces yo había comprendido que, como hacían Debbie y Teófilo, la propia imaginación es fuente de inspiración.

El puente

En el verano anterior al nuevo milenio, un experimentado arquitecto mejicano, famoso como diseñador de puentes, se encontraba en el aeropuerto internacional Benito Juárez en viaje a Texas para participar en una reunión sobre un proyecto para construir un puente sobre el Rio Grande. Al llegar a la puerta de embarque se unió a la fila para abordar el avión. Una mujer joven, maya, con un talego de tela de colores que le colgaba de un hombro, se colocó detrás de él. Mientras esperaban para presentar la tarjeta de embarque y entrar en el avión, el arquitecto puso su maletín en el suelo y escribió algo en una libretita de bolsillo. Cuando lo fue a levantar, el maletín había desaparecido. Se volvió para mirar detrás de él y vio que la mujer maya, con el talego colgado al hombro, se alejaba a toda prisa, sosteniendo el maletín. Se echó a andar para seguirla, pero cuando estaba a punto de alcanzarla, ella dobló una esquina bruscamente y se adentró en un área solitaria del aeropuerto donde había dos hombres, también mayas, quienes al parecer la esperaban. Los dos hombres flanquearon al arquitecto.

—Esto es un secuestro amistoso —uno de ellos dijo.

Iban vestidos con camisa blanca y pantalones grises.

—¿Quiénes son ustedes? —preguntó el arquitecto.

Como respuesta, recibió un empujón en la espalda para que se pusiera en marcha. Una furgoneta Volkswagen esperaba afuera del edificio con el conductor al volante y el motor al ralentí. La mujer maya se subió al vehículo y se sentó en el asiento de al lado del conductor, mientras que los dos hombres, con el arquitecto en el medio de ellos, ocuparon el asiento de atrás. Uno de ellos le vendó los ojos con un pañuelo.

—Va a ser un viaje largo, así que tome un trago —el otro hombre dijo y agarró una botella de mezcal de una caja con licores que había en la furgoneta, la acercó a la boca del arquitecto y le forzó a que bebiera un buen trago.

En poco tiempo, el arquitecto se quedó dormido, aunque despertaba a intervalos, pero enseguida se topaba con la botella entre los labios, y el alcohol le volvía a inducir el sueño. Cuando llegaron al punto de destino, los secuestradores cargaron con el arquitecto, borracho como una cuba, y todos bajaron del vehículo. Luego lo transportaron a volandas como su fuera un saco de harina hasta un pequeño edificio de adobe y cañas y lo depositaron, junto con el maletín, en una petaca que había dentro para que durmiera la mona.

Cuando despertó era ya el día siguiente. La luz del sol, junto con gorjeos de pájaros, rumor de conversaciones y un olor mezcla de café, tortillas y frijoles se filtraban por la ventana abierta. Estaba desorientado, sin idea de dónde se encontraba. También sentía hambre y necesidad de orinar. Afortunadamente en la vivienda había un baño con retrete y agua corriente. Entonces se cambió de ropa, que sacó de su maletín, y salió fuera de la caseta. Vio gente sentada en el suelo alrededor de una hoguera.

—¿Quiénes son ustedes? —preguntó.

—Pertenecemos al pueblo Tzotzil —uno de ellos que parecía el jefe contestó en español.

—¿Y qué lugar es éste?

—Este territorio pertenece a la municipalidad de Ocozocoautla, Chiapas. Formamos parte del Consejo del pueblo
indígena.

El arquitecto comprendió que se encontraba en territorio
de selva tropical. Se mantuvo de pie en frente de ellos y en
silencio hasta que el jefe hizo un ademán para que se acercara
y comiera. Él reconoció a los dos secuestradores que lo trajeron
hasta allí. Mientras comía, tortillas y frijoles, y bebía café, la
gente Tzotzil continuó conversando en su idioma sin prestarle
atención. Cuando se recompuso, los del grupo se levantaron,
y el jefe le dio señas para que les siguiera, y el arquitecto anduvo, mezclado entre el grupo, sacudiéndose a cada paso los
mosquitos de la cara.

Un par de kilómetros más tarde, el grupo se paró y sus
miembros se alinearon en semicírculo. Para el arquitecto, el
espectáculo que se contemplaba no podía resultar más absurdo:
Una altísima escalera de madera, pintada de blanco, a la que
le faltaban algunos pedazos de los rieles se levantaba en medio
de un pequeño claro, rodeada de árboles oscuros, de modo
que la blancura de la escalera contrastaba con la oscuridad del
lugar. El arquitecto levantó los ojos con la esperanza de ver algo
interesante al final de la escalera, pero ésta terminaba estúpida-
mente, sin nada más que la bóveda natural que formaban un
cúmulo de nubes rosadas. Allende el lugar, el horizonte aparecía
despejado, pero en la proximidad del pie de la escalera se veía
una cañería de la que emanaban chorros de agua que se esparcía
por el terreno abrupto.

El arquitecto alzó la cabeza y miró al grupo de gente for-
mado en semicírculo con gesto inquisitivo.

—El Gobierno nos facilita agua para el regadío. Nosotros
controlamos el gasto —dijo el jefe.

—Parece razonable —contestó el arquitecto y, desconcertado, dirigió su mirada hacia el tope de la escalera.

—El final de la escalera nos sirve de ventana al mundo —dijo el jefe y añadió—: Le hemos traído a nuestro territorio para que usted lo vea con sus propios ojos.

El arquitecto no dijo nada, pero negó vigorosamente con su cabeza en resistencia a subir. En ese momento, un hombre, que llevaba una soga atada a la cintura, se separó del grupo, se le acercó y, en un abrir y cerrar de ojos, pasó una parte de la soga alrededor de su cintura, dejando una longitud de aproximadamente un metro entre los dos. A continuación, el hombre Tzotzil le forzó a aproximarse a la escalera, y, en silencio, ambos subieron los peldaños en tándem. Al alcanzar el tope de la escalera se detuvieron por unos instantes y enseguida descendieron. Cuando tocaron tierra otra vez, el hombre nativo desató la soga que los unía. Entonces, el jefe habló de nuevo:

—Lo que queremos es que el Gobierno del Distrito Federal de México apruebe el presupuesto necesario para construir un puente que cruce el rio que usted ha visto desde arriba de la escalera.

El arquitecto avanzó un par de pasos hacia el jefe con actitud humilde y dijo:

—Entiendo lo que me dice.

—Queremos un puente para que se nos haga más fácil el intercambiar comercio con nuestros hermanos del otro lado del rio.

El arquitecto afirmó con la cabeza; luego respiró hondo y al cabo dijo:

—Entiendo lo que me dice.

El jefe movió la cabeza afirmativamente.

—¿Qué requieren de mí? —preguntó el arquitecto.

—Vamos a dejar que vuelva a la Ciudad de México con un mensaje para el Gobierno Federal, y su misión es convencer a las autoridades de la necesidad de construir un puente en este lugar.

—Entiendo lo que me dice —dijo el arquitecto.

El jefe Tzotzil movió la cabeza afirmativamente.

No existen registros referentes a la intervención del arquitecto en el Gobierno Federal, pero, pocos años después, el llamado Puente de Chiapas se construyó en el punto exacto donde los Tzotzils lo habían anticipado.

El ciervo

Me gustaría que alguien le dijera a esta gente que yo no estoy loco. Por más que repito mi historia, nadie me cree. No hace ni dos horas que la policía me trajo a este hospital mental en detención provisional bajo la sospecha de que constituyo un peligro para los demás.

Yo me he criado en Montana, y en mi familia, todos somos cazadores, incluso mis dos hermanas mayores. El año pasado saqué la licencia de caza mayor, y mi padre me regaló el rifle de mis sueños. "Vas a ser un buen cazador, Hijo", me dijo.

Mi padre me facilitó el contacto con un guía de caza aquí en Nuevo México, donde me encuentro estudiando en la universidad. Antes de que mi padre me regalara el rifle, mi sueño era jugar al baloncesto. Mido uno noventa y tres de estatura, pero solo peso setenta y siete kilos, por lo que algunos de mis compañeros dicen que estoy muy flaco para ser buen jugador. Por eso, voy mucho al gimnasio para desarrollar más mis músculos.

Desde que tengo el rifle, sin embargo, mi ideal ha cambiado. Ahora sueño con cazar un gran venado y ganar un trofeo de caza mayor. Por eso, ayer, llamé al guía que me recomendó mi padre y acordamos juntarnos en su campamento que queda algunos kilómetros más allá del pueblo de Taos.

Así que hoy en la mañana, temprano, me puse mi vestimenta de caza, coloqué el rifle en el maletero del coche y conduje hasta el lugar de la cita, donde llegué poco antes del mediodía. Una fina capa de nieve cubría el terreno. El cielo estaba despejado, y una suave y fría brisa traía olor a pino. El guía y yo iniciamos la marcha hacia el sur, y pasado el mediodía llegamos a una zona rocosa donde había un cúmulo de álamos con las hojas de un atractivo color amarillo.

¡Uau! El paisaje era maravilloso. Yo sugerí hacer un alto para disfrutar de la vista. Pero mi guía dijo: "Si de verdad tu quieres ser experto en caza mayor, debemos otear y dirigirnos hacia el valle". Y hacia allí nos dirigimos.

Anduvimos unos cinco kilómetros más cuando empecé a notar que la vegetación era más abundante y de un verde más intenso que lo que habíamos visto hasta entonces. El guía dijo: "Cerca de aquí debe correr un arroyo". Yo eché una ojeada a mí alrededor y fue en aquel momento cuando descubrí huellas de animal ungulado cruzando el sendero por el que caminábamos. Alerté a mi guía, quien comentó: "Un alce solitario y sediento se dirige hacia el arroyo". Mi corazón dio un vuelco. Seguimos la línea de huellas hasta un punto en el que el sendero se bifurcaba y las huellas desaparecieron. Acordamos cada uno seguir una de las dos rutas.

Yo avanzaba lentamente, manteniendo la respiración superficial y el rifle listo para disparar tan pronto como mi objetivo se hiciera visible. La dificultad estaba, sin embargo, en que cada dos por tres me parecía ver un ciervo: en alguna roca oscura, el ramaje caído de los árboles, la penumbra originada por la luz que se filtraba a través de las zarzas… Hasta que de repente, a unos cuarenta metros de mí, medio oculto por arbustos, discerní la presencia de un magnífico animal, un ciervo adulto de cornamenta formidable que tan pronto aparecía como desaparecía, como si se tratara de una visión. Yo me sentía como hipnotizado por su presencia, hasta que me di cuenta de que el ciervo podría darse media vuelta y correr monte arriba. Así que mantuve los ojos en las huellas y también me guié por el olfato.

Después de poco más de una hora de seguimiento, el venado solitario cambió de dirección, y, en mi determinación de rastrear las huellas, caí en un barranco. Oí el sonido de agua corriente y pensé que provendría tal vez del arroyo del que habló mi guía. Entonces escalé la pared de la zanja para alcanzar la superficie del terreno de nuevo y localizar al venado. Cuando alcancé el nivel de la superficie y miré a mi frente me quedé helado al ver la cabeza y cuello de un ciervo, provisto de una cornamenta monumental, que permanecía inmóvil unos pasos más allá del borde del barranco donde me encontraba, como una silueta superpuesta contra el vasto horizonte que, en aquel momento, aparecía nublado. ¡Qué cornamenta tan magnífca!

Desde mi posición, apenas alcanzado el borde del barranco, no vi nada más que el busto y más allá las copas de los árboles. No reflexioné, pero me las arreglé para sujetar el rifle en posición de tiro, apunté a dónde pensé que quedaba el corazón del ciervo y apreté el gatillo. ¡Ay, ay!, inmediatamente oí. ¡Dios mío!, me dije, he herido a alguien. Me quedé de piedra. Hice un esfuerzo y conseguí salir del barranco. Entonces vi un hombre de mediana edad que yacía en la hierba, agarrándose con fuerza el muslo izquierdo. Lleno de aprehensión, corrí hacia él. Vi que la sangre se filtraba a través del paño de sus pantalones vaqueros y que las lágrimas resbalaban por sus mejillas.

Eché mano de mi cuchillo de monte y comencé a rasgar la tela de sus pantalones alrededor de la herida, y enseguida me di cuenta de que era superficial, pero aún así quise ayudarle en todo lo posible.

—Voy a llamar a una ambulancia —dije

—Y yo voy a llamar a la policía —replicó.

Ambos permanecimos en el mismo lugar sin encontrar modo de comunicarnos. Yo me percaté de su enfado para conmigo y traté de justificar mi acto diciendo que no le había visto cuando disparé, que yo creí que disparaba a un alce y no a él. Pero el dijo que le parecía que yo estaba mal de la cabeza. A mí no me gustó su parecer. De repente sentí el deseo de salir corriendo, y estuve a punto de dejarle allí tendido, cuando oí el sonido de sirenas y me lo pensé mejor.

La ambulancia y coches de la policía llegaron al mismo tiempo. Los agentes comenzaron a interrogarnos. Yo oí decir al herido que él era un fotógrafo profesional que estaba en misión de trabajo, que se encontraba fotografiando el tótem con el ícono de la cabeza de un ciervo que podían ver allí, el mismo que yo tomé como verdadero cuando disparé y le herí. Uno de los policías se me acercó. Yo le conté mi punto de vista, pero desde el comienzo, tuve la impresión de que el agente no me creía. Entonces, el proceso se aceleró: la ambulancia se llevó al fotógrafo al Centro de Urgencias, y a mí me trajeron a este hospital mental en el coche de la policía bajo la sospecha de que estoy mal de la cabeza y constituyo un peligro para los demás.

Quisiera encontrar a alguien conocido para que les diga a estos facultativos que yo no estoy loco, que solamente soy un novato en materia de caza mayor y que me queda mucho por aprender después de causar este accidente. Espero que esta gente del hospital entiendan mi situación antes de que mis padres, mis amigos y todo el mundo que me conoce se enteren de dónde me encuentro y pierda mi reputación de hombre cabal.

El caminante y el halcón

Cuando la luz y la sombra alcanzan un marcado contraste, el calor quema la maleza, y los guijarros crepitan bajo la suela de las botas, un joven ornitólogo, su rostro y brazos bronceados por un despiadado sol del desierto, camina por un sendero solitario. Dos horas antes, marchaba por un desfiladero entre castaños y plantas de hojas anchas, siguiendo el curso del pájaro sílfide de cola larga, una especie única de colibrí, para, si la oportunidad se presentase, capturarlo. ¿Cómo fue que perdió su curso y ahora se encuentra en este caluroso valle?

Con la palma de su mano, el joven se limpia el sudor de la frente. No obstante, está disfrutando de la experiencia: la vista de las lejanas colinas, el dorado campo, el verde cactus con su fruta roja, el sonido de sus pasos... ¿Pero cómo ha llegado él hasta aquí? ¡La Sílfide azul lo hizo! Con los ojos de la mente, él ve otra vez aquel insecto azulado, excepcionalmente grande, que, surgiendo de un arroyuelo que corría justo al borde de la vereda por la que caminaba, gira hacia él, y su pálida cara, como de muñeca, lo mira fijamente: "Yo soy una sílfide, y en nuestro mundo, nos protegemos los unos a los otros. Deja al colibrí en paz". El viento le trae estas palabras a sus oídos, en tanto que el gigantesco insecto bate sus alas. En aquel momento, una fuerte corriente de aire lo desplaza. Y ahora, aquí está, caminando por este sendero polvoriento.

Está tratando de orientarse cuando un pájaro grande, posado en la punta de un cardo solitario, acapara su atención. Es un halcón. Se acerca al pájaro. ¿Qué verá en mí un ave de rapiña? El halcón aprieta sus garras con fuerza. El ornitólogo admira su cuerpo alargado, sus plumas de color castaño, su pico curvado en la punta y sus poderosas garras. Lentamente, se le va acercando aún más, agarrando las tiras de cuero de su mochila, y entonces ve manchas de sangre en la pechuga. Se detiene al borde del sendero, en frente del halcón, el cual adopta una pose arrogante y desafiante. El pico aparece manchado de sangre también. El joven aborrece lo que está viendo: el halcón ha atrapado una paloma blanca, que sangra, moribunda, entre sus garras. De nuevo, aparece la Sílfide azul, aleteando en el aire entre él y el halcón: "Renuncia a tus intenciones de capturar el colibrí de cola larga. Mira lo que le está pasando a esa paloma blanca"—una suave brisa le trae estas palabras.

Mucho que aprender, reflexiona el caminante, y otra vez apela a su intuición para encontrar su rumbo.

Alimentando a la familia

Ir en autobús a trabajar me es más ventajoso que conducir porque el autobús para cerca de mi apartamento y del hospital donde trabajo como ayudante de cocinero.

Yo tengo 21 años. La mayor parte de la gente que viaja en el autobús es mayor que yo. Casi nadie habla, solo intercambiamos algunas miradas. En particular, hay un señor mayor, delgado, de pelo canoso, aunque abundante, que acapara mi atención. Usa gafas de lentes redondas sin montura y tiene aire de filósofo. Siempre está en el autobús cuando yo subo.

Ayer, una mujer joven, sus hombros cubiertos con un chal ajado, estaba sentada en el banco que hay bajo la marquesina de la parada del autobús. La mañana estaba soleada. Un niño de unos 5 años, de pelo largo y sucio, que le tapaba las orejas y le bajaba hasta los ojos, jugaba con un perrito terrier en la acera. Yo me situé de pie a la derecha de la mujer.

Un autobús llegó y paró. No era ni el mío ni el de ellos. Reanudó la marcha. Después que se fue, yo levanté los ojos y vi un hombre grueso, vestido con una camisa azul, desgastada, y pantalones de pana, que salía de un McDonald, situado al otro lado de la calle, enfrente de nosotros. Se paró de pie al lado de su camioneta y comenzó a desenvolver un bocadillo McMuffin.

—Psst —la mujer del chal chistó al niño, levantando la barbilla hacia donde estaba el hombre grueso.

El chiquillo comandó al perro, y ambos atravesaron la calle, libre de tráfico en aquel momento, corriendo. Niño y perro rondaron alrededor el hombre grueso por un tiempito hasta que el terrier dio un salto acrobático y le arrebató el bocadillo de las manos. Hecho esto, el animal salió corriendo con la comida entre sus dientes.

—Yo se lo voy a traer de vuelta —dijo el niño, mientras corría detrás del perro.

El hombre se limpió sus dedos grasosos en los pantalones.

—No te molestes, chaval, el perro ya tiene la lengua en ello —gritó y caminó de vuelta al restaurante.

El terrier dejó caer el trofeo a los pies de su ama. Ella lo recogió y lo dividió en tres partes. Mi autobús llegó, y yo subí a él. A través de las ventanillas traseras vi que los tres, sentados en el banco, disfrutaban del bocadillo. ¡Fascinante! Pensé.

Esta mañana, antes de tomar el autobús, por capricho, fui al mismo McDonald y compré un bocadillo McMuffin. Salí y me paré en el bordillo de la acera mientras lo desenvolvía. Como ayer, la misma familia estaba bajo la marquesina de la parada del autobús, mirándome. Antes de que parpadeara tres veces, el niño y el terrier estaban a mi lado. Dado que yo ya sabía lo que buscaban, ofrecí mi bocadillo al chiquillo. Pero él lo rechazó con gesto de disgusto, y el perro orinó en mi zapato. Frustrados, ambos regresaron al lado de la mujer.

Mi autobús llegó a la parada, y yo crucé la calle justo a tiempo para tomarlo. El filósofo estaba sentado en uno de los asientos delanteros. Intercambiamos una mirada.

—Usted les interrumpió su método —dijo.

Yo me quedé helado.

El filósofo estaba leyendo un libro titulado ¨El Discurso del Método¨, de René Descartes.

—¡Esclarecedor! —exclamé y me abrí camino hacia el fondo del autobús.

El hombre barrigudo

El hombre barrigudo piensa que él es un barril. Su creencia le viene de un sueño repetitivo que tiene desde hace muchos años. El hombre se cree lo que sueña. Cuando se mueve, oye un gorgoteo de líquido dentro de su estómago. Mientras duerme, el barril rueda sobre el eje de su cama y choca con la punta de su bota o con la botella de cerveza dejadas en el suelo. Pero el hombre barrigudo apenas si nota las magulladuras. Medio dormido, se levanta del suelo, vuelve a la cama y descansa por algún tiempo. Por la mañana, se levanta, entra en el cuarto de baño, se para frente al inodoro, abre el grifo del barril y orina. Después va a la cocina y se toma la primera botella de cerveza entera de un trago para comenzar la jornada y rellenar el barril. A medida que transcurre el día, el hombre hace una pausa entre lata y lata de cerveza y recuerda que hubo un tiempo en que trabajaba y tenía esposa y amigos. Pero lo despidieron del trabajo y también perdió el afecto que una vez sintió por su mujer y amigos. Al final del día, el hombre barrigudo siente que su vientre se vuelve tenso como cuerdas de guitarra, teme que el barril se rompa y piensa si necesita un refuerzo, pero cuando se vuelve a dormir, sueña el mismo sueño.

Un regalo de amor

Dado que nos acercamos a la fecha de su cumpleaños, bella señora, yo fui a la *Tienda de la inspiración*. Quería elegir un regalo que le encantara. Empujé la puerta, pero me la encontré cerrada con llave. La empujé de nuevo, pero no cedió. Este inconveniente amenazó con arruinar mi imaginación. Pues ha de saber, bella señora, que yo la imagino a usted como nunca podría imaginar a ninguna otra mujer. Noche tras noche sueño con usted, y en mis sueños siempre se la ve dulce, lo mismo si aparece flotando en una rosada nube que recostada en un diván de purpureo terciopelo.

Desde la *Tienda de la inspiración*, me dirigí a la *Tienda de lo común*. Me mostraron anillos, collares, pulseras… todo me pareció vulgar, sin ningún acento. "¿Por qué gime?", la dependienta preguntó. Mi pensamiento voló a usted, a su viveza, su sonrisa angelical. Pensé en las noches de verano, los dos tumbados en la arena de la playa bajo la luz de la luna, con el bálsamo de sus labios sobre mi piel, envuelto en su ternura y con las gaviotas, amantes de la luna, volando alrededor nuestro. "La luz fluorescente irrita mis ojos", le contesté.

Con la imaginación desgastada, en un último atento, mis ojos se tropezaron con esta perla que aquí le traigo, bella señora. Le ruego la acepte como un regalo de amor.

El árbol solitario

El calor del verano ha quemado la espiga en el campo y teñido de marrón las hojas caídas. Cada mañana él camina hasta el granero. El sonido del crujido de la arena bajo las suelas de los zapatos pisando el terreno le recuerda un par de botas de combate que calzaron pies más jóvenes. Mira hacia atrás. ¿Tal vez descuidó percatarse de ese par de botas olvidadas en el porche? Pero detrás de él solo ve una nubecilla de polvo que se eleva unos centímetros del suelo, remolina sobre su eje y desaparece sin dejar rastro. Él sigue su camino.

El último día del verano, antes de entrar al granero, hace una pausa y escucha el gorjeo de los pájaros. El repiqueteo proviene de unos árboles cercanos que se ven detrás de una tapia que separa su granja de un parque público. Él se imagina que los pájaros le dicen: *busca, no te rindas.* Dentro del granero, troncos de leña, esperando el invierno para alimentar la chimenea, se apiñan en el rincón detrás de la puerta; fardos de heno llenan los estantes; rastrillos, escobones, arneses para la caballería, todo está en su lugar como siempre. Un largo espejo con un fino marco de metal cuelga detrás de la puerta trasera. No se acuerda de quién fue la idea de colocarlo allí. Se para de pie frente al espejo: un hombre alto, de piel curtida por el sol, anchos hombros y manos firmes. Luego, con el fin de que entre la brisa y refresque el granero, entreabre la puerta. ¡Dios mío! Por un momento, el espejo le trae el reflejo de un soldado en uniforme de guerra, calzando botas de combate, la cara y forma del cuerpo semejando las suyas propias. Entrecierra los ojos para concentrarse. "Quién…"". Se vuelve para mirar afuera. Enfilando la línea de reflexión del espejo ve las largas y gruesas raíces expuestas de un pequeño árbol solitario que habita la superficie de la tapia de piedra. La imagen del soldado se desvanece y el granjero cierra la puerta y sus ojos. Y cuando los abre de nuevo se ve asimismo en el espejo con las marcas del luto en ellos. Dándole la espalda al espejo, comienza a trabajar vaciando sacos de trigo en un rincón del granero.

El Perro de raza mixta

Durante una de las visitas a la perrera, Elisa, de pie frente a las barras que separaban el público de los compartimentos con los perros, apuntó a uno de ellos, tristón, de raza indefinida, que estaba solo en su cubículo. Miguel, su marido y logopeda, quien estaba parado al lado de su mujer, echó una mirada al canino, hizo pucheros con los labios y arrugó la nariz. ¡Detestable!

—¿De verdad te gusta ese perro?

—Sí, me gusta —contestó ella.

Se habían conocido a través del Internet en enero del 2004; se gustaron y comenzaron a salir juntos. Sus relaciones sexuales, ambos estuvieron de acuerdo, fueron satisfactorias, pero qué decir de sus personalidades, ¿serían compatibles, si decidieran formalizar sus relaciones? Para probarlo, decidieron vivir juntos a lo largo de las cuatro estaciones del año. Para ello, firmaron un contrato de renta y ocuparon una pequeña casa en la zona de la Bahía de San Francisco. Tuvieron éxito, y en Febrero del 2015 se casaron. El tenía cuarenta años, no muy alto pero bien proporcionado y de aspecto sano. Ella había pasado de la edad fértil; petisa, de ojos negros y piel pálida se asemejaba a una de esas antiguas muñecas de porcelana alemanas. Ninguno de los dos había estado caso antes y no tenían hijos.

Un empleado de la perrera, un hombre joven, de manos grandes y rostro curtido, se les acercó.

—Se llama Siba —dijo, refiriéndose al mismo perro—. Si quieren —continuó— yo puedo llevarla al patio para que ustedes interactúen con ella.

Elisa movió la cabeza afirmativamente. El hombre sacó el perro del cubículo y ellos le siguieron hacia afuera. La idea de adoptar un perro se les ocurrió unos seis meses después de que se casaron; más para disfrutar de su compañía durante sus excursiones al aire libre que como perro guardián.

—¿Cuántos años tiene esta perra? —Miguel preguntó.

El empleado se abstuvo de contestar hasta que soltó a Siba y la dejó corretear por el patio vallado.

—Unos diez años, nuestro veterinario calcula que tiene —dijo entonces.

Al oír la edad del perro, Miguel enseguida se volvió a Elisa.

—Cariño, yo creía que buscábamos un galgo joven, no un perro viejo y desgarbado como éste.

Algunos años antes, Miguel tuvo un galgo italiano, fino y rápido como el diablo, un placer verlo correr.

—¡Oh! No digas eso, Miguel.

Él puso su atención en el sucio y lastimero perro: era blanco con manchas de color naranja repartidas por la cabeza, el dorso y las patas. No se lo podía creer. ¿Sería que Elisa estaba pasando por momentos de confusión mental?

—¿Pero cómo puede ser que te guste este…?

En aquel momento, Siba, con trote destartalado, se les acercó y se tropezó con las piernas de Miguel, interrumpiendo su frase. Él la empujó con el pie y con tal fuerza que su acción más pareció una patada que un empujón. La perra se quejó por un instante, luego orinó en el césped y enseguida vino hacia Elisa y llena de contento se puso a danzar a sus pies.

—No seas brusco con el perro, por favor —dijo Elisa a su marido.

A Miguel le faltó poco para decir que a él el perro no le gustaba en absoluto.

—¡Maldito perro! —murmuró.

Siba, juguetona alrededor de Elisa, dio dos o tres ladridos amistosos, y Miguel notó que le faltaban algunos dientes, y los que aún poseía se habían vuelto amarillos. Chascó la lengua en desagrado.

—¿Cómo es posible que te vuelques por un perro tan lastimoso?

—Pues porque sobre gustos no hay nada escrito.

Miguel no contestó. Se preguntaba si la diferencia en el gusto por los perros que existía entre ellos no sería sino solo una muestra, algo así como la primera golondrina que anuncia la llegada de la primavera, entre otras diferencias no percibidas todavía.

Una vez que el cuidador llevó a Siba de vuelta a la perrera, Elisa se dirigió a la oficina de adopción, y Miguel la siguió. Un empleado de mediana edad, de espeso bigote negro y amigable sonrisa, se encontraba detrás del mostrador, y ellos se le acercaron. Miguel se llevó las manos a los bolsillos y se paró de pie junto a su esposa, mirándola con ojos incrédulos mientras ella comunicaba al empleado su interés por adoptar al perro. Súbitamente, Miguel sintió una ola de calor que le ascendía por la espina dorsal y le cegaba. Se encontraba a punto de explotar cuando el empleado intervino:

—Sucede —dijo— que esta perra no está disponible para adopción.

A Miguel esas palabras le sonaron más propias de un árbitro de boxeo que de un trabajador en la perrera. Elisa respiró profundo, apoyó los codos en el mostrador, echó la barbilla para adelante con el fin de mirar en la pantalla del ordenador y preguntó:

—¿Por qué no?

—Esta perra está enferma —dijo el hombre después de confirmar la información que tenía.

Mientras tanto, Miguel hacía esfuerzos por mantener la calma, al tiempo que trataba de hallar qué postura debería él adoptar en la situación de conflicto que se avecinaba; le parecía inverosímil que su mujer tomara una decisión unilateral y fuera a adoptar, contra toda lógica, un perro enfermo.

—No obstante —el empleado prosiguió— si un perro está enfermo, pero alguien lo quiere adoptar, a veces permitimos llevarlo a casa por unos días para consultar con un veterinario antes de adoptarlo.

Elisa se volvió para mirar a Miguel y puso una sonrisa de compromiso, sus chispeantes ojos negros hablaban por ella de su intención de hacer lo que el empleado acababa de explicar.

—Cariño —Miguel se apresuró a decir— ¿Por qué ese capricho? ¡Estamos frente a un perro enfermo!

—Pero a mí me gusta esta perra —Elisa no dudó.

—Ya veo —dijo el hombre y paseó sus ojos del uno al otro como si se tratara de dos boxeadores en el cuadrilátero.

—Ya veo —Miguel dijo también, aunque no estuvo seguro de qué era lo que él veía.

Al final, en aquel atardecer veraniego, Miguel y Elisa salieron de la perrera llevando a Siba de una correa corta. A medida que avanzaban por el aparcamiento hacia el coche, la sinfonía de ladridos proveniente de los perros de adentro se desvanecía lentamente, y Miguel se sentía como pasajero en un barco que acababa de zarpar hacia playas desconocidas. Cuando llegaron a su vehículo de tres-puertas, pusieron a Siba en el maletero, visiblemente nerviosa, y Miguel lo puso en marcha.

—Debemos parar en alguna clínica de perros cercana —Elisa dijo mientras buscaba la dirección en Google.

—Está bien —Miguel asintió secamente, dudando de su poder de persuasión para disuadir a su mujer de sus absurdas pretensiones.

Había un hospital de urgencia para animales a unos tres kilómetros de donde se encontraban ellos, y Miguel condujo hasta allí. El veterinario, Dr. Rosado, un hombre de mediana edad, bajo y regordete, en uniforme quirúrgico de color verde claro, salió a recibirlos en el hall de entrada. Elisa tiró de la correa para acercar a Siba a los pies del veterinario mientras ella le explicaba el problema. El Dr. Rosado la escuchó atentamente, y enseguida condujo a ellos y a Siba a la sala de examen.

—La perra tiene un absceso en el recto —dijo cuando concluyó su examen clínico.

Elisa y Miguel se miraron con cara de no entender el significado del hallazgo.

—Es accesible a la extirpación quirúrgica —el Dr. Rosado dijo mientras se lavaba las manos.

—¿Cuánto nos costaría? —preguntó Miguel.

—Alrededor de mil quinientos dólares —contestó el veterinario mientras se secaba las manos.

Miguel se llevó una palma sobre la frente con cara de alarma. Incurrir en tal gasto resultaba una desfachatez. Nunca antes Elisa había empujado el límite de su tolerancia en tal grado. ¿Por qué hacerlo ahora?

—¿Tiene riesgos? —preguntó Elisa.

—Todas las operaciones quirúrgicas conllevan un riesgo, pero si tenemos suerte y todo sale bien, podemos dar la perra por curada —contestó el doctor Rosado.

Miguel se dijo así mismo que a él no le gustaba aquel perro en absoluto.

—¿No le importa, doctor, si mi mujer y yo lo hablamos a solas antes de tomar una decisión? —preguntó.

—Adelante, por favor.

Salieron de la sala y fueron otra vez al hall de entrada.

—Bajo mi punto de vista —Miguel dijo con energía— adoptar un perro que está enfermo no tiene sentido.

Se encontraban de pie en medio del hall. Elisa miraba a su marido a la cara como si hubiera anticipado su reacción.

—No hay marcha atrás, Miguel —dijo en voz baja como temiendo que alguien estuviera escuchando.

—¿Qué quieres decir? Por supuesto que nos podemos retractar —No podía creer que ella se aferrara a un razonamiento tan ilógico. Ta vez su cabeza no le funcionaba bien. ¿Le pasaría algo de lo cual él no se había percatado?

—Tú fuiste testigo —dijo ella— del afecto que Siba me mostró en el patio de la perrera, y…

—¡Todo eso no es más que sentimentalismo! —En aquel momento a Miguel no le importó que se le notara enfadado. Elisa parecía dar a entender que el perro la había elegido como dueña y señora.

—Cubriré los gastos de la operación con mis ahorros — dijo Elisa.

Tal declaración tomó a Miguel un poco por sorpresa. Si ella pagaba la cuenta, no había duda de que se declaraba a sí misma el ama del perro; sin embargo, él, Miguel, todavía habría de vivir bajo el mismo techo. ¿En qué estaría pensado?

—Pero, Elisa, no se trata solo del dinero. Es que…

Se le vino a la mente en aquel momento que estaba dando no solo con los deseos de su mujer sino que también con la alianza que se había establecido entre ella y el perro, que él mismo había visto desarrollarse.

—Haz lo que mejor te parezca —concedió.

De vuelta en el despacho del doctor, Elisa le dijo, para asombro de Miguel, que su marido y ella estaban de acuerdo con que operara a Siba. Así que, arreglaron la admisión de la perra como paciente y ellos se fueron a casa.

Aquella noche, Miguel no pegó ojo. No podía quitarse de la mente el pensamiento de que adoptar un perro enfermo era una temeridad. ¿Cómo iban a cuidarlo? Se pasó la noche dando vueltas en la cama hasta el punto que su mujer se despertó. Entonces él trató de convencerla de la futilidad de seguir adelante con tal empresa, pero ella no respondió, sino que se acomodó de nuevo en la cama y enseguida se durmió hasta que sonó el despertador. Cuando se levantaron, ella dijo que iba a tomar unos días libres (trabajaba como encargada en una tienda de electrodomésticos) para ir a recoger a Siba y cuidar de ella. Miguel pensó, pero no habló, que, definitivamente, Elisa había asumido el título de dueña del perro.

Aquel día, avisada de que Siba estaba lista para el alta, Elisa fue a recogerla. Un empleado sacó a la perra, que llevaba un collar isabelino de protección, a la sala de recepción. Elisa la miró con ojos espantados, pues, con aquel tan grande collar de plástico en forma de embudo, Siba parecía un ser de otro planeta. El empleado dijo que, de acuerdo con el doctor, Siba estaba lista para el alta, aunque con antibióticos y bajo la condición de seguir tratamiento con un veterinario. Elisa estuvo de acuerdo. Luego pagó la cuenta y salió. En el coche, acomodó a Siba, que todavía estaba adormecida, en una manta extendida en el maletero y condujo a casa.

De pie en el medio de la cocina, mirando a la perra, y la perra a ella, parecía que Elisa se preguntara qué debería ella hacer a continuación. Determinó llamar a Miguel al trabajo.

—Me pregunto dónde debemos instalar a Siba para dormir.

—Decide tú, Elisa. Es tu perro.

—Todavía se la ve muy débil para dormir afuera…

—Haz lo que te parezca mejor —Miguel concluyó.

Elisa decidió arriesgarse a dejar a Siba sola en la cocina por un rato, aprovechando que todavía estaba adormilada, e ir a la tienda de animales más cercana para comprar una cama para perro, un collar y una correa. Cuando Miguel volvió a casa, después del trabajo, halló la cama colocada en un rincón de la cocina y a Siba en ella. Durante la noche, sin embargo, la perra deambuló por donde quiera. Elisa se levantó varias veces y trató, con poco éxito, de calmarla. Miguel se percató de que el perro enfermo no solo les iba a alterar el ritmo del dormir, sino también su intimidad.

Al día siguiente, Elisa pidió una cita con la clínica para animales, de modo que la primera salida de Siba fue para visitar al veterinario de la comunidad. Olfateó el umbral de la puerta de entrada y rehusó seguir adelante hasta que Elisa la animó con palabras cariñosas. Nada más entrar a la sala de espera, un espacio de unos seis o siete metros cuadrados, Siba se dio de narices con un bulldog de piel oscura, y se zarandearon el uno al otro como pelea de ciervos hasta que Elisa y la dueña del otro perro, una mujer de mediana edad y de apariencia humilde, se las apañaron para separarlos. Un momento después, el asistente de veterinario, un hombre joven, delgado, llamó al bulldog. Después vino el turno de Siba.

Con cuidado, el asistente de veterinario levantó a Siba del suelo y la colocó sobre la mesa de observación, y el doctor, un hombre de aspecto sano, de unos cincuenta años de edad, procedió a examinar a la paciente siguiendo su propia rutina, sus dedos deslizándose sobre la piel de la perra como tentáculos y él concentrándose en la cicatriz quirúrgica.

—Todo va bien —dijo con acento polaco, una vez dado por terminado el examen clínico, y añadió—: En un par de días ustedes pueden desprenderla del collar sanitario.

—Gracias, doctor Ku…

—Kurboranowsky —dijo el veterinario y añadió—: Puede llamarme Dr. K. para abreviar.

—Gracias, Dr. K. —dijo Elisa y, un tanto atorada, condujo a Siba hacia la salida.

En su camino de vuelta a casa, Elisa se paró en la tienda de animales y compró algunos juguetes para perros con el fin de tener a Siba entretenida mientras Miguel y ella se iban a trabajar. Pero pronto estuvo claro, sin embargo, que Siba no era una perra juguetona. Durante el día, correteaba en el jardín de la trasera de la casa y ladraba a toda creatura viviente que se le cruzaba. Cuando se cansaba se tumbaba al sol, apoyada contra alguna pared y dormía largas siestas. Las noches se hacían más problemáticas porque no le gustaba dormir en su cama. Elisa extendió una manta sobre ella para hacérsela más cómoda, pero no sirvió de nada. La situación se hizo estresante para ambos esposos, y Miguel, sin que encontrara mucha resistencia por parte de su esposa, optó por dormir en el sofá de la sala de estar.

Llegados a ese punto, Elisa, quizás alarmada por lo mal que iban las cosas entre Miguel y ella, llevó a Siba a la tienda de animales y la dejó que olfateara las camas colocadas en la estantería hasta que pegó la nariz en una de ellas, hecha de tela de tartán, y Elisa la compró. Con ello se arregló el problema de las noches y Miguel volvió a dormir con su mujer. No obstante, él era consciente de que, debido a la perra, algo, lo cual no podía o no quería definir, estaba cambiando en sus relaciones.

Un día de agosto, Elisa fue al centro para encontrarse con un par de amigas y llevó a Siba, ya sin el collar isabelino, consigo. Todos se sentaron en una terraza para tomar café. Por precaución, Elisa había atado la correa a la pata de su silla. De repente, sintió un tirón que la sacó del asiento y fue al suelo, mientras Siba escapó, arrastrando tras de sí la silla, en persecución de un caniche que camina al otro lado de la calle. A mitad de camino, la correa se enrolló entre las piernas de una mujer que por allí transitaba, y ella, la perra y la silla rodaron juntos por el asfalto. Enseguida se acercaron otros transeúntes y los rodearon.

—¡Dios mío! —La señora exclamó mientras se levantaba del suelo—. ¿De dónde se escapó este perro?

La escena empezaba a tomar un aspecto teatral.

—Pues, estábamos allí… —Una de las amigas de Elisa señaló con el dedo la terraza donde se habían sentado—. La perra vio el caniche…

—Mi marido y yo, —Elisa la interrumpió— hemos rescatado esta perra de la perrera. Estamos tratando de familiarizarnos con ella. Siento mucho…

—Bueno, bueno. Al menos no estoy herida —dijo la mujer.

—Lo siento mucho —repitió Elisa y extendió los brazos como si quisiera incluir a todos los presentes.

Cuando los curiosos escucharon estas palabras, comenzaron a dispersarse, Elisa se hizo cargo de Siba, sus dos amigas retornaron la silla a donde pertenecía, el caniche desapareció de la escena y el espectáculo finalizó.

Cuando Miguel volvió a casa aquella noche y su esposa le contó durante la cena lo sucedido, no pudo aplacar la ira que le invadía.

—Francamente, Elisa, estoy harto de este perro.

—Ese es tu problema, Miguel. Siba no es un perro impecable. Tiene sus defectos, y tú no puedes perdonar que los tenga.

Miguel se revolvió en su silla. Puso el tenedor sobre la mesa, alcanzó el vaso de vino que tenía en frente del plato y se lo bebió de un trago.

—¿Por qué he de aguantar esta mierda? —murmuró.

—Depende de ti, Miguel, el valorar las cosas de forma realista y no dejar que te sobrepasen.

Miguel se irguió, llevó sus pies debajo de la silla y empujó ésta hacia atrás de forma abrupta. Me está diciendo que el problema no es de la perra, sino mío, pensó. Se levantó.

—¡Yo no soy quien ha adoptado este estúpido perro! —Salió del comedor.

Desde el enojo durante la cena, los esposos vivían en silencio, pero en un silencio tenso, y de nuevo cesaron de dormir en la misma habitación, aunque continuaron compartiendo las excursiones al aire libre durante los fines de semana. El Parque Regional Joaquín Miller, que les quedaba muy cerca de donde vivían en Oakland, se convirtió en su principal destino. Al principio, Miguel tuvo la esperanza de que Siba fuera a trotar por aquellos senderos con agilidad, pero su optimismo se desvaneció cuando, durante las siguientes pocas excursiones, se dio cuenta de que la perra se movía de forma desgarbada sobre el terreno. Se preguntaba si Siba alguna vez destacaría en algo.

Otro día, en el mes de octubre, se encontraban caminando por un sendero estrecho a lo largo de un cañón, por el fondo del cual corría un arroyo, cuando, de repente, Siba echó a correr precipicio abajo y a poco se quedó enganchada entre las zarzas. Elisa recurrió a su marido para ayudar a liberarla, pero Miguel reaccionó perezosamente, y fue solo con gran dificultad que lograron rescatarla.

—Yo no creo que esta perra sea *normal* —Miguel refunfuñó.

—Bueno, no es para tanto. Es más fácil ver la viga en el ojo ajeno que…

Miguel no escuchó más. Tratándose de su sentimiento hacia la perra, estaba claro que a su mujer no le importaba un comino, y cualquier intento de reconciliación a ese respecto era una batalla perdida. No obstante, se las apañaron para mantener su compostura y continuar la excursión. Siba, tal vez percibiendo el desencanto de su amo, se mantuvo a raya durante el resto del camino, olfateando las yerbas y los excrementos de animales. Cuando regresaron a casa, Miguel estaba exhausto, más debido a las confrontaciones entre ellos que al ejercicio físico. Se preguntaba por cuánto tiempo iban a durar discutiendo sin que algo se rompiera en su matrimonio.

Otro día, también en el parque, Siba se disparó delante de ellos en persecución de alguna presa. La pista la llevó a toparse con una pasta de excrementos recientes de vaca en la que se revolcó, de manera que, cuando volvió a reencontrarse con sus amos, apestaba.

—¡Esta perra se ha rebozado en mierda! —Miguel puso cara de disgusto.

—Siba es solo un animal.

—Así es. ¿Pero por qué insististe en adoptar un animal tan estúpido?

A Miguel se le pusieron los carrillos rojos. Elisa esperó unos momentos antes de responder y luego dijo: —Lo hecho, hecho está.

—¡No! —Miguel dio una patada a una piedra que rodó en la dirección de Siba y le golpeó el costado—. Lo que se ha hecho se puede deshacer.

—¡Cálmate! En cuanto lleguemos a casa la bañamos.

—No seré yo quien la toque. ¡Qué asco!

Cuando regresaron al coche, Miguel se negó a que la perra entrara; el hedor lo impregnaría todo, dijo. Elisa, sujetando a Siba por la correa, refunfuñando, trató de rebatir la decisión de su marido, al mismo tiempo que ella misma trataba de subir al coche con Siba. Pero Miguel no se ablandó. Subió el primero, cerró la puerta, lo puso en marcha y arrancó de estampida como alma que lleva el diablo.

Viéndose sola en el parque con la perra, a Elisa no le quedó otra alternativa sino caminar a casa con Siba. Cuando llegó, Miguel no estaba allí. Condujo a Siba derecho al patio y la bañó, aplicando abundante champú y restregando el pelo vigorosamente hasta que estuvo segura de que no quedaban trazas del mal olor.

Una vez satisfecha de su trabajo, Elisa llevó a Siba adentro de la casa y le echó de comer. Después fue al garaje para ver si el coche estaba ya allí; pero no estaba. En aquel momento, le sonó el móvil. Era un oficial de la policía de tráfico que llamaba para notificarle que Miguel tuvo un accidente de coche a la altura del Puente de la Bahía. "Conducción temeraria", dijo el oficial cuando Elisa le preguntó qué había pasado, y añadió que Miguel había intentado cambiar de carril a gran velocidad pero calculó mal la distancia que le separaba del otro vehículo y giró muy rápido hacia la derecha para evitar una colisión de modo que el frontal de su coche chocó violentamente contra el parapeto de la carretera. La ambulancia lo llevó al Hospital Provincial en San Francisco con una pierna rota, y su coche está listo para el transporte a un garaje de reparaciones. ¿Tenía ella alguna preferencia a qué garaje llevarlo?, le preguntó. "No", respondió Elisa.

Después de las alarmantes noticias que había recibido al teléfono, Elisa se mostró muy inquieta. Hizo planes para dejar a Siba en una cercana guardería para perros y a continuación fue a alquilar un coche y se puso en camino para ver a Miguel en el hospital.

El accidente le causó una fractura del tobillo, que ya se la habían tratado y enyesado. "No un gran problema" dijo él, aunque añadió que por algún tiempo tenía que hacer rehabilitación física y pedir la baja por enfermedad. Elisa le condujo a casa al día siguiente. Durante el viaje, ella manifestó que estaba dispuesta a deshacerse de Siba. Miguel dijo que, si a ella no le importaba, él preferiría hablar de ello más tarde porque se sentía cansado y quería echarse un sueño.

El patio de la casa incluía un pórtico de unos cuarenta metros de longitud, con suelo de baldosines mejicanos de color ocre. Un vallado de madera construido a lo largo de los flancos y la trasera del patio marcaba sus límites, y unos cuantos arbustos con camelias, repartidos por aquí y por allá, completaban el entorno. En este ambiente, Miguel comenzó a practicar los ejercicios de rehabilitación, siguiendo las explicaciones que el terapista le había facilitado, mientras que su mujer iba a trabajar. Corría la última semana de Octubre. Apoyado en muletas, Miguel daba pasos minúsculos a lo largo del pórtico. Siba lo observaba desde un rincón mientras que él ignoraba su presencia a propósito.

Un par de días más tarde, sin embargo, la perra se le acercó y comenzó a caminar a su lado. Él la dejó hacer y pronto la acción se convirtió en un juego: de vez en cuando, Siba aceleraba su marcha, dando algunos pasos hacia adelante, y Miguel se daba prisa por alcanzarla, y así prosiguiendo, se dio cuenta de que tal práctica se hacía entretenida y que aceleraba su mejoría.

Se pasó una semana sin que los esposos hubieran vuelto a hablar del asunto de desprenderse de Siba, según Elisa lo había referido en el coche mientras conducía a Miguel de vuelta a casa desde el hospital, aunque ambos se las habían apañado para zurcir sus desavenencias sin dejar costuras.

—Yo creo que pronto voy a encontrar un hogar para Siba —Elisa dijo una noche a principios de noviembre.

Se habían sentado alrededor de una pequeña mesa que tenían en el porche con un vaso de vino. El sol decaía detrás de las colinas de Oakland. Miguel se sorprendió así mismo acariciándole las orejas a la perra por primera vez.

—¿A qué hogar te refieres? —preguntó y paró de acariciar a la perra. Extendió la mano para alcanzar una anchoa de un plato con aperitivos que Elisa había preparado para acompañar a la bebida.

—Hay un joven que trabaja en la guardería a quien Siba le encanta. Dice que a él no le importaría llevársela a su casa si decidimos desprendernos de ella.

Miguel levantó los ojos hacia el horizonte del oeste —girones de nubecillas grises flanqueaban otras más grandes y blancas— y distraídamente volvió a acariciar las orejas de Siba.

—¿Y a ti, qué te parece? Se preguntaba asimismo qué habían hecho mal para dejar que un perro quebrantara su matrimonio.

—Depende de ti, Miguel. Yo estaré de acuerdo con lo que decidas.

—Tengo que admitir que Siba me ayuda con los ejercicios. Parece como si entendiera lo que hago. Esperemos un poco más antes de decidir.

Elisa le dedicó una amplia sonrisa. Se levantó de la silla y se encaminó hacia el interior de la casa.

—Voy a poner la mesa para cenar —dijo, acariciando la nuca de su marido según pasó.

Una semana después, Miguel se levantó una mañana, fresca pero soleada, con ansia por salir a caminar al aire libre. Andaba ya sin las muletas y deseaba comprobar cómo le iría bajo el cielo raso. También sentía curiosidad por ver si Siba se comportaría de la misma manera que lo estaba haciendo en el porche, lo cual le entretenía y le ayudaba.

Point Isabel es una pequeña península en la Bahía de San Francisco, que alberga un grande parque para perros, senderos fáciles de transitar y otras aéreas recreativas. Miguel estaba familiarizado con la zona. Mientras Elisa trabajaba, él llevó a Siba al parque. Comenzó a caminar despacio por un sendero bien señalado sobre terreno plano en dirección al agua. Siba le acompañaba, pegada a los pies, como lo había hecho en casa, lo cual le puso muy contento. Los perros cobradores se afanaban capturando las pelotas de tenis que sus amos les tiraban desde el suave precipicio al borde del canal de agua que allí se formaba, el cual dividía la península en dos mitades.

Faltando pocos metros para alcanzar el canal, Siba, aparentemente estimulada al ver la actividad de los perros cobradores, corrió para unirse a ellos, pero se tropezó con las rocas al borde del precipicio y se cayó al agua. Enseguida se hizo evidente que no sabía nadar; de manera ineficaz, trataba de mantener la nariz a flote. Miguel no supo qué hacer. De repente, un joven se zambulló en el agua y la empujó a flote hasta la orilla. Una vez en tierra, empapada y temblando, Siba proyectaba una estampa lamentable. Algunos de los presentes se acercaron con sus perros para verla.

—¡No sabe nadar! —uno de los presentes dijo riéndose.

Miguel sintió renacer su desprecio por Siba.

—¿Saben? —un hombre entrado en edad, barbudo, dijo. Y enseguida añadió—: A los perros se les puede enseñar a nadar.

Miguel comprendió que lo que el hombre barbudo había dicho era verdad, que los perros pueden aprender un montón de cosas si se les da el entrenamiento apropiado. Él había entrenado al galgo italiano que tuvo; con las mismas, podría entrenar a Siba también. Poco a poco se iba dando cuenta de que no podía culpar a su mujer porque se hubiera encaprichado con Siba. 'Sobre gustos no hay nada escrito', ella había dicho. El

que él tratara de cambiar el gusto de su mujer por la perra
era la causa de las desavenencias entre ellos. Razonó que no
era posible el percatarse de todos los aspectos del carácter de
una persona simplemente por vivir juntos durante las cuatro
estaciones del año; lleva más tiempo el conocer mejor a una
persona, y se preguntaba si ello no sería también verdad para
conocer mejor a un perro.

Sin más interés por permanecer en el parque, se dirigió a la
salida. Siba le siguió como si nada hubiera pasado. No era una
perra impecable, como Elisa había dicho, pero tampoco era su
culpa el que no lo fuera. ¿Por qué no se le había ocurrido a él,
durante los cuatro meses que tenían a Siba, el entrenarla? Salió
del parque y se dirigió a casa. Recapacitó que debería compartir
con Elisa sus deducciones.

Caminos tortuosos

Yo me incorporé como becario al Instituto Salk en San Diego, California, desde Toronto, en 1990. Tenía treinta años. Keylor Montes, de Buenos Ares, fue mi mentor. Él tenía cincuenta años y había trabajado en el Salk desde hacía veinte. Ambos éramos biólogos, y desde entonces hemos trabajado en investigación juntos durante veinte años más.

Cuando me presenté a Keylor, pensé que se parecía a Carlos Gardel, el legendario cantante de tangos. "Bueno" —dijo él cuando le comenté acerca de mi impresión. Y añadió: "No se cantar, pero me gusta tocar el clarinete". No obstante, con 1,90 de estatura, fino de talle, de pelo liso y negro peinado hacia atrás, ojos oscuros y cejas espesas, se asemejaba, en la memoria que yo guardaba por películas y fotos, a Gardel, excepto en que la perenne sonrisa del cantante yo veía reemplazada en Keylor por una atenta y serena expresión. Con el tiempo, ganó peso y le salieron canas, pero su atenta y serena expresión permaneció.

Nada más jubilarse, a los setenta años, en diciembre del 2010, Keylor y Marina, su esposa por treinta y seis años, fueron de vacaciones en un viaje que incluía la Argentina, y me envió mensajes y fotos de los lugares que iban visitando. Pensé que estaban disfrutando de un muy merecido descanso.

Cuando regresaron, nos invitaron a Laura, mi mujer por diecisiete años, y a mí, Pablo Gascony, a una velada en su casa de La Jolla. Querían compartir sus experiencias con nosotros, y Keylor deseaba ponerse al día con lo que estaba pasando en el laboratorio.

—Nada nuevo allí. Estamos ocupados, como siempre —le dije, y enseguida: — Pero nos morimos por saber acerca de vuestro viaje.

Estábamos a mitad de febrero. Habíamos llegado un poco antes de la puesta del sol, y, dado que la temperatura era buena, nos sentamos alrededor de una mesa con aperitivos y bebidas en el porche. Ni Laura ni yo habíamos estado en Buenos Aires, así que ella les preguntó acerca de su visita a aquella ciudad.

—Cuando fuimos a Boca, ya sabéis, el barrio donde Keylor nació y se crió en Buenos Aires —Marina saltó— él dijo que quizá nos deberíamos ir a vivir allí.

Keylor levantó sus ojos hacia me con expresión apologética como si él no tuviera el derecho de alejarse del laboratorio. Yo iba a decir que, por supuesto, era natural que quisiese ir allí, cuando Laura se me adelantó: —¿No es cierto? Quiero decir lo entrañable que resulta el lugar donde uno se crió.

Aunque con poca convicción, Marina afirmó con la cabeza. Miré dentro de mí para ver si la declaración de Laura también me concernía, si en algún momento yo me había sentido como que quisiera volver a Toronto después de jubilado, pero no, no era así. Bien es verdad, sin embargo, que la idea de jubilarme no había entrado en mi mente.

—¿Qué harías allí? —pregunté a Keylor.

Nos sirvió vino antes de contestar.

—Supongo que podría encontrar un trabajo docente a tiempo compartido, o algo parecido, en el Instituto de Biología en Buenos Aires, donde yo trabajé antes de venir a California, para mantenerme ocupado.

Me apresuré a alcanzar la bandeja con aperitivos y coger un canapé relleno con queso de cabra frito para masticar y así evitar decir lo que tenía en mente: que lo que él había dicho no tenía mucho sentido, que él podría obtener un puesto docente o administrativo en nuestro Departamento, y quizá con un contrato más ventajoso que en Buenos Aires y sin el estrés de tener que salir del país.

—De cualquier manera, eso no me preocupa por ahora —dijo Keylor, mirándome como si me hubiera leído el pensamiento.

Un silencio siguió a sus palabras hasta que Laura se encargó de romperlo.

—¿Qué otros lugares visitasteis que os gustaron?

La pregunta indujo un cambio de conversación. Hablaron de lugares que visitaron en Miami y Nueva Orleans hasta que se levantó un vientecillo frío, y Laura empezó a estornudar. Para entonces ya habíamos disfrutado de la velada y consideramos prudente el despedirnos y marcharnos.

De camino a casa, mientras yo conducía, Laura me preguntó si yo creía que Keylor iba a volver al Instituto Salk y ocuparse en algo, quizás como voluntario. Le dije que me parecía que sí. "Mira a Marina", le dije, "ella está contenta trabajando de voluntaria en el Museo". Ambos estábamos familiarizados con la actividad de Marina, trabajando como voluntaria en el Programa educacional del Museo Marítimo. Lo cual había iniciado nada más jubilarse hacía algunos años.

Un mes después, me enteré por Keylor de que iban a hacer otro viaje, esta vez por la costa de México. Durante ese viaje, otra vez él se mantuvo en contacto con nosotros por medio de mensajes de texto y fotos. En esa ocasión, sin embargo, percibí un sutil cambio en su modo de expresarse. "Hoy", escribió, "me senté en la playa durante la puesta del sol mientras Marina se bañaba. La luz crepuscular daba al agua un tono misterioso, y dorado al firmamento". Esas palabras me parecieron más propias del poeta que del científico.

A su regreso, tres semanas más tarde, invité a Keylor a comer en un pequeño restaurante cerca del laboratorio, donde nos gustaba ir a veces, y le mencioné mi observación acerca de las palabras que él había usado.

—En México me di cuenta de que no permanecemos los mismos a través de nuestras vidas —dijo.

Yo le echaba de menos en el laboratorio y, en verdad, no estaba seguro qué me quería decir.

—¿A qué te refieres?

—A que vivir libre de ataduras profesionales es un privilegio.

Me sentí decepcionado y a la vez incierto sobre qué esperar. Dos meses antes de su jubilación, Keylor sufrió varios problemas de salud. Primero tuvo un episodio de vértigo por lo que necesitó ir al hospital y le dejó sin equilibrio e incapaz de andar sin ayuda durante varios días. Poco después de volver al laboratorio, sufrió un ictus que le causó el verlo todo borroso y doble, y además los médicos le diagnosticaron presión arterial alta. Así que, siguiendo el consejo médico, se jubiló en diciembre del 2010.

Antes de que Keylor se enfermara, habíamos comenzado un proyecto de investigación sobre la conducta adquirida en gatitos desde su nacimiento. Yo comprendí su razón para jubilarse, pero en el fondo esperaba que me echara una mano con el trabajo una vez recuperado.

—¿Quizás no te sientes totalmente recuperado? —le pregunté al tiempo que le miraba atentamente a través de la mesa, tratando de observar cualquier cambio en su aspecto físico. Pero solo vi la misma expresión de serenidad; si acaso, solo las áreas canosas de su pelo aparecían un poco más extensas.

—Yo me encuentro bien. Simplemente me viene el deseo de experimentar con aquello que no lo pude hacer mientras estaba en activo.

Yo sabía que Keylor siempre tuvo una vena de competitividad y no me lo imaginaba dedicado solamente a vivir un estilo de vida placentera.

—Está bien, Keylor, tú sabrás lo que haces.

Yo siempre he respetado las opiniones de Keylor, incluso cuando no estoy de acuerdo con él. Pero aquel día, la conversación que tuvimos durante el almuerzo me hizo sospechar que tal vez se estaba volviendo senil. Aunque, a decir verdad, enseguida me sentí mal por pensar así, especialmente cuando insistió en pagar la cuenta.

Por algunas semanas no supe de Keylor. Estuve ocupado en el laboratorio y regresaba a casa tarde. Por coincidencia, Laura también estuvo muy ocupada, así que no nos veíamos mucho. Una noche, sin embargo, en el mes de mayo, mientras cenábamos, Laura comentó que Marina la había llamado acerca de Keylor.

—*Quel est son problème?* —pregunté distraídamente.

Estábamos hablando en francés; nuestros padres proceden del Canadá francés. Laura y yo nos conocimos en el Consulado de San Diego, donde ella todavía trabaja como coordinadora de viajeros canadienses en conexión con entidades de negocios en California. Nos casamos tarde, cuando ambos teníamos treinta y tantos. Según es también el caso del matrimonio Montes, no tenemos hijos, pero a todos nos gustan nuestros trabajos.

—Marina dice que Keylor está deprimido.

—¿Qué quiere decir?

La noticia acaparó mi atención, y por un momento, la sospecha de que Keylor se estaba volviendo senil se apoderó de mí otra vez.

—Ella piensa que el estar desocupado le está trastornado.

Estábamos cenando salmón asado con patatas.

—¿Te apetece otro filete de salmón? —le ofrecí después de servirme segundos.

—Sí, por favor.

Serví un filete de pescado en su plato y más vino blanco en nuestros vasos.

—Me sorprende —dije—. La última vez que Keylor y yo comimos juntos me pareció que se sentía feliz de la vida.

—Pues parece que ya no es así. Deberíamos invitarlos a casa a tomar té.

Yo estuve de acuerdo.

Vinieron a casa en una tarde de domingo y tomamos té en la sala de estar. Keylor y Marina se sentaron en el sofá y Laura y yo en dos sillones en frente de ellos; todos nos acomodamos alrededor de una mesita auxiliar en la que Laura había colocado una bandeja con el juego de té. Keylor aparentaba sentirse inquieto. Al principio él y yo hablamos del trabajo en el laboratorio mientras Marina y Laura charlaban de sus cosas. Él me dio algunos consejos acerca de cómo proceder con un experimento con el que yo me encontraba un poco perdido, lo cual se lo agradecí.

—¿Qué es lo que te sucede, Keylor? —Laura le preguntó a bocajarro.

Keylor volvió la cara hacia ella con expresión de sorpresa.

—¿Por qué no le cuentas? —Marina le animó.

Keylor dudó. Primero se volvió hacia mí como si yo fuera el que hacía la pregunta y luego dijo: —Lo que pasa es que… el no hacer nada me pone nervioso.

—Pero yo pensé… —me callé por un momento; luego seguí—: que lo que tú buscabas era tomar las cosas con tranquilidad y disfrutar de la vida.

—Sí, pero haciendo solo eso no me llena.

Me sentí desarmado. ¿Cómo se le podría ayudar? Keylor se levantó del sofá y fue hasta el balcón.

—Tengo que involucrarme en algo significativo —dijo mientras miraba por el balcón.

—Algo útil para llenar sus días, eso es lo que él quiere decir —dijo Marina, todavía sentada en el sofá, tomando sorbos de té.

—A mi me parece que el problema es de fácil solución. Keylor debería reincorporarse al laboratorio —dije, sintiéndome victorioso.

Un silencio se extendió en la sala durante el cual Keylor cabizbajo retornó a ocupar su asiento en el sofá. Marina le tomó la mano como queriendo consolarle.

—Keylor hallará lo que busca por sí mismo —dijo Laura en tono reconciliatorio.

Cuando se reanudó la conversación, nos concentramos en explorar posibles planes de acción, pero Keylor no participó. No obstante, una vez que se marcharon, yo me sentí esperanzado de que él decidiría volver al laboratorio y trabajar con nosotros, su equipo, 'en alguna capacidad' como Laura había dicho en febrero. Después de todo, él había probado tener una gran capacidad para adaptarse y copar con cualquier situación que se presentara cuando se trataba de alcanzar su objetivo.

No se presentó, sin embargo. Se pasó una semana, más o menos, cuando, preocupado por su estado de salud, le llamé. Todavía le estaba dando vueltas al mismo asunto, es decir, que se encontraba desocupado y necesitaba encontrar algo significativo para hacer. Otra vez le sugerí que debería darse una vuelta por el laboratorio. Pero él desestimó la idea y dijo: —Tal vez sea verdad el que debo tomarme la vida con calma, viajar y disfrutar.

Marina intentaba sacar a su marido del estado de desánimo en el que se encontraba. Con frecuencia nos telefoneaba a la

salida del trabajo para compartir sus preocupaciones con nosotros.

—No puedo figurarme, por el amor de Dios, qué es lo
que él busca —dijo en una de las veces que llamó; estábamos a
finales de mayo, y añadió—: Sé que no es ni dinero ni prestigio.
Nada de eso le inmuta en el presente.

Yo no podía borrar de mi mente el pensamiento de que
Keylor debería volver al laboratorio, y así se lo comuniqué a
Marina.

—Pongámoslo en claro, Pablo —dijo— Él no está interesado en hacer eso.

Tomé en serio las palabras de Marina y, después de terminar de hablar con ella, le confié a Laura mi confusión. ¿Estaba
Keylor senil? ¿Trataba de apropiarse una nueva identidad? Un
montón de preguntas se amontonaron en mi mente aquella
noche. Sin embargo, solo una respuesta parecía clara: Keylor
iba camino de entrar en una nueva fase en su vida. Pero yo lo
veía mal enfocado y, estando ya entrado en edad, temía que el
tiempo no le diera de sí. ¿Qué haría yo en su lugar —me preguntaba— si tuviera que hacer algo fuera de mi especialidad?
De cualquier modo, cuando Laura y yo nos dispusimos a acos-
tarnos, me di cuenta de que mi conversación la había alterado y
dejé de hablar. Tomé una píldora para dormir y me acosté con
la esperanza de quedarme dormido rápidamente.

Pasó tiempo sin que supiéramos de Keylor. Al comienzo
del verano, nos sorprendió con la noticia de que quería convertirse en consejero para escritores de ciencia ficción. "Ayudar
a escritores a entender algunos conceptos científicos que luego
ellos puedan aplicar en sus relatos podría aplacar mis ansias
intelectuales", nos dijo. Tal decisión, tan repentina, resultaba,
cuando menos, intrigante. Yo entendí su punto de vista, sin
embargo, y, por tal, estuve de acuerdo con sus planes. Pero

su entusiasmo por el cometido no le duró mucho. Un mes más tarde, me confió su frustración con el trabajo. "No puedo afirmar que esta actividad merece la pena porque el escritor es también el creador y yo me limito a actuar como una aguja calibradora: las ideas del protagonista son erróneas, o caen fuera del rango científico, y así sucesivamente", dijo.

Keylor abandonó esa actividad. Según yo le escuchaba, mientras me relataba sus quejas, también recordé que él siempre había acometido cualquier proyecto nuevo de forma sistemática; la espontaneidad con la que actuó en esta ocasión podría haber sido la causa de su fracaso. En aquellos momentos, comprendí que uno paga un precio por cambiar su identidad, por intentar redefinirse.

A primera vista, el hecho de que Keylor cesara en su reciente actividad parecía algo sin importancia, pero Marina dijo que otra vez él se volvió mohíno y empezó a hablar de estar malgastando su vida en balde al no tener algo útil en que ocuparse. Me dio por pensar en que Keylor estaba entrando en un círculo vicioso de comenzar y enseguida terminar nuevos proyectos. ¿Por qué desearía cambiar el destino de su vida? ¿Qué otra cosa, a parte de su maestría en biología, podría aportarle satisfacción personal a su edad? Marina también dijo que el hecho de sentarse bajo el enrejado de parra en el patio, mientras tocaba el clarinete, le levantaba el ánimo un poco. Ella se preguntaba si tal vez el emprender un nuevo viaje de vacaciones sería de ayuda, y yo le dije que lo más probable era que sí.

Los esposos Montes fueron de vacaciones a Portugal. Marina era de ascendencia portuguesa y hablaba el idioma. Keylor la conoció en la librería de nuestro Departamento, donde ella trabajó como consultora de bases de datos hasta que se jubiló. Cuando se casaron, ella estaba divorciada desde hacía varios años. Ellos eran felices, aunque ninguno nunca tuvo hijos.

Cuando regresaron de Portugal hacia finales de Julio, nos invitaron otra vez a su casa, en un ambiente muy parecido al que habíamos experimentado a mediados de febrero cuando volvieron de Argentina. Como el tiempo era ahora caluroso, Laura y yo nos quedamos hasta la media noche. Los dos estaban contentos y Keylor habló por un largo rato acera de lo mucho que habían disfrutado escuchando a los cantantes de Fado en los restaurantes donde cenaron y también acerca del placer de dejarse perder por las viejas calles de Lisboa.

No obstante, una vez de vuelta en casa, Marina reanudó sus actividades como voluntaria y Keylor su rumia acerca de qué hacer con su vida. Por algún tiempo contempló la posibilidad de trabajar como voluntario. "Tal vez en un museo, como Marina, o en la biblioteca pública", dijo. Por alguna razón, sin embargo, la cual él nunca me dijo, no llevó a cabo el propósito y su pesquisa en pos de "algo significativo" comenzó a sonar como un disco roto; tanto era así que cuando, en agosto, se le ocurrió el plan de usar su tiempo para traducir artículos sobre investigación biológica del español al inglés, tomé su declaración con un grano de sal. "Con un poco de práctica, supongo que podría subirme al burro", dijo. Por otro lado, pensé que su nuevo plan estaba más a tono con su nivel de competencia y me mostré optimista acerca de sus posibilidades de éxito. Pero Keylor tampoco tomó esa avenida. Dijo que la traducción no daba margen para innovar, "porque el traductor ha de mantenerse fiel al autor que es el cerebro creador".

En total, el interés de Keylor por hacerse traductor científico se desvaneció. En ese punto, yo me pregunté cuándo iría él a entender que la posibilidad de sobresalir en algo, que con tanto afán buscaba, recaía en el uso de su experiencia como biólogo. A su edad, ¿en qué otra clase de individuo podría él transformarse? Pero él estaba, a mis ojos, tan enfocado en su peregrinación para encontrar "algo significativo" en que emplearse, que sus méritos pasados, por muy sobresalientes que fueran, no los tenía en consideración.

Perdida la esperanza de que Keylor volviera, en cualquier momento, para ayudarnos a registrar los datos obtenidos a través de los experimentos, durante el resto del verano, me concentré en terminar el proyecto de investigación que habíamos diseñado juntos el año anterior y dejé de preocuparme por él. De modo que, cuando al comienzo del otoño, Laura y yo nos enteramos por medio de Marina de que Keylor dedicaba la mayor parte de su tiempo en casa a tocar el clarinete fervientemente, ninguno de los dos le dimos mucha importancia. "Al menos el tocar música le tiene entretenido", dijo Laura. Pero cuando, dos semanas después, Marina también nos comunicó que habían asistido a un concierto de clarinete, de Mozart, en el Teatro de las Artes y que Keylor había escuchado al clarinetista sin parpadear como si no hubiera oído esa música antes, me di cuenta de que había algo en ello que le obsesionaba. Así que, el hecho de que, desde entonces, Keylor echara horas practicando el clarinete no vino de sorpresa. Pero el que saliera de casa solo para encontrarse con otros músicos en la comunidad era harina de otro costal. Hasta que Keylor me llamó un día para decirme que se había unido a una banda musical.

Poco antes de la Navidad, Keylor nos envió, a Laura y a mí, una invitación para asistir a un concierto de arreglos de música popular, interpretado por su banda, en uno de los escenarios temporalmente levantados para la celebración de una serie de 'Conciertos junto al mar.' El programa incluía música de los Beattles y otras piezas, tales como *Life in a Glass House*, de Radiohead, que requerían la participación de uno o más clarinetes. Laura y yo lo disfrutamos. Cuando terminó, Keylor apoyó su clarinete en las rodillas mientras se secaba el sudor de la frente con un pañuelo que sacó del bolsillo. Después se levantó de la silla y junto con los otros músicos de la banda hicieron una reverencia ante los asistentes. Recibieron un grande aplauso.

Aquella misma noche, Keylor nos pidió a Laura y a mí a que por favor les acompañáramos a él y a Marina a cenar en el restaurante *Boca*, en San Diego, para celebrar el éxito. Antes de empezar a cenar, brindamos con champagne; después, en la conversación, Laura y yo expresamos nuestra admiración por su interpretación durante el concierto.

—¿Cómo es posible —le pregunté— que seas capaz de tocar tan bien con tan corto tiempo de practicar?

—Bueno, Pablo, uno ha de preguntarse qué es posible hacer.

—De acuerdo. Pero llegados a cierta edad…

—A pesar de la edad, o debido a la edad.

El camarero trajo una gran bandeja con parrillada y la colocó en el medio de la mesa. Cada uno de nosotros eligió los trozos de carne que más nos apetecían y nos servimos.

—Entiendo lo que dices, Keylor —Laura intervino—, pero tocar el clarinete es algo muy diferente de investigar en biología.

Yo afirmé con la cabeza, de acuerdo con el juicio de Laura.

—Yo siempre he disfrutado tocando el clarinete —Keylor dijo, y yo recordé que él ya había dicho eso mismo cuando nos conocimos.

Extendió el brazo para alcanzar el cesto del pan que había en la mesa. Marina, con el cuchillo y tenedor listos para cortar la crujiente chuleta de cerdo que se había servido, nos echó una sonrisa como diciendo que su marido era capaz de salir con éxito en todo lo que se propusiera. Muchas veces había yo sido testigo de sus ansias de salir victorioso en el trabajo y disfrutar del proceso al mismo tiempo. Pero en aquel momento, pensé que estábamos comparando manzanas con naranjas.

—Sin embargo, Keylor —dije—, Biología es nuestra especialización.

—Sí. Pero ello no te dice lo que yo he sido antes.

Reflexioné en sus palabras. Yo siempre quise ser biólogo. Recordé, sin embargo, que de joven me apasionaba el atletismo. En una ocasión, gané una medalla de oro en los 400 metros lisos en competición nacional, lo cual hizo que me sintiera orgulloso de mí mismo y me viniera el deseo de repetir la hazaña. Por entonces yo me consideraba un atleta.

—Lo pasado, pasado está —dije—. Uno debería concentrarse en el presente.

—Eso depende —contestó Keylor e hizo una señal al camarero para que regresara a la mesa.

—¿Depende de qué? —Laura, que seguía la conversación con interés, preguntó.

—Pues depende de…

En aquel momento el camarero se acercó a la mesa. Keylor le pidió una servilleta, porque la que estaba usando se había empapado de champagne al servirlo, y luego concluyó: —Depende de lo que nos dé satisfacción en la vida.

Me di cuenta de que lo que Keylor buscaba desde que se jubiló era algo que le aportara satisfacción personal, no era dinero ni prestigio, como ya lo había mencionado Marina.

—Suponiendo que yo esté de acuerdo con lo que dices, Keylor —propuse—, dime, ¿Por qué has cambiado el rumbo de la búsqueda para encontrar tu satisfacción?

—Recuerda, Pablo, que yo no elegí cuándo jubilarme.

Por supuesto que lo recordaba, le iba a decir cuando Laura saltó: —Pero, Keylor, podías haber vuelto al Instituto y emplearte en la enseñanza o algo así.

—Por un tiempo pensé hacer eso, como sabéis, pero la curiosidad, el deseo de encontrar algo diferente, de imaginar nuevas formas de hacer las cosas y la propia inspiración me llevaron, de alguna manera, a ponerme al día con la música y tocar el clarinete.

Permanecimos en silencio mientras saboreábamos el postre y luego Keylor dijo: —Tuve la suerte de encontrar un grupo de buenos músicos, unirme a su banda y practicar juntos.

El camarero se aproximó a la mesa de nuevo y preguntó si deseábamos alguna cosa más. Keylor nos miró a todos interrogativamente y luego, dirigiéndose al camarero, dijo: —No, muchas gracias.

—Me consta que Keylor podría tocar en una orquesta —Marina comentó con candor cuando nos disponíamos a salir.

—Bueno, querida, el ansia por tener éxito a veces nos conduce a creer que somos mejor de lo que realmente lo somos —Keylor se apresuró a decir y añadió: —Además, como ya dije, no era prestigio lo que yo necesitaba, sino algo significativo.

Una vez afuera del restaurante, Laura y yo felicitamos otra vez a Keylor y nos despedimos.

Cuando conducíamos de vuelta a casa, Laura dijo: —Supongo que es un canje.

—¿Lo que Keylor ha hecho, quieres decir?

—Sí. Se necesita echarle valor. ¿Harías tú algo parecido cuando te jubiles? —Laura volvió la cara hacia mí para ver cuál era mi reacción.

Me tomé un momento para reflexionar y luego dije: —Es difícil decir. No cabe duda de que he aprendido un montón de la trayectoria que Keylor ha seguido. Pero por ahora, yo estoy contento con lo que hago. ¿Y tú?.

—Es difícil decir para mí también. Supongo que debemos esperar y ver qué pasa.

Dejamos el asunto en ese punto y permanecimos en silencio hasta que llegamos a casa, cinco minutos más tarde.

El viejo barrio del abuelo

Luis Montiel, criador de perros, y el posible comprador de su negocio se habían intercambiado textos y emails. Aquella tarde, sin embargo, el comprador llamaba porque quería echar un buen vistazo a la instalación antes de tomar su decisión.

Ana, hija única de Luis Montiel, y su nieto de 8 años, Marcelo, también habían llegado de visita.

El comprador inspeccionó cuidadosamente la instalación, el estado de la contabilidad, las medidas de higiene y el ambiente general. Tomó notas acerca de los recintos del parto, de los perros y cachorros y del stock de comida. Él y Luis Montiel hablaron de negocios.

Cuando el comprador se marchó, la familia se trasladó a la casa de Luis, situada próxima a la instalación de su negocio, en San Bernardino, California, y se sentaron alrededor de una mesa de madera en el porche para charlar y tomar chocolate caliente con bizcochos.

—¿Te pasa algo, papá? —Ana había notado que su padre parecía estar triste.

—¿Pasarme algo? No. Solo que no puedo decidir si vender o no mi negocio.

—Bien visto, papa, yo creo que deberías venderlo. Falta poco para que cumplas los ochenta. ¿No crees que sea tiempo de que te jubiles y te tomes la vida con calma?

—Abuelo, ¿vas a vender tus perros? —Marcelo preguntó.

El muchacho había mostrado curiosidad por los cachorros de su abuelo desde que era un bebé.

Ana había traído a la mesa una bandeja con una jarra llena de chocolate caliente, tres tazones y bizcochos. Luis Montiel mojó un bizcocho en el chocolate, algo que a él y a su nieto les encantaba hacer. Levantó los ojos y miró a su nieto como si necesitara considerar las palabras antes de responder.

—Tu abuelo está un poco cansado de cuidar a sus perros —Ana se le adelantó a decir. Se había sentado junto a su hijo y frente a su padre. Enseguida añadió: —Lo ha hecho durante muchos, muchos años.

Ana echó una mirada al fino y escaso pelo canoso de su padre y las arrugas de la frente y las manos. Quiso añadir, pero no lo dijo porque pensó que Marcelo era demasiado joven para comprenderlo, que su padre había sido un infatigable criador de perros durante más de cincuenta años. Ella sabía que su padre había disfrutado mucho con su profesión y se las apañó para vivir de ello. Pero por los últimos dos años, desde que murió su madre, después de que estuvieran casados por tan largo tiempo, ella había notado que su padre se fatigaba con facilidad y estaba perdiendo su entusiasmo por el negocio.

Mientras tanto, Marcelo miraba a su madre con curiosidad y luego volvió los ojos a su abuelo tratando de averiguar de qué iba la cosa.

—Cuando sea un poco más mayor, voy a cuidar de tus perros, abuelo —dijo con autoconfianza—. No se los vendas a ese hombre que vino a verte —añadió y puso sus manos alrededor del tazón lleno de chocolate, adoptando un tono como si se tratara de negocios.

—Cariño, lo que dices es muy bonito —Ana dijo y añadió: —Y yo sé que lo dices de todo corazón. Pero falta mucho hasta que tú crezcas lo suficiente como para que puedas ocuparte de los perros de tu abuelo.

Marcelo puso cara de fastidio y rechazó el juicio de su madre como falso.

—Pero, mamá, papá y tú decís que cada mes yo crezco un poco más.

—Bueno, eso es verdad, pero…

Parecía que su madre iba a contrarrestar el razonamiento de su hijo, cuando Luis intervino: —Lo que tu madre quiere decir es que una vez que aprendas todo lo que hay que aprender en la escuela y crezcas hasta convertirte en un fuerte mozo hablaremos de ello.

—Ya estoy fuerte. ¡Mira! —Marcelo flexionó su brazo derecho y cerró el puño fuertemente para hacer resaltar su pequeño bíceps y enseñárselo a su abuelo.

Ana se impacientó un poco con la pesadez de Marcelo de querer cuidar de los perros. Pensó que su insistencia hacía que su padre se sintiera incómodo.

—Abuelo, ¿tienes los perros desde hace mucho tiempo?

—Sí, desde hace mucho, mucho tiempo.

Ana se levantó de su silla e hizo intención de entrar en la casa.

—Ve y díselo —dijo, dirigiéndose a su padre según iba de camino, y añadió que Santi, su marido, aquella noche tenía que trabajar hasta tarde y ella iba a hacer algo de cena y comer allí antes de que Marcelo y ella se fueran a casa.

Luis asintió con la cabeza. Sabía que lo que su hija quiso decir era que le contara a Marcelo la historia de cómo se hizo un criador de perros, la cual también había contado a la familia y los amigos innumerables veces. Por momentos, sin embargo, permaneció en silencio. Marcelo, expectante, le miraba con ojos muy abiertos.

—Cuando yo tenía tu edad —Luis Montiel rompió el silencio sin más preámbulo— vivíamos en un barrio donde habían otros muchos niños y…

—Como que… ¿Eran tus amigos?

—Bueno, pues… Jugábamos juntos después del colegio. Marcelo se volvió pensativo y dijo:

—¿Dónde jugabais, en un parque?

Luis tomó un sorbo de chocolate.

—Si continuas haciendo tantas preguntas, no podré terminar la historia antes de que tu madre nos llame para cenar.

—Ya no haré más preguntas.

—Está bien, escucha. Lo que te voy a contar sucedió en mi viejo país. Entonces no teníamos un recinto para jugar dentro de un parque. En el barrio donde vivíamos había mucho terreno y…

—¿Había animales? —el nieto no pudo contenerse de preguntar.

—Por supuesto que había animales. Nos encantaba atrapar grillos y saltamontes y lagartijas… —Luis visualizó, en su imaginación, el edificio de apartamentos, construido con piedra dorada, donde vivió de niño con sus padres, rodeado de una grande explanada, donde jugaban al futbol, y caminos polvorientos que conducían, a través de las huertas, hasta el rio, donde iban a pescar. Pero comprendió que debía acortar su relato— Y…

—¿Había también perros?

—Bueno, el tema de los perros vino más tarde.

—¿Cuándo?

—Te lo diré si prometes no interrumpir.

—Lo prometo —Marcelo estaba entusiasmado de oír el relato de su abuelo. Nervioso, empezó a jugar con la taza de chocolate.

—Cuando yo estaba ya a punto de terminar la educación secundaria, uno de los niños, Daniel, nos mostró algo que él había aprendido de un pastor en el pueblo de la sierra donde la familia pasaba los veranos.

—¿Qué?

—Cómo usar la honda. ¿Sabes de lo que hablo?

Aunque Marcelo no estaba seguro, afirmó con la cabeza. Luis se quedó mirando fijamente a su tazón, ya vacio de chocolate, en frente de él, con expresión ensoñadora.

—Soñaba que a medida que pasaba el tiempo yo manejaba la honda cada vez mejor —dijo en voz baja.

—¿Tirabas bien, abuelo?

—Sí, claro. Era capaz de dar en el tronco de un pequeño abedul a una distancia de cuarenta o cincuenta metros. ¿Sabes lo que es un abedul? Son esos arbolitos de tronco blanquecino que tú seguramente has visto en el parque.

—¡Hala!

Marcelo no sabía bien cómo era un abedul, o cuán lejos era la distancia de cuarenta o cincuenta metros, pero creía al abuelo y admiraba su destreza.

—Pero un día sucedió algo —Luis siguió en voz más profunda. Esperaba otra pregunta de Marcelo, pero el niño permaneció en silencio, pendiente. El recuerdo de lo sucedido, sin embargo, entristeció a Luis. Pero no quiso defraudar a su hija y continuó.

—¡Eh!, —dije a Daniel— ¿ves aquel perro allí lejos? —Luis se iba animando otra vez.

—Sí, lo veo —contestó Daniel— Los otros niños también lo vieron. Era un perro pequeño pero fornido, que correteaba a través de la explanada, lejos de nosotros. Yo apunté y Daniel me gritó: "¡No tires! Si le das en la cabeza lo puedes matar. —Aquí, Luis se tomó un respiro.

—¿Le diste en la cabeza?

—El tiro le golpeó el pito.

La perplejidad se adueñó de Marcelo. No sabía a qué atenerse acerca de lo que oyó. Le parecía que era algo a la vez de risa y serio.

—¿Le diste en el pito? —Necesitaba cerciorarse para resolver su ambivalencia.

Luis Montiel se percató de la confusión de su nieto, a causa de su relato, y decidió suavizar el drama:

—El perro se llamaba Toby —dijo con voz más alegre.

Marcelo puso cara de estar contento otra vez.

—¿Toby? —preguntó.

—Así es. Era de unos vecinos a quienes mis padres conocían.

—Me gusta el nombre, Toby —Marcelo se arrodilló en el asiento de la silla y apoyó los codos sobre la mesa, deseoso de oír el resto de la historia.

—Bueno, pues verás. Me sentí horrible de lo que había hecho. A partir del golpe, el pobre Toby tuvo problemas para orinar. Los otros niños no dijeron nada de lo que había pasado y nadie lo supo. Pero yo se lo dije a Toby.

—¿Se lo contaste al perro, Abuelo? —Marcelo no podía entender cómo eso era posible.

—Toby —le cuchicheé al oído mientras le acariciaba las orejas— Yo soy quién lo hizo. No quería hacerte daño, solo asustarte un poco. Lo siento muchísimo. Te quiero mucho.

Marcelo escuchaba con toda atención, sus ojos húmedos de lágrimas.

—¿Qué dijo Toby? —preguntó.

—Pues…Él meneaba la cola, muy contento. Nos hicimos íntimos amigos. Le dije que yo iba a cuidar de él desde aquel momento, y también de todos los perros del mundo.

Marcelo afirmó con la cabeza.

—Yo voy a cuidar a tus perros, abuelo —dijo de todo corazón.

Luis Montiel sacó un pañuelo de su bolsillo. Disimuladamente, se secó un par de lágrimas que le resbalaban por las mejillas. Entre tanto, Ana volvió al porche; la cena estaba lista. Luis se levantó y entró en la casa.

—Mamá, le he dicho al abuelo que voy a cuidar de sus perros —Marcelo le dijo a su madre mientas entraban en la casa. Ana le acarició su pelo negro sin decir una palabra.

La casa de Berta

En la primavera de 1985, Berta tenía 90 años y hacía quince que era viuda. En aquel tiempo, los que vivían en Morondo, un pueblito localizado en un área de terreno llano y árido de la Provincia de Castilla, eran gente mayor. Habían trabajado en las tareas del campo, en la periferia del pueblo, hasta que se jubilaron y ahora vivían a paso lento, sin estrés.

Berta vivía sola en la misma casa que su marido y ella habían comprado siete años después de que se casaron, una casa construida de cemento y ladrillo, con una fachada descolorida debido a las inclemencias del tiempo. La casa tenía un corral en la parte trasera con un gallinero, dos cerdos, tres cabras y un montón de conejos.

Berta y su marido también trabajaron en el campo, arando, sembrando y recogiendo el fruto, a sueldo. No tuvieron hijos, pero siendo ellos gente estoica, sin vicios, apegados a sus obligaciones, tradiciones y supersticiones, vivían en paz con ellos mismos y su entorno.

—Ya no doy abasto para terminar todo lo que hay que hacer —una mañana de mayo de aquel mismo año le dijo a su hermano Guillermo, tres años más joven.

Durante la enseñanza secundaria, Guillermo ayudaba a sus padres con el trabajo del campo. Una vez finalizados los estudios, ansioso de marcharse del pueblo y buscar aventuras, se alistó en el ejército. Sin mucha instrucción como soldado, fue de voluntario a Marruecos y participó en la Guerra del Rif. Un año y medio más tarde, resultó herido en combate, no por las balas enemigas, sino por el malfuncionamiento de su propio fusil. Perdió el antebrazo izquierdo. Aunque se le concedió una baja honorable y una modesta pensión, la ocurrencia, intermitente, de dolor fantasma le atormentaba —él nunca entendió por qué el brazo amputado podía dolerle— y le limitaba la capacidad para trabajar y ganar un sustento decente.

—Yo puedo ayudarte —dijo él.

De pie junto a la puerta por fuera de la casa mientras ella regaba unas pequeñas parcelas de tomate y de cebollas que todavía sembraba al frente, él levantó los ojos hacia las tierras labradas que se extendían por todo el alrededor y que pertenecían o bien a los terratenientes o bien al Gobierno. Esparcidas entre caminos tortuosos, se veían las casitas de los trabajadores. La vista le trajo a la memoria su lucha por trabajar aquellas mismas tierras con solo un brazo y se entristeció.

—Tú estás muy ocupado con cuidar de tu mujer —Berta dijo.

A su regreso a Morondo de la guerra en la colonia africana, Guillermo se casó con una paisana, Sara, de su misma edad, a sabiendas de que ella era diabética. Se adaptaron a vivir una vida simple, y por muchos años, Berta y su marido les ayudaron en lo que pudieron. Aunque se las apañaron para vivir de forma independiente en su modesta y pequeña casa, Sara se estaba quedando ciega debido a la diabetes y necesitaba ayuda con los quehaceres de la casa. Su marido era el único soporte.

—¿Qué vas a hacer entonces?

Él sabía que Berta no se encontraba bien tampoco. Aunque baja de estatura, tenía un cuerpo robusto y una mano firme.

Pero los fríos inviernos y abrasadores veranos contribuyeron a que sufriera de artritis, lo cual, junto con su edad avanzada y todo el quehacer en la casa, la huertita y el corral, acabó por disminuir su energía y sus movimientos.

Ella no contestó. Cuando terminó de regar, cerró el grifo, que estaba empotrado en la pared, y enrolló la manguera en el soporte.

—Hala —dijo— El regado está concluido. Echarle de comer a las gallinas es lo siguiente.

Anduvo hacia la trasera de la casa. A mitad de camino, entró en el cobertizo, recogió un cubo medio lleno de semillas y lo llevó apoyado en la cadera hasta el gallinero. Guillermo le siguió los pasos.

—Las tareas de la casa son las que más me cansan —dijo ella y esparció granos de semilla entre los pollos.

—Vas a necesitar alguien que te ayude.

Después de que su marido murió, Berta siguió siendo autosuficiente. Pero ahora, sin embargo, ella se daba cuenta de sus limitaciones, y Guillermo con frecuencia tocaba el tema de que su mujer y él podrían vender la modesta casa en que vivían y cambiarse a vivir con ella. Él podría ayudar con las tareas domésticas y cuidar de los animales. Pero Berta no estaba de acuerdo, y él no insistía. Si alguien contradecía su punto de vista, que ella basaba más en intuición que en conocimiento, respondía con arrogancia y rechazo. Aún así, Guillermo suponía que si Berta falleciera antes que él, la propiedad pasaría a ser suya por jerarquía genética.

—¿Ayuda de quién? —preguntó ella.

Guillermo no dijo nada. El cacareo de las gallinas le fascinaba. Las miraba en silencio mientras Berta vaciaba el cubo.

—¿Ayuda de quién? —repitió.

Abstraído, Guillermo trataba de decodificar las vocalizaciones de los pollos.

—¡Perdón! ¿Qué? ¡Ah, sí! —Se recordó— Vas a necesitar a alguien que te ayude con el trabajo de la casa.

Ella negó con la cabeza y le echó una mirada que él interpretó como un rechazo de su sugerencia. Berta comenzó a andar de vuelta a casa y Guillermo hizo lo mismo a su vera. Se pararon por un momento en el cobertizo para dejar el cubo.

—¿Sabes? —dijo ella— Amanda me ayuda un poco.

—Amanda es nuestra prima. Eso no es lo que yo digo.

Guillermo no dudaba de que Amanda ayudara a Berta un poco, pero esa no era la clase de ayuda que él creía que ella necesitaba, no sería suficiente. De niña, Amanda se mostró perezosa y eso hizo que no aprendiera en la escuela, y ahora a sus 75 años, gorda y glotona, andaba y se movía lentamente. No servía para nada, pensó, y le sobrevino una sensación de impotencia. A pesar de todo, siguió tratando de convencer a Berta de que ella necesitaba más ayuda.

—¿Te quedas a comer? —Cortó la conversación con impaciencia cuando llegaron a la puerta.

—No, gracias. Sara me necesita. Debo irme.

Amanda era una persona muy representativa de Morondo. Era hija única, nunca se casó y siempre vivió con los padres. Después que su padre, quien había estado enfermo por años, muriera, ella siguió viviendo con su madre hasta que ésta también falleció. Cuando se quedó sola, Amanda comenzó a visitar a Berta, y después de un año de que murió su madre, las autoridades de la localidad mandaron derribar la casa donde vivía debido a su condición ruinosa. Dada la carencia económica y de recursos personales para sobrevivir, en la primavera de 1985, Amanda terminó por irse a vivir con Berta.

—Amanda es una santa —los vecinos le decían a Guillermo— Le va a servir de mucha ayuda a Berta.

A parte de la familia, el Padre Jaime, el cura párroco, un puñado de vecinos y gente que iba a la iglesia con frecuencia, todos pasados de los 65 años, Amanda a penas si tenía otros contactos sociales. Siempre había sido así con ella. De joven, sus padres la empujaron para que trabajara en las labores del campo, pero ella se mostró reacia y solo trabajó por unos años y con bajo sueldo. Las malas lenguas difundieron el rumor de que Amanda nunca tuvo una relación amorosa.

—Ya veremos —Guillermo solía responder a los vecinos— Yo conozco bien a nuestra prima. A ella le gusta la complacencia y…

—Tú tienes esposa —los vecinos le salían al paso— De viejos, el vivir solo es muy duro.

Para Guillermo, Amanda, perezosa, egoísta y torpe, distaba mucho de ser una santa. Por otro lado, no acertaba a entender por qué él se resistía a aceptar el arreglo que de forma natural las dos mujeres habían iniciado.

Hacia el final del verano, durante las visitas a su hermana, Guillermo se dio cuenta de que la casa estaba sucia, los platos permanecían amontonados sin lavar y una capa de polvo cubría los muebles. Él comprendía que la capacidad de su hermana para hacer las cosas declinaba con rapidez, pero ¿qué pensar de la de Amanda? Una tarde soleada y seca, Guillermo llegó a la casa de su hermana para mostrarle a Amanda cómo cuidar de los animales y limpiar el corral, para ahorrarle a Berta el tener que hacerlo a riesgo de caerse. Después de ello, los tres entraron a la cocina, hicieron unos bocadillos y se sentaron a comerlos.

— ¿No ves, Amanda, que esta casa está sucia? —Guillermo se atrevió a decir.

—No veo cual es el problema —contestó Amanda.

—Bueno, pues parece que vas a necesitar ayuda con las tareas de la casa. Se da el caso que Sara y yo sabemos de una mujer latinoamericana que…

—¡No! Esas extranjeras vienen aquí, se apañan de todo lo que pueden y se vuelven a sus países. La gente habla de ello en la iglesia.

Guillermo se acordó del comentario que una de las vecinas había hecho unos días antes, que Amanda no era callejera, y no dijo nada. ¿Pero por qué rechazaba la ayuda que se le ofrecía? Terminaron de comer los bocadillos y Guillermo se marchó.

Durante el otoño, Guillermo observó que la casa de Berta caía en más abandono. Todavía se preguntaba por qué Amanda rehusaba la ayuda que se le ofrecía. Berta no le era de mucha ayuda tampoco ya que su viveza se iba apagando. Él no sabía qué hacer. Aunque no era religioso —cuando perdió su brazo también perdió su fe— conservaba las tradiciones del lugar, y consultar con el párroco era algo que la gente del pueblo hacía cuando se encontraban afligidos.

El padre Jaime era un castellano pelirrojo, alto y delgado, nacido de padre irlandés, emigrante, y madre castellana. De adolescente entró al seminario en la capital de la provincia, y cuando se ordenó de sacerdote aceptó el encargo de párroco de la iglesia en Morondo. Se ganó la confianza de la congregación por su dedicación y esfuerzo para resolver los problemas ajenos, y se mantuvo siempre alerta a las eventualidades del pueblo. Cincuentón por entonces, todavía era de buen ver y se mantenía lleno de energía. Recibió a Guillermo en su oficina, anexa a la sacristía.

—Padre Jaime —comenzó diciendo Guillermo— ¿Qué me aconseja debo hacer para restaurar la higiene y el sentido común en la casa de mi hermana? Amanda no mueve un dedo para mejorar la situación.

—¿Está Berta contenta con Amanda?

El cura se ocupaba en abrir sobres de un montón de correspondencia que se esparcía por su mesa de despacho.

—De eso no estoy seguro.

—¿Qué podría ir mal? —dijo el sacerdote. Con el abrecartas señaló una silla al otro lado de la mesa para que Guillermo tomara asiento.

—Tal vez —continuó éste después de sentarse— usted pueda persuadir a Amanda a que cambie su conducta.

El padre Jaime cesó de abrir las cartas. Levantó los ojos.

—Amanda —dijo— no tiene malicia o intereses mundanos.

Guillermo estuvo de acuerdo en que Amanda no tenía vicios; no obstante, la casa de su hermana se mantenía sucia y maloliente desde que ella vivía allí. Si eso no era debido a malos hábitos, ¿a qué, entonces, se debía?

—No sé que pueda pasar en el futuro —dijo— pero sé que algo va mal en el presente.

El padre Jaime retiró la correspondencia lentamente hacia los lados y agarró una caja de madera con tabaco que tenía encima de la mesa.

— ¿Un puro? —Le mostró la caja de tabaco a Guillermo.

— No, gracias.

El cura encendió el cigarro e inhaló el humo con deleite.

—Veré qué puedo hacer para mejorar la situación de tu familia —dijo y le echó otra chupada al cigarro puro— Mientras tanto… Cambió la conversación para hablar de asuntos de su iglesia y los sucesos en el pueblo.

Después de que Guillermo salió de la oficina del párroco, pensó que éste no se había tomado en serio el problema que le manifestó. En vano persistió en su propósito de cambiar la aptitud de Amanda para convencerla de ser más activa en la casa. Sin embargo, la situación empeoraba. La suciedad había llegado a invadir incluso hasta las hendiduras de debajo de las puertas; restos de comida manchaban las paredes; las bolas de pelusa se acumulaban debajo de las camas y así sucesivamente. La parsimonia de Amanda le exacerbaba. Ella respondía a las sugerencias de cómo hacer para mejorar su eficacia de un modo simplista e impreciso que a él le llevó a concluir que ella no era persona de fiar. Más aún, Amanda tampoco ponía atención a su propia salud. Se quejaba de múltiples dolencias. Guillermo intentó hacerla ver la importancia de ir al médico y seguir sus recomendaciones, pero ella ni mostró iniciativa para hacerlo ni paró de quejarse. Él veía que con Berta cayendo en una pasividad patológica y una inconsciencia de lo que sucedía a su alrededor, la casa pronto se convertiría en una pocilga.

Al aproximarse la Navidad, el padre Jaime acostumbraba a hacer una visita anual a aquellos feligreses que necesitaban alguna ayuda. Durante estas visitas, se enteraba de lo que sucedía en el pueblo. Y así, por ejemplo, se enteró de que una adolescente estaba embarazada, pero nadie *sabía* de quién. Él conocía a la joven de vista, de verla en la iglesia de vez en cuando y siempre le había parecido que era una muchacha devota. Las malas lenguas, sin embargo, dijeron que el embarazo fue el resultado de la lujuria, dañando su reputación.

El embarazo de esta adolescente y sus consecuencias ocupaban la mente del padre Jaime cuando éste llegó a la casa de Berta. Nada más entrar, se vio sacudido por un penetrante olor a orina que inmediatamente hizo que su atención girara del problema de la chica embarazada a la circunstancia que Berta y Amanda vivían. Echó una mirada a su alrededor y comprobó que la casa estaba muy sucia. Se acordó de la visita que Guillermo le hizo en su oficina; ahora, él tenía evidencia de lo que Guillermo trató de comunicarle. De vuelta a su iglesia a pie, el sacerdote revisó mentalmente los pecados que había contado entre sus feligreses.

Para los servicios religiosos de Nochebuena, la iglesia estaba repleta. Berta, para entonces débil como un pajarillo, no pudo asistir, pero Amanda estaba presente. El padre Jaime habló, durante el sermón, de la lujuria, y todo el mundo parecía saber a quién tenía en mente. Después, de forma sutil, se refirió a la pereza y dijo: "Descuidar el cuidado de las personas queridas es un pecado". Guillermo se dio cuenta de que una de las vecinas de Berta, sentada al lado de Amanda, se volvió a mirar a ésta con expresión de perplejidad.

Sara, quien sentía más que veía el ambiente, pues para entonces ya estaba tan ciega como un murciélago, dijo a su marido cuando salieron de la iglesia: "Supongo que te habrás dado cuenta de que muchos de los comentarios del padre Jaime iban dirigidos a tu familia".

—La pregunta es si Amanda también se habrá percatado de ello —contestó él y le tomó de la mano para guiarla a casa.

Al comienzo del nuevo año, bien debido a pecado o pura pereza, Guillermo juzgó que la casa de su hermana se mantenía en status quo. La idea de buscar ayuda legal para poner fin a la situación cruzó su mente. En un frio atardecer de enero, recibió la noticia, a través de una vecina, de que Berta se encontraba enferma. Cuando llegó a la casa, halló a su hermana en cama, confundida, quejosa y respirando con gran dificultad. Amanda, sentada a su lado, se ocupaba, de forma ceremoniosa, en secarle el sudor de la frente con un paño. Un hedor impregnaba toda la habitación.

—¿Cuánto tiempo lleva enferma? —preguntó Guillermo.

—Hace tres días que comenzó con diarrea.

Guillermo reflexionó y enseguida preguntó: "¿Has llamado al médico?

—Ella no quiere ver al médico —Amanda habló sin apartar sus ojos de la cara de Berta.

Al otro lado de la cama, Guillermo se aproximó a la enferma, inclinó la cabeza, apartó gentilmente el paño que tapaba su frente y observó su cara de cerca. Berta hacía un gran esfuerzo para respirar, y el vacio emocional que manifestaba su rostro le asustó.

—Yo creo que está muy enferma —dijo así que se enderezó y añadió en tono sarcástico: "Pero esperemos que se cure por sí misma. ¿No es eso lo que esperas?

—Yo hago lo que puedo —respondió Amanda.

Guillermo caminó hacia la puerta, pero primero de salir, volvió la cabeza y dijo: "Por favor, mira a ver si alguna vecina puede venir y ayudarte a cambiar las sábanas y esparcir algún desodorante en la habitación. Apesta. Yo volveré con el médico.

Al anochecer, Guillermo llegó con el doctor Benítez, el médico del pueblo, un hombre cincuentón, grueso, de mediana estatura y manos grandes. Dos vecinas, quienes habían venido a ayudar a Amanda a adecentar la habitación, respetuosamente salieron de ella cuando el médico entró. Sin más palabras, éste procedió a tomarle el pulso a Berta y examinar la elasticidad de la piel. Luego sacó el estetoscopio de su maletín de cuero, deslizó la campana por debajo del camisón de la paciente y escuchó el sonido de los pulmones y del vientre. Cuando terminó su examen, sacudió la cabeza y apretó los labios. Metió el estetoscopio otra vez en el maletín, se frotó las manos con desinfectante y dijo: "Malas noticias".

Amanda suspiró y comenzó a lloriquear.

—Por favor… —Guillermo se acompañó de un gesto para que ella saliera de la habitación, lo cual hizo.

—¿En qué puedo ayudar? —Guillermo entonces le preguntó al médico.

—No se puede hacer mucho. Tiene neumonía y deshidratación. Con la edad que tiene, esos problemas hacen que esté confundida. Voy a pedir el traslado al hospital.

Guillermo sabía que el doctor Benítez se refería al hospital más cercano, que se encontraba en otra localidad a unos cuarenta kilómetros de distancia.

—Yo creo que la ambulancia tardará unas tres horas en llegar. El personal del hospital está ocupado con el traslado de otros enfermos de la región que necesitan ingresar —dijo el doctor Benítez y añadió "Mientras tanto, llámame si ves que se pone peor.

Una vez que el médico se fue, Amanda y las dos vecinas que le habían ayudado antes con la limpieza entraron en la habitación. Mientras esperaban a la ambulancia, Berta empeoró y respiraba con gran dificultad. Sucedió tan rápidamente que expiró después de tan solo unos minutos de agonía. Las tres mujeres se movían en la habitación con cautela como si Berta solo estuviera dormida. Alisaban la ropa de la cama y tocaban los pies de la difunta a través de las sábanas con delicadeza, mirando su cara para cerciorarse de que en verdad estaba muerta. Emitían lamentos. Una de las mujeres le dijo a Guillermo con voz queda que la difunta, en vida, tuvo un corazón de oro.

El doctor Benítez, una vez notificado del fallecimiento de Berta, regresó al amanecer pero se limitó a firmar el certificado de defunción y se fue. A la salida del sol, Guillermo fue a su casa y poco después volvió con Sara, y todos se prepararon para el velatorio. La noticia de que Berta había muerto se extendió por el pueblo. Vecinos y amigos llegaban en grupitos para rendir homenaje al difunto y dar el pésame a la familia. Guillermo fue al mortuorio a elegir un ataúd y comprar flores. El padre Jaime ayudó con las disposiciones para el entierro en el cementerio sito en la trasera de la iglesia.

Durante el funeral, la iglesia estaba iluminada con velones y el candelabro con poca luz. Guillermo, de pie detrás de un improvisado pódium, junto al ataúd, adornado con coronas de flores, elogió las virtudes de Berta mientras estuvo en vida. Mientras hablaba, notó con el rabillo del ojo que Amanda, de rodillas en el banco, gimoteaba y parecía abatida. Una onda de compasión anidó en su corazón, y le pareció que el padre Jaime, quien también se encontraba cerca del pódium, notó su repentina reacción.

Después del funeral, la gente comenzó a salir de la iglesia a través de los portones que daban al cementerio adjunto. Guillermo pidió a Sara que se agarrara de su brazo y anduviera lista junto a él porque quería alcanzar a Amanda. Y así que la alcanzaron, él dijo: "Me imagino que ésta es una dura pérdida para ti. Si te sirve de ayuda, quiero que sepas que puedes venir a nuestra casa por el tiempo que necesites".

—Gracias —Amanda contestó rápido—Pero la casa de Berta ahora es mi casa.

Un escalofrío trepó por el espinazo de Guillermo. Quería abofetear a Amanda con su única mano. Pero su mujer le pellizcó en el brazo y esto hizo que se calmara y disminuyera el paso.

—Nunca pensé que Amanda fuera capaz de tal desfachatez —dijo enrojecido.

—Para ella, esa es su casa, mal que nos parezca —dijo Sara.

—¡Es un descaro!

—Olvídate. Estamos aquí para enterrar a tu hermana.

Guillermo comprendió que aquel no era el momento adecuado para hablar de asuntos de pertenencias. Se encontraban al pie de la sepultura que pertenecía a la familia. El padre Jaime, ataviado con sotana negra y casulla dorada, de pie al lado del féretro, leía una oración del libro de devociones que sostenía en sus manos. Cuando metieron la caja mortuoria en la sepultura, un asistente pasó una pala a Guillermo, quien la agarró con su única mano, y, ayudado por el mismo empleado y siguiendo el ritual de costumbre, echó la primera palada.

Al faltar Berta, Guillermo se sintió todavía más disminuido como persona, como si hubiera sido mutilado otra vez. Aunque el temperamento de Berta fue distinto al suyo, ambos se habían llevado razonablemente bien. Ella y su marido les habían ayudado a él y a Sara a salir adelante en la vida, eso era algo por lo que él estaba muy agradecido y que nunca olvidaría. Pero más allá del hecho de ir a vivir a la casa de Berta, lo cual él consideraba que era su derecho, y cuidar de la propiedad, se sentía moralmente obligado a preservar el legado de su hermana y su marido.

En el transcurso del invierno pasaba a diario por la casa de su difunta hermana, para el desagrado de Amanda, y haciendo la vista gorda ante la inmundicia acumulada, iba al corral y echaba de comer a los animales, lo cual hacía con mucho gusto. En las ocasiones en que se topaba con su prima, sus interacciones, breves y ariscas, le convencieron de que ella se mantenía firme en quedarse con la casa. Iba a necesitar un plan de acción legal para echarla de allí. Maldijo el día en que se alistó como voluntario en el ejército y fue a la guerra en las colonias. Si en lugar de ello se hubiera quedado en el pueblo, ahora se sentiría un hombre completo con dos brazos para trabajar, sin miedos y sin amarguras. Se dio cuenta de que estaba envejeciendo, flaqueando, y se peguntó cual iba a ser su suerte y la de su mujer. Estas preocupaciones le martirizaban. Sara no era de mucho consuelo tampoco. Decidió consultar acerca de ello con el padre Jaime.

—Por favor, sírvete más sopa. Matilde, mi nueva ama de casa, es una excelente cocinera —dijo el padre Jaime, quien había invitado a Guillermo a comer.

Mientras saboreaba la sopa, Guillermo, sentado enfrente del cura, iba dando rienda suelta al decir de su congoja. Al cabo, centró el tema en el asunto de la casa de su difunta hermana.

—Voy a necesitar la ayuda de un abogado —dijo y puso atención a la reacción de su anfitrión, cuya cabellera pelirroja, ojos azules, y buenos modales en la mesa le daban apariencia de una persona de confianza

—Eso podría suponer una eternidad —dijo el cura. Sostuvo la cuchara llena de sopa en el aire mientras miraba a su invitado y añadió: "Además, ¿de dónde vas a sacar el dinero?

—¡Ajá! Hombre de poca fe —Guillermo se aventuró a decir. Dibujó una leve sonrisa y en tono más serio añadió: "Los ahorros que Berta tenía en el banco han pasado a ser de mi pertenencia. No es que sea mucho dinero, pero lo quiero invertir en el rescate de su casa.

Se hizo un silencio durante el cual Matilde, la regordeta y madura ama de casa, trajo una cacerola con estofado a la mesa. El padre Jaime no había estado seguro de si Guillermo, con solo una mano, sería capaz de manejar el tenedor y el cuchillo simultáneamente, y le había pedido a Matilde que por favor cortara la carne en pedazos pequeños antes de cocinarla. Cuando ella salió, el padre Jaime cogió el cucharon y sirvió primero a su invitado y luego así mismo, deleitándose con el aroma. Guillermo se sintió agradecido de no tener que usar el cuchillo. Disfrutó comiendo el estofado relajado.

—Un noble plan —el padre Jaime dijo.

Animado por la respuesta, Guillermo continuó: "Quizá usted pueda convencer a Amanda para que deje la casa antes de que yo empiece con eso.

—Quizá deberíamos dejar el asunto en manos de Dios.

—¿Qué quiere decir?

—Yo puedo decir una misa y tu hacer una novena.

Guillermo bebió de su vaso. Dijo 'yo no tengo fe' y volvió a poner el vaso en la mesa.

El padre Jaime también bebió agua de su vaso.

—No puedo echar a Amanda de la casa sin ninguna ayuda —dijo.

Se hizo un silencio entre los dos hombres mientras seguían comiendo. Un sentimiento de impotencia invadió el alma de Guillermo otra vez. A su edad, ya no le quedaba mucho tiempo de espera para ver si recobraba la fe antes de encontrar una solución a su problema.

—Ya veremos —dijo.

Continuaron charlando, pero el padre Jaime se las apañó para desviar la conversación hacia las cosas del pueblo.

Guillermo había disfrutado de la comida en casa del padre Jaime, pero se sintió defraudado del resultado del encuentro. El cura había querido atraerlo a los rezos en la iglesia antes de comprometerse a ayudarlo. Soledad, tristeza y resentimiento hacia su prima le afligían. Se sentía abandonado del cielo y de la tierra, incapaz de tomar alguna acción.

No fue a la casa de Berta por varios días hasta que el pensamiento de que los animales en el corral tendrían hambre le remordió la conciencia y una mañana fue allí de improviso. Se le cayó el alma a los pies cuando vio la cantidad de suciedad acumulada por todas partes. A continuación, mientras Amanda se iba a la iglesia, él se ocupaba en limpiar el espejo de cuerpo entero en el recibidor, lavar los platos en la cocina, organizar los estantes en la despensa, sacudir el polvo de los muebles y así sucesivamente. También regó las plantas, cuidó de los animales y barrió el corral. Tenía la esperanza de que su dedicación para adecentar la casa de Berta sirviera a Amanda de estímulo para hacerse más diligente. Pero después de un mes de fatiga sin que ella hubiera movido un dedo, él decidió buscar ayuda legal. Determinó usar los ahorros de Berta para conseguir su objetivo.

Por suerte, el doctor Benítez le puso en contacto con un abogado que tenía su oficina en el mismo lugar en que estaba el hospital, y Guillermo fue hasta allí en autobús.

—Si existe un testamento en el que su difunta hermana le legó el usufructo de su propiedad, no habrá ningún problema —dijo el abogado, un hombre de buen ver, de unos cuarenta años.

Para Guillermo, esas eran palabras gordas. Entendía la palabra testamento pero no usufructo.

—¿Si ella me legó? —preguntó.

El abogado puso una sonrisa de disculpa y dijo: "Eso quiere decir que si te concedió la casa".

Sentado frente a frente con el abogado, a través de su mesa de trabajo, de madera de caoba, Guillermo le miraba con ojos entornados, reflexionando.

—¿Puede probarlo? —el Abogado preguntó en un tono de voz un tanto retador.

Guillermo bajó su mirada.

—¿Probarlo?

—Sí. Busque el testamento original o una copia del mismo.

Guillermo comprendió que no le quedaban argumentos ni preguntas. Estuvo de acuerdo en buscar el documento y la consulta terminó.

Un mes le llevó a Guillermo primero de pedir una nueva consulta con el letrado. No tenía mucho que añadir a lo que ya se había tratado la primera vez puesto que no había encontrado ni el original ni ninguna copia del testamento de Berta en ninguna parte de Morondo donde buscó.

—Ocupar una vivienda ajena sin permiso es un delito —dijo el abogado y añadió: "Aún hallando evidencia de que la propiedad le pertenece, todavía lleva mucho tiempo el resolver estos casos porque la parte contraria tiene derecho a contestar la decisión del juzgado".

Guillermo nunca había participado ni observado un juicio. Estaban en el verano. ¿Se refería el abogado, en cuanto a resolver el problema, al otoño o más tarde? La ceguera de Sara iba a peor, y él deseaba sacarla de la minúscula y ruinosa casa donde vivían y cambiarse a la casa de Berta donde Sara podría moverse más fácilmente.

—Y a lo largo del proceso, la acusada, Amanda, podrá permanecer en la casa —el abogado habló de nuevo.

—Y si no encontramos el testamento, ¿cuánto tiempo se llevaría? —preguntó Guillermo.

—Sería mucho más largo. No puedo decir exactamente.

—Seguiré buscando —Guillermo se hizo consciente de que estaba siendo impulsivo, pero al mismo tiempo comprendía que no había razón para echarse atrás. Si Berta había autorizado al banco a transferirle sus ahorros a él, uno esperaría que ella hiciera lo mismo con la casa.

Confiando en su suerte, decidió retener al abogado y seguir sus consejos. Después de su tragedia en la Guerra del Rif, esta sería la pelea más desafiante que estaba a punto de emprender. Se sintió listo para la lucha. Y combatió durante todo el otoño y el invierno y todo a lo largo del siguiente año. Luchó contra la obcecación de Amanda de no querer desistir de vivir en la casa de Berta. Peleó contra la alianza que los vecinos establecieron con su prima, y contra la aptitud ambivalente del padre Jaime. Con todas sus fuerzas bregó con todos los que se oponían a su causa legal hasta terminar exhausto, hasta que le volvió el dolor fantasma en el brazo amputado. Pero confiaba en su abogado.

En el invierno de 1988, finalmente, se celebró un juicio en la Audiencia del Juzgado sito en la localidad de su abogado. El defensor público se hizo cargo del caso de Amanda puesto que se la consideró persona indigente. El doctor Benítez y el padre Jaime y algunos de los vecinos fueron llamados a declarar como testigos. Al final, el fallo fue favorable a Guillermo y sentenció a Amanda a desalojar la propiedad. Pero su abogado presentó una apelación contra la sentencia ante el mismo Tribunal y el proceso siguió.

—Sin el condenado testamento, nuestra probabilidad de ganar el caso es escasa —dijo el abogado.

—Ya veremos —dijo Guillermo.

En la creencia de que ganaría la batalla legal, y temeroso de quedarse sin dinero antes de que el proceso llegara a su fin, vendió las cabras de Berta, y dos meses más tarde hizo lo mismo con los cerdos y los conejos. Pero no tuvo el nervio para vender las gallinas. Su abogado le aseguró de que él podía obrar así porque Amanda no contribuía a pagar los gastos de la casa. Para Guillermo, Amanda no había cambiado ni una pizca desde que Berta murió. Iba a la iglesia y al mercado pero hacía un mínimo de tareas domésticas. Siempre había dependido de otros para ganarse la vida. Había aprendido a asumir el papel de víctima e inventar historias que parecieran reales para despertar un sentimiento de compasión y culpabilidad en los demás.

En su imaginación, él veía a Sara y así mismo viviendo en la casa de su difunta hermana; allí, Sara se movía con más facilidad—se había negado a usar un bastón para ciegos— y él escuchaba el cacareo de los pollos. Tal vez podría aprender a descifrar lo se decían. Soñaba con estas escenas.

Seis meses después, el abogado citó a Guillermo a que viniera a su oficina. El Juzgado había revisado la apelación admitida en primera instancia.

—El juez no encontró evidencia para apoyar la pretensión de Amanda de que tiene el derecho a vivir de forma permanente en la casa de Berta —dijo el letrado.

A Guillermo se le iluminó la cara. Vio su oportunidad. Se le abrió el cielo. En su opinión, la casa de Berta le pertenecía a él por ser el pariente más próximo.

—No sin prueba de que usted es el dueño —el abogado dijo.

Por unos instantes, la respiración de Guillermo cesó y el corazón le dio un vuelco.

—¿Qué quiere decir? —preguntó.

—Por supuesto, podemos seguir la pauta…

Guillermo no podía concentrarse. De repente, la escena de la guerra en la que resultó herido revivió en su mente, y la intensidad del dolor fantasma subió a las nubes tan rápidamente como un cometa en un día ventoso.

—¿A qué pauta se refiere? —preguntó.

—Naturalmente…

Pero Guillermo ya no oía las palabras del abogado.

—Ya veremos —balbuceó. Se levantó de su asiento, al otro lado del pupitre de caoba del letrado, y respetuosamente salió del despacho.

El padre Jaime había seguido el pleito entre Guillermo y Amanda con imparcialidad. Sara opinó que ese era su deber como párroco, pero Guillermo creía que el cura tenía un poco de fariseo. De todos modos, no le importó que el padre Jaime ayudara a Amanda, cuando el desahucio se llevó a cabo, a entrar en la única residencia para mayores disponible para la gente pobre de Morondo. El doctor Benítez y el padre Jaime habían llegado a un acuerdo con el administrador de una residencia para mayores situada en la vecindad del hospital para que aceptaran a los ancianos de Morondo que carecían de medios para cubrir sus necesidades.

Próximos a la Navidad, Guillermo recibió la noticia de su abogado de que basándose en la ley de sucesión por herencia el juez había determinado otorgar a él y a su mujer el derecho de usufructo de la casa de su difunta hermana. No obstante, él no podría vender la casa hasta que no demostrara estar en posesión del testamento de la difunta que incluyera la autorización de venta.

Guillermo dijo a Sara que por favor se preparara para la mudanza. De repente, a ella le entró pánico. Cada vez que él traía el tema a colación, ella entraba en una situación de un miedo increíble y juraba que no podía controlarse. Temía salir de su casa.

Guillermo sacó fuerzas de flaqueza y fue a la casa a diario. Barrió el suelo, limpió el polvo de los muebles, aseó el corral y se entretuvo mirando a las gallinas. A medida que pasaba el tiempo, sin embargo, las idas a la casa se hicieron cada vez menos frecuentes. Terminó por vender los pollos, y, al cabo, un buen día, cerró las puertas y ventanas con candado y cesó de ir allí. No podía probar ser el dueño; por tanto, para él la casa dejó de existir.

La casa dejó de existir para todo el mundo en el pueblo. Quedó abandonada, los cristales de las ventanas rotos, el techo medio colapsado y el corral repleto de yerbajos y escombros.

La gente se refería a ella indistintamente como *la casa de Berta, la casa de Amanda,* la *casa de Guillermo* y *la casa sin dueño.* No podían creer por qué las autoridades permanecían irresolutas, dejando que la propiedad entrara en un estado de ruina. Pero hasta donde alcanza la memoria, nadie levantó un dedo para encontrarle una solución.

List of First and only Publications

"El Teso village": The Acentos Review (acentosreview.com), August 2015.

"The Ambler": The Literary Nest (theliterarynest.com), October 2016.

"The Hiker and the Hawk": Aester & Ichor (aesterandichor. com), February 2017.

"Palmiro": Adelaide Literary Magazine (adelaidemagazine.org), May 2017.

"Three Black Birds": Adelaide Literary Magazine (adelaidemagazine.org), July 2017.

"Ernestine's Struggle": Adelaide Voices Short Story Award Finalist, 2017.

"Never Too Late": Adelaide Literary Magazine (adelaidemagazine.org), August 2018.

"An Old Cemetery": Adelaide Literary Award Anthology, vol. I., 2018.

"Marie": With Painted Words Magazine (withpaintedwords. com), Jan-Feb. 2018.

"The Deer": With Painted Words Magazine (withpaintedwords. com), March 2018.

"The Bridge": With Painted Words Magazine (withpainted-words.com), July 2018.

"Lucas Parra": Adelaide Literary Magazine (adelaidemagazine. org), October 2019.

"A Beautiful Afternoon in April": Adelaide Literary Award Short Stories, February 2020.

"At the Gate": With Painted Words Magazine (withpainted-words.com), January 2019.

"The Easel on the Beach": With Painted Words Magazine (with-paintedwords.com), October 2019.

About the Author

José L Recio was born and raised in Spain, where he studied medicine. He specialized in clinical neurology and initiated a career in neuroscience research. In conjunction with other researchers, he published several papers in specialized American journals. When he was in his mid-thirties, he left Spain for California on an International Fellowship and joined a neuro-behavioral research team at UCLA for two years. Personal and sociopolitical circumstances induced him to make a change in career orientation. He entered a Residency Training Program at

Loma Linda University, California, and from there, he became an American Board Certified Psychiatrist. He has practiced in several communities in Southern and Northern California and participated in teaching activities as part of several Continued Medical Education programs. More recently, he developed an interest in creative writing. Some of his fiction reflects emotional and psychological personal experiences, transferred to literary characters in different life contexts; other pieces are the result of mere fantasy. In the process of becoming bilingual and bicultural, he writes in and translates into both English and Spanish. His short stories have appeared in several literary journals such as Adelaide Literary Magazine, Los Acentos Review, The Literary Nest, and With Painted Words. "Ernestine's Struggle" was named *Adelaide Voices Short Story Award* finalist, 2017, and "A Beautiful Afternoon in April" in *Adelaide Literary Award Short Stories*, 2018. "An Old Cemetery" was included in *Adelaide Literary Award Anthology*, 2018. José Recio and his wife currently live in Pasadena, Los Angeles, where three of their four children also live. In addition to working, reading, and writing, they enjoy outdoor activities such as hiking with their whippet, and traveling.

www.ingramcontent.com/pod-product-compliance
Lightning Source LLC
Chambersburg PA
CBHW022348020726
47500CB00002B/174